"You think they might hold the answer to Serafino's implant?"

Captain Tasha Sebastian retrieved her third cup of coffee. "What do you need me to do?"

"Keep Kel-Paten out of Sickbay as much as possible, for one," Eden replied.

"That means you won't be seeing much of me. Where I go, he goes these days. What else?"

Eden took a deep breath. "As you said, Kel-Paten has no great love for telepaths, or for Psy-Serv. I have reason to believe he has an extensive personal library of Psy-Serv's history, their methods, their means, everything. I need access to those datafiles."

"You think they might hold the answer to Serafino's implant?"

"Maybe not Serafino's specifically, but at least its medical pedigree."

Sass pursed her lips and regarded her friend carefully. "You're asking me to break into the admiral's security locked datafiles. Files that are probably loaded with every defensive hacker trap he could create with his mega-million credit mind. Files that probably have more security devices, hidden alarms and fail-safe programs than anything else in civilized space, Psy-Serv's own databanks included."

"Yes."

"Files that are located in his quarters, which are again no doubt the most secure location on this ship; hell, probably in this fleet."

"Yes."

Sass shrugged. "Piece o' cake. Anything else?"

What reviewers are saying about COMMAND PERFORMANCE...

Award-winning books and stories by Linnea Sinclair:

WINTERTIDE by Megan Sybil Baker
2001 EPPIE Award Best Fantasy Novel
2001 Sime~Gen Gatemaster's Award Best Fantasy Novel
2000 PEARL Award finalist
2001 Dream Realm Award finalist

FINDERS KEEPERS by Linnea Sinclair
2001 Sapphire Award
2001 PEARL Award
2001 Dorothy Parker RIO – 2nd Place

Gambit by Linnea Sinclair
Grand Prize Winner, Third Annual *Romance and Beyond Fiction* Contest
2nd Place (tie) 2000 Sapphire Awards, Short Story category

Macawley's List by Linnea Sinclair
First Prize Winner, Third Annual *Romance and Beyond Fiction* Contest

How I Spent My Summer Vacation by Linnea Sinclair
First Place (tie): *Futures Magazine* Short Story Contest

COMMAND
PERFORMANCE

by

Linnea Sinclair

NBI
NovelBooks, Inc.
Douglas, Massachusetts

NBI

Published by
NovelBooks, Inc.
P.O. Box 661
Douglas, MA 01516

NovelBooks Inc. publishes books online and in trade paperback. For more information, check our website: www.novelbooksinc.com or email publisher@novelbooksinc.com

Produced in the United States of America.

Cover illustration by Linnea Sinclair
Edited by Anita York

ISBN 1-59105-064-2 for electronic version
ISBN 1-59105-089-8 for trade paperback

This bit of space opera silliness is dedicated to:

'Doc' Janie, RN, the best friend an unorthodox spacefleet captain could ever have;

Daiquiri, my Maine Coon cat, who should have been named 'Tank';

Dr. Alexander Keith and the staff at Advanced Wellness, the best friends an author's aching shoulder could ever have;

And as always, to Rob, husband of infinite patience who after more than 20 years, still finds me amusing.

CHAPTER ONE

SHIP'S GYMNASIUM, TRIAD HUNTERSHIP *VAXXAR*

There might be worse things in the galaxy than a lethal alien virus, Captain Tasha Sebastian mused as her Chief Medical Officer angrily paced the huntership's locker room aisle. Evidently an admiral with an attitude, and an agenda, was one of them. Especially when that admiral's actions directly impeded finding a cure for that same lethal virus.

"People are *dying*, Sass." Doctor Eden Fynn flung her hands wide in exasperation, narrowly missing smacking her hand on the metal wall. Her honey blonde hair, normally tucked neatly behind her ears, was tousled and unruly. Her lipstick had either been chewed off, or left on the rims of too many cups of tea—all sure signs that the *Vaxxar's* CMO wasn't happy.

Sass fully understood why. The Nar'Relian virus had proved to be a stubborn puzzle. Then the admiral provided an additional obstruction to its solution. She scrubbed at her face with one end of the towel draped around her neck before responding. "The Triad's priorities have often been different than ours. And they do make up half the Alliance."

Eden didn't seem to hear her. "I'm so close to finding a cure. But now *he* announces we're going in the complete opposite direction. All because some damn pirate turned informant has decided to go on an unscheduled vacation!"

The admiral's announcement had also, and not for the first time, forced Sass to delay her regular zero-g racquet-lob game. It was almost as if he saved all his senior staff meetings for when she was off-duty.

A politically savvy friend had warned her, when she'd agreed to

1

accept command of a huntership in the newly formed Alliance fleet, that just because the Coalition-Triad war was over didn't mean former enemies would stop sniping at each other. She'd hoped the threat of invasion by the Illithian Empire would create cooperation, not conflict. But Admiral Branden Kel-Paten, the former *Triadian* admiral, seemed to have made it his personal mission to trip her up whenever he could.

This latest was a little more serious than her disrupted racquet-lob schedule, however. This involved an outbreak of a lethal virus all through Coalit...that is, Alliance space. It was, as Doc Eden Fynn had said, life and death. Eden could save lives—if she had indeed found a cure.

It was a life and death issue to Admiral Kel-Paten, too. He wanted Jace Serafino—*that damned pirate turned informant*, to quote Eden— dead. He'd all but said so in the staff meeting earlier.

She rested her hand briefly on her CMO's shoulder. "Let me see what I can do." Her commbadge trilled as if to punctuate her words. It took Sass a moment to find it under her towel, clipped to the neck of her pink workout shirt. "Sebastian."

"My office. Five minutes." The admiral's familiar deep voice brooked no argument, and was also, considering she was still off-duty, not unexpected. She wondered what crisis he'd uncovered now, just to occupy what was left of her free time.

"By your command, sir." Sass tapped it off and caught Eden's wry grin. "What?"

"Good shirt."

Sass looked down. *My name's No, No, Bad Captain. What's Yours?* was clearly visible now that she'd removed her towel. She grinned back. Maybe she could present Kel-Paten with a crisis of her own. "Want to try double-teaming him?"

Eden fell into step with her. "If he still refuses to change course, there's no reason I can't use one of the shuttles, take a med team with me, and—"

The red alert sirens erupted as the corridor doors irised open, stopping Eden in mid-sentence.

Sass slapped her commbadge. "Captain here. Status, Mister Rembert!"

"Incoming energy wave. Eight-point-two on the Graslan scale. McAbian residue readings—"

"On my way. Captain out."

Sass bolted down the corridor for the lifts, her heart pounding. She didn't have to hear the residue reading figures. An eight-point-two Graslan wave was more than enough to tear a huntership the size of the

Vaxxar apart.

She almost collided with the tall, dark-haired man in a black Triad uniform as she lunged out of the lift. Kel-Paten. He slanted her one of his infamous scowls before grabbing her elbow and forcefully guiding her through the double sliding doors that led to the upper-level of the bridge.

The two-tiered, U-shaped command center of the huntership was already frenzied with activity. Voices were terse, commands clipped. Every screen streamed with data.

Kel-Paten hadn't released her arm. "You're out of uniform."

She was also off duty, but the possibility they were at death's door prevented her from reminding him of that fact. There wasn't time to argue with him. Again.

She offered him a brief "acknowledged" as she headed for the closest scanner station to check incoming data. What she saw wasn't pretty, but they had time. Five, maybe ten minutes to try some fancy dancing that could either save their lives or send them to their graves in infinitesimal pieces. She glanced over her shoulder. Kel-Paten had slid into the left command seat. With a practiced familiarity, he thumbed open a small panel covering the dataport in the armrest and linked into the ship's systems through the interface feeds built into his wrist. He frowned slightly, then his eyes flared bright with that eerie, luminous hue that signaled his cyber systems were at full power. He was spiked in, as much a part of the huge huntership as the drives, scanners and bulkheads.

Except, unlike the drives, scanners and bulkheads, he could talk.

She turned back to her console, knowing he could hear her just as well from there as if she were seated next to him.

"Kel-Paten, my data shows a major energy disturbance at oh-five-seven-point-four."

"Oh-five-seven-point-four-three-two," the voice through her commbadge stated; yet she knew if she turned, Kel-Paten's mouth wouldn't be moving. "Preliminary residual shock waves created no perceptible damages. Ship integrity is sound. Secondary waves—"

"Damn!" Sass swore as she was thrust abruptly sideways. She clung to the wide console with both hands.

"Forward shields down to eighty-five per cent," a crewmember's voice announced below her.

"Acknowledged!" came both her reply and the admiral's.

She tapped furiously at the console. Kel-Paten was no doubt eons ahead of her calculations in his inner journey through the data, but he looked for the known, correlating and synthesizing.

She looked for the unexplainable.

It was one of the reasons they worked so well as a team, in spite of the fact they'd been on opposite sides for over ten years: she had a knack for understanding the illogical data; he was brilliant in instantly utilizing the available data. Granted, his cybernetically-enhanced thought processes were a million times faster than hers, but he was linear where her analysis tended to do pirouettes and somersaults.

"Tell me what we *don't* have, Kel-Paten," she said tersely. The huntership shuddered as another line of shock waves impacted against its shields.

"Energy signature is not indicative of ionic storm formation. No indication of natural stellar trauma."

"Space-time rift?" she ventured, her fingers rapidly tapping instructions into the sensor pads.

"Highly improbably with no previous black hole activity recorded in this quadrant."

"We might just be making history then, admiral," she quipped as she scanned the results of her latest data request. "We have abnormally high levels of McAbian particle residue at the sub-atomic level."

"Stellar wind shear—"

"This ain't no damned stellar wind shear," she barked as the *Vax* heeled hard to port and everyone's stomach made corresponding lurches to starboard. "Kel-Paten, help me out here. Look at those damned levels!"

The few seconds of studious silence from the admiral were filled by the sounds of voices around her: reports of minor hull damage on Deck Seven; a fluctuation in shield integrity portside; two crewmembers with broken arms on Deck Ten. Down in Sickbay, Eden would be up to her pretty blue eyes in contusions and broken bones, Sass knew. After this, they'd both need a pitcher of iced gin!

"McAbian levels are increasing at the rate of seventeen parts per nanosecond," Kel-Paten reported. "Probability of vortex formation is eighty-seven point six-five percent in the next ten minutes."

At his words, a chill surged up Sass's spine. A vortex—a hole violently torn in the space-time continuum. It could be anything from the universe farting to the birth of a major black hole as the result of a dark star implosion perhaps hundreds of thousands of light years away. And here they were, stuck at the wrong place at the wrong time with nowhere to go but down the galactic shitter.

"Can you spike out, Kel-Paten? We have to do some fancy dancing. I need you at the con."

"Agreed. Acknowledged."

"Rembert!" She called to the science officer two consoles down. "Monitor this station—we've got a rift coming."

The tense look in the officer's eyes reflected her own concern. She slapped at the shipboard comm button on her seat's armrest before she took the seat next to Kel-Paten. His pale eyes were losing their eerie luminescence.

"This is the captain. Secure all decks. Repeat. Secure all decks. We're on a rift horizon. Sebastian out."

She turned to him, asked the question whose answer could well seal their fate. "How big?"

He'd swung open the small comp screen attached to his seat and watched the data closely. "Projected diameter of thirty-seven point two kilometers, given the current state of emissions."

"How close are we to center?"

"One-six-five-three-oh point nine five kilometers from the epicenter; again, given—"

"I know, I know! Did you re-work the shields?"

He glanced at her. "Of course. They're back at optimum."

"Well, praise the Gods and pass the peanut butter," she said, noting the undisguised superiority in his tone. "Remind me to tell you how much I love you, Kel-Paten. *If* we live through this."

The ship lurched sickeningly again. Alarms wailed and the data on her screen relayed everything she didn't want to know. This was a different kind of reminder, a deadly one.

One that stated that when huntership met vortex, vortex usually won.

CHAPTER TWO

Remind me to tell you how much I love you, Kel-Paten.

Something in Kel-Paten's chest tightened sharply at her quip. He struggled to maintain his usual impassive expression. He'd wanted to hear her say those words for so long that even now, laced with sarcasm, and in the midst of an emergency situation, they still had the power to send waves of heat rolling through his body.

He swallowed hard and forced his gaze away from the petite blonde woman in a captain's uniform, and back to the comp screen on his left. It took a moment for him to refocus his vision. When he did, he saw that Sass had already taken the hyper-drive engines off line and dropped power on the impulse engines to eighty per cent.

Good girl. The mistake most novice—and nervous—captains made when encountering a rogue energy field was to buck it full bore. That only resulted in tearing the ship apart. It was better to ride the field, navigate the energy waves. But that took some very delicate handling.

Both civilized and uncivilized space was littered with debris from ships whose captains had tried to tackle Lady Nature head on. His ship, he knew with complete certainty, would never be one of them.

Not as long as either he or Tasha Sebastian was in command.

He checked the status in Engineering. "Warp core secure," he reported; then changed screens with a tap of his finger. "Fifty-five seconds to primary flare."

"Great," Sass intoned, following the same data on her screen. "The galaxy decides to fart while we're sharing its undies."

There was a ripple of nervous laughter from nearby crewmembers. He felt some of the tension on the bridge abate, in spite of the seriousness of their situation. He wondered if he should chance a commiserating smile but she'd already swiveled around and was nodding at several officers, Triad and United Coalition.

"I love you all, you know that," she announced blithely.

"Yes, ma'am!" came back several replies from around the bridge.

A high-pitched beep returned his attention to his screen. "Thirty-five seconds." He glanced again in her direction. Was she aware of how little time they had left? She regarded him questioningly. The words he ached to say died in his throat. He turned back to his comp screen and wondered, not for the first time, if he were going to die without ever being able to tell her how he felt.

"Ten seconds," she reported.

"Switching helm control to manual." He keyed in his clearance code.

She finished hers, nodded. "Helm control on manual. The admiral has the con. Hang on, boys and girls. It's going to be a rough ride."

He watched the primary flare explode on the ship's forward view screen like a thousand suns colliding in some crazed dance, streams of energy suddenly spiraling outward. Without thinking, he reached for her, locking her small hand in his. When she turned to him, he called up all his courage and said her name. "Sass, I—"

The *Vaxxar* collided with the full force of the expanding vortex. His words were lost in the wailing of alarms and groaning of metal bulkheads straining under impact as the ship lurched violently, first to port, then to starboard.

Bridge lights flickered and went out, though it was only microseconds before auxiliary emergency lighting kicked on, bathing everything in a murky red glow. The ship lurched again; two crewmembers went sprawling down the stairs. Only Kel-Paten's firm grasp on her hand kept Sass from flying out of her seat. A pressure vent ruptured in a lower wall panel, sending a mushroom of hot, moist air across the bridge.

The fingers of Kel-Paten's left hand moved in rapid staccato over the control pad at his seat as he coaxed the huntership through a series of snake-like maneuvers.

Sass had both his data and her own on her comp screen and adjusted the braking vanes with her right hand as he called them out to her.

"Three percent, port and starboard."

"Three percent, sir," she responded.

"Steady as she goes. I'll need a ten percent increase on my mark in eighteen point two seconds." He paused, watched the numbers flick by in familiar yellow-green. "Mark!"

"Vanes at ten percent, sir."

The *Vax* seemed to glide then, for a moment, before another shock wave sent her careening to port.

"Damn it!" Sass swore, jolted out of her seat, almost landing in Kel-Paten's lap.

Muttering something about "opportunities lost", he picked her up and set her back in her seat.

She looked at him. "Sir?"

"I want to try feathering the aft braking vanes." He'd lost his grasp on her hand and knew this wasn't the time to claim it back.

Her questioning gaze turned to one of understanding. "Do it."

There had to be forty different edicts prohibiting the feathering of braking vanes in the Triad's operational manuals. He'd probably authored thirty of them. Braking vanes on hunterships weren't designed to be feathered, to be angled in such a way to let energy flow over them instead of stopping it. Vanes were there to *create* resistance, not decrease it. Vanes feathered had been known to shear off, taking whole sections of the hull with them. Or create vibrations that threatened the stability of a ship.

At least, that's what they did under normal, logical circumstances. But the eye of an erupting vortex was not a normal, logical location.

"Retract forward vanes," he ordered.

"Vanes retracted," she replied and the ship began to shimmy in response.

Immediately, reports of structural slippage were heard around the Bridge. Kel-Paten ignored them.

"Invert aft vanes, fifteen percent."

She tapped at her screen. "Fifteen."

"Let's start with a five percent pitch, Sebastian, then give me a two percent increase on my marks."

"Affirmative, Kel-Paten. At five."

He watched twenty seconds click by on his vision field.

"Mark."

"At seven."

Twenty more seconds.

"Mark."

"At nine. Must be jelly 'cause jam don't shake like this," she added.

"Mark."

"At eleven."

At nineteen percent, the shimmying noticeably subsided. He could feel the helm responding to his commands. At twenty-seven percent, the *Vax* seemed to find her space-legs again. Overhead lighting flickered back on and at least five of the fifteen-odd alarms ceased to wail.

It was an encouraging sound. Almost as encouraging as...Well, he could think about her words, later. Right now, he had a damaged ship to deal with and two of his officers demanding his input at Damage Control.

He pushed himself out of his seat and headed for the Lower Bridge. They had lived through the worst of the vortex. Someday, perhaps he would remind her of what he'd waited for more than a decade to hear her say.

UPPER BRIDGE, COMMAND SLING, THS *VAXXAR*

It took almost two and a half hours from the moment of the first flare for the huntership to finally clear the vortex and for operations on the Bridge to return to some semblance of normality, with only the never-ending litany of damage reports hinting at the severity of what the ship and her crew had experienced.

"Bridge to Sickbay. Hey, Doc. Come up for air, yet?" Sass could almost see Eden's responding grimace to her question.

"We're still treading water, captain, but I think we'll make it," said Eden's disembodied voice over the comm. "Briefly, we have four concussions, fifteen broken arms, eight broken legs, three steam burns, and more bumps and bruises than I have space in my medical logs to record."

"Nothing more serious?"

"Gods be praised, no!" Eden said.

"Sounds like you earned this week's pay anyway, Doc. Keep me informed. Sebastian out."

She flicked off the comm, leaned back in her seat and let out the sigh she had been holding in for she didn't know how long. The sound must have drawn Kel-Paten's attention. He turned from where he stood at the upper bridge railing.

"I'd like to do a physical inspection of ship's damage," he told her after a lengthy moment of silence.

Why not? she thought. Hell, it was only 0145 in the morning. She'd been on duty since 0800; about seventeen and a half hours straight, save for her racquet-lob game. She glanced down at her pink sweat pants and realized she was still in her *No! No! Bad Captain!* shirt. A hands-on of the ship would probably take another two hours. After that, she could fall directly into bed, still in her sweats and wake up two hours later for her ritual workout with Eden Fynn. Still in her sweats. How convenient! She grinned in spite of the dull ache between her shoulder blades.

She stood, stretching, saw Perrin Rembert almost walk directly into a pylon at the sight and dropped her arms abruptly. Well, it wasn't as if she was naked under the t-shirt; she had an exercise top that matched her shorts: pink. But from the distance it must look...oops! Ah, well.

Kel-Paten waited for her by the bridge doorway. Well, not quite at the doors. It was as if something had stopped him dead in his tracks just before the entry to the corridor.

"Want to start in Engineering?" she offered.

"Engineering?" he repeated. "Um, no. No." He ran his hand over his face. "Let's start in Sickbay. Engineering after that."

The suggestion surprised her, though she said nothing as she followed him down the corridor to the lifts. Sickbay was where she would've started after any trauma on board the *Regalia*; her crew's welfare always came first. But Kel-Paten...it was well known he rarely showed up in Sickbay except under the direst of circumstances. Maybe, she mused, all that shimmying had finally shaken some compassion into that cybernetic system of his.

If it had, he might be willing to give credence to her and Eden's request to send a med-team back to Farside Station. They may have bested a vortex, but they still had a virus to fight. And Kel-Paten had some damned runaway pirate named Serafino to find.

SICKBAY, THS *VAXXAR*

Eden Fynn was too tired to hide her surprise when Kel-Paten showed up in her E.R.. His dislike of medical facilities was well known. She didn't blame him. If someone had cut off her arms and legs when she was a teenager and replaced them with bio-cybernetic limbs, she'd not have pleasant memories of the place either. However, any comment she might have made was preempted by an emergency call from the bridge.

Again.

Kel-Paten moved immediately to the intraship vidscreen on the nearest wall, with Sass only steps behind him.

"Status, Mister Kel-Faray," he ordered the round-faced First Officer.

"It's an unidentified ship, sir. We seemed to have dragged her out of the vortex with us. She's badly damaged and breaking up."

"Life forms?"

"Four, humanoid, and one's fading fast. But it won't matter if the ship—"

"Lock a transbeam on all survivors. Transport them directly here to Sickbay. And send a full security team." He glanced to his left. "You're about to have a few more visitors, Doctor."

"We can handle it," was her professional reply. Already, her med team angled equipment into position.

Four broad beams of light shimmered in rainbow colors before coalescing into human forms on top of the emergency diagnostic tables. Blue-coated personnel swarmed around them, with Eden heading her own team at the first diag bed. She ran the medicorder briefly over the still form clothed in a tattered gray spacer's uniform. An elderly man who had died from his injuries minutes before being transported.

She recorded time of death and moved automatically to the next bed, her scanner parading the important data before her eyes:

Male. Humanoid. Forty-one years of age. Six foot three and one-half inches. Two hundred twenty-two pounds. Respiration was fast, but not life threateningly so. Blood pressure elevated.

The medicorder categorized his injuries: concussion, broken left wrist, some minor internal bruising to the left side. She was about to move on—he'd make it on his own for now—when her patient stirred and groaned softly.

Immediately, she reached out and laid her hand gently against his face, which felt stubbly from several days' growth of beard.

"Shhh," she crooned, aware that Sass had come up next to her and leaned over the man. "You're safe," Eden continued. "You're going to be all right. You're on board the Alliance ship *Vaxxar*."

Jet dark lashes fluttered against bruised cheekbones.

"Admiral," said Kel-Faray's voice from the vidscreen. "We have a positive ID on the ship that broke up."

The lashes parted, revealed startlingly deep blue eyes. Not pale like the admiral's, but dark like the jeweled waters of the Isarrian Ocean.

Something buried deep under several layers of professional medical training in Eden's mind sent her a message: *Damn, but this guy is gorgeous!* Right from the tips of his scuffed boots, to the gray pants that hugged well-muscled thighs, to the torn shirt that revealed a flat, hard stomach, to the square jaw with that damnably attractive cleft, to his jet dark hair that had escaped its careless tie and now lay against his shoulders...he was unequivocally gorgeous.

Quickly, she shook herself back to reality and mentally readjusted her 'doctor's cap'. "Just lie still. You've been injured and—"

"The *Vaxxar*?" The man's voice rasped painfully. He licked at dry lips.

"Go ahead, Kel-Faray," Kel-Paten said from where he stood at the comp screen.

"Yes, you're on the *Vaxxar*," Eden repeated calmly.

The man's gaze seemed centered on her chest. Eden belatedly realized her blue labcoat had come undone, revealing the thin v-necked shirt underneath. His gaze shifted towards Sass's pink t-shirt with its unorthodox logo and came back to Eden again.

"We believe the ship destroyed was Captain Serafino's ship, the *Novalis*," Kel-Faray's voice informed Sickbay.

Kel-Paten turned and a low, bitter expletive escaped his lips. The sound drew the man's attention and slowly, painfully he turned his head in Kel-Paten's direction.

In three strides Kel-Paten was next to Eden. "Serafino." He spat out the name, anger tingeing every syllable.

Jace Serafino responded with a cocky, lopsided grin. "It's good to see you, too, Tin Soldier. And you are...?" He grasped Eden's hand and brought it to his lips.

Eden stared in shock. *This* was the damned pirate? The morning's staff meeting outlining the mission to find him had clearly detailed all his sins...but hadn't provided, she realized with a start, one clear holoimage of the man. She wasn't sure even a clear one would've done him justice.

She drew her hand away immediately. "I'm Dr. Fynn, Chief Medical Officer."

He laughed softly at her discomfort, then coughed from the effort.

"Captain Serafino," Eden said sternly, "you really must—"

"Wait. Don't trank me out yet, sweetling." His voice rasped. "*No! No! Bad Captain!*" he read out loud. "Gods, this has to be Sebastian." He winked at her.

It was Sass's turn. "Captain Serafino—"

"Damn, Kel-Paten, I really have to compliment you," he said, turning away from her. "A truly creative and inspiring choice of uniforms for your officers."

And with that pronouncement, Jace Serafino promptly passed out.

CHAPTER THREE

CORRIDOR, SICKBAY DECK, THS *VAXXAR*

Tasha Sebastian lengthened her stride in an attempt to keep up with an angry Kel-Paten, who barked orders into his commbadge on their way back to the bridge.

"I want every bit of debris you can find, do you understand me? Every bit that's out there, lieutenant!"

They turned the corner. Two gray-clad maintenance crew dove out of their way.

No need for my morning jog with Eden, Sass thought as she trotted alongside, listening to the salvage crew lieutenant try to reason with Ol' No-Excuses Kel-Paten.

"I don't care what the current equipment limitations are, lieutenant! If you have to, you get *out* there with every Gods-damned sieve from the Gods-damned galley and bring me everything that may have been even remotely connected to the *Novalis*!"

They reached the lifts, both breathing hard. Sass considered taking her pulse and jogging in place. She certainly was in appropriate attire, but doubted that Kel-Paten, standing with his hands shoved in his pants pockets and scowling fiercely at the closed lift doors, would find her actions the least bit funny.

That she found them downright hysterical only told her how bloody tired she was.

With all the activity on board—emergency repair crews, relief shift personnel, medical personnel—the lifts were bound to be delayed. Of course, she knew none of this mattered one iota to Kel-Paten, who had now added impatient foot tapping to his repertoire of *fierce-scowl* and *don't-mess-with-me-hands-shoved-in-pockets* attitude.

She propped herself up against the wall next to the lift. The metallic sheeting was pleasantly cool against her bare midriff and she closed her eyes, pleading with the Deities for five seconds of peace and quiet and silence. Well, as much peace and quiet and silence as one could expect after what the *Vaxxar* had just gone through. But after all her years in space, the continuous chatter over shipboard comm requesting *Lt. So-and-So* to report to *Such-and-Such* or advising *Team Whatever* that the *Who-Gives-A-Lubashit Drill* was about to commence, no longer even registered in her mind.

Kel-Paten's deep voice, laced with undeniable bitterness, did.

"I gather you do not find the sudden appearance of the *Novalis* disturbing?"

Sass opened one eye, peered up at him. His gloved hands had left his pockets and were crossed over his chest. Classic defensive posture. *My, we're a bit testy this morning, aren't we?* And Gods, it *was* morning— about 0230 or later if the aches in her body were correct.

She closed her eye. "I find," she said, after a deep breath and the requisite counting to ten which was supposed to help but never really did, "the sudden appearance of the *Novalis*, and Captain Serafino, to be a major annoyance right now."

"Sebastian—"

Pause.

Oh, get a life! she thought wearily. *I really, really wish you would just get…a…life!* Reluctantly, she shoved herself away from the wall. "With all due respect, admiral, the appearance of Serafino at our doorstep has certainly saved us the time and expense of going to look for him. Do I find that a bit odd?" She rephrased his earlier question. "Yes, I find it odd. But disturbing?" She shook her head. "Not yet, not at this juncture and without further information."

"You mean you don't find it disturbing that within twenty-four hours of when *we* were commissioned to find Serafino—he suddenly shows up?"

No, I don't have your rampant paranoia, she thought as the lift signal pinged. *But Eden does have a virus to cure and this will only delay us more.* This morning's meeting had detailed the two hundred and fifty thousand credits that Serafino had allegedly absconded with. It was part of the Alliance's payment to him for undercover services that had never been rendered. The Triad Ministry of Intelligence was having furzel-fits over it. No doubt they'd want Serafino delivered for prosecution, and that meant, again, going in the opposite direction of the latest virus outbreak on Farside Station.

Kel-Paten stepped back, allowing her to enter the empty lift first. He gave the voice command for the bridge as the doors closed.

"Admiral, I will not jump to conclusions before I have all the facts and, right now, we don't have all the facts. We *are* in the quadrant where Serafino was last sighted, according to HQ's report. You yourself suggested at the staff meeting a few hours ago" —*Gods, was it only a few hours ago?*— "that it was your opinion that we weren't far behind him. Actually, it seems we were in front of him because somehow he got piggybacked to our—oh, never mind." He was giving her one of those sideways-warning looks. She decided to glare back up at him.

They were still glaring at each other when the lift pinged again to signal they'd reached Deck One. She didn't wait for him to step back to allow her to exit, but barged past him and strode down the corridor.

"Sebastian!" he called after her.

She stopped just short of the bridge doors and turned. A smile? Was that a glimpse of a smile just now leaving his face? She must be more tired than she thought. Ol' No-Excuses Kel-Paten never smiled. He scowled.

"Let's...let's get some coffee," he offered, waving his hand towards the other end of the corridor. "My office. I need to do some thinking aloud. I do it a lot better if you're there to punch holes in every theory I come up with."

"Sure," she said, unable to hide the note of surprise in her voice at his sudden change of tone. "I desperately need some coffee right now."

"Agreed." He slapped the commbadge on his shirt. "Kel-Faray, the captain and I will be in my office. I want an update on all damage reports in fifteen minutes. And everything and anything that Salvage comes up with on the *Novalis* as soon as you hear from them."

ADMIRAL'S OFFICE, THS *VAXXAR*

Sass had her back to him, leaning one hip against his office wall while she waited for the replicator to kick out two cups of coffee. Kel-Paten permitted himself a few moments of pleasurable indulgence at the sight, then clicked open the comm on his console before he totally forgot why the Keltish Triad had bestowed the rank of admiral on him. "Dr. Fynn, Kel-Paten here. What's the status on Serafino?"

"He regained consciousness briefly," Fynn told him, an undercurrent of exhaustion in her voice. Sass pushed a steaming cup across the desk towards him, then sat. He nodded and focused on the CMO's report.

"We've given him a sedative and he's resting comfortably. His injuries are serious but not life-threatening."

"Good. Your orders, Doctor, are to keep him alive, but that's all. Just keep him alive long enough so I can have the pleasure of killing him. Kel-Paten out."

He sifted through a short line of messages from various division commanders that had blinked on his comp screen just as he finished with Fynn. He could've spiked in through the interface in the armrest of his chair and downloaded the information directly into his memory, but Sass was there, sitting, sipping coffee, watching him.

He knew what he was. He knew she knew what he was. He just didn't like reminding her of it. Spiked in, he'd be on full cybe power, and his eyes would take on a luminescent hue. He'd had no choice on the bridge earlier when they'd encountered the threat of the vortex. But he had a choice here.

"I apologize for the delay." He reached for his coffee as he turned away from the comp screen. "But there were a couple—" And he hesitated, stopped in his mental and verbal tracks by the enigmatic grin on Sass's face. "—a couple of things I was...um, Sebastian?"

Sass wiped the grin off her face and pulled herself upright in her chair. "Oh, sorry. When I'm tired, the mind wanders, you know."

"Looks like it wandered into a rather pleasant place," he commented as blandly as the suspicious and jealous thoughts bouncing around in his head would permit. *What, no, who had she been thinking of?* The look on her face had been absolutely blissful—like a furzel licking fresh cream off her whiskers.

"Just a couple of ideas I've been playing around with," she replied with a shrug.

He hoped like hell it wasn't ideas about one of his Engineering officers. "If I can be of any help..." he offered, all the while knowing that if she ever *did* confide in him that she was interested in someone, he'd be duty-bound to kill the man. Or at the very least transfer him to the farthest reaches of the galaxy where nothing, human or otherwise, would ever wish to be.

He would have no choice. And while he was at it, he'd send that bastard Serafino with him.

Serafino. A thought occurred to him, so chilling that even the mouthful of steaming coffee he took did nothing to melt the rock hard feeling that had suddenly lodged in the pit of his stomach.

Had Sass been thinking of Serafino?

Serafino's effect on—and prowess with—women was legendary.

Kel-Paten hadn't missed the wink Serafino had given her, had seen the way Serafino's gaze had raked over her half-naked form...

She'd been reluctant to leave Sickbay; wanted to check on the rest of the crew there, she'd said, and he had to all but order her to return with him to the bridge.

Serafino.

He hadn't realized he'd spoken the name aloud until he heard Sass's voice.

"What about Captain Serafino?" she asked. "Besides the fact that he's here and our house guest for a while."

House guest? He'd prefer to see him an occupant of the morgue. He tapped at his screen, bringing up a series of folders on Serafino. All intelligence gathered by the Triad over the last fifteen years.

"Just what do you know about Serafino?" he asked. "Not," he touched the screen, "what's written here. But what do *you* know? Have you meet him before?"

"Probably not that he'd remember."

"You've met before." The tone of his voice dropped the room temperature about forty degrees.

"My life's been full of interesting characters. It's part of my job description."

"You find Serafino interesting?" He steepled his fingers in front of his face and peered at her from over their black-clad tips.

She sighed. "I thought you wanted to run some theories by me."

Why are you being evasive, Sass? Then, out loud: "I do. And I will. Tell me why you find Serafino interesting."

"Why not? You find him disturbing," she challenged. "I think interesting might fit right in there. Especially when you consider the circles he's run around the Triad, the U-Cees and the Illithians for years. And, oh yes, the T'Sarii. Let's not forget the T'Sarii. In some ways, I admire his...creativity," she added with a flip of her hand.

He closed his eyes briefly. Creativity? Unorthodox methodology was more like it, and not unlike his own Sass in that. A devil-may-care attitude. *Of course* she found Serafino interesting. What woman wouldn't?

"So you've met before. How many years ago? Just how well did you know him?" He fired the questions at her.

Anger flared in her eyes. She sat upright. "I don't know what you're getting at, but if you're accusing *me* of any collusion with Serafino—then let's just come out and say it right now, shall we? And cut all this twenty-questions lubashit."

17

"You can check my service record. And you can talk to my crew on the *Regalia* and on the *Goldstar* and all the other ships before that and you will find that I have never and will never sell out my allegiance to the U-Cees—or the Alliance, or whoever the hell we are now!" She slammed her fist down on the armrest of her chair, punctuating the end of her sentence.

Before he could reply, she rose to her full five feet in height and pointed her finger at him. "*You* think that because the *Novalis* shows up right after we get ordered to find him that *I* leaked that information to him somehow, don't you? That's what you meant when you said you found his 'sudden appearance disturbing', isn't it?"

"Sebastian—"

"Why would I do that," she continued, leaning her hands on his desk, "and drop him just-so-pretty in your lap if I were working with him? That would make no bloody sense!"

"Sebastian—" He wiped one hand across his face.

"Do you really think I'm that stupid?"

No, but he'd begun to wonder about his own mental faculties. Somehow he'd lost control of this discussion several minutes back, and he wasn't quite sure how or where. His discussions with Sass often contained heated exchanges; though not the kind of heat he'd have liked. They'd clashed, amicably, for years. Yet there was something different in her forcefulness this time. An element of hurt, or fear?

"I don't think you're stupid. Now sit down."

She sat, though he could tell by the way she folded her arms across *My name's No! No! Bad Captain!* that she was none too happy about it. Or with him.

"I don't think you're stupid," he repeated. "I just need to know how you know Serafino, and from where."

"From Queenie's," came the terse answer after an equally tense silence.

Queenie's? The name had a faint ring of familiarity but he couldn't place it. "What's Queenie's?"

"A whorehouse and casino on Farside Station." She leaned back in her chair. "Don't look so shocked, Kel-Paten. I spent two years with U-CID doing undercover work. I have a knack for ferreting out illegal arms sales."

"I've heard." He tapped his fingers against his mouth. He'd read and damn near memorized her personnel file, knew about her training with the United Coalition Intelligence Division. But her mention of casinos brought up his old fantasy of taking her to T'garis, the Triad's casino world.

"It's in my personnel file," she reminded him.

"And Serafino was..."

"A player. I doubt he'd remember me. That was almost fifteen years ago. Plus, even if he did, he wouldn't remember me as 'Sebastian'. I didn't even—" And she stopped, gave her head a small shake. "—I couldn't use my real name," she added quickly. "We all had nicknames. That's what we used."

"Sass," he said.

"What? Oh, yes." She nodded. "Everyone called me 'Sass'."

He tapped his fingers against his mouth again before speaking. "Appropriately descriptive."

She shrugged. "I won't argue that." She drew a deep breath. "Have we cleared up any possible charges of treason against me? Or should I anticipate spending the night in the brig, just to be safe?"

Oh, Sass, he thought, *how very appropriately descriptive.* He now knew more, yet knew nothing. He'd never doubted her loyalty to the Alliance or her crew for a moment. That had never been the issue, though she'd thought it was.

It was her allegiance to himself that had him bone-chilled worried.

"I don't think the *Vax's* brig could hold you," he answered truthfully.

That finally evoked a small smile from her. "Not for long," she agreed. "Now, are you finally ready to discuss whatever it is you think we should be working on?"

He shook his head, closing his eyes briefly. Even with his eyes closed, those damn yellow numbers still glowed in the lower left corner of his vision: 0342.15.20. No matter how many numbers were attached, it was still very very late.

Or very very early.

He always had the option of switching to his surplus power supply to stay awake for another thirty-six to forty-eight hours. Under normal conditions, he rarely slept for more than four hours a night.

But Sass had no auxiliary cybernetic power supply. And any feasible and productive time for discussion had long since passed.

"No," he said. "It's late, Sebastian. Your temper's sharp and my mind is not right now." He waved her off. "Go get some sleep."

"You sure? Look, Kel-Paten, I'm sorry I popped off at you like—"

"I'm sure. Go."

"I really *am* sorry."

"I doubt it," he said and forced his mouth into what he hoped looked like a smile. It wasn't an expression he was used to wearing, and it felt as if his mouth fought him every time he tried. "If you ever stopped arguing with me, I'd worry because I'd know there was something very wrong."

"Okay." She eased herself up out of the chair and headed for the door. "We'll pick up where we left off tomorrow morning—today. Morning. Hell, you know what I mean!"

"Oh-eight-thirty, this office," he told her as the door whooshed open.

"Oh-eight-thirty?" she squeaked.

"Oh-nine-thirty, then. In uniform. And on time."

"Who, me?" she asked in mock innocence then saluted him, hand over her heart. "By your command, admiral."

"Dismissed," he replied and then, ever so softly, and only after the door had closed, said a gentle benediction: "And may the Gods keep you in their care."

That had been his private blessing to her for years, so much so that it was almost automatic, though rarely spoken out loud. Yet this time, he added extra energy to the plea. Something about Serafino's appearance bothered him. Something more than just the fact that the man was a pirate, a rogue...a decidedly romantic figure.

Something about Serafino bothered him deeply. He steepled his hand in front of his mouth and tried to identify the source of his disquiet.

He couldn't. And that bothered Admiral Branden Kel-Paten, the infamous Tin Solider, even more.

CHAPTER FOUR

SICKBAY, THS *VAXXAR*

Halfway through downloading a report regarding the medical status of Serafino and his crew, Eden Fynn came to the conclusion that there must be, at the very least, a racquet-lob game going on somewhere in Sickbay. A *silent* racquet-lob game, which only Captain Tasha Sebastian could see. Or was trying to see.

The booted foot propped against the edge of Eden's desk rocked the captain's chair, now tilted at a precarious angle, back and forth, back and forth. It was a motion, Eden noted, that was in direct relation to the sound of Sickbay's doors opening:

Phwoosh.

Sass tilted back, head turned slightly for a second.

Thwip. The doors closed. Sass sat forward.

Phwoosh.

Sass tilted back.

Thwip.

Sass sat forward.

Given the amount of traffic through Sickbay on a normal day—and they were less than twenty-four hours after the vortex rift incident—there was always a lot of *phwooshing* and *thwiping*. Most of which Eden had long ago learned to ignore.

But the captain's seesawing movements were, after all the stress of the day before, just a bit more than Eden could take. However, she at least waited until Sass was in the *thwip* stage before she reached over her desk and grabbed the older woman's boot.

Startled, Sass almost went ass over teakettle right out of Eden's office.

"Hey! What are you—?"

"What are *you* doing?" Eden chimed in. "Are you rocking yourself to sleep down here? Or am I missing Fleet finals in racquet-lob being played in my ER?"

"I'm—? Oh, sorry!" Sass grinned sheepishly and dropped her foot to the floor. "It's *him*," she explained with an upward wave of her hand that delineated something larger and taller. "I swear to the Gods he's following me around. If I go down to Engineering, five minutes later, there he is. If I'm in the Mess having tea, bingo. He shows up. He's driving me—how do you like to put it? Nucking futz?"

"This is something new?" Eden asked in obvious disbelief.

The answer was preceded by a sigh. "No, just worse. And I'm just getting less tolerant, losing my patience." She rubbed the heels of her hands over her eyes. "I really popped off at him last night. This morning. That was wrong. Unprofessional. I should know better than to let him push my buttons. But his paranoia is getting to me."

"Paranoia?"

"Yeah, you know. Questioning everything I do, everywhere I've been, everyone I talk to...paranoia. I think he thinks I'm going to wholesale Triadian secrets to the Kalfi, or some such lubashit."

"Like what?"

"Like what?" Sass repeated. "I don't know. I don't even know what secrets the Kalfi would be interested in. Or don't already know."

"No, not that. What kind of questions—what makes you think Kel-Paten is paranoid?"

"You mean besides the fact that he insists on personally reviewing just about every damn report I write? Or tries to fill up what little spare time I have doing this-that-or-the-other thing with him where—and I know this is true—he can keep an eye on me? So I don't go wholesaling stuff to the Kalfi." She raised her eyes in a pleading gesture. "Like yesterday, after the staff meeting. 'I'll require your attention for a moment longer'," she mimicked, lowering her voice in a bad imitation.

Eden chuckled.

"Multiply that by one hundred and you've got my week."

Eden nodded. She understood Sass's frustration. She also had her theories about Kel-Paten's reasons, but she wasn't sure enough to voice them. Especially if she were right, and the bio-cybernetic construct in charge of the newly formed Alliance Fleet actually *was* experiencing emotions. Then she, as Chief Medical Officer, might just have to Section Forty-Six him. She didn't think that would go over well in the Triad part of the Alliance. It might even start another war. Then a puzzling virus would be the least of their problems.

"Then when he finds out I knew Serafino—"

"You *know* Serafino?" The information surprised Eden.

"Gods, not you, too!" Sass groaned. "Yes, I knew Serafino. Past tense. Briefly. I worked at Queenie's, years ago, remember?"

Eden nodded.

"He was a player. I knew the name that went with the face, that was all. Didn't mean a whole lot at the time; his kind at Queenie's wasn't exactly unique."

"Would Serafino remember you?"

"I doubt it. Why?"

"Because I'm a little worried about his condition," Eden admitted. "He regained consciousness—briefly—after you left. I was working on the T'Sariian, Dr. Monterro was attending Serafino. Did what was necessary to make him comfortable. Nothing out of the ordinary. Trouble is, he should have fully come out of it by now, or at least be showing some signs... I don't know. Maybe, because of his physical condition—" he was incredibly fit, Eden had noted. "—he's strong, very strong, very healthy. An older, weaker man might require more time. Not Serafino."

"You don't ride through a vortex flare and come out smelling like a blossom," Sass pointed out. "And the *Novalis* wasn't the *Vax*."

"True, but—"

"But, what? Talk to me, Healer." Sass leaned forward, lowering her voice. "You've picked up something, are sensing something, and you don't like it. I've known you too long, Doc. What do we have here?"

"I wish I could answer that," Eden said truthfully, folding her hands. "It's nothing I've encountered before. But whatever it is, it's keeping him unconscious. I just thought that, if he knew you, if he heard a familiar voice, it might draw him out."

"I could try standing next to him and say 'place your bets, please' or 'ante up' but I don't think that's really going to help."

"No, probably not," Eden admitted. "I—uh-oh." She reached for a stack of reports to her left and quickly dragged them to the middle of her desk. Her voice, when she spoke, was a bit louder than normal and almost authoritative. Eden did many things extremely well. Acting was not one of them.

"—and I think that if we can make the crew understand the importance of proper nutrition...oh, hello, admiral. Can I help you with something?"

"Doctor."

23

Sass raised her eyes in a pleading gesture before turning in her chair.

"Sebastian," Kel-Paten said. Pause. "I didn't realize the doctor needed to report to you concerning the crew's nutritional requirements."

"We were covering a number of topics," Sass told him blandly.

Eden quietly replaced the report into the stack, hoping the admiral hadn't noticed the large graphic of a furzel on the top. It was a report on the pet-rescue system she'd designed for the few domesticated animals allowed on the *Vax*, including Sass's furzel and her own. Had Kel-Paten seen the graphic and tied it in with her words, he would no doubt think they were going to serve sliced furzel in the Mess Hall.

"You'll be off duty shortly, Doctor." It was a question, but as with most questions posed by Admiral Kel-Paten, it was issued in the form of a statement.

Eden glanced at her watch. "Yes."

"Then I'm sure you have things to attend to before leaving."

No, she'd done most of them, anticipating Sass's arrival so they could then have dinner in the Officer's Mess together. "Actually, the captain and I were—"

"I'm afraid I'll be requiring—" and at this point, Sass turned her head so that only Eden could see, and exactly mouthed Kel-Paten's words. "—Captain Sebastian's attention at this time."

Then Sass stood and faced Kel-Paten so Eden would have time to recover from her coughing fit. "I don't suppose it can wait until after dinner? I made plans to—"

"I'm sorry, but you'll have to cancel those plans. I'll have something to eat brought to the Ready Room."

Sass sighed theatrically. "Ahh, dining by starlight, eh, admiral?" The *Vax's* Ready Room had large floor-to-ceiling viewports set into the outer wall. "How can I resist such an invitation?" And with that, she waltzed out of the office, singing strains from a corny but romantic musical number that had been popular many years before.

The mask dropped. Eden saw it. Kel-Paten's usual impassive expression had suddenly blurred into something heavily tinged with emotion as Sass had turned her face up to his, coquettishly, and purred about being unable to resist his invitation. And Eden had seen more than that. She'd seen the auras that only she, or another like her, could see.

Kel-Paten's aura pulsed with an intensity not unlike the hot flare of the vortex he'd fought yesterday.

He was fighting this, Eden realized, but it was a losing battle. She didn't need her ability to read auras to see the hunger in his eyes as he watched Sass leave Sickbay.

He looked back at Eden for a brief moment, as if he were about to say something. Then it was as if he realized what had happened: the perpetually flippant captain had responded, as she often did, with sarcasm. And he'd misread her, badly, because he wanted to…badly.

But this time, Eden had witnessed it.

Section Forty-Six.

The mask fell back into place.

"If you'll excuse me, Doctor." He inclined his head slightly.

"Of course."

Eden leaned back in her chair after he left and released the tension of the past few moments with a large sigh. Sass's natural lighthearted and often flippant attitude was going to lead her into big trouble. Sass teased everyone, but Kel-Paten was not something you teased. She doubted if teasing was even in his emotional programming. Which meant he was subrouting all his responses through whatever last known human emotional levels had been present when the psycho-cybernetics had been added.

Which would have been when he was around sixteen or seventeen years old.

Eden groaned out loud.

Paranoia? No, Kel-Paten wasn't suffering from paranoia.

He was suffering from adolescence!

EDEN FYNN'S QUARTERS, THS *VAXXAR*

Something bothered Eden all through dinner with Caleb Monterro and Dannar Kel-Minra, but she couldn't quite place what it was. Dann, a lieutenant in navigation, was pleasant, about her own age and made no attempts to disguise his interest in her. He was a kind and gentle man, and kind and gentle enough not to push himself on her or make her feel uncomfortable in any way.

But he didn't make her feel anything else either. In the years since her divorce, she couldn't truly remember a man who had. Though she'd known, and dated, many nice men.

Who were…nice. But that was all.

She prowled about her quarters after dinner and wondered if that's what made her feel so restless. Her life was fulfilling in all areas except one: romance.

Maybe she expected too much. She hadn't signed on with Fleet while still in medical school because she'd been husband-hunting.

She thought about taking a sedative—she had the night before only because of sheer exhaustion. But tonight, other than that odd restlessness, she felt better, more rested, with just the usual aggravations of a huntership CMO. So a cup of Orange Garden tea and the comfort of Reilly, her large black furzel, nestled against her, was all she needed. Not surprisingly, she fell asleep shortly after her head touched the pillow.

Or she thought she did.

Over the years, she'd tried many times to figure out if the space she now occupied—this gray, hazy yet palpably solid space—was real or just a dream.

It never felt like a dream. It felt as if she stood in a large, dimly lit room. Or building. Yet she had no sense of walls. But she had a definite sense of floor and, as she'd done for years, she took a few steps forward once she realized where she was.

She wasn't afraid. This wasn't a frightening or lonely place. Rather, it was a place of immense peace, immense calm. A waiting place. An in-between place.

There was always a gentleness in the gray mists about her, as there was now. It was a place that calmed her mind and often, when she was troubled before sleep, she would wake, if that's what she did, to find herself here. And she knew that if she waited long enough, thoughts or images would come into her mind. She wouldn't physically see them— she'd never physically seen anything here except for the soothing gray mists.

Except now.

She almost stumbled over him in the fog, sensing his presence more than seeing it only moments before they collided—she, moving dreamily forward and he, just rising from his seat. And then there was the warm and very reassuring pressure of his hands on her arm and about her waist as he drew her against him, then back down to the bench.

A bench. A stone bench.

And a man.

Jace Serafino.

"I'm sorry, I—ohmygods!" she gasped as she recognized the deep blue eyes staring intensely at her.

She was dreaming, she had to be dreaming. But her hand, now pressing against the soft fabric of the shirt covering his chest, felt the presence of a heartbeat.

He studied her face. "I...know you." Like Kel-Paten, it was a question, yet a statement.

She nodded. "Dr. Eden Fynn, CMO on the *Vaxxar*." And winced when she heard the formality of her own tone. *Why the hell didn't you just add 'reporting for duty'?* she chastised herself mentally.

Jace was smiling at her. "Why didn't you?" he asked.

"Why didn't I—" And she stopped, frozen by the realization that he'd heard her thoughts.

You're a telepath. She whispered the thought in her mind.

Yes. Like you.

Like me? He was wrong! *I'm...I'm not a telepath.* To be a telepath in the Triad was to be feared, to be manipulated. You were either an agent with Psy-Serv, or you were declared legally insane. *I'm a healer, an empath! I'm—*

You're here, aren't you? His question was gentle, as gentle as the hands that now rested against her waist. She knew she should object to this sudden familiarity, except that it didn't seem all that sudden. The way he held her, the way he'd guided her to the bench, even the way he now used that light, teasing tone in his voice—his mind-voice—raised no internal alarms in her. Even her doctor-patient concerns didn't exist on this level.

This telepathic level. This *here* which she had known all her life and now didn't understand.

Here? she questioned.

In Novalis.

She shook her head. *I don't understand. The* Novalis *was your ship.*

Novalis *is a place. This place. I named my ship after it.*

How did you...how did you know the name? Did you name this place?

His soft chuckle was audible. *The Ancients named this place, I think. Or maybe the Gods did. It depends on which legend you're taught. Don't your people have songs about it?*

I don't know. Not that I remember. But I wasn't raised...my father was human.

Ahhh. He touched his fingers lightly on the left side of her face, first at her temple, then twice on her cheek, about an inch apart. His thumb came to rest under her chin.

She was trembling. She knew what he'd done and who—no, *what*, he was. She had felt his touch beyond her mere physical existence, though the physical sensations were admittedly pleasant.

He'd marked her. It was an ancient benediction; a ritual blessing some said was older than the U-Cees, older than the Triad. It was a blessing of a Nasyry warrior-priest that denoted safekeeping: "May the Gods keep you in their care" were the words that often accompanied it.

Innocuous words, but said by a Nasyry they carried power.

A power that hadn't been seen or heard from by either the U-Cees or the Triad in over three hundred years.

"Who are you?" She spoke out loud now, afraid what her thoughts would reveal.

He looked at her quizzically and withdrew his hand from her chin. "Jace Serafino, last time I checked."

"You're Nasyry."

His eyes narrowed for a moment. "Your studies have not been totally lacking, Doctor."

"I...no. There were things I've wanted to know."

"Self-taught, Healer?"

"Mostly, yes."

His hand was back, cupping her face. She felt his feather-light touch in her mind.

You're a touch telepath, Doctor, do you know that? At least, you are with me. You can link to my thoughts by touching me.

I'm an empath, she repeated.

The two aren't mutually exclusive. You experience your strongest empathic readings when you touch your patients, don't you?

Yes. But in Sickbay, I tried with you. There was nothing.

A small smile. *I beg to differ. You underrate yourself. Especially in that delightful outfit—do you always wear see-through clothing in Sickbay? And I found that touch of blue lace rather memorable...*

Eden saw what he'd seen as he flashed the mental image to her: she'd chosen that shirt for comfort and had forgotten that its low-cut neckline would gape when she leaned over. And the blue lace—Gods, that bright blue bra of hers!

That's—that's not what I meant!

You blush beautifully. I'll have to keep that in mind.

Captain Serafino—

Jace. There was a firm but friendly insistence in his tone.

She sighed. *Jace, I received no telepathic readings from you in Sickbay. Why?*

A waft of negative emotion now; a slight tension from him that quickly faded. *That was Psy-Serv's best effort.*

Psy-Serv? You're agent for them? A frisson of fear ran up her spine before she could stop it.

No! His answer was emphatic. *May the Gods strike me dead if I ever...*

He drew her against him, fitting her against his broad chest, his face resting in her hair. She could feel the warmth of his breath on her neck and it was calming, reassuring, like the gray mists around her.

And there was something else: safety. Protection. Like the ritual blessing he'd traced on her face, he now wove a pattern of wholeness in her mind. Eden imagined that she couldn't feel more protected were one of the Gods to suddenly come down and cup her in His hand. There was a tremendous power in this man called Jace Serafino. And a tremendous benevolence.

Suddenly he tensed, his breath catching hard as sharp pains, thin and cutting as microfine wires, laced through his body. He thrust her from him, but she grabbed for his hand.

"Eden, don't, Gods, Eden don't, it might kill you!" he rasped.

"Jace, what is it? What's wrong?" Where they touched her flesh stung and tingled, like a thousand insects dancing a fandango of death on her skin.

He managed a pained smile. "Psy-Serv. Years ago." He gulped for air. "An implant. There's an implant. That's why you can't—"

He slid to the ground, his body shaking. "Oh, Gods. Eden, help me!"

Then he disappeared.

She bolted out of her bed, rudely dislodging the sleeping furzel. She pulled on her workout shorts and the nearest sweatshirt, grabbing for her sneakers and commbadge. It trilled just as she exited into the corridor.

"Sickbay to Fynn! We've got a Code Red on Captain Serafino!"

"I know, Gods damn it, I know!" she barked back at the tiny transmitter. "I'm in the lift and on my way!"

CHAPTER FIVE

SHIP'S GYM, THS *VAXXAR*

Sass called it the "Kiss Your Ass Good-bye" stretch—bend over, grab your ankles and try to yank your head through your legs. That was Sass's position when she saw Eden walk in. Well, perhaps 'walk' wasn't the right word. Even from her upside-down vantage point, the CMO's method of perambulation was better categorized as 'trudge'.

And Eden Fynn rarely trudged.

A tall full-figured woman of a comfortable beauty, Eden Fynn had sparkling blue eyes, golden blonde hair, a well-proportioned distinctly feminine form and, as had been overheard more than once from the lips of various male crew, "legs that didn't quit". But, of course, that reference had nothing to do with the act of walking, an act that Eden wasn't performing with her usual bright gait. Especially not at 0630 when she normally bounded in to the gym to accompany Sass on their morning jog.

"Captain, we need to talk," Eden said as Sass slowly straightened out of her stretch.

Captain. Eden only called her 'Captain' in the presence of pompous muckety-mucks (like the admiral) or when both of them were totally trashed and trying like hell to act sober.

Or when there was a problem. A big, *big* problem.

Sass took an intuitive leap based on the fact that Eden was still in her Sickbay scrubs: "Serafino."

A confirming nod.

"He's...still alive?"

"Yes. Don't ask me how or why, but yes."

"Kel-Paten didn't—"

"This has nothing to do with Kel-Paten. At least, not at this point," Eden said with a tired sigh.

"Then what does it have to do with?"

Eden's answer was barely audible. "Psy-Serv."

"Oh, damn." That wasn't a term Sass wanted to hear. She grabbed her friend by the elbow. "My office. No. My quarters." The latter was the only place she could be sure Kel-Paten wouldn't barge into, unannounced.

The replicator in the captain's quarters dutifully produced a steaming cup of tea and a cup of darkly pungent Mahrian blend coffee while Sass sat at the small dining table, hands folded, and listened to Eden's recitation: her inability to use her empathic senses to diagnose Serafino; her nagging feeling of something being very wrong; and her inexplicable encounter with Jace Serafino in a place called 'Novalis'.

"Tell me again," Sass said. "This place, this is not just a dream. You'd know a dream from, from whatever this is."

Eden plucked one of the plump lushberries from the bowl in front of her. "I guess you could liken it more to a meditative state; an 'out of body experience'. I, you'd have an existence there.You can touch and feel things."

"Like when Kel-Paten spikes in. He's on the bridge but he could also be in engineering."

"Sort of," Eden agreed. "Except that he's not physically in both places."

"And you are."

"Yes."

"Okay. More like a simdeck program. Simdeck programs have substance. Temporary substance, but substance."

Eden thought for a moment. "If Kel-Paten were to spike in to the simdeck and recreate himself—"

"Which is illegal," Sass cut in.

"Yes, which is illegal. But if he did that while he was spiked in and was also physically on the bridge, and then had a secondary substantial existence on the simdeck—that's probably the closest to what I'm talking about."

Sass sat back in her chair, popped a large purple lushberry in her mouth. "Damn!" She chewed thoughtfully. "So okay, so you do this. I mean, you are Zingaran. How did Serafino get there?"

Eden waited until Sass swallowed the berry. "He's a telepath," she stated.

Sass felt her jaw drop open. "Ohhh, damn."

"I know."

"You mentioned Psy-Serv." Sass's words came quickly, her brain pumping out worried thoughts even faster. "If Serafino's a telepath—and you're sure of this, I assume—If Serafino's a telepath, and the Triad, I mean, the Alliance, had ostensibly hired him for the Illithian mission, that means he's on their payroll, which means he's also on Psy-Serv's payroll...am I right on this? Are you following me?"

"Yes. I mean, no, he's not on Psy-Serv's payroll. He's on Psy-Serv's shit list."

The proverbial light of knowledge clicked on in Sass's brain. "A rogue telepath."

"I think that's probably correct."

"You *think*—?"

"I'm not sure. We hadn't gotten that far into an explanation when his physical body in Sickbay had a seizure. Courtesy of Psy-Serv. That much he did manage to tell me."

"Courtesy of Psy-Serv?"

Eden nodded. "There's an implant in his brain. It doesn't show up on any of my med-scans—that's how treacherous it is. I had to use other methods to find out what little I know. It's triggered by the resonance of any telepathic activity and makes such activity excruciatingly painful."

"But you said he met you, telepathically, in this Novalis place. How could he if he has this implant?"

A sigh of frustration blew through Eden's lips. "I don't exactly know right now. It's one of the things I'm working on. He seems to be able to override it for short periods of time."

"Why did Psy-Serv put it there?"

"That I don't know either," Eden admitted.

Sass grabbed Eden's empty cup along with her own and stuck them in the replicator port. "Tea, Orange Garden blend, and coffee, double black, Mahrian," she ordered. Then, as the beverages materialized, "Behavioral implants have been used with homicidal psychotics."

"That was outlawed over sixty-five years ago. I even checked my medical journals on that."

"Lubashit." Sass handed the steaming cup to Eden and sat back down at the table. She held Eden's gaze with her own for a moment, then looked away. "There were cons on Lethant who had them. There was talk that they should have done that with me. I don't know if I ever told you about that."

"Only that it was a horrible experience," Eden replied.

Sass' eighteen-month stay on the U-Cee's prison world—a desolate, lawless wasteland populated by what the legal system adjudicated to be human filth—wasn't easy for her to talk about. Not even now. Not even with Eden, who was one of the few people who knew the truth.

"Were they recent implants?" Eden asked, bring Sass's thoughts back to the present problem at hand.

Sass shrugged. "Depends on what you call recent. I was there seven years ago. Gods, was it only seven? Seems like yesterday." She tilted her head back and downed the last of her coffee. "How time flies when you're having fun." She smiled thinly. "Anyway, to answer your question, yes, seven years ago they were still doing brain implants as a way of behavior control. They had a med facility on Lethant."

"I don't suppose they'd risk doing them on Varlow," Eden mused.

"Right next door to HQ? Hell, no. The public outcry would've toppled the government faster than a fleet of Triad hunterships. Oops, sorry. I forgot; we're one of them, now. But where were we?" she asked, her fingers pinching the bridge of her nose for a moment. Talking about Lethant invariably gave her a headache. "Oh, yes. Serafino. The implant. Are we sure we're not dealing with some serious psychosis here? I take it you want to remove the implant."

"I think if I don't, it'll kill him."

"Are you sure if we do, he won't kill us?" Sass challenged.

"At this point, relatively sure."

"Kel-Paten's not going to like 'relatively'," Sass said.

"Kel-Paten...Sass, I need a favor." Eden leaned over the table towards her friend. "I don't want the admiral brought in yet."

"Because of his well-publicized hatred for telepaths? I can understand your concern, but Eden, he hates Serafino pretty thoroughly already. I don't see where telling him Serafino's a telepath is going to add to that much."

"It's not just Serafino," Eden answered quietly. "I'm a telepath, too."

This time Sass's mouth gaped all the way open. "But..." she managed finally. "How?"

Years ago, Psy-Serv had set up their own system of identifying telepaths and drafting them into service. The official line that it was all volunteer, yet no one knew of any telepath who had said no, and lived. And just in case someone tried to hide his or her talents, Psy-Serv routinely scanned the populace, starting in grade school, for the slightest twinge of telepathic ability.

If there were 'rogue' telepaths, and there were always rumors there were a few, it was because they had grown up outside the system, on desolate rim worlds, never being exposed to formal schooling. Or regular medical exams.

Sass knew what that was like.

But Eden had been raised in a nice little dirtside colony and had attended all the proper schools and all the proper birthday parties. And that was the center of Sass's question—how had Eden escaped Psy-Serv's scans?

"I'm not sure," Eden said. "But I think it's because I'm half-Zingaran and was recognized as an empath when I was still small. Whatever they sensed from me they probably just chalked up to empathic talents.

"That, and I don't really remember experiencing what Serafino calls Novalis until I was in my teens, maybe thirteen? Fourteen? The telepaths I'd heard about developed their talents much younger, around four or five."

"But when you went for your Fleet physical, didn't they scan you again?"

"Yes. But...I don't know. That's something else I don't have an answer for right now."

"But you're sure?"

Eden nodded slowly. "That I'm telepathic? Gods help me, yes I am. Though obviously not well trained or I wouldn't be running into the problems I have now."

"With Serafino."

"I'm hoping I can contact him again. I'm hoping he may have the answer to the implant."

Sass retrieved her third cup of coffee. "What do you need me to do?" she asked when she returned to the table.

"Keep Kel-Paten out of Sickbay as much as possible, for one," Eden replied.

"That means you won't be seeing much of me. Where I go, he goes these days. What else?"

Eden took a deep breath. "As you said, Kel-Paten has no great love for telepaths, or for Psy-Serv. I have reason to believe he has an extensive personal library of Psy-Serv's history, their methods, their means, everything. I need access to those datafiles."

"You think they might hold the answer to Serafino's implant?"

"Maybe not Serafino's specifically, but at least its medical pedigree."

Sass pursed her lips and regarded her friend carefully. "You're asking me to break into the admiral's secure locked datafiles. Files that are probably loaded with every defensive hacker trap he could create with his mega-million credit mind. Files that probably have more security devices, hidden alarms and fail-safe programs than anything else in civilized space, Psy-Serv's own databanks included."

"Yes."

"Files that are located in his quarters, which are again no doubt the most secure location on this ship; hell, probably in this fleet."

"Yes."

Sass shrugged. "Piece o' cake. Anything else?"

"If you get caught, we'll both be court-martialed, you know that."

"No," Sass replied. "We won't both be court-martialed. If I get caught, I go down alone."

"Sass—"

"No buts about it, Fynn. I survived Lethant. If I get caught, and it's still an 'if', they'd probably send me back there, or someplace like it that the Triad has, since it would be a Triadian officer's secure files I violated. In any case, as I said, I've done Lethant. Been there, done that, bought the vidloop, as they say. And I can tell you, you wouldn't survive. Nothing against you, but you weren't raised like I was."

Eden shot her a look that clearly stated she was in disagreement with Sass's opinion. "It's not an issue," Eden said, "because, number one, you won't get caught, right?"

At the optimistic pronouncement, Sass grinned broadly.

"And number two, if you are, I'd bet you Kel-Paten won't tell a soul."

Sass burst out laughing. "Lubashit! Are you kidding? He'd be so righteously pissed that my biggest problem would be talking him out of venting me out the port exhaust just so I could be formally court-martialed!"

<^>

No, Eden thought as she trudged a little less wearily back to her quarters, the last thing on Kel-Paten's mind if he found Sass in his quarters would be any kind of disciplinary action. Unless of course it involved silk whips and Sass in a black leather bustier…

No, No, Bad CMO! she chided herself as she stripped off her scrubs and stepped into the shower. Her friend never did strike her as the 'whip and leather' type. With Kel-Paten, there was no telling where his fantasies lay. Eden had a feeling that as long as they included Sass, in person and in his cabin, he wouldn't give a hoot for what she'd be wearing. As long as it could be removed quickly.

She glanced at the clock on her nightstand and told the computer to wake her at 1330 hours. That would give her about five hours of sleep, which she desperately needed. And with Serafino sedated after the seizure, she felt safe that she wouldn't be meeting up with him in Novalis right now.

They both needed a good night's sleep.

EDEN FYNN'S QUARTERS, THS *VAXXAR*

The last thing Eden remembered was Reilly snuggling against her arm, purring loudly. Then Jace was rising from the stone bench, hand outstretched to greet her.

"I hoped you'd be here." He took her hand in his as they sat down. "I thought I might have scared you away." He smiled, but it was a smile touched with a nervous tension.

"You shouldn't be here," she said, the concern in her voice evident. "I don't know if I can pull you back from another seizure."

"I overstayed my limit last time, I'm sorry. But—"

"Your limit?" Then her guess had been right. He had a way of temporarily bypassing the implant.

He nodded. "Twelve minutes and fifteen seconds is max at the moment. I try to keep an internal clock running, but it got away from me last time. It's just been so long..." he closed his eyes briefly. "I have so much to tell you, so much to explain. I just don't know if there's time."

A feeling of deep loneliness emanated from him.

"You haven't been in touch with another telepath in quite some time." It wasn't a guess. She was primarily an empath.

"More than four years. Not since Bianca."

"Bianca?" she questioned and immediately an image flashed into her mind: a woman, dark-haired and beautiful. She recognized the azure-blue eyes. They were like Jace's. She felt the bond of strong affection he had for his older sister. And she also realized how much more could be transmitted telepathically than through words. In those brief moments when she experienced Bianca Serafino, she completely sensed the woman's personality—her serious, protective nature towards her wayward younger brother; her deep love for her son, Jorden. She saw, no *felt* him, too. All this in a matter of seconds.

And then she felt Jace's fear and his anger and knew that the implant had something to do with Bianca.

"It was a trade," he said out loud. "My life, or my talents, for hers and Jorden's. He's a lot like me, you know," he mused sadly. "Scares the hell out of her sometimes, she used to say."

"Used to?"

A feeling of loss. "I haven't seen her in four, almost five years. I don't even know if she's alive, although I was promised as much. Still, Psy-Serv is Psy-Serv. No one dictates to them. Not even Captain Jace Serafino." He squeezed her hand and she knew he needed just to feel her warmth right now.

She squeezed back. "You said you needed my help. What can I do?"

"In eleven minutes? Oh, Eden, I do need your help but understand you may have to take a lot of furzel-naps to get the whole story."

"But couldn't you, couldn't we talk in Sickbay? Jace, the seizure was serious but unless we mistime this meeting now, the implant shouldn't activate again. I hope to have you responsive by tomorrow."

A sad smile crossed his face. "When you talk to me tomorrow, I won't know half of what I need to tell you. The implant does more than just prohibit telepathy."

"You won't—?"

He shook his head. "I probably won't even remember your name. Eden, the Jace Serafino you have in Sickbay is only part of the person I am. I'll be honest with you right now. It's not my better part." He brought her hand to his lips and lightly brushed them across her knuckles. "Gods, woman, you are a gorgeous creature. I think I've told you that, haven't I? And yes, you are blushing beautifully again. The Jace Serafino 'out there'," he continued, with an upward nod of his head as if Sickbay were off somewhere in the distance, "is a rake and a scoundrel who has only one use for beautiful women. It's not friendship and right now, Eden, I really, really need a friend. I just wish you were ugly. It would make dealing with you so much easier."

"Captain Serafino," she said, gently withdrawing her hand from his, "we are both professionals. There's no reason we can't work together in that atmosphere."

"No, of course not." He laughed. "You underestimate yourself, Doc. But then, you probably have a fleet of men who tell you that daily."

"We're getting off the subject," she warned.

"You do that to me." The twinkle in his eyes was unmistakable.

"Jace!"

"All right. Back to business. We have seven minutes. I'll talk or transmit, whatever is easier. You listen."

She nodded.

He was, as Sass had termed it, a 'rogue' telepath. He and his sister were the products of a liaison between a Nasyry priest and a highborn but rebellious daughter of a wealthy Kel family.

But the Nasyry haven't been present in this System in several hundred years, Eden pointed out.

The Nasyry come and go as they, as we *please,* was his answer. *We use the space-time continuum as a means of travel. A 'yesterday' to us may be one hundred and fifty years ago to you.*

Why aren't you with your people? Couldn't they help you?

A twinge of anger mixed with shame. *They have no love of half-breeds.*

Then you and Bianca—

She's all I have. She and Jorden. He has my 'talent', by the way—his mother doesn't. Which may be how and why Bianca made the one big mistake in her usually orderly life and that was her Psy-Serv lover. Jorden's father. That's how this whole thing started.

Eden saw and felt how the quiet, methodical woman had been totally unprepared for the handsome and flamboyant Psy-Serv agent who'd swept her off her feet—solely to gain access to Jace. It had taken the agent twelve years; twelve years of pretending to love Bianca, twelve years of playing father to a son who meant nothing to him. Twelve years for Bianca to trust him enough to arrange for him to meet with her brother, who by then had already established a reputation for himself as a daring mercenary.

Jace had hated the man on sight and later blamed himself for Bianca's marriage. He'd spent little time with his sister over the years; the nature of his 'career' keeping them out of touch for long periods. The first time he ever saw his nephew was the first time he met with Bianca's husband. He was in importing and exporting, the man had told Captain Serafino. Perhaps they could do some business together?

So good was this agent, so strong were his talents, that even Jace didn't pick up on the fact that he was a telepath. Not until it was much too late.

And then he was given the choice—work with us…or your sister and her son will die.

That had been a little over four years ago. Jace made the only choice he could have.

You're the only telepath I've found since that time, he told her. *The only one not with Psy-Serv. There is so much you need to know, Eden. It's almost providential you're on the* Vaxxar, *that you have access to everything this ship represents and can do. I need your help, I really need your help, or else more than just the Triad, and this new Alliance, will suffer.*

He raised her hand to his lips, kissing her wrist this time, then spoke out loud. "I'm just about at my limit here. Trust me, Eden, but do yourself a favor and keep your bedroom door locked. My 'evil twin', you know!" He grinned.

"I've asked Sebastian to help," she said, ignoring the pleasurable little chills that ran up her spine at his touch.

"If you trust her, then I do too."

"I think Kel-Paten has some files, some med files from Psy-Serv. They may give me some insight into your implant. Do you have enough time to tell me what you know about it?"

In a micro-second an image of a small red and silver device flashed into her mind along with the words: *That's all I saw; that's all I know.*

It's a start, she told him encouragingly.

He drew a deep breath. *I have to go.* His lips brushed against hers in a feather-light kiss just as he disappeared.

Next to her, Reilly shifted his considerable furry weight, demanding more bed space that she automatically granted him. He rubbed his soft face against her arm, sensing that his humanmommy was not quite asleep and not quite awake. If he nudged her a bit more, perhaps a can of food might appear.

But no, she only sighed and settled deeper into the coverlet. Reilly sighed also, purred for a while and snuggled closer, only to be dislodged a bit later.

Mommy up?

But no, humanmommy wasn't up. But something...something was. Golden eyes narrowed, searched the shadows of the cabin.

Protect mommy. Must protect mommy.

Then it was gone.

Reilly slept lightly after that, furry ears alert, twitching.

Must protect mommy.

CHAPTER SIX

ADMIRAL KEL-PATEN'S OFFICE, THS *VAXXAR*

Eden disliked being called into the admiral's office, especially when it was only a half-hour after she'd awakened. Especially when she hadn't even finished her first cup of Orange Garden tea yet. And especially when she plotted with two captains against him.

At least, that was the way Eden's overactive conscience viewed the situation.

She acknowledged Kel-Paten's request from the vidcom in her cabin, gulped down the rest of her tea and, with a quick glance to make sure Reilly had sufficient food and water to last until dinner (woe be unto her if the always vocal furzel didn't!), headed down the corridor to the lifts.

In the few minutes it took her to reach the bridge deck, she mentally catalogued what Kel-Paten might want of her. The rareness of his appearances in Sickbay was matched only by the rareness of his requests to deal with his CMO personally.

Most likely, she mused as she exited out into the main corridor, he wanted to discuss either Serafino's condition (she had been required to log a report on his seizure) or the condition of his two surviving crewmembers: a middle-aged T'Sarii male whose internal injuries included a punctured lung, and a Keltish engineering techie in his late twenties with a broken jaw and shoulder. Only Eden's orders as CMO had kept them, to date, safe from the admiral's interrogation skills.

She smiled at Timmar Kel-Faray, the *Vaxxar's* amiable First Officer, who exited the admiral's office just as she arrived.

"You here to see him?" Timm Kel-Faray asked after the doors closed behind him.

There was no question as to who "him" was. She nodded. "Another command performance."

"Heard you had a rough night, Doc. Thought you'd still be sleeping."

"So did I," she replied, then changed the subject. "Anything come in from Farside Medical on your shift?" She'd shared her frustrations over the troublesome virus with the First Officer a few days ago.

"Not that I know. The Bridge usually doesn't comm me when I'm in conference with the admiral." He nodded behind him. "He's in one of his moods again. Sorry."

That was one thing Eden had noticed shortly after coming on board the *Vaxxar*. Both she and Sass had been prepared for the usual protectiveness and loyalty a crew would exhibit towards their captain, or in this case, their admiral. With Kel-Paten, they found there was an undeniable loyalty and unequivocal trust, but also an undeniable honesty. The bio-cybe commander-in-chief was well respected. But Eden knew of no one who considered him a friend.

She smiled her thanks then, assuming her best professional mien, laid her hand against the office door scanner. It read her identity and the doors parted to allow her entry.

The admiral was at his desk, head angled slightly away from her, but she clearly saw the eerie luminescent glow in his eyes. He'd been spiked in, probably looking for the latest reports on Serafino. Or tracking Sass's location on the ship. Or both. Eden knew he was quite capable of doing both, and many more things, simultaneously.

"Doctor." He leaned back in his chair and motioned to one of the two empty chairs across from his desk, his eyes once again their usual pale blue.

Eden sat and rested her folded hands properly in her lap. "Admiral, what can I do for you?"

"Serafino, I gather, is still unconscious." As usual, he wasted no time with pleasantries or small talk.

She'd checked with Sickbay immediately upon awakening and so had an answer for him. "Correct."

He glanced briefly at what she recognized as her report on the comp screen. "Do you have an explanation for the sudden decline in his condition?"

None that I'm going to give to you at this moment, she thought, then out loud: "Dr. Monterro and I have some theories, but I don't want to get into them until we can present you with something conclusive."

"Such as—?"

Mistrust. She empathically read that, coming strongly from him. She was dancing around the facts and he knew it. Damn! She fished around for something close enough to appease him.

"It is possible he had a previous brain injury that was aggravated by his injuries sustained in the vortex flare." Well, that was somewhat the truth, after all. The implant could be considered a previous injury.

"Or—?"

Damn him! No wonder Sass headed for her gin stock so quickly at the end of each day. She tried to remember what little she knew of Serafino—the physical Jace Serafino, rake and scoundrel.

"It could also be the result of trefla addiction or an overdose." Potent and dangerous recreational drugs were a well-known pastime for many 'rim-runners', as mercenaries and other fringe spacers were often called. Trefla crystals were one of the more popular. When she'd performed her volunteer work at the clinic on Farside Station, she's seen first hand just what it could do.

Kel-Paten seemed to accept that. He touched the comp screen with one black-clad fingertip. Her report on Serafino vanished; another report appeared in its place.

"T'Krain Namar." He said the name of the T'Sarii crewmember and looked back at her.

"Master T'Krain still has difficulty breathing, not to mention speaking. Sir. He needs at least another twenty-four hours on the respiratory regenerator."

"I need some answers before the next twenty-four hours, Doctor, and with Serafino unresponsive and Kel-Pern sedated," he told her, leaning forward across his desk, "I don't have a lot to choose from. I'll be down in Sickbay at 1630 exactly, Doctor. I expect to have T'Krain available for questioning."

"That's not possible—"

"Then do the impossible!" he barked.

Something in Eden snapped. Maybe it was the tone of his voice, the tone of someone who knew he was making an unreasonable request, and didn't care. It reminded her of several bad tempered adolescent boys she'd had to deal with on Station Triad One, when she and Sass had arrived there to attend the Peace Conferences almost a year ago. There had been a minor accident; an escalator had malfunctioned, causing two major injuries and several minor ones. One of the teenage boys had suffered a small facial laceration. She'd been attending to a shabbily dressed elderly woman with a broken hip and crushed left ankle when the boy had roughly grabbed her shoulder, almost turning her around.

"Healer!" He'd been frowning, much like Kel-Paten was now. It was a petulant frown, his typically dark Keltish eyes focusing on the signature blue-stone ring on her left hand that bespoke of her craft and her heritage. "We're already late for the party and this stupid thing breaks down, and look what it does to me! Just look!"

And he'd pulled his other hand away from his face, revealing a long thin gash that had left a smudge of blood on his palm. "I'm scarred for life! Do you know who my father is? He'll sue! We'll own that stupid company who made that lubashit escalator!"

She'd quickly removed his hand from her shoulder. "You'll be fine. Just go wash your face." And she'd turned back to the old woman, only to find herself spun around again.

"I said, do you know who my father is? You don't deny my requests, Healer!"

She'd grasped his thin wrist forcefully. "I have a severely injured patient here, young sirrah. I told you. Go wash your face. Now—"

"Do you know who I am?" he shrilled at her.

"Yes. You are a rude, foolish, ill-mannered and ill-bred child, badly in need of a spanking. And if you do not leave me alone to attend to my patient, right now, I will administer that spanking myself. Right here, in front of all your friends. Do I make myself clear, young man?"

The teenage boy blinked. There was something about the authority in her voice that even he recognized, and probably, in all his spoiled and pampered life, had longed for from one of his parents. And had never received. "Y-y-yes, ma'am. Doctor."

She'd turned back to the old woman, the sound of the boy's departing footsteps drowned out by the solitary applause of her friend nearby.

"Bravo, Eden!" Sass had halted in her ministrations to one of the less injured to offer her approval. There were chuckles also from a couple of security officers on the scene.

"These high-pocket politicians' kids, people just don't tell them 'no' because of who daddy or mommy is," a short, pudgy officer remarked. "Might do them good to hear 'no' a little more often."

Just as it might do the admiral good to hear 'no' a little more often as well. She squared her shoulders and met Kel-Paten, blue stare for blue stare.

"Admiral Kel-Paten," she said from between clenched teeth, "you may run this ship, you may run this Fleet, you may even run this entire Triad, for all I know. But I will tell you one thing you do not run, and that is my Sickbay. My patients' lives are not to be hazarded by whatever political machinations you may currently be involved in. You will talk to Master T'Krain, Master Kel-Pern and Captain Serafino when, and only when, I give you medical clearance to do so. Rest assured you will have that clearance at the earliest opportunity that I deem to be safe. But know that is my decision and my decision only. Do I make myself clear?"

Kel-Paten blinked at her—a blink not unlike that ill-tempered teenage boy's. And for the first time she wished she wasn't just a touch-telepath. She'd give anything to know what was going on in his mind right now. The little her empathic senses picked up showed confusion, with a small bit of admiration.

"Perhaps I didn't explain myself well," he began.

My oh my oh my! she thought. *Is the unshakable admiral backing down?*

"No one is more aware of your concerns than I am," she offered him. "But it was your order that I keep Serafino and his crew alive, at all costs, just so that you could have the pleasure of killing them. I have to assume that 'at all costs' includes even yourself. Sir." She smiled but it was not a warm smile, and he knew it.

He leaned back and steepled his gloved hands in front of his face in what she had come to recognize as a typical Kel-Paten gesture.

"You wouldn't have given that answer to Captain Sebastian," he said after a moment, but there was no accusatory tone in his voice. If anything, he seemed amused.

"Captain Sebastian would have known better than to make that request," she told him.

"Captain Sebastian has not had the aggravation of Serafino in her back pocket for the past fifteen years," he said. "Nor a veritable flock of petulant Triad Senators who expect, no, *demand* the impossible out of me simply because I am Kel-Paten." He looked at her from over steepled fingertips and raised one eyebrow. "If I can't intimidate you into getting what I want, dare I ask for your sympathy?"

His mouth twisted and with a shock Eden realized the Tin Soldier was trying to smile! It was a small smile and a bit crooked, she admitted. Barely visible between his gloved hands, but it was there. She saw it.

He could be almost charming if he ever gave himself half a chance, she noted. She wondered if he'd ever tried that crooked half-smile of his on Sass.

"You have more than my sympathy, admiral. You have my complete cooperation, as long, and I must repeat this, as long as you allow me first to do what I'm here to do. I promise I'll never try to advise you on tactical or military matters..." And she let her sentence drift off, knowing he could fill in the rest as well as she could.

He nodded. "When do you expect I'll be able to speak to either Kel-

Pern or T'Krain?"

"I think within forty-eight hours is reasonable and safe."

"And Serafino?"

"His condition is more fragile until we can identify whatever unknown factor or factors caused the seizure." It was a great non-answer and she congratulated herself on it.

"Understood, Doctor." He touched the comp screen, dumping its contents. "I have nothing further. Dismissed."

She stood. "By your command, admiral."

"Doctor Fynn." His voice stopped her just as his office doors slid open. "Tell Captain Sebastian she's trained you well. Very well."

She didn't try to suppress her grin this time. "It's not totally the captain's doing, sir. I spent my university summers as a camp counselor. Dealing with Triadian officers is not all that different from tending to teenagers."

And with that, she stepped out into the corridor, the doors whooshing softly closed behind her.

SICKBAY, THS *VAXXAR*

With a frustrated sigh, Jace Serafino folded his telepathic self back inside his mind. There was so much he had wanted and needed to share with the *Vaxxar's* CMO, and he'd let himself get distracted by a too soft mouth, a blush of pink on pale cheeks, by the very womanly roundness of her body. That wasn't like him. Well, that *was* like the human Captain Jace Serafino but not the Nasyry Jace Serafino. He was a highly disciplined, well-trained warrior.

All that had gone to hell when he'd touched minds with Eden Fynn.

He'd been totally unprepared for her impact on him. It wasn't just her physical beauty; he'd known many women as sweetly beautiful as the Zingaran healer. In fact, he'd known women who were so exotically beautiful that their very entry into a room caused all conversation to cease.

But then, as his often-so-wise sister would point out, an eight-foot tall, three-hundred pound foul-smelling grenkbeast entering a room would also cause all conversation to cease.

That wasn't necessarily the hallmark of beauty, and he'd never really understood her comment until he met Eden.

Eden Fynn didn't cause all conversation to cease. She caused his heart to start beating again. She caused him to want to find a garden and pick the perfect bloom, just for her. She caused him to search his repertoire for the witty phrase, the play on words, just to see her smile. She caused him to feel young and silly and foolish and he couldn't seem to get enough of her. His twelve-minute time limit was going to drive him out of his mind.

Literally. Because if the Nasyry element of Jace Serafino felt that way, the human, womanizing, certified rake and scoundrel element of Captain Jace Serafino was going to go completely out of control once he "woke up".

He'd tried to warn her; would have to warn her more. The last thing he wanted to do was hurt her, and hurt her he would. There was no room in the human Captain Jace Serafino's life for the kinds of emotion, the kind of commitment she made him want. There was a price on his head, in more than just the Triad, or now, the new Alliance. Strewn across civilized space were a series of individuals who would not hesitate to strike out at Serafino through his feelings for Eden. Just as they had through Bianca and Jorden.

He couldn't let that happen, again.

But Gods, how he wanted her! How he wanted to know, just once in his life, what it would be like to be loved, truly loved, by a woman like Eden Fynn. He needed her warmth, her compassion, her intelligence. And her innocence; oh yes, there was an innocence in her that comes only from a truly loving heart. It was a rare, rare quality. That was what he'd first noticed when their minds had touched, and it had sent his jaded senses reeling. He felt that he'd spent his entire life in a dank and musty room, and suddenly a window had opened, and it was spring and every fruit tree was in blossom outside.

He'd gotten drunk on her perfume of gentle innocence and he was now, he knew, a confirmed alcoholic. Or Eden-holic. A mental chuckle echoed in his thoughts but it was tinged with sadness.

Why now? Why when his life was in such a wretched state? He wanted to offer her the sun, the moon and the stars...and all he could bring her was pain.

He sighed, physically sighed this time as the damage from the seizure faded. His other wounds had healed; he was Nasyry and had the enhanced Nasyran recuperative powers. Even now, his ears picked up the sounds and voices in Sickbay. Eden's voice was one of them. A warmth flooded his veins at the sound.

She was discussing with someone named Cal the fact that Captain Serafino's vital signs were rapidly improving.

You want vital, Eden my lovely, come here and I'll show you vital! The thought and accompanying sensation raced through his mind before he could stop it.

A surge of heat flowed from his mind-body directly into Eden. She'd been standing near the foot of his bed, close enough that he heard her surprised intake of breath as his heat touched her.

Jace felt her question the sensation and tried to throw a mental bucket of cold water on him, but it didn't work. His physical senses were coming around too quickly, and he was now aware of her perfume and the soft sound of her breathing as she moved closer to him.

He groaned softly but audibly.

There was a slight click as Eden placed her med-scanner on a nearby table. With his psychic senses, he could 'see' her as she leaned over him. "Captain Serafino? This is Doctor Fynn. Can you hear me?"

His mouth moved slightly but no sounds came out.

He shifted his focus. On the wall above his bed, the diagnostics panel rapidly kicked out data on his improving condition as the sensors built into the bed monitored his physical changes.

Eden leaned across him to key in some adjustments.

"Cal," she called out, her fingers tapping in instructions, her attention on the readout, "I think Captain Serafino is about to return to the land of the living—ohh!"

He yanked her down on top of him, his mouth hard against hers, his tongue taking advantage of her surprised exclamation to probe her warm sweetness. His left hand had already threaded its way into her hair, his right arm tightening around her waist.

Warm. Soft. Sweet. She was all these things, this woman.

The man she'd called Cal looked up from the file in his hand. "Yes, it appears he has returned," he commented lightly.

His warm, soft, sweet woman tried extricating herself from his passionate embrace. He lost his grip. She fell off his bed and landed squarely on her rump on the floor with a very unprofessional exclamation.

She was still sitting there, glaring up at the bed when Jace rolled over and, propping himself up on his side, extended one hand down to her.

"Come back up here, nurse. I think I need a little more of your special medicine."

"I think you've had quite enough 'special medicine', Captain Serafino," she snapped at him, ignoring his hand and his chuckles as she pulled herself off the floor.

He liked what he saw; womanly curves accented by the well-fitting black and tan jumpsuit uniform that even her shapeless blue labcoat couldn't hide.

"Fynn," he said, reading the nameplate on her coat. "Does Fynn have a first name?"

She squared her shoulders. "Yes. It's 'Doctor'. Now, please lie back down. I'm going to have Dr. Monterro run some tests on you."

He rested his head against the pillow. "Dr. Monterro, eh? What a coincidence! Two people in the same Sickbay with the same first name."

She shot him a withering glance. He grinned broadly in answer. She snatched the med-scanner from the table and thrust it towards the other doctor as he walked in. "I'll go advise the captain that Serafino is awake."

Eden...sorry. He reached out, softly, haltingly into her mind just as she exited Sickbay. She turned, startled, then shaking her head, strode out into the hallway.

He didn't know if she'd heard him, or had turned for another reason.

He didn't know...he couldn't remember what it was he didn't know.

DECK TEN, THS *VAXXAR*

At Eden's request, the ship's computer had informed her of Captain Sebastian's location in Drive Thruster Maintenance in Engineering Deck Ten, though by the time Eden arrived Sass had left maintenance and walked down Deck Ten's main corridor on her way back to the Bridge.

"Just making my rounds," she told her CMO.

"Alone?" Eden asked with a smile.

Sass chuckled. "Oddly enough, yes. The admiral's in the middle of a vidconference with both Captain Kel-Tyra and old Admiral Rafe Kel-Tyra. I heard Rissa put the link through. I thought I could use the time to check on some of our people without 'Himself' breathing down my neck."

"Well, I've got some good news and some bad news," Eden said, carefully lowering her voice.

"Want to discuss it over tea in the Lounge?" Sass asked.

Eden nodded, and nothing further on the subject was said until they were seated at a quiet table next to one of the floor-to-ceiling viewports in the Officers' Lounge on Deck Eight Forward, two steaming cups before them.

"Okay. What's up?" Sass asked.

"Serafino." Literally, she thought, remembering the telling hardness of his body beneath hers. "He's awake. He was right about his memory. He didn't even know my name."

"So your link with him is broken now that he's awake?"

Eden remembered the soft, sad apology in her mind and shook her head. "I don't believe so but I think it'll be more difficult. When his physical body was unconscious, his subconscious or telepathic sense had free rein. Now that he's physically awake, his conscious mind will dominate. It's only when he releases his conscious mind, during sleep, for example, that his telepathic sense will be active. Though after he woke up just now he was able to, very briefly, contact me. But I could feel it was a strain."

"Do you know anything more on the implant?" Sass kept her voice low.

"You have a copy of the drawing I made of the unit as he showed it to me and the results of my research through our computers. Other than the three possibilities I listed, nothing. I'm sorry to have to give you so little to go on."

"I'm not going to have time to do any specific searches when I access Kel-Paten's files, anyway, so don't worry about it, Eden. It's going to be a 'get and grab'. I'm going to dump whatever I can find and hope to hell you can use it." Sass sighed. "I figure some time in the next three days I'll make an attempt to get in. I wish I had had more notice about this vidconference with Kel-Tyra—Rohland usually keeps the admiral chatting for a while. That would have been an ideal time to get into his quarters and access those data files."

"He's going to interrogate Serafino and T'Krain tomorrow. Kel-Pern is still out of commission," Eden said. "Maybe then—?"

"Maybe, but I have a feeling he's going to want us there when he talks to them. You, for your empathic readings as to who is telling the truth and who isn't. And me because I'm more fluent in the street lingo dialect of T'Sar that T'Krain speaks than Kel-Paten is. The admiral can handle his own in a diplomatic situation with the T'Sarii, but this T'Krain is as far from a book-fed highbrow as you can get. I doubt if he could even converse with one of his own educated people."

"T'Krain's Standard is pretty bad," Eden admitted. "Though he does have an impressive command of our swear words."

"Yeah, well I think the 'fuck you very much' is Serafino's doing. Probably his idea of a joke."

Eden sipped at the last of her tea. "Captain Serafino certainly does have an interesting sense of humor."

"Around the admiral, that could be fatal," Sass warned. "You'd better get the message to him to behave himself or that implant will be the least of his troubles."

Behave? Eden had no idea how she could get Captain Serafino to behave. His inner self didn't seem to be doing a very good job of it, if their recent encounter was any proof.

"I don't think Kel-Paten appreciates being called the 'Tin Soldier'," Sass was saying, referring to Serafino's brief but notable comments when he was first transported into Sickbay.

"I'm sure Serafino knows that. I'm equally as sure that's why he said what he did. It's like he wants Kel-Paten to get angry."

"I thought 'cybes couldn't experience emotions," Sass said. "I mean, I've seen Kel-Paten act as if he's angry. But I thought it's just all some response simulation program. Why would Serafino care about that?"

"I don't think it's a simulation," Eden said carefully.

"Kel-Paten?" Sass looked at her incredulously. "It has to be. He's a 'cybe."

"I'm an empath," Eden countered. "And he's not just a 'cybe, not in the sense you mean. There's still a lot of human biology there."

"You're telling me you've sensed genuine anger from him?"

More than just anger, but Eden didn't say that. "Yes."

"I was under the impression...hell, the U-Cees built their strategies around the fact that, between the cybernetics and Psy-Serv's emo-inhibitor programs, Kel-Paten is one six-foot-three deadly emotionless son-of-a-bitch. That was the whole point of him, don't you see?" Sass asked, her index finger making the point in the air. "No emotions to sway decision making. Only hard, cold clinical facts. Data in, data out."

"You've seen him lose his temper," Eden said.

"And I've heard your medical diag comps use a compassionate tone of voice when interviewing patients, and a firmer tone response if a patient starts to babble on too much. There are a couple of programs in Engineering that have a definite warning tone. I even know of bar-'droids in the high priced Glitterkiln casinos that tell jokes. And laugh. That doesn't mean they feel anything. Those are response simulations, Eden. Mimicry. Not feelings."

"I know."

Sass looked quizzically at her. "What are you telling me here? Does Kel-Paten need a tune-up or do we have a Section Forty-Six situation?"

Section Forty-Six. Eden had read the regulation so many times the key phrase stuck in her mind: behavior, attitude and/or reactions clearly in contradiction to the accepted norm.

"As I don't have access to his full medical profile," Eden told her, "I can't answer that."

"So in the meantime," Sass said, "we're going into a potentially explosive situation between a lethal 'cybe who just might have a screw loose, and a rogue telepath who has the ability to pick up and use that very flaw. Lovely!"

Would Jace sense the same emotions she had in Kel-Paten? Of course he would. Eden hadn't even thought of that; she gave herself a mental kick. But could he use that information? His subconscious, telepathic self would sense it, yes, but would he be able to transmit that to his conscious self?

With a sinking feeling she knew he could, just as he'd sensed her discomfort after he'd kissed her in Sickbay and then sent his apology. There was communication, albeit limited, between his telepathic level and normal level.

When it was important enough.

And she knew that when it came to the fifteen-year feud between Kel-Paten and Serafino, it was definitely important enough.

CHAPTER SEVEN

BRIDGE, THS *VAXXAR*

"All I know, admiral, is that Doctors Fynn and Monterro still have tests to perform on Serafino. They don't want anything to occur that could cause him to relapse."

Kel-Paten glanced down at Sass as she stood next to him on the bridge. Her face was in profile to him. She watched the starfield flowing by the large forward viewport as the *Vaxxar* traveled at sub-light speed towards the nearest Fleet Base on Panperra Station.

He hated when he couldn't see her eyes when she spoke. He was learning, sometimes the hard way, to read her expressions, the nuances between her words and thoughts. True, he'd been trained—he liked that word better than programmed—to correctly interpret over one hundred and forty human facial expressions and another sixty-seven non-human ones. But these classifications were useless when it came to Tasha Sebastian.

He needed to know more than the fact that her facial expression designated, for example, mild amusement. He needed to know if that amusement were directed at him or against him; if it were an amusement she felt he'd understand and wanted to share with him; if something he said or did was the source of that delightful pixie-ish smile. He needed to know if he made her feel something.

And nothing in his progr—his training allowed for that.

Right now, the little he could see of her face told him she'd adopted her "professional expression"—a noncommittal, almost bland mien. She simply reported the facts as she knew them, and had no opinions of same.

Or else she had deep opinions and wasn't about to share them with him. He'd known her long enough, studied her long enough, to see that also as a viable option. It was at those times he felt the most left out. She didn't trust him enough to share her concerns with him.

Or, like most of his crew, she believed he wasn't capable of caring.

He was. She'd taught him that, too.

So he probed, asked a few more questions about Serafino's condition, and got nowhere. Except that now she thought he didn't have any faith in Fynn's medical abilities.

"I assure you, Sebastian, I have a great respect for the doctor's assessment here. However, her focus is different from ours." He liked that as soon as he said it. It aligned Sass with him under the heading of "Command", breaking from her usual allegiance with the CMO.

"As I understand it, we'll have nothing to focus on if Serafino is comatose again. Or dead." She looked at him briefly, a slight raising of one eyebrow as if to say, 'Are you following me on this, flyboy?'

She hadn't called him "flyboy" since the peace talks. Before that, it had been one of the names she'd taunted him with from the bridge of the *Regalia*. Flyboy. An ancient aviator term for heavy-air fighter pilots. The first time she'd leveled it at him he'd taken offense, but she'd used it so often after that that it had become almost a term of endearment. At least, he liked to think of it that way.

Now, all he rated was the raised eyebrow.

"I only intend to question the man, not torture him," he told her.

"At least not yet, eh, Kel-Paten?" she replied, her voice lowered a bit and with a hint of a smile.

"Sebastian." He paused.

"Kel-Paten," she replied and then paused in turn.

This game was one of their few rituals that had continued after the peace talks. He would say her name, followed by the appropriate warning-filled pause whenever something she said or did warranted his supposed disapproval. And she would reply with his name, either matching his warning tone or, more often, mocking it.

This time it was the latter.

"When we reach Panperra he'll be turned over to Adjutant Kel-Farquin," he said, watching her carefully for her reaction. "That should be torture enough."

She choked back a laugh at his comment, which told him she remembered what he did. Homer Kel-Farquin's whining, nasal voice and supercilious manner had been one of the low-points in the peace talks. Kel-Paten would steeple his hands in front of his face every time the adjutant would launch into one of his obnoxious diatribes. After one such painful session, Sass had sarcastically complimented Kel-Paten on his ability to appear so focused on Kel-Farquin's every word.

"I am not focused," he'd told her without expression. "I am sleeping."

He'd been rewarded then with one of her—heart stopping—smiles. Not dissimilar to the one now teasing across her lips.

"Why, Admiral Kel-Paten," she drawled. "I heard you were so impressed with Kel-Farquin's oratory talents that you ordered copies of every one of his speeches from the peace talks."

"I believe," he countered dryly, "that would be grounds for a Section Forty-Six."

"Unless one had a justifiable reason for ordering them. You know," she said, continuing their verbal game, "those tapes may contain the very thing we need to defeat the Illithians."

He thought for a moment. "A subliminal transmission of their contents into Illithian space could be very effective," he posited, matching her feigned concern.

"Or considered cruel and inhumane methods."

A slight shrug. "Who would be left to complain?"

"There might be a few. After all, I found copious amounts of gin to be a workable antidote."

He glanced down at her. "I slept."

"And well I remember your ingenious defense. Better than mine. No hangover."

"It's a methodology I developed after a long association with Triad politicians. Let my experience be your guide."

She clasped her hands behind her back and rocked on her heels. "I'll keep that in mind for your next staff meeting."

Had he misread her? Was she aligning him in her mind with the likes of Homer Kel-Farquin? He wasn't sure until she grinned up at him.

"Gotcha!" she said softly.

Smile back at her, his heart prodded, but his brain and his lips refused to cooperate. By the time he'd managed to edge up one corner of his mouth she'd turned away from him, her attention on a nav-tech on the lower tier of the bridge. There was a problem with some incoming data. She stepped quickly down the stairs.

Some of her warmth, however, lingered behind.

Gotcha.

Yes, indeed.

EDEN FYNN'S QUARTERS, THS *VAXXAR*

The deeply luminous yellow eyes staring at Eden relayed only one message: Feed Me. As usual, Reilly had maneuvered into position at the head of Eden's bed exactly five minutes before her cabin lights would flicker on at their preprogrammed time of 0600 hours. So it was his purring, and the occasional tap of a soft paw against her face, that functioned as her wake-up alarm—or pre-wake-up alarm. And a much more pleasant one than the tinny computer voice that would intone, just as the cabin lights would reach full brightness, "It is oh-six-hundred, Doctor Fynn. Would you like Orange Garden or Sunrise Spice this morning?"

She was opening Reilly's 'Tuna Platter Supreme' when the question was posed.

"Orange Garden," she answered, and only then realized that she'd slept through the night with no contact with Jace.

That information warranted a mental *Damn!* There was so much she still needed to know about him, not the least of which was his physiology. The *Vaxxar's* med files contained little information on the Nasyry. There were things that troubled her, such as unknown compounds in his blood analysis that could be results of the implant. Or could just be the Nasyran norm.

And here it was, 0610 hours, and she had no answers.

It was one more thing, then, she'd have to ask Sass to look for in Kel-Paten's datafiles. If anyone had information on the Nasyry, the Tin Soldier did.

The ship's gym was empty. It was agreeable to both women to use the treadmills rather than the simdeck jogging programs, which were crowded this early in the shift. They choose side-by-side machines facing a large viewport that, as the gym was located in the aft end of the ship, gave them a backwards vista of the *Vaxxar's* journey.

"What's our ETA at Panperra?" Eden asked while they were still in a slow jog and conversation was comfortable.

"Late tomorrow, about 2030 hours," Sass answered. "But we're too large to dock there. Access will be by shuttle."

"I suppose any R & R is out of the question." Panperra had a few good pubs that Eden wouldn't mind spending some relaxing time in.

"With Kel-Paten, I think that's a given. At least for me. You remember what happened on Triad One."

Eden did. The Triad HQ had been their last stop before embarking on their present mission. Sass, Eden, Cisco Garrick and several other former crew from the *Regalia* had planned a great evening of pub-crawling and pool halls. That had come to an abrupt halt when Kel-Paten had shown up at their first stop and attached himself to Sass's side. She and her people, he had stated, knew little of the station and Triad ways. To which Sass had retorted that whether one got shit-faced on U-Cee gin or Triadian gin, it still gave you a bitch of a headache in the morning.

Finally Sass had waved off her friends, told them to continue on without her. She'd informed Eden later that she'd spent the rest of her much-awaited shore leave with the admiral in the very sedate Triad Officer's Club, sipping watered down gin and discussing military strategy.

"If you're lucky," Sass continued as they both increased their inclines, "you won't be stuck with Homer Kel-Farquin. Chances are, I will."

"Hazards of the occupation," Eden quipped. "Maybe you can convince Kel-Paten afterwards that you need a couple of good rounds of iced gin. Tell him it's your doctor's orders."

"I doubt very much if he'll let me catch up with you and Cal and Cisco, if any shore leave is approved at all."

"Bring him with you," Eden told her.

Sass shot her an incredulous look. "Surely you jest."

"I jest not. Bring him with you."

"Why ever would I want to do that? Don't you think I see enough of him as it is? Or are you looking to file me for a Section Forty-Six?"

"Hardly," Eden grinned, starting now to puff a little as the treadmill's speed picked up. "I just think...I have a couple of new theories on our Tin Soldier and this may answer some questions."

They both jogged in silence for a few minutes.

"The emotional programming thing, you mean," Sass said finally. Sweat beaded on her forehead.

"Umm-hmm."

"What are you planning to do? Get him drunk and see if human emotions surface?"

Eden dabbed at her face with her towel. "Hadn't thought of that. Not a bad idea."

"Great!" Sass panted. "And the next morning...not only will he be...his usual miserable self...but his usual miserable self...with a hangover!"

Eden laughed and coughed at the same time. Laughing and jogging were not the two most compatible activities. "Well, actually..." she said, thinking out loud, "his cybernetics...probably don't permit...his getting drunk...or allow a toxic reaction."

"You mean...he's too bloody perfect...for a hangover?" Sass laughed and coughed now too. "How incredibly...annoying!"

"Speaking of....annoying...having some problems....with Captain Serafino."

Sass snatched her towel from the treadmill's safety bar and wiped her face before looking at Eden. "Such as?"

"There are some...physiological questions...I can't answer."

"Implant?'

Eden shrugged as best she could while jogging. "Could be."

"Then...what?"

"Sass...what do you know...about the Nasyry?" She lowered her tone even though there was no one near enough to hear.

"The Nas...oh, lubashit!"

Eden nodded.

"He's...?"

Eden nodded again. "Well, half...anyway."

"Damn."

"It's not...in any of my...reports," Eden told her. "And I'd like...to keep it that way."

"Got it," Sass said. "No need to report...unconfirmed suspicions."

"Well put, captain." Eden grinned.

"Who else knows?"

"Cal. That's all."

"And the med files...here?"

"Damnably...incomplete."

Sass shook her head knowingly. "I guess...I'm adding this...to my shopping list."

"If you don't mind."

"Your wish...Doctor...is my command," Sass said breathlessly. The treadmills were cranked all the way up and it was difficult to hear, let alone talk, over the pounding of two pairs of sneakered feet.

They finished their workout without further conversation, other than the friendly acknowledgments to two crew members who'd started their own workouts on nearby machines.

That left only the short trip in the lift and down the corridor to their cabins to shower and change and start their day by 0800.

Eden's quarters were closer to the lift; the captain's quarters farther down the corridor, next to the admiral's and the Ready Room. They stopped at Eden's door.

"Are we talking to Serafino today?" Sass asked.

Eden shook her head negatively. "Not Serafino, not until Cal and I can pin down those unknown readings in his blood. I'm thinking..." she hesitated for a moment, pursing her lips as she attempted to convince herself she was on the right track. "I'm thinking of trying to make some form of telepathic contact with him today, maybe after you and Kel-Paten talk to T'Krain. I figure whatever discussion follows will keep Kel-Paten busy enough not to hover around Sickbay, waiting for me to give him clearance on Serafino. Especially if you'll run interference."

"Got it. But can you make contact with Serafino while his physical self is still awake?"

"It's not the easiest way," Eden agreed. "But he said something about my being a touch-telepath. He managed to reach out to me yesterday, shortly after he woke up. I heard him clearly in my mind, though it was very brief." A very brief apology after a rather startling encounter, Eden remembered. "If I can strengthen that link through physical contact—"

"Not an altogether objectionable task, Doctor," Sass teased, her eyebrows raised. "I haven't seen that much of him, but what I have seen is damned nice to look at."

Eden pulled herself up to her full height and looked haughtily down at the shorter woman. "I am a professional, Captain Sebastian!" she teased back.

"Keep a bucket of cold water handy," Sass retorted, punching her friend good-naturedly on the shoulder before she headed towards her cabin.

"For him or for me?" Eden called out to her.

Sass stopped at her cabin door. "For both of you! And should you need any help—"

She quickly ducked inside to avoid the balled-up gym towel hurled at her by the professional Dr. Fynn.

TASHA SEBASTIAN'S QUARTERS, THS *VAXXAR*

Once inside her cabin, Sass was met by another moving projectile. This one was fur covered and known as Tank.

"No, you can not have any more food!" Sass told the small black and white furzel who *murrupped* and purred and wove in and out of her legs on her way to the shower. She'd discovered Tank curled inside a container of hover-tank repair parts shortly after they'd left Port Bangkok. Upon inspecting the fidget, as baby furzels were called, Dr. Fynn had pronounced him healthy (once he was minus a rather large colony of fleas) and about five months old.

Now, Tank happily inhabited the captain's cabin. He flopped down on her bed when she emerged from the shower, presenting his belly to be rubbed. She obliged. His loud purr filled the room, softening as he fell asleep.

"You," Sass said, giving him one last stroke, "are spoiled." She grabbed a clean jumpsuit from her closet. Her commbadge pinged as she pulled on her boots.

She tapped at it. "Sebastian."

"Kel-Paten here. I'd appreciate it if you could be in my office as soon as possible."

It wasn't even 0800 yet and still a full hour away from her usual 0900 briefing with the admiral. She knew an interview with one of Serafino's crewmembers was on today's schedule, however. That was no doubt going to be the highlight of the admiral's day and he probably couldn't wait to talk about it.

"You promise me coffee and I'll do anything," she responded.

There was a moment of silence, then: "That can be arranged."

"Good," she replied. "On my way. Mahrian blend, black."

A hissing sound stopped her before she reached the door. She spun around. "Tank?"

Another hiss, and a low growl.

She headed back to her bedroom. "Tank?"

The long furred fidget's back was arched, his ears flat to his head. Sass followed his wide-eyed gaze...and saw nothing. Nothing but the starfield outside her cabin viewport.

"What's the matter? You just realize you're in the spacelanes?" She patted his head, shook her own, and left.

Kel-Paten didn't like to be kept waiting. And she really could use a hot cup of coffee.

ADMIRAL'S OFFICE, THS *VAXXAR*

He knew how she took her coffee just as he knew how she took her gin and what vegetables she liked and how seedless black grapes, chilled, were one of her favorite snacks. After eleven years of following her, challenging her and studying her, he knew all of those minute, concrete details.

But he still, no matter how hard he tried, didn't know how to read between the lines of those light-hearted quips of hers. *You promise me coffee and I'll do anything.*

He wanted desperately to believe that even a mild flirtation existed in those and many other things she said to him, as he tried to ignore the fact that she also frequently traded quips with others. He wanted desperately to believe he wasn't the "Tin Soldier" to her, wasn't a cybernetic construct that so many of his crew viewed as simply another extension of the ship. He wanted to be real and warm and as human as he could to her, and had no idea how to do that without making more of a complete fool of himself than he already had.

So as much as possible, he kept her with him, in unscheduled meetings, extended conferences, detailed inspections and whatever other ways he could think of to commandeer her time.

He heard her step through his office door just as he retrieved two hot cups of coffee from the replicator set in the far wall. He held one out. She accepted it with a bright smile and sipped at it as he stood in silent, appreciative appraisal in front of her. Then she moved towards the chair in front of his desk, and there was the light, seductive scent of sandalwood in the air around her. He could see where her short hair was still slightly damp at the nape of her neck. He had to willfully restrain himself from reaching out to touch it.

He took his own chair and placed his cup on the desk to the right of the datafiles he'd pulled as an excuse for this discussion. He granted himself another moment of the silent pleasure of just looking at her before clearing his throat and selecting a thin crystalline file, pushing it into the appropriate data slot. "As long as we have to be on Panperra, we might as well acquaint ourselves with some of the adjutant's recent projects."

Sass groaned loudly. "If this is one of Kel-Farquin's reports, I'm going to need a lot more than just coffee to get through."

"If this were Kel-Farquin's, I would've brought pillows," he replied blandly, his tone hiding the deep pleasure he felt at her responding wide smile. "No, this is some data on the recent ion storm activity which Panperran sensors were in prime position to record. Now..."

Sass leaned on the edge of his desk in order to better read the data on his monitor. The incisive analysis he'd spent over an hour perfecting fled from his mind.

"Now..." he began again, but her face was inches from his own and he could, if he wanted to, and oh, how he wanted to, close that gap by pretending to reach for a datafile. Their faces might even brush. Their lips...

"Now?" she asked.

Damn her, damn her! He'd worked and reworked the storm data just to be able to show her he wasn't the linear, narrow, by-the-book analyst she often accused him of being. He could use his intuition, he could be creative, he could...

He couldn't remember anything of his painstakingly crafted theory about ion storms and wormholes.

"This is a large storm," he blurted out.

One-point-four-million credits they had spent perfecting his flawlessly synchronized cybertronic brain interface and that was the best he could come up with.

She cocked her head slightly to one side. Perhaps she knew of the amount and was just now realizing what a tremendous waste of funds it represented. "Sure is."

He cleared his throat again. Maybe his creative theory was hiding in there and the act would release it. It didn't. But his one-point-four-million credit brain was packed with linear, logical deductions and before he could stop it, they flowed from his mouth. Just as they always did.

Besides, if he didn't keep talking, if he didn't keep quantifying the data and redacting it, he was going to kiss her.

That, he knew, would impress her even less than his dry recitation.

"If there's nothing else, admiral?" she asked after a half hour of facts that could have been found in any fleet cadet's textbook.

He'd failed, lost yet another chance to show her he was more than the Tin Soldier. It was almost as if his very bio-cybernetics thwarted him at every turn. Betrayed by his own body. He turned quickly, and with a few quick touches on the comp screen, he called up a selection of files of unknown subject matter, only peripherally aware they were there. But at least it looked as if he were doing something productive. "Nothing else. Dismissed, Sebastian."

Sass inclined her head slightly. "By your command, admiral."

He waited until the doors whooshed closed before he let his head fall wearily against the high back of the chair. Why was he so incapable of being human around her? He'd yet to manage anything more than a smile and even that was an effort. Was he fighting his own fear of rejection...or something else? Something he didn't want to think about.

What if his humanity had been programmed out of him?

CHAPTER EIGHT

SICKBAY, THS *VAXXAR*

T'Krain Namar's leathery face brightened as Eden entered his sickbay cubicle. "Fynn, yes doctor. You are. How?" he asked in his best broken Standard.

It took Eden a moment to rearrange the words. "Fine, thank you, Master T'Krain. And how are you feeling this afternoon?"

"Easier. Pain. Now breathe. Yes. No more." His thin faced nodded rapidly.

Okay, let's decipher this one slowly, Eden told herself. "You are in less pain when you breathe, is that correct?"

The thin face nodded again.

"Good. Stay still for a few moments while I check some of your readings." She held the med scanner near his chest and watched the figures dance across the small screen. Everything appeared as it should be, for a T'Sariian male of his age who'd been through the injuries he'd sustained. She told him as much, adding, "Then there's no reason Admiral Kel-Paten shouldn't be able to talk to you. I believe he has a few—"

"Kel-Paten!" T'Krain suddenly sat straight up in bed. "No! Fear! No! Wrong. Do cannot! Release sick, now I am!" He coughed profusely and theatrically.

"Master T'Krain—"

"Help! Help! Out let! Rather no die, sick! Sick!"

"You're perfectly fine, Master T'Krain," Eden said with a strong but soothing tone in her voice.

Bony brown hands grasped the sleeve of her lab coat. "Stay! Me with,

Fynn doctor! Stay, human! Die! All we die now! Soldier Tin, all we die!"

She patted his arm reassuringly, her touch bringing with it the strong sense of fear pervading the T'Sariian. "I'll be right here the whole time. The admiral just has a few questions. There's nothing to be worried about."

It was at this point Cal Monterro stuck his head through the cubicle doorway. "The admiral and Captain Sebastian are here to see T'Krain, if you'll permit it."

Yellow eyes bore into hers. "Now? Here?" A keening sound escaped his lips. "Lost, lost! Is lost all! Is lost all!"

"In spite of the noise, Dr. Monterro, I believe Master T'Krain can withstand a few questions," Eden told him as she tried to dislodge the T'Sariian's long fingers from her wrist. She was unsuccessful in that endeavor until she heard the muffled footsteps come up behind her. T'Krain drew back against his pillow as if a battering ram had shoved against him. He wrenched the bed covers quickly up under his chin.

Kel-Paten assumed his usual military stance, hands folded behind his back, on the left side of T'Krain's bed and nodded for Eden to stay in place across of him. Sass came up and stood more casually on the left, one hand resting on the footboard.

"Master T'Krain, I hope you've found our medical facilities adequate to your needs," Kel-Paten began, his deep voice deceptively calm.

Yellowed eyes flicked from the admiral to Sebastian and back again. "Sick, sick," he said weakly.

Eden had no trouble picking up a palpable sense of impending dread. Clearly, the T'Sariian was terrified, but whether it was because of who was in the room or because of what he knew, she couldn't tell at the moment.

"Dr. Fynn is doing all she can—and she's one of the best CMOs the Fleet has," Kel-Paten replied with a nod to Eden.

"Save me, why you? Later kill if!" T'Krain wailed.

Kel-Paten regarded T'Krain quietly for a moment and Eden wondered if he, too, was having trouble unscrambling T'Krain's sentences. "I am sure you wish to give the Alliance your full cooperation," Kel-Paten said finally. "Therefore, you'll be in no danger and receive our every protection."

"Later me know I! Kill you will!"

"The Triad—the Alliance has no real interest in you, Master T'Krain," Kel-Paten said and Eden noted with a mental grin that she and Sass weren't the only ones who couldn't keep straight which team they played on.

"We need to know what you can tell us about Captain Serafino," Kel-Paten was saying.

Angular shoulders shrugged in a jerky movement. "Know? Know? What you I tell, know? All you, everything, Soldier Tin! Know always! Namar, small, small, stupid!"

"I don't think you're stupid, T'Krain Namar," Kel-Paten said smoothly. "I think you're intelligent enough that someone like Captain Serafino would want you on his ship. Would trust you."

"Trust? Hmmph!" The T'Sariian jerked his chin in the air as he spoke. "Trust? Orders, orders, orders, no! Question not! This, yes do, question? Not!"

Eden saw Kel-Paten glance at her for confirmation. She nodded. As far as her empathic senses could tell, T'Krain was telling the truth. Serafino gave him orders and that was all. He wasn't allowed to question.

"What kinds of orders, Master T'Krain?"

Another nervous shrug. "Here go we! Here go we!" His voice climbed at the end of each sentence almost comically. "Course this, yes take. Course that, take no. Here go we!"

As T'Krain spoke, Eden had her first sense that the T'Sariian was, if not lying, then definitely omitting some facts. She shifted position enough to catch Kel-Paten's brief attention, and the captain's as well.

Sass spoke before Kel-Paten could. "T'Krain. *Enk rankrintar narit t'sor enarin.*"

It took Eden a moment to translate the insult; one she knew only because she'd heard Sass used it before: your tongue and your brain are no longer friends.

Sass's pronouncement unleashed a flood of T'Sariian words from T'Krain who, in his excitement, evidently forgot his professed frailty and, releasing his death grip on the coverlet, waved his hands excitedly as he spoke.

Eden caught only a few words: Money. Betrayal. Hunter. Hunted. And Serafino's name along with a few others: Admiral Kel-Varen's for one. But it wasn't the words she needed to understand; it was the emotions behind them. She signaled to Sass what she knew with a system they'd devised years before—fingers open. Fingers closed. Truth. Lies.

The hard tone left Sass's voice. She moved closer to T'Krain. Kel-Paten stepped back a bit as she inched next to him, yet still within reach of the T'Sariian. Eden knew the admiral's presence, his lethal presence, was one of the reasons T'Krain was talking at all.

T'Krain laughed at something Sass said, and seemed to relax. Eden's hand remained open. T'Krain was telling the truth, whatever that was at this point.

But his next words were laced with a totally different feeling. Eden closed her hand into a fist and, just a quickly, there was a guttural utterance from Sass.

T'Krain hissed something back that sounded equally as nasty. His right hand swung out to grab the captain.

Kel-Paten intercepted the movement with cybernetically enhanced speed, his black-gloved hand clamping onto the narrow wrist. "Touch her and you die," he growled menacingly.

The T'Sariian paled under his leathery, amber skin as he drew in one, long, noisy breath of air, no doubt feeling it was his very last. But when, after a few moments, he was able to take a second breath, and then a third, albeit shaky one, he parted his lips into a taut, stiff smile and puffed out several strained laughs.

"Heh. Heh. Heh. Joke. Yes? Kidding." His gaze went from Kel-Paten to Sass. Then he let out a long sigh, as if some deep understanding had just dawned. "*Esry'on tura?*" he asked her as Kel-Paten released his wrist.

Sass frowned and shook her head. "*Nalk,*" she replied emphatically. No.

Two emotional responses hit Eden at the same time. From T'Krain, it was surprise and disbelief.

From Admiral Kel-Paten, it was a similar jolt of surprise, but with a distinct twinge of regret, of frustration that seemed out of context with what had been happening in the room. Whatever it was, it had been caused by T'Krain's last question, which Kel-Paten had obviously understood, along with Sass's definitive "no". An interesting combination, Eden noted. Something else to ask Sass about.

"I think we have all we need to know from Master T'Krain at this time." Sass looked at Kel-Paten and nodded.

He inclined his head slightly, but said nothing.

Eden turned to T'Krain. "We appreciate your cooperation. Thank you."

The thin face nodded rapidly. "Fuck you very much! Fuck you very much, too!"

It was the only Standard phrase he knew in its proper word order, and it was definitely a memorable one.

DR. EDEN FYNN'S OFFICE, SICKBAY, THS *VAXXAR*

Kel-Paten's first impulse had been to flatten the T'Sariian for his insulting parting comment. But the small blonde grabbed his arm and propelled him through the doorway before he could do much more than let out an exasperated grunt.

"He doesn't mean it, not the way he said it! Serafino !" She shoved him down into a chair in the CMO's office. "Serafino—or someone—just taught him that to be funny. He doesn't know what he's saying."

She referred to T'Krain's parting "Fuck you very much". He knew that, yet it took a moment for her words to sink in, and for him to shift his focus from the overly excitable T'Sariian to the woman who had now had him pinned in the office chair. Her hands pushed against his shoulders, her legs were planted between his own, and their combined weight caused the chair to tilt backwards slightly, bringing her face inches from his. Their thighs touched in an undeniably intimate manner and he suddenly forgot everything—Serafino, T'Krain—everything except how little effort it would take to pull her against him and sear her with the rush of heat that coursed through his body.

"Sebastian." His voice was a raspy whisper and the pause that followed hinted at a deep pain he hadn't meant to let surface.

She straightened. "Admiral? You okay?" she asked softly.

He closed his eyes. His thumbs for a brief moment traced the lifeline of her pulse. He nodded, gently removing her hands from his shoulders and holding them together before releasing her, letting her step away.

"I'm fine." He ran his hand over his face then abruptly pushed himself out of the chair, turning his back to Sass as he sifted disinterestedly through a small pile of case files on Fynn's desk.

"We need to go over T'Krain's information." His voice sounded strong, almost harsh, angry again. It was always easier to be angry. "Get Dr. Fynn—"

"I'm right here," the CMO said.

He spun around, almost colliding with Sass, and saw Fynn leaning against the doorframe.

"Look, I'm sorry for dragging you in here like that." Sass briefly touched his arm. "And," she added, one hand towards Eden, "for so rudely commandeering your office, but I really thought we were about to witness a murder." She grinned.

He waited for Fynn to respond to the smile. He wasn't the only one to notice she didn't. And he had a very bad feeling about just what Fynn had been noticing.

Sass's frowning gaze went from Fynn to him, then back to Fynn again. "Just what is going on here?"

"I think," Eden said, "that we're all just waiting to find out what

T'Krain told you. You were, after all, the only one who understood what he said." She took her seat and straightened the files on her desk that he'd disturbed.

Sass sat also. He remained standing, and Sass looked up at him. "Sorry. I thought you spoke...you didn't understand any of it?"

He chanced a glance at Fynn. Sass and Eden Fynn were friends, close friends. And the latter was an empath who'd been standing in the doorway for the past few moments while he'd let his thoughts, and emotions, run rampant in regards to the former. Again.

Fynn knew. This time he was sure. The look on her face when he saw her in the doorway told him everything. She knew. And if she knew, then Sass would know, and...he didn't want her finding out that way. Not from a medical practitioner who knew what he was, who would advise Sass that his feelings were an aberration, a programming glitch that could be rectified. Fynn could order that. That's what med techs did.

He had to learn to control his feelings when Fynn was around. He stuffed the last remnants of pain back into his emotional strongbox and turned his mind to the matter, and question, at hand.

"I only understood a few words once T'Krain got going," he admitted and leaned back against the office wall, crossing his arms over his chest. He couldn't sit down, couldn't sit so close to Sass in the small confines because every time he did her warmth seemed to wash over him and he was caught like a drowning man in a rip tide. "His dialect is too..." he stopped, searching for the right word. That rarely happened to him. This was a very frustrating day in more ways than one.

Sass tilted her chair back and looked up at him. "It's not the dialect. T'Krain actually speaks an ancient form of T'Sar. Like our using 'thee' and 'thou', only worse. There are a couple of remote, fundamentalist colonies that still speak that way. Plus they often invert the subject and predicate."

"Throw cousin from the window a kiss?" Fynn volunteered.

"Exactly," Sass agreed. "Or maybe you could say, 'Thee shouldst throw thy cousin from thy window a kiss.' That might be even closer."

"Well, T'Krain did some 'kissing and telling', but some of it he kept to himself," Fynn noted. "There were more than a few deceptions thrown in there."

"You caught them well," Sass told her with a smile. "Damn, but you're good! And damn if he didn't like that one bit."

"Did T'Krain know you were there to read him empathically?" Kel-Paten asked Fynn. Maybe the Zingaran doctor had still been thinking of the T'Sarii. Maybe she hadn't been tuned into his emotions. Maybe. He doubted it.

"I made sure he thought I was there strictly as a medical professional, but he is T'Sarii, admiral. Many of them have a low level empathic sense."

Gods, no. He'd forgotten that fact. The Illithians were the usual enemy-of-the-decade, and therefore his required focus. Not the ineffectual, quirky T'Sarii.

With a deep sense of impending doom, he realized that would explain T'Krain's earlier question, *'Esry'on tura?'* Is he your lover? He'd understood the question, but thought T'Krain had asked it because he'd reacted when T'Krain had struck out at Sass.

But the T'Sarii evidently had been reading more than just his physical response. He'd picked up on the emotional response as well.

While Fynn was scanning T'Krain, T'Krain had been scanning him.

And Sass, with her eclectic linguistic abilities, had fully understood the question as well. *'Esry'on tura?'*

He prayed she wouldn't understand as well the real reason behind it.

"All right." He ran his hand over his face in a weary gesture. "T'Krain. Tell me what happened in there with T'Krain."

T'Krain Namar was a small time opportunist, small time arms dealer and small time mercenary. He'd known of Serafino through mutual contacts for many years; he'd only been asked less than one year ago to serve as navigator on the *Novalis*. He didn't particularly know why; he didn't particularly care. He'd been low on funds at the time and working for Serafino was no less painful than working for any other human. Plus, he'd always admired the man's rakehell attitude and allegiance to the only thing that T'Krain himself really cared about: money.

At least, that's all he thought Serafino had cared about. But working closely with him for the past year, he'd come to believe that more than just cold, hard cash motivated the mercurial captain. Revenge motivated him and it was a revenge involving a woman. No, he didn't know who the woman was, or why, out of the scores that flocked through Serafino's cabin, one in particular would mean more than the rest.

T'Krain also said that he knew that Serafino had a deep contact somewhere in the Illithian Federation. It had been what the Alliance had hired him for. Serafino had been honest about that much with the T'Sariian but was definitely evasive when it came to exactly whose side he was working on. T'Krain said Serafino told him that "he didn't have a need to know" and T'Krain had accepted that, as long as he was paid.

And as for payment, he was under the impression the two hundred fifty thousand credits was only the beginning. There was more coming—

Serafino had intimated as much. But he'd never said from where.

"How did they end up in the vortex?" Kel-Paten had ventured as far as the edge of Eden's desk, where he perched safely several feet from Sass, and directed his question to her.

"Let me state that before that, his association with Serafino had become strained," Sass explained. "They'd been to Panperra a couple of times. T'Krain had been allowed to come and go as he pleased. But now—I guess it was about a month ago—he was confined to the ship, or could leave the ship in Serafino's presence only.

"Further, T'Krain said—and it may only be he's saying this as some kind of excuse—he said that Serafino's personality started to change. He'd forget things, or people. Became very mistrustful."

"Trefla," Kel-Paten snorted. One of the side effects of the illegal drug was a skewed, disjointed personality.

Sass shrugged. "T'Krain had decided he'd had enough and was going to jump ship, but Serafino hounded him, wouldn't let him out of his sight. Then, without warning, broke dockage and headed, as far as T'Krain knew at that point, to nowhere. Except that Serafino fed T'Krain exact coordinates. Exact coordinates that put them right at the epicenter of the vortex."

"Why would he do that?" Fynn asked.

Kel-Paten answered. "To use its power, doctor. There's scientific evidence that if we can harness a vortex, we can use it as a form of intergalactic travel. Faster than the hyper-warp drives we currently have." It had been a theory he had been actively working on for many years and believed, that had it not been for the war, he would've gotten much farther. It was one of the reasons he had been so amenable to the peace talks.

But not the only one.

"Anyway, according to T'Krain," Sass continued, "when the *Novalis* reached the coordinates, the vortex was just starting to form. T'Krain has no idea how Serafino knew it would and he was surprised, he swears, to see the energy signature come across the sensors. That was one of the answers that Eden couldn't give me a definitive reading on."

"Sometimes," Fynn explained, "an individual's recollection of an incident is a stronger emotional experience than the exact veracity of the recounting. That usually happens in times of great fear or horror. Details could be added on; erroneous details that are really lies, but because the sensation 'fits', and because the overlaying emotion is so strong, the details become as if they're true.

"We talk," she said, gesturing to herself, "about 'first level' and 'second level' feelings. A strong second level feeling could drown out a weaker, even though factual, first level feeling."

"I'm somewhat familiar with the terminology," Kel-Paten said. The 'somewhat' was an underestimate. He was more familiar with elements of psycho-synthesis than he cared to remember.

"T'Krain said he was also just as surprised to see our energy signature," Sass continued, "though Serafino didn't seem concerned. At least, not until his ship began to break up. Everyone was in bad shape at that point and yes, they were trying to make a blind jump through the vortex. But when the ship began to break up, Serafino took the helm and did what he could to get her within our sensor range. And the rest, we all know."

Kel-Paten turned slightly on the corner of Fynn's desk and looked down at her. "What's your base reading on T'Krain and where does his V-level peak?" Base reading. V-level. Those were Psy-Serv terms and he used them deliberately. He wanted Fynn to know he'd long ago done his homework on empaths, mind talents.

"My base on the subject is slightly higher because he's T'Sarii and not humanoid," she told him in her best clinical recitation. "I also have to factor in Captain Sebastian's linguistic appraisal of the origin of his dialect. If he was Fundamental T'Sarii, that adjusts his base further upward. Fundamental T'Sariis had a strong religious training that emphasized a clannishness and rigid morality. The fact that T'Krain had left the colonies and now associated with humanoids meant he had gone through some serious family schisms. Without further probing, I'd put his base at a delta-gamma range that will accept a fair amount of delusional rationalization as fact in order to survive.

"His V-level I'd put low, at maybe a four or five. He was probably exiled or excommunicated from his colony. He now has to rebuild his self-esteem. So he will say what it takes to aggrandize himself, or to warrant praise from someone he's talking to."

"Given that?" he prompted.

"Given that, I'd say about eighty per cent of what he told Captain Sebastian is a probably true recollection, keeping in mind he has some tiered second level reactions in there. Once the computers translate the vid-transcript of the session, I'll overlay my readings and stat it to your offices." She nodded to Sass then to him. "But that probably won't be until tomorrow."

"Tomorrow's acceptable," he told Fynn, pushing himself away from her desk. He stopped behind Sass's chair and rested his hand lightly on its back. "We'll leave you, then. You have more than enough work to do." He swiveled Sass's chair to face the door before she could object. "Come along, Sebastian. You're with me."

He waited, favoring her with one of his usual glares, until she offered a half-hearted wave to the CMO and fell in step with him as he strode through the doorway.

She turned before he realized he was ahead of her. "Comm me when you're ready for dinner," she called back through Fynn's open doorway. "Give me prelims on T'Krain, then."

"Will do." Fynn nodded as her doorway slid closed.

Sass stepped back towards him. He uncurled his fingers from the fist he'd consciously made, motioned her towards the corridor as if his world hadn't just taking a nose dive into a black hole.

Eden Fynn could give Sass a lot more than prelims. He needed Fynn busy and away from Sass as much as possible until he could figure out a way to do some damage control. He was afraid that her empathic readings on the T'Sariian weren't the only things she would discuss with her captain as soon as they were alone. And he didn't know what he feared worse: Sass's scorn, or pity when the Zingaran CMO told her just how hopelessly in love the Tin Soldier was with her.

Or Fynn's resultant order to Section Forty-Six him, removing him from command of the *Vaxxar*, and removing Sass from his life.

CHAPTER NINE

SICKBAY, THS *VAXXAR*

Eden took a half hour to review updates on the virus on Farside Station. There was little chance, with Serafino and all that had happened, the *Vax* would head back there now. But that didn't mean she couldn't work on the data. The virus still plagued her, pun intended, she noted with a mental nod. However, Serafino's situation, and warnings, bothered her more.

Which was why a visit with him was next on her schedule.

She worked on the virus data just in case Kel-Paten returned unexpectedly. It wouldn't do to have him find her in Serafino's hospital room, so shortly after their interrogation of T'Krain. That would definitely take some creative explanations, but not more creative than what she'd devised as a means to initiate telepathic contact with Serafino without either harming him (she would set the alarm on her wrist watch for ten minutes) or exposing herself (literally) to the amorous advances of his 'evil twin'. She needed a way to keep the physical Serafino busy while she reached out for the telepathic one.

And it had taken considerable creativity to find a way. Creativity and a history lesson.

She caught Cal's eye as she strode towards Serafino's room and nodded slightly. He nodded back. They'd already discussed what she had to do and he, too, had set his alarm. But his was set for eleven minutes, at which time he would physically go in and break the contact between her and Serafino if he had to. Neither doctor knew for sure if Serafino would survive another seizure.

The security lock read her palm print and granted her entry. Serafino had been scanning a vid-mag on the swivel screen that pulled out from the wall by his bed and looked up when she entered, a broad smile on his face.

"Well, if it isn't one of the Doctor twins, and my favorite at that! Have I told you how beautiful you look today, beautiful?"

"Yes, Captain Serafino. You told me this morning." She avoided looking at him and concentrated instead on the data on her hand held medicorder. She wanted to make sure, very sure, that he was strong enough to withstand her telepathic attempt.

"You can tell me how perfect I am. I don't mind," he teased.

She glanced at him and thought regretfully how true that really was. He was undeniably perfect. Tall. Dark. Handsome. To-die-for blue eyes. Owning a pair of those herself, she'd never before succumbed to their reputed charms. But his were different; a deep azure blue with flecks of green and gold, graced by long dark eyelashes. Oddly sensitive and compassionate eyes set in a distinctly masculine chiseled face that tended to an early beard shadow. Which only made him look more handsome and more rakish.

"Actually," she told him, beginning to enjoy the charade, "you're not all that perfect." She sighed and then became quiet. Patients hated that sigh, she knew. That worried-medical-doctor sigh. And they hated it even more when the doctor subsequently became quiet.

"Hmm," she mused out loud, pretending to concentrate on the readings in her hand.

"Hmm?" he questioned.

"Hmm."

"Is that a good 'hmm' or a bad 'hmm', my lovely doctor?"

She shrugged. "Not sure."

"What do you mean, not sure? You're the doctor—the Chief Medical Officer, if I'm correct." He smiled, but it was a tense smile.

"You are. Correct, that is."

"And what else am I, Doc?" he queried. "Look, I got bumped around a bit. But that doesn't warrant being locked up in here."

His high security confinement disconcerted him. She and Kel-Paten knew it would.

"It's for your protection," she told him, making an adjustment to her medicorder.

He tried to peer at its screen but she angled her body away.

"My protection, eh? Look, I'm on your side, remember? Your Council hired me."

"That's something you'll have to discuss with Admiral Kel-Paten," she told him.

"I'd love to. Bring him on. Bring on a whole army of Tin Soldiers. When are you going to let me talk to him?" He'd made this request before, and had received the same response before.

"When I give you medical clearance, captain, and you're not there, yet."

"Why?"

"Not sure." They were back where they started and that's just where Eden wanted him.

He leaned against the pillows and groaned. "Okay, Doc, what is it? I'm a big boy. You can tell me. Am I pregnant?"

His query—and expression—was so comical that Eden laughed out loud in spite of her desire to focus on her mission. "No, but I'm glad to see you still have a sense of humor."

"You have a sexy laugh, Doc."

"And you, Captain Serafino," she said, moving in for the kill, "have something that is confounding my best scanners. So I'm afraid I have no choice but to resort to drastic measures."

He frowned. "Explain."

"We can't get a definitive reading on your body temperature. There's something in your system—and I've seen it in rare cases—that scrambles the medicorders."

"Something—like what?"

"Electrolyte levels have been known to do that," she lied.

"Which means—?"

She pulled out a long, antique glass thermometer. "I have to take your temperature. Manually."

"Manually?" He stared at the instrument that bespoke of a time long ago of scalpels and sutures and things that actually hurt. "What's that thing?"

"A thermometer. An oral thermometer. Open wide..."

His eyes almost crossed as he stared at it. "I will not. You're not putting that thing in my mouth!"

"Are we afraid, Captain Serafino?" she cooed.

"Afraid? Lubashit, no. It's just that nobody's used those things in centuries, Doc. Where did you get your medical degree, anyway?"

"The same place you got your captain's license. Send away twelve box-tops from Starry Loops cereal and you can be anything your heart desires. Now say ahhh."

He clamped his mouth shut. "No," he said through tight lips.

Eden stood back, eyed him in mock anger and tapped her foot. Then, reaching into her other lab coat pocket, she pulled out a much larger and longer thermometer.

"Fine," she said, holding it out for him to see. "You don't want to say ahhh, we can do it another way. This is a rectal thermometer." She stressed the word 'rectal'. "Roll over."

Serafino actually paled. "You must be out of your friggin' mind."

"Then say ahhh," she told him.

He said 'ahhh'.

When she was sure the thermometer was securely under his tongue, and that he wouldn't bite the thing in half, she surreptitiously tapped at the extra commbadge in her pocket, sending a signal to its coded twin on Cal Monterro's desk. Serafino was under control. Now came the hard part.

She took his wrist in her hand as if to take his pulse. Again, an ancient medical practice in an age of scanners and sensors and sonic surgery.

"What now?" he mumbled around the thermometer.

"Shh! I told you, you mustn't talk. Lie back and close your eyes. I need your heart rate to relax so I can take your pulse. The more you fight this, captain, the longer it's going to take. And if I can't get a good reading out of that oral thermometer, I'll have no choice but to use—"

He fell back abruptly against the pillows, his eyes tightly closed.

She let her hand encircle his wrist and used the blinking red numbers on her watch to let her mind fall into a light trance. His breathing slowed, and so did hers until they were matched in rhythm. She called his name. *Jace?* She had a brief floating sensation and then a comforting warmth.

Eden! What in bloody hell did you stick in my mouth?

She shot him a mental grin. *Had to shut you up somehow. Would you have preferred the other orifice?*

She felt him grin back; a small tickle of warmth in her mind as he sent his words: *Damn you, woman. A doctor and a comedian.* She felt a question forming. *How did you...how did you know this would work?*

Shutting you up, or contacting you through touch-telepathy? No, sorry, we don't have much time and I'm being silly. There are some Zingaran manuals on telepathic healings. It was an avenue I had to try. Jace, we've got some problems, not the least of which are some compounds in your blood I can't get a reading on. My med files have so little on Nasyry physiology. I don't know if you have a severe infection I can't find or it's just normal. That's the first thing, she told him and then waited.

Eden, I'm sorry. I don't have an answer on that. I feel fine, if that's any help.

He felt her disappointment. *Not to a doctor. But we have other avenues.*

We?

Sass—Captain Sebastian. We think Kel-Paten has accumulated some impressive files on Psy-Serv over the years. Sebastian's going to go in and get them.

You can call her Sass. I know who she is. I know about Lethant and what happened on Farside. She has quite a reputation on the Rim.

That wasn't something she was here to discuss and told him so. But it was something she would warn Sass about. She knew there were parts of Sass's past the captain would rather forget. And other parts that would put her in serious jeopardy if the wrong person were to learn of those facts.

He evidently caught her concern. *I don't kiss and tell, Doc.* A big mental grin. *What else do you need to know? We're at about six minutes and running.*

I have Cal on stand-by, timing us. Jace, I can't try to remove that implant until I know more about your blood composition. Anything you can remember from past physicals will help me. If not now, and I know we don't have the time, then the next chance you get to contact me.

Understood. Whatever you can do, love, know that I appreciate it. And I don't blame you for anything that might go wrong. I know I'm a big unknown here.

Not for long if Sass can get that data from Kel-Paten's files. In the meantime, I need to know how you by-pass the implant. Maybe I can help in some way, extend your time.

A flood of information came to her—Nasyry mind control rituals plus a healthy dose of cyber-circuitry tricks. Much of it meant nothing to her, especially the technical data. That would be child's play to Kel-Paten, she knew, but asking his help right now was out of the question. Still, it was an area that Sass was well versed in. She felt his agreement.

Tell Lady Sass that Shadow sends his regards. It was almost time to break contact.

She wondered if she said 'ante up' whether you'd remember her?

From Queenie's? Tell the little card shark I sure as hell do! Tell her I said she ought to play Kel-Paten in a sudden death round of Starfield Doubles for the control codes to the Vaxxar. She'd win, no doubt.

She sent him a smile. *Will do, captain.*

It's Jace, he reminded her firmly. *And, Eden...*

Yes?

Our game is strip poker. I will reach you later, love...

The contact was gone.

She opened her eyes and gently released Serafino's wrist, then tapped at the commbadge in her pocket. Her watch told her she had forty-eight seconds to go.

Forty-eight seconds more and she could have killed him.

"Captain Serafino," she called softly.

Bright blue eyes suddenly opened. And looked a bit dazed. There was, she knew, some residual from the telepathy.

She plucked the thermometer from his mouth, glanced at it and pretended to make a note on the nearby med scanner. When she looked up, he was still watching her.

"You know, Doc, I keep thinking that I know you from somewhere." His voice had momentarily lost its usual arrogance and was closer to who she knew as "Jace". "I keep thinking," and he licked his lips as he thought for a moment, "that we were more than just friends."

She shook out the thermometer and placed it back in her pocket. "In your dreams, Serafino. In your dreams."

She retrieved the med-scanner and headed for the door, palming the security lock back on as the door closed behind her. But Jace Serafino was far from safe; not from the damned implant in his head, not from Admiral Kel-Paten's probing. She could no longer deny the admiral the right to do the latter; she had only vague ideas what to do about the former.

With a sigh, she sent a note to Kel-Paten upgrading Serafino's condition. Providing she was present, she would permit him to be interviewed.

A message waited for her when she returned to her office. The admiral requested her presence at in interview in the Ready Room at 1845 hours. Dinnertime, to be exact.

And it looked as if Jace Serafino was going to be the main course.

CHAPTER TEN

READY ROOM, THS *VAXXAR*

It was a repeat performance; a repeat command performance. Only this time the players weren't in Sickbay but in the Ready Room; the small but efficient conference room just aft of the bridge. A more fitting place than Sickbay to interview the former captain of the *Novalis*; at least in Kel-Paten's mind. Here the admiral felt comfortable, surrounded by the familiar and functional—the dark, oblong table; the repetition of cushioned chairs; the comp screens set in at regular intervals into the tabletop. Familiar and functional without the annoying clicking and beeping of Sickbay diagnostics, too reminiscent of a place and time he'd just as soon forget.

No, the *Vax's* Ready Room was a place in which he felt in total command, and he didn't want to be anything less when confronting Jace "Shadow" Serafino.

And confront he did. Especially after Serafino accused the Triad of selling out to the Illithians.

"Perhaps, captain," Kel-Paten all but spat out the title in disgust, "I choose not to believe your story. You have a reputation for many things in this sector. Veracity is not one of them."

Jace Serafino looked over the tips of his boots, which were propped in a comfortably disrespectful fashion on the edge of the table. "Perhaps," he replied in a tone equally as deadly as Kel-Paten's, "that's because the quality of truth in this sector has often depended upon the quantity of money willing to purchase it. Admiral." Serafino smiled, the effect at once disarming yet cunning. "The Triad chooses to hear and see what suits the political machine at the moment, and is willing to pay any amount to insure that fantasy. If you'd ever chance to venture out of this safe and sterile little world you've created for yourself, you'd know everything I've been telling you is true."

He jerked his chin towards the wide viewport where Sass had been leaning for the last half-hour. "If you'd ever taken the time to listen to her, she'd tell you. Unless she doesn't trust you, either."

Kel-Paten refused to let himself look at Sass, refused to see what might be an acknowledgment in her eyes. "I have an excellent rapport with all my officers. And crew," he replied firmly.

"Your crew," Serafino put in smoothly, "is terrified of you. Most of your officers are Triad born and bred and brainless. If you've got a chance in hell to survive," he continued, raising his voice over Kel-Paten's angry growl, "you're going to have to listen to the likes of me. And them." He nodded first at Sass and then at Eden.

Kel-Paten leaned his fists against the tabletop and glared at Serafino. "If the U-Cees had proof of Triad collusion with the Illithians, don't you think they would have brought out that fact at the peace talks, or in council?"

"The U-Cee politicos are as ignorant and blind as you are, Tin Soldier. And they, like you, rarely venture from their tidy and orderly little domains to see how the real universe lives. But for some reason, you've now got on this ship—and maybe I know a little more about your crew than you do," he mused out loud with an appraising glance at Sass, "certain people," and he looked now directly at Eden, "who have significant experience in the real universe. G-level and below, as we say in the trade. Not your A-level military docks on station, or your C and D-level private money docks, or even your respectable freighter bays on E-level. But let's go below G, Kel-Paten. Let's take a walk down to where the methane-breathers flirt with the oxys, where trefla is as common as fleas on a furzel. Work the rim worlds, like the Doc here has, though maybe she won't admit that to you, either. But she knows, they both know."

Serafino turned casually to Sass. "You've come a long way since Queenie's."

"Up or down, Serafino?" Sass replied lightly. "Coming from you, that comment could mean anything."

Serafino laughed heartily. Kel-Paten tamped down his annoyance and used the moment to glance quickly at a series of discreet hand signals from Fynn. Yes, Serafino was telling the truth, or at least believed everything he said. Not only the accusations about the Triad but about Sass's knowledge and undercover experience.

He knew about that. Hell, he'd researched everything he could about Captain Tasha Sebastian for years: she was the orphaned child of wealthy parents, schooled by the top private tutors, recruited into the Coalition Military Academy and graduating top of her class, with honors. She spoke almost as many languages as he did, spent two years in deep intelligence work. Which explained some of the gaps in her history he'd never been able to reconcile.

He knew all this; had always seen her background as the perfect complement to his own. It disturbed him not only that Serafino knew as well, but seemed to know more.

"Captain Sebastian," Kel-Paten said, disliking the easy laughter that had flowed between Sass and Serafino, "is not the one who took two hundred and fifty thousand credits. And ran."

Serafino shrugged noncommittally. "If I hadn't, would you have come looking for me? I highly doubt it. That, Kel-Paten, was my insurance policy. Your people wanted to send me on a one-way trip to hell. I had no intention of accommodating them."

"You didn't have to accept the mission," Kel-Paten shot back.

"If I hadn't they would have killed me. Probably sent you to do that, now that I think of it. You would've liked that, wouldn't you?"

Kel-Paten's eyes narrowed. "It would have been my pleasure." That would only leave Dag Zanorian to plague the galaxy. A considerable improvement, in his estimation.

A theatrical sigh escaped Serafino's lips; he leaned back in his chair and, glancing over his left shoulder, raised his gaze to Eden Fynn. "See what abuse I have to put up with, Doc? Can't you feed him some 'nice' pills, or something? Or, I know!" And he snapped his fingers and turned back to Kel-Paten. "We'll just reverse the polarity on your batteries! You know, kind of a bio-cybe attitude adjustment hour!"

Kel-Paten slammed the back of the chair against the table with such force that both Sass and Fynn jumped. Serafino only readjusted his outstretched legs slightly and appeared equally as unconcerned as Kel-Paten rounded the corner of the table and stopped, black-gloved hand pointing threateningly in Serafino's direction.

"I have had," he said, each of his words punctuated with bitter anger, "just about enough of your insubordinate shit, Serafino." In three long strides he was at Serafino's side and about to grab a handful of rumpled white linen shirt when a smaller hand clasped onto his wrist. He froze, not by any force of strength leveled against him, but because of a look of disapproval in a pair of green eyes.

"Branden," Sass said softly, "he's playing you. He's no use to us dead. Yet."

She'd stepped between them, but still firmly held his wrist. Even though she had to see the slight haze of luminous blue in his eyes. He'd switched over to full cybernetic function, right after he had slammed the chair into the table and headed for Serafino.

With the slightest of movements he could toss her across the room. Or sear her with a touch, and she'd be dead before she hit the floor.

He knew she knew that, yet here she was, all five-feet of her, standing between him and the object of his wrath while holding onto his wrist—with no more concern in her demeanor than if she were about to follow him onto the dance floor.

It was the second time that day that she had initiated physical contact with him, and though Kel-Paten wasn't deluding himself that this or her earlier encounter with him in Fynn's office were anything more than a normal reaction of one fellow officer to another in a stressful situation, it was still something no one else had done since he'd been in the Academy. People—not his crew, not his staff, not his officers—people just didn't like to touch him. They didn't want to. Never knew when those power implants in his hands might activate and their last thought would be one of intense searing pain. Yet he could have told them that that could only happen if his cybernetics were 'powered on'—something he knew anyone could tell by the change of hue in his eyes.

Sass knew that. She'd known it before she ever came on board as an Alliance captain, because she had access to all the intelligence the U-Cees had on him. So she knew that...and yet here she was, ignoring the telltale blue glow. It was as if what he had wanted for so long to happen was now happening: she was seeing him, accepting him, not as a 'cybe but just as Kel-Paten. Just as Branden Kel-Paten.

It would have almost, almost been an optimistic thought were it not for the intense disapproval evident in her eyes.

Kel-Paten didn't know if she viewed him as human or 'cybe, but whichever it was, she was extremely disappointed. And more than a tad pissed.

That cut at him like no ion lance ever could.

He drew his hand away from hers—not sharply, not in any way to cause alarm—and then without glancing at either Serafino or Eden, strode quickly from the Ready Room. The door whooshed closed behind him.

<^>

Eden Fynn let out a slow, soft sigh of relief. The sound was not lost on Serafino.

"Is he usually this testy or is it that time of the month?" he drawled.

Sass perched on the edge of the table not far from his boots and crossed her arms over her chest. "You owe me one, Serafino. You are very, very lucky to be alive right now."

He gave her a confident smile. "The Tin Soldier and I go back a long time. He's threatened me before."

"Then you should know better than to push him right now," Sass said. "If what you've been telling us is true—about high level corruption in the Triad—than you should be looking to us, to him, for help. Alienating him will get you nowhere. Except dead."

Serafino considered her words for a moment. Then with a glance back at Eden: "Ahh, so it's good cop-bad cop here, eh? And what's your role in this little play, Doctor? I hope you're the one they assign to rehabilitate me."

"You know, Captain Serafino," Eden said, stuffing her hands into her lab coat pockets, "you would have made a great used star-freighter salesman."

He laughed. "Or politician?"

"Or double agent," Sass intoned lightly.

He looked back at the small blonde. "No." The smile faded from his face. "I'm no saint, Sebastian, but then neither are you. You've moved in the same circles I have; you know how to check on what I've told you. Your Tin Soldier boy there," he said with a nod towards the closed doors, "the Triad bought him and built him and owns him. He can't even think in those directions until all that Triadian propaganda is shaken loose out of him.

"You're right," he continued. "I need his cooperation. Hell, I need this damn ship, if you want to know the truth. I'm not the only one that Faction I told you about is looking to permanently deep-six. He's on the list—or will be. Little by little, they will take out anyone they feel could stand in their way. He's an unknown, the Tin Soldier is. Too powerful for the likes of them—tell him that."

"And I suppose," Sass asked, "you're going to tell me I'm on that list, too?"

"Why the hell do you think they put you on the *Vax* in the first place?" Serafino asked her. "They figured he'd do the job for them. Which is very reassuring to me because it proves that they're not infallible; they can make mistakes. They've misjudged this whole situation, haven't they?"

"Serafino, I still don't know who this 'they' is you're talking about." Sass unfolded her arms and pulled herself away from the table. "And I really don't know what 'situation' you're referring to, unless it's the fact that the admiral and I were adversaries at one point, and let me stress the word 'were'. Keep in mind we're both professionals; career officers. We have our duties and perform them to the best of our abilities. And if that means cooperating with someone we once viewed as an enemy, we can do that. *I* can do that. And that's something—if you want Kel-Paten's help—I strongly suggest you start to learn."

She tapped at the badge on her jacket. "Security Team One to the Ready Room." She looked at Eden. "Cisco will escort Captain Serafino back to Sickbay. I'll see you in forty-five minutes in the Officers' Mess," she added.

Serafino looked at Eden as the doors closed again.

She motioned with one hand towards the corridor. "Captain?"

He pulled his feet off the table. "She has no idea, does she?" he asked as he stepped next to her. "But you do."

"I don't know what you're talking about. I—"

"Kel-Paten," he cut in. "You could file a Section Forty-Six on him, probably. 'Cybes aren't supposed to have those kinds of emotions."

"I didn't feel his anger at you was out of place," she said mildly, but something that looked like surprise flickered briefly across her face. A face he'd like to explore with his fingers. His mouth.

He forced himself to remember they were talking about the Tin Soldier. "Anger?" he asked. "Oh, there was heat there, but it wasn't from anger. And it wasn't directed at me."

The doors opened and Cisco Garrick stepped in. "Doctor?" Two burly security officers moved to flank Serafino on either side.

"Ah, yes, table for five, please," Serafino quipped as they headed into the corridor.

He grinned when Eden shook her head in exasperation.

They were in the lift, heading down to Sickbay when he felt something struggle within himself and was suddenly compelled to touch her mind. He interrupted her conversation with Trav Kel-Ranag, a security officer who'd showed considerable interest in the CMO in the past few minutes.

He only wants in your pants, darling, Jace purred, his telepathic intrusion startling her.

She managed to keep from tripping over her own tongue in answering Kel-Ranag's question about a new holo travel program before replying silently. *And you don't?* she shot back with no little irritation.

He chuckled. *Most definitely, but at least I'm enough of a gentleman to let you know first what an unacceptable scoundrel I am! I did warn you to lock your bedroom door.*

Jace—are you telling the truth?

About wanting you? Absolutely. I—

No, damn you! About the corruption in the Triad defense ministry. About that senator—

*I'm surprised you have to ask that question, Eden. But since you have...*He flashed a series of images to her; not the least of which was a scene of Minister Kel-Sennarin leaning over a table in a dark and dingy bar, with two Illithian agents on the other side.

The contact was abruptly broken by the lift doors opening and Garrick grabbing Serafino's arm, guiding him down the corridor to Sickbay. He leaned into the officer, feeling lightheaded from the effort to contact Eden.

It had been a risk to attempt the contact. He hoped she'd caught it all, desperately hoped she'd caught it all.

They were all dead if she hadn't.

CHAPTER ELEVEN

DECK ONE CORRIDOR, THS *VAXXAR*

Sass had spotted Cisco Garrick and his team as soon as she stepped out into the corridor.

"Get Serafino back to Sickbay with the least amount of trouble," she told him, her mind also on another bit of trouble. But one that had occurred a half hour earlier.

Kel-Paten. She'd seen the 'cybe officer angry before. Hell, she'd known him for over ten years. Much of his anger had been directed, during those same years, at her and the *Regalia*.

But something more than anger had seethed through the Ready Room. And whatever it was had almost jeopardized their interrogation with Serafino. She fully intended to find out what, and why, that was.

That being her primary focus, she headed down the corridor to the Admiral's office once she was sure Garrick and his team understood their instructions.

She laid her palm against the door scanner and waited the few microseconds while it confirmed her identity and reported same to the occupant—if there was one—of the office.

There was. She was granted entry by the almost silent sliding of the double doors into the wall.

The lighting in Kel-Paten's office was unusually dim for being occupied, and occupied it was by the tall form silhouetted against the floor to ceiling viewport. At sublight speed, the starfield was a black vista dotted with the silver-blue of stars. The stars seemed to move slowly; Kel-Paten did not, but remained standing, his back to her, his arms braced on either side of the viewport. He didn't turn when she entered, nor even after the doors whooshed closed. Yet he had to know she was there; his office doors wouldn't have opened without his verbal command.

Something was wrong, very wrong. She bit back the sarcastic opening lines she'd prepared and waited for him to acknowledge her. But he didn't, so she leaned against the back of one of the swivel chairs opposite his desk, knowing from experience that it would squeak.

But that, too, elicited no response.

"What happened back there, Kel-Paten?" she asked finally.

A tense shrug, more silence; then: "I lost control," he said, his back still to her, an unusual hesitation in his voice, as if the very act of speaking were difficult. "I thought that was obvious."

"That's not like you," she replied, the anger she'd so carefully cultivated suddenly waning. Damn it all, he wasn't even putting up a fight! Everything in his stance, his tone, screamed defeat. This wasn't the Kel-Paten she'd known for ten years.

"I imagine," he said after a moment, "that Dr. Fynn is ready to Section Forty-Six me about now."

"I don't think so. I made it look as if we were playing good cop-bad cop. Serafino thought he was real cute by picking up on that." At the mention of the name, she saw Kel-Paten's shoulders tense, and his hands, still braced against the viewport, clench. She thought of all the years, all the countless times she and the Tin Soldier had traded barbs over their respective ships' vidscreens—and all she'd ever been treated to was his usual impassive response. His typical 'cybe response; a slight frown, or raising of one eyebrow.

And yet here he was, almost going into a full-circuit melt-down.

Maybe a Section Forty-Six wasn't such a bad idea.

"Look, do you want me to handle Serafino from here on?" she offered. "We should be transferring him over to Homer within twenty fours hours. I can—"

"No!" He swung around to face her and she noted with surprise the luminous blue glow in his eyes. He either was still powered up since the session in the Ready Room, or had just now powered up. And if he had just now...

Something was very wrong, not the least his overreaction to Serafino. There'd been other things before that, she realized, other times when he'd displayed what could only be categorized as 'human emotions'. True, Eden had pointed out that Kel-Paten was still half human, but wasn't that human half supposed to be totally controlled by the cybernetic enhancements? Not to mention the psych-programming.

It was one of the reasons she'd always felt secure in dealing with him. She'd spent years studying him, her adversary until recently. She'd educated herself on bio-cybernetics, emo-programs. She respected—no, was in awe of his finely crafted, expertly created intelligence.

She'd also believed that his Triad crew, yielding to him as they always did, had never challenged him to his full capacity.

That's why she argued with him, had tested him for the past six months. And she felt their cooperative efforts to break free of the vortex were proof she'd been right. Utilization of the braking vanes had been an intuitive step for his programming.

But perhaps accessing that intuition had also broken down his safeguards. What did he just admit to her? That he'd lost control. That was *not* Kel-Paten. That was *not* the Tin Soldier. And she was not terribly thrilled with that realization.

He stared at her, that eerie glow in his eyes.

She remembered how he'd hinted he'd thought she had something to do with Serafino's appearance in the quadrant. He still might not be sure whose side she was on.

He still might view her as the enemy. There was a time the U-Cees had.

"We both can handle Serafino." He stepped away from his desk as he spoke.

As if in tandem, she took another step back towards the door.

"I think it's *important* we both handle Serafino," he continued.

His office comm buzzed, Rissa Kel-Faray's soft voice breaking the tension. "Sir. Admiral Rafe Kel-Tyra's responding to your request on translink four."

"I'm sure that's important," Sass said. "By your command." She nodded formally and was out the door before he could grant, or withdraw, permission, Serafino's warnings echoing darkly in her mind.

OFFICERS' MESS HALL, THS *VAXXAR*

"Drinking our dinner, are we?" Eden climbed the short flight of steps to the captain's private table in the Officers' Mess, her dinner tray balanced in her hand. Support Services had integrated several recipes that Eden had offered, the hearty vegetable stew and accompanying thick cheese-bread on her tray only two of them.

Sass's tray, by comparison, held only a tall glass of iced gin. And a mutilated lime wedge.

The captain looked up as Eden took the seat across from her. "Sit down, Doc. I think we may have a problem."

To underscore her point, she activated the privacy field around the table as soon as Eden sat, the pale yellow lights in the floor signaling to anyone nearby that the two officers didn't want to be disturbed. The sonic buffer itself would prevent them from being overheard.

The smile immediately dropped from Eden's face. "What happened?"

Sass gave a short, dry laugh. "I think the correct response is: 'you tell me'. No, I'm sorry, let me just run some questions by you, some issues, and you tell me what you think."

Eden nodded and Sass continued. "I'm sure you've noticed, as I've bitched about it to you enough, that Kel-Paten has been on my case since we came on board. We've discussed whether or not he completely trusts us, and by 'us' to some extent I mean the U-Cees. I told you how he just about accused me of creating the vortex just to bring Serafino to this ship.

"And after tonight, I think you can pretty clearly see just how much he would love to be the cause of Serafino's termination."

"Yes, but—" Eden started to say.

"No, wait. Please. You've also been reading Serafino for us, for me, though this whole thing. I'm relying heavily on your appraisal. Everything you've told me leads me to believe that Serafino is telling the truth, to the best of his knowledge, about possible collusion between the certain people in the Triad and the Illithians. At least, in certain very sensitive areas. Is that right?" She stabbed the lime wedge with her swizzle stick and pointed it at Eden.

"Well, yes."

"Well, yes? Eden, I don't like the sound of 'well, yes.' What else do you know?"

"Serafino and I had brief contact right after your session," Eden replied and described the images that had been flashed to her mind of the Illithian agents and the Triad Defense Minister.

"Oh, lubashit." Sass closed her eyes briefly. "Eden, Kel-Paten reports directly to Kel-Sennarin."

"So?"

"So, you didn't see what I saw when I chased after him about a half hour ago. I was, I don't know, confused about his reaction to Serafino. No, about the *intensity* of his reaction. The intensity of his overreaction. Are you following me on this?"

Eden was, and she hadn't even had any caffeine. She suspected she'd known Sass too long.

"I went to his office to get some answers. If he wanted to play good cop-bad cop, fine, but tell me first, okay? But when I got there, Eden, it was strange. The office lights were dimmed. He was staring out the viewport; didn't even turn when I came in. And when he finally did, I saw he was still in his 'cybe mode."

"That's not that unusual," Eden offered. She'd studied much of the same intelligence as Sass had on Kel-Paten, only from the medical and cyber-medical viewpoint. "The cyber interface functions as an emotional discipline—"

"Like he was going to emotionally discipline Serafino just now? Lubashit, my dear friend." She waggled the lime at Eden again.

"I don't know what you're getting at."

"Then think back about what Serafino told us just before I left. That this 'Faction', as he calls them, eventually intends to take out Kel-Paten, but first they wanted Kel-Paten to take out me. And I don't mean to dinner."

Oddly prophetic statement, that, Eden thought. She was going to have to tell Sass what she'd sensed from Kel-Paten. "You're basing your conclusions on one false premise," she began but Sass cut her off.

"I think not. You don't know the way he looked at me just now, in his office. It makes too much sense."

"But—"

"But do you think Serafino's telling the truth?"

"I know he's telling the truth," Eden replied quickly.

"Then you have to see that Kel-Paten's part of it. That's why he wanted Serafino dead, and dead before I could talk to him. That's why he went after him in the first place. C'mon, the two hundred and fifty thousand credits Serafino stole is small frack to the Triad.

"Eden, we have to get that implant removed and we have to remove it tonight," Sass continued. "Before we get to Panperra, before we're supposed to turn him over to Kel-Farquin. Because, one, I don't know if Kel-Paten will let him live that long. And two, the only way we're going to know the whole story is when Serafino's freed of that device. Serafino, the total Serafino, knows the whole story. What we have now is a physical body that remembers part of it and a telepathic connection that can't stay on line for more than ten minutes." Sass drew a deep breath. "I may not, *we* may not have that much time."

"You can't seriously think Kel-Paten would harm you," Eden asked pointedly. "There'd be questions, inquiries—"

"He's Kel-Paten. *The* Kel-Paten. And with Kel-Sennarin behind him, there'd be no questions."

Eden started to reply…then stopped. Could she be wrong? Could she have misread Kel-Paten's emotions? After all, she'd never 'sensed' a 'cybe before. There weren't any other ones to 'sense'. She knew the millions of credits and hundreds of hours spent on his psych programming. Much of it designed by Psy-Serv's best. Wouldn't they have also, then, created a 'scrambler' much as all ship's communications systems had? A Triad huntership broadcasts a message to set up an ambush in such and such a sector at such and such a time, and if that same message were intercepted by 'unfriendly factions', it would read like a recipe for her best fruit pie.

She had to consider that was a possibility. And it was a possibility that could only be uncovered completely by a telepath. Like Jace Serafino.

Yet Jace had also intimated that he'd sensed 'a certain heat' coming from Kel-Paten in regards to Sass. But he wasn't working with his full capacities, either.

No, Sass was right. They had to remove that implant and they had to do it now.

"We need that data from his files," Eden said.

"I know." Sass licked her lips. "I checked his schedule. He logged in for an inspection tour of navigation and stellar cartography. He will probably also ask, no, *demand* that I accompany him. I can't be with him, and in his cabin, at the same time. And I can't refuse to go with him, because then he might go back to his cabin and find me there."

"We need a way to keep him busy and free you up."

"Exactly. That's why I want you to make me sick."

"I beg your pardon?"

"What's the herb, it's got that weird name, that raises your body temperature? We used it when we got ditched out in the snowfields that time. I want you to give me enough, just enough, to simulate a raging fever. Something that when I weakly collapse in front of him will register to his cybernetic sensors as real. And register on Sickbay's diags as real. And then you're going to lock me up in one of your med rooms and not permit him to see me for at least four hours, during which time I'm going to have to climb up through the ship's interior ducting all the way to his cabin, break in, infiltrate his security, download half the universe and get back to Sickbay in time for my miracle cure."

"Sass—"

"Don't look at me like that, Fynn. You knew I was nuts when you signed on board with me years ago."

"Yeah, but—"

"Yeah, but nothing. You have the hard part of keeping Kel-Paten from going back to his cabin. And if he does, you've got to alert me right quick." Sass leaned over the table. "Got it?"

Eden suddenly smiled and tapped her juice glass against Sass's now empty one. "Feels like old times, girl. Feels like old times."

MAIN LIFT BANK, THS *VAXXAR*

Sass leaned back against the cool metal walls of the lift and closed her eyes. That foul smelling herbal compound of Eden's had kicked in several minutes ago, first with a feeling of lightheadedness that had just progressed into a rather unpleasant dizziness.

Admiral Kel-Paten, she noted, was in his usual spit and polish military stance, gloved-hands behind his back. It wasn't until the lift doors opened on Nav Deck that he turned, expecting her to step in front of him.

By that point, she felt the small beads of sweat trickling down the side of her face.

"Tasha?"

There was an odd hoarseness to his voice, Sass thought, or maybe the herbs affected her hearing as well.

"Tasha, are you all right?"

"Don't think so," she whispered. Her knees gave out and she slid towards the floor.

The next few moments progressed through a hazy, moving fog. Kel-Paten dropped to his knees and suddenly she moved upwards, his arms under her legs and around her back.

He must have slapped at the emergency comm link because she recognized, though dimly, its discordant trill.

"Kel-Paten to Transporter Room! I need an emergency transport to Sickbay. Lock on my commbadge and Captain Sebastian's. Now!"

And there was the familiar hum and momentary disorientation as her physical form merged with beams of light...and re-emerged as physical form in Sickbay.

Eden looked totally surprised. Sass fought the urge to wink at her friend but her eyes didn't seem to want to cooperate. "Admiral! What happened?"

"I don't know."

I passed out, she wanted to say, but her mouth didn't seem to be working either.

Caleb Monterro motioned them into the nearest diag room.

"She just passed out," Kel-Paten said.

Do I hear an echo? No, that would be Eden's job, hearing thoughts.

Her back bumped against something hard. The diag table, she assumed. An annoying beeping sound commenced. Definitely the diag table, kicking on and downloading her vitals.

Kel-Paten's face hovered over hers. "We had an inspection tour of Navigation scheduled." He looked at Monterro then Eden. "She seems to have—"

"A fever. A very high fever." Eden glanced at the readouts on the wall above the bed. "Admiral, I'm going to have to ask you to leave now."

"Is this serious?"

"I don't know." Eden ran her scanner over Sass's chest. "But you have to leave."

"If it's serious, I want to stay."

Get him out of here, Eden!

As if on cue, Eden shot Kel-Paten a reproving look. "You have to leave, admiral."

"No, I—"

"Kel-Paten, you're wasting my time. And hers. I'll send Dr. Monterro out shortly if we know anything."

Kel-Paten nodded as if in a trance. "Yes, of course. I'll be in your office, Doctor. Thank you."

The doors whooshed shut. Cal palmed on the security lock. Eden rolled up Sass's sleeve and removed the small transdermal patch she'd placed there, covering the reddish area with a new patch.

"You will," Sass heard Cal say to Eden, "explain all this at a later date."

"Promise, Doc." She smiled at him. "The captain said she'd even bring her best gin. Now go out there and keep the admiral occupied, like we planned. And for the Gods' sakes, let me know immediately if he leaves Sickbay."

It was a few minutes before the fog dissipated from Sass's vision and her mouth felt connected to her brain again.

"How are we feeling?" Eden crooned teasingly.

"We feel like lubashit on a lemon." She pushed herself up onto her elbows. The room tilted only slightly. But her head pounded and her stomach felt as if it had been through a shredder. "I supposed I could say I've had hangovers worse than this, but I honestly can't remember when. Okay, hand me my gear, will you?"

She removed her uniform jacket, stripping down to her dark gray t-shirt. Into the pockets of her fatigue pants and into the small pouches on her utility belt she stuffed the few things she would need, the last of which was a small bag of fidget treats.

"You left Reilly in my cabin, right?" she asked Eden.

"He and Tank were playing 'run round the table' last I saw them."

"Excellent. They'll both earn their keep tonight." Sass glanced at her watch. "I've got about three and a half hours. Don't worry—after this they'll probably name some medical deity after you." She hoisted herself into the large square air-duct. "Get some sleep, Doc. By the time my night's over, yours will just be starting. You've still got to operate on Serafino after this."

"Piece o' cake," Eden quipped, echoing Sass's earlier optimism. "Just watch your ass out there."

"Yes, ma'am." Sass flashed her friend a wide grin and shoved herself into the small dark tunnel, ignoring the hundred or so things that could yet go wrong.

Including what one 'cybe admiral—a very deadly 'cybe admiral—would do if he caught her hacking into his private files in his cabin.

CHAPTER TWELVE

SICKBAY, THS *VAXXAR*

Kel-Paten stared at the docupad containing the four hundred page report Dr. Monterro handed him. "That's all we know on the Nar'Relian virus. Most of it's conflicting. Dr. Fynn and I have been trying to correlate some of the data in our spare time."

"And you think—?"

"It's our first guesstimate, given the symptoms. Please keep in mind, admiral, we could be totally wrong. Dr. Fynn is administering some tests, and as we know more, I'll be out to advise you. We could very possibly be wrong." Monterro nodded. "By your command—"

"Yes, of course." Kel-Paten waved one hand distractedly and then scanned the first page of the report. A fatal virus, almost always proceeded by a sudden onset of a high fever. In the few cases that did not result in death, the patients were inexplicably paralyzed, as if their life essence had been sucked out of them.

He stopped reading. He couldn't read anymore. Gods, he couldn't lose her! Not like this. They hadn't had enough time together. He'd never even told her he loved her.

They had to be wrong; Fynn had to be wrong. The diags had to be wrong. There was some other explanation. There had to be.

She would be fine.

Sass would be fine.

He held onto that thought like a prayer, like a mantra. Since the 'cybe operations he'd considered himself a soulless creature, too intelligent and sophisticated to believe in the Gods that had spurned him.

Yet now he prayed, pleaded, promised the Gods anything if only she would live.

And then prayed some more, that if she should die, they take his own life as well.

TASHA SEBASTIAN'S CABIN, THS *VAXXAR*

"Okay, Reilly, now that's a good fidget," Sass whispered as she watched the larger animal squeeze into the conduit duct too small for any human form. Reilly fit, but just barely, and she knew if it hadn't been for the handful of treats she'd thrown through the grating he wouldn't be making the journey at all.

Behind him, Tank bounded quickly, not one to miss any hint of a meal. She'd positioned two small lasers on the furzels' collars and as they pushed in frustration against the grating that separated them and their snacks, she operated the lasers remotely, punching small holes in the grating's frame.

"Oops, sorry, almost scorched your ear fur there, Tank!"

"*Mrrrrrupp!*" the fidget responded.

There was the muffled thud of the grating hitting the floor. The two animals leaped down into the admiral's cabin and devoured the few small treats.

"Okay, now!" she called hoarsely, having given them enough time to finish their food. "Out time, furzels! Out time!"

It was a trick Eden had taught Reilly back on the *Regalia* and she'd subsequently taught to Tank. "Out time" meant the furzels could have their freedom, run loose in the corridors. But to earn that, they had to open the cabin doors.

Which they did by making a mad dash across the room and throwing their small bodies against the manual lock override to the right of every ship's cabin door.

It often took several tries.

Thumpety-thumpety-thumpety-thumpety THWACK! Thud.

A furzel ran, hit the wall and fell to the ground.

Thumpety-thumpety-thumpety-thumpety THWACK! Thud.

Thumpety-thumpety-thumpety-thumpety THWACK! Thud.

In-between the 'thumpetys' and the 'thuds' Sass made her way back to her cabin and out her own door. She monitored their progress on the small comm link on Tank's collar and prayed no one would see her, or hear the bizarre noises coming from the admiral's cabin.

Thumpety-thumpety-thumpety-thumpety THWACK! THUMP!

She'd have to speak to Eden about Reilly's weight problem. That last one almost sounded as if he might crash through the bulkhead.

Thumpety-thumpety-thumpety-thumpety THWACK! Thud.

Swoosh.

The cabin door opened. The furzels raced out. The captain stepped in.

SICKBAY, THS *VAXXAR*

Eden turned off the bed's diag systems as soon as Sass left, fluffed the pillow and leaned against it with a quiet sigh. It had been a busy week and it was far from over. A short fidget nap, as Sass had recommended, would do her some good. She'd dozed about five minutes when she heard the door lock cycle. She opened one eye.

Cal stuck his head in, noted her position and quietly slipped inside.

"He's looking through the reports on the virus," Cal told her.

"Lucky him," Eden replied, stifling a yawn.

"He looks miserable."

"So was I when I read them. Lousiest bit of medical research I've ever seen," she said.

Cal leaned against the wall, folding his arms across his broad chest. "I didn't mean it that way, my dear. I mean the admiral looks extremely upset over Captain Sebastian's supposed condition."

"The admiral," Eden noted, "had several good reasons to be upset, not the least of which is the captain's supposed condition. I just wish I could get a clear reading on whether it's a 'good' upset or a 'bad' upset."

Cal caught her slight frown. "I take it you're having problems placing him in an empathic category. Being 'cybe, he might not react in ways we'd understand."

"Tell me about it!" She stretched her arms over her head. "His being programmed by the Triad's Psy-Serv only makes it that much more difficult. You've seen his med files, Cal, and I'm sure you saw the same gaps I did."

"So much for their unequivocal trust of the U-Cees."

"Sass said the same thing. Looks like we all have a lot to learn."

Cal went back out to keep an eye on Kel-Paten; Eden relaxed into the pillow again.

A little early for bedtime, or are we napping?

The gray mists cleared. Jace had one leg propped up against the stone bench, leaning one hand on his knee. She came and sat down next to him.

No, actually it's just about bedtime, but you're right, this is a nap. I'm going to pull a late-nighter, on your account, Captain Serafino.

Jace, he reminded her patiently. *Do you have a problem with first names, Eden, or just mine?* He was smiling, and because the telepathic contact was so clear, so strong, she saw his smile as well as felt its warmth.

I have a problem, she told him gently, *with such familiarity with a patient.*

We're friends, Eden.

I'm not disputing that. She was becoming genuinely fond of the playful, telepathic Jace Serafino. *But even friendship, real friendship, takes time. Through trial and error, so to speak. And the Jace I know 'here'*, she motioned to the gray mists, *is not the Jace Serafino I've been encountering 'out there'.*

I've been misbehaving, have I? He sat down next to her, his hands clasped between his legs, and gave her his most innocent look.

She laughed. *That's putting it mildly. You did have a rather nasty run-in with Kel-Paten.*

Ah, the Tin Soldier. No, he and I have never gotten along.

Jace, how much do you remember, how much are you aware of what your physical body is doing?

You mean do I remember my conversation with Kel-Paten in the Ready Room earlier? Some. I know you were there, and Sass was. Like speaking now with you, I can't be involved for more than my time limit. So I try to fade in and out, keep myself out of trouble. You can tell, can't you?

Eden nodded. She'd noticed a slight difference in Captain Serafino's reactions from time and time and suspected the internal Jace had a hand in that.

Can you read Kel-Paten? she asked.

He shrugged. *Sometimes better than others. There's a strong cybernetic overlay that Psy-Serv designed to prevent just that.*

Gods, she'd suspected as much. *A scrambler?*

He nodded. *That's as good a way of describing it as any. There's also shielding; any telepath worth his salt can shield, prevent being read by other telepaths. But since Kel-Paten's not telepathic, he can't do that. Hence, the scrambling system, as you put it.*

When I remove the implant, I may ask you to do what you can to read Kel-Paten.

Whoa, whoa! He held up his hand as if to stop her words. *Talk to me, my pretty doctor. The last we talked about removing the implant we were still in the discussion stages. Why the rush all of a sudden? Do you intend to be my widow before I can even make you my bride?*

Eden ignored the little butterfly that made a brief appearance in her stomach at his words. She had neither the time nor the interest in anything romantic right now. *Sass believes Kel-Paten may have documentation relative to the implant in his files. She's chasing down the information, literally, right now. If she finds what I can use, I'm going to have to try, Jace. You've given us too many warnings about this faction in the Triad. You've also suggested that Kel-Paten might be involved. And that Sass's life, and most likely yours and mine as well, is in jeopardy.*

You, 'out there', know only half the story and you, 'in here', know the other half. We need to put you back together, Jace Serafino. We need to know what you know.

Kel-Paten's permitting this? he asked.

She shook her head and flashed him the mental image of the admiral beaming into Sickbay with Sass in his arms, and her subsequent 'recovery' and escape through the conduit duct.

Jace rolled his eyes. *Gods, I should have known! I've heard some pretty wild stories about you two.* He touched her chin, tilting her face up to his. *Well, my Eden, if I'm to die, then let it be in your arms.*

Your optimism overwhelms me.

Eden. He gently stroked her face, his touch causing a trail of heat across her skin. *This implant is serious business. I don't doubt your medical expertise. I'm just too familiar with Psy-Serv's deviousness.*

I will not risk your life. Unless Sass brings me exactly what I need to remove the implant, you'll remain a split personality for a while longer. I will not endanger you in any way, she repeated.

You endanger me every day, every hour. His thumb traced the outline of her lower lip, then softly his mouth followed where his thumb had been.

For a brief moment, Eden ignored all her mental warnings about men like Jace and let herself sink into his gentle, wonderful kiss. But when she felt the warmth of his tongue probing her mouth, she turned her face away and grasped his hands, which had been getting far too familiar, in her own.

Jace, please don't—

Why? Don't you know what you do to me?

Yes. No. I mean, yes, this is a wonderful fantasy, but Novalis is not real life, not for me. And you're not...the same. Out there.

A sad smile crossed his face and he brought her hands to his lips, grazing her knuckles with a kiss. *I'm a rotten son-of-a-bitch out there, Eden. I've warned you to keep your bedroom door locked.*

And you question why I'm saying 'no' now? she asked somewhat wistfully.

And you question why I'm trying? Eden, a woman like you would never love the Jace Serafino out there. Do you understand why you, and this time, are so precious to me?

And what happens when I remove the implant? Which Jace Serafino will become the real one?

I don't know, he replied honestly. *I was pretty much the same son-of-a-bitch before the implant. Not someone you would've liked. What the implant has done is forced me to look at myself. And it's allowed me to be, with you, someone maybe I would've been, if my life had been different.*

So I don't know, Eden, who you're going to get when you've put me back together. I just hope, no matter what, we can still be friends.

She smiled and started to reply, when he continued: *Because I have this real fear, you know, of rectal thermometers!*

Regretfully, Eden let their link fade. She lay quietly, still feeling his touch on her hand, on her face.

Seeing his teasing smile, when he spoke of his fear of rectal thermometers.

Eden had a fear as well. Sass might be in trouble, deep trouble. Jace had confirmed her suspicions about Kel-Paten's personal psychic shield. It was very possible the affection she sensed in him when Sass was around was a deception.

It was very possible, should he find out what she and Sass were up to, he'd kill them both.

CHAPTER THIRTEEN

BRANDEN KEL-PATEN'S CABIN, THS *VAXXAR*

Sass straddled the swivel chair in front of Kel-Paten's small desk and typed in a generic access code. The recessed comp screen emerged from the desktop, its electronic 'eye' winking on for retinal verification. Quickly, she ran one finger over her lips and smeared a light film of lipstick across the small portal.

"Retinal confirmation temporarily off-line," the tinny computer voice intoned softly. "Please respond with verbal verification procedures."

She'd already taken the wad of chewing gum from her mouth and stuck it directly over the microphone input.

"Retinal and verbal verification procedures temporarily suspended," she typed into the keyboard. "Computer, run Inoperative Systems Simulation—Emergency Access Procedure Number Three Seven Four at this time."

It wasn't an unusual request. She'd run many sims on the *Regalia* designed to train computers and crew what to do in event of a partial or—Gods forbid!—total systems failure. She'd run two such sims from her office here in the *Vax* in the first few months she'd been on board. Just like the manual override on each cabin door, there had to be an alternate way of getting out. Or getting in.

Right now, she needed in.

Dutifully, the ship's computer system responded. She implemented some basic tests just to get further into the program before trying to bamboozle it into letting her into Kel-Paten's coded files.

His cabin lights winked on and off; his cabin temperature raised and lowered. His replicator even produced a nice, hot cup of Mahrian Blend, black, which she sipped gratefully while moving the program through its paces. She glanced at her watch—she had a little more than two and a half hours left. A lot of time, but yet not. She had no idea what she'd find, or how much, once she got in.

"Computer," she typed in, "Initiate Emergency Data Transfer Simulation Program."

"Please verify through retinal scan," the computer replied audibly. She'd not dampered its voice, only her own.

She typed her answer. "Computer, retinal scan off line. Repeat. Initiate Emergency Data Transfer Simulation Program."

"Authorization code required to initiate. Respond with code," the computer said.

She knew that was the next level of security; hell, she'd designed the *Reg's* programs to respond in a similar manner. But what the *Vax* had that the *Regalia* didn't was Kel-Paten, a bio-'cybe who physically spiked in to the computer systems. She drew a small coiled wire from one of her pockets and quickly disconnected the keyboard, inserting a coupler and reconnecting the keyboard through that. The other end of the coupler she patched into the small port set into the arm of Kel-Paten's custom-made chair.

"Derive code from terminal location," she typed in. "Retinal and verbal functions off-line during simulation."

There was a moment of tense silence. Had she tried this from any other terminal, including her own office, Sass knew she wouldn't be able to gain access. But she was banking on the fact that Kel-Paten felt his personal quarters were totally secure. And she was banking on her knowledge that he usually spiked in—a "spike" that she hoped she had just recreated—as far as the computer was concerned.

"Access granted," the computer intoned softly and Sass let out a corresponding sigh. Then: "Damn bitch, but you're good!"

It was all relatively easy pickings from there.

True to form, Kel-Paten's files were disgustingly well organized. She popped a portable datadrive into the download port and initiated copy-file commands. It would have been easier and quicker to tag files and have them sent to her own data files; but that would have left a trail. This way, any trail led to his own computer, and stopped there. Her datadrive had been carefully created so to leave no input ID.

One of the more interesting things she'd learned to do on Lethant.

There was a ton of data referencing Psy-Serv; an almost equally large amount of data on Serafino. She copied both directories and went surfing for more.

"Med Files-BKP" and "BKP-Personal" also were snatched. She'd just discovered an encrypted file titled "Sass" when her badge trilled.

"Sass! Eden here. We lost him!"

"Bloody damn!" She flicked off the comp screen. It slid back into the desk top, but the green light on her drive still flashed, the unit working, pulling data. She heard the smart click of the cabin door lock recycling. She dove under the desk, fitting her small form into the kneehole, and shoved her com badge down the front of her shirt. If it beeped now, she was toast.

Cabin lights flicked on. Heavy footsteps moved across the carpeted floor as the door swooshed closed.

Damn! Shit! Sonofabitch! Sass ran through every swearword she knew in five languages. *Frack! Grenzar! Antz-k'ran! Trock!*

She listened to the sound of a drink being poured. Thank the Gods she'd finished her coffee and disposed of the cup in the recyc. She heard a cabinet door *thwump* closed, a short spate of footsteps and then the *fwoosh* of couch cushions as a body sat down into it.

Great! Just my luck; the Tin Soldier's poured himself a drink and is now going to sit and watch a season's worth of Zero-G Hockey reruns or something. Eden! she cried out mentally. *Get me...no! Get him out of here!*

He couldn't stay in his cabin. Granted, it was the end of the working day, past dinner and all that happy lubashit. But didn't he have to be somewhere, do something? *Aren't I dying in Sickbay? Doesn't he care?*

If nothing else, it was a bitch to find command staff replacements on short notice. Surely he had to appreciate that?

Scrunched into the kneehole of the desk, small beads of sweat trickling down her chest, Sass cautiously eyed the small drive. It was still downloading and for the life of her she couldn't remember if it beeped when it finished. Or not.

The 'or not' would be a relief. Any other option would take a lot of explaining. If she lived long enough.

The tiny green light on its cover panel blinked on-off on-off. At each 'on' she breathed in. At each 'off' she held her breath. Why couldn't Kel-Paten have been listening to music, or turned on a vidshow? Anything that made noise! But no, he was sitting in silence, a silence far too loud for her liking.

A commbadge trilled. For a moment her heart stopped and she clasped her hands over her chest to muffle any further noise. But it wasn't her badge that had been activated.

"Kel-Paten here."

"Admiral, this is Dr. Fynn."

Sass squeezed her eyes shut tightly. *Eden, oh Eden! Get me the hell of out here!*

The couch fabric rustled. "Go ahead, Doctor."

"I would appreciate it if you'd return to Sickbay, admiral. I think we may have some good news in a half hour or so."

A half hour or so. That was Eden's way of telling her to *Get the Hell out of the Badlands and do it Now*!

"On my way, Doctor!" Kel-Paten replied. Sass heard the clink of a glass against the tabletop.

Thank you! Thank you! Thank you, Eden you gorgeous broad you! You genius! You wonderful woman! Sass waited a few seconds after the cabin doors swooshed closed before extricating herself from under the desk. The kink in her back complained painfully.

"*Beep-ta-beep!*" said her datadrive.

She almost jumped out of her skin. "Up yours and the equinnard you rode in on!" Sass snatched the drive from the port. She tapped at the desk and the vidscreen popped up. She grabbed at the pink gum and quickly wiped her sleeve over the lipstick smear then popped the screen back down again.

The duct grating she'd already replaced when she'd first come in, but she checked it again just be to sure and then did a quick visual to see if there were any other traces of her visit. There were none—it was as if she'd never been there.

She spied a glass of Excelsior brandy on the table on her way towards the door. Expensive stuff. So that's what he'd been drinking.

Drowning his sorrows, or toasting Captain Sebastian's demise?

"What the hell." She downed half the contents, then wiped her lip print and fingerprints off with the tail of her shirt.

She was out the door and back in her cabin just in time to find Reilly and Tank doing a reprise of "run around the table".

"How did you—?" But of course, the furzels couldn't answer how they'd gotten back in her cabin. Usually they made their way down to hydroponics where either she or Eden would eventually retrieve them, as they had always done on the *Regalia*. "You guys know more secrets than I do!" she told them. Then, stuffing the datadrive in her shirt, she climbed into the larger access ducting that opened into her bedroom closet and made her way down the maintenance ladders to the lower deck that housed Sickbay.

Caleb Monterro waited for her. "Quick!" He tossed her the silver hospital gown. She stripped off her clothes, not caring what he saw or didn't. He was, after all, a doctor and one who had tended to her many times over the years.

He stuffed her clothes and the drive into a small hamper next to the bed as she slid beneath the covers. Just at that moment, Eden stuck her head in the door.

She nodded at Sass. Sass nodded back.

Then Eden turned. "Admiral," she said, "you can see Captain Sebastian now. But only for a few moments."

Kel-Paten strode past Eden without so much as a 'by your command.'

"Tasha." His voice had a noticeable rough edge to it. "How are you feeling?"

"Like hell," she replied, her voice equally as breathy. After all, she'd only just finished scaling twelve flights of maintenance ladders. Thanks the Gods it was *down*!

He cleared his throat. "Doctor." Eden looked at him. "I would like to be able to speak to Captain Sebastian. Alone."

"I'm sorry, admiral, but the captain is still not out of danger completely. She requires medical monitoring at this time. If my presence disturbs you, then you will have to tolerate Dr. Monterro's."

They needed to tolerate somebody's as protection, until she could find out what Kel-Paten had in his files.

"Is there a problem in Navigation?" Sass asked, feigning concern over an inspection tour she knew damn well hadn't occurred.

"No, it's not that." He started to reach for her but he stopped as Eden stepped up to him.

"Whatever it is, it can wait until the morning," Eden told him firmly.

He glanced one more time at Sass.

"She'll be fit for duty so soon?" he asked Eden.

"She can rest in her quarters for the next shift or so. By the time we make Panperra, she'll be fine." Eden motioned to the door. "Admiral, if you don't mind...?"

He turned to Eden just before he reached the door. "What time are you releasing her?"

"Probably sometime after breakfast, depending upon how she fares during the night."

"I'll be here at 0900 to escort her."

"That won't be necessary. One of my nurses can see her to her cabin."

"I'm sure your staff has more pressing concerns. Doctor. I'll see her safely back to her quarters myself." He squared his shoulders and stared down at her.

"Admiral, Captain Sebastian will be released if and when I say she is released, and if and when she is, she will be released to no one other than one of my medical staff. I'm sure *you* have more pressing concerns."

"Actually, I don't. I'll be here at 0900. And I will accompany one of your staff, and Captain Sebastian, back to her quarters."

Sass didn't think he would murder her in front of witnesses. Obviously, neither did Eden. "I'll call you in the morning," the CMO said. "And advise you if she's ready to be released. Now, if you'll excuse me, I still have a lot of work to do."

Kel-Paten's icy gaze went from Eden to her, causing a chill to flit up Sass' spine. But no, not a chill. Something else. Something different.

Because his gaze wasn't the least bit icy at all.

CHAPTER FOURTEEN

SICKBAY, THS *VAXXAR*

Sass let out a sigh she didn't realize she'd been holding when the door closed behind the Tin Soldier. Then she lunged for her clothes. There was a lot of work yet to be done.

"How much were you able to get?" Eden held out the small datadrive.

Sass finished pulling on her boots then accepted it, holding it in her line of sight and squinting. "Won't know 'til I get back into this thing. I don't think it's wise for me to use your office in case you-know-who pops back in. But Cal's office is in the back and doesn't have your glass walls. Right?"

Cal's office it was. Eden brought in another cup of coffee and left Sass alone to start unraveling the data.

She made a backup copy first, just in case fail-safes or traps existed. There were over fifty directories, some with names she recognized, but most had only numbers. Nothing blatantly labeled: Psy-Serv Secrets.

Would've been nice. A block of files with Triad Med Ministry transit tags caught her eye. They were also security locked. She unlocked them, bundled them and shot them over to Eden's personal inbox.

Twenty minutes later, a noise caused her to look up. Eden, in her doorway. And not with fresh coffee, damn! But a distinctly pinched look about her eyes.

"Trouble?"

"I've worked through much of what you sent me. From odds and ends I've been able to put together, it looks like Psy-Serv has been experimenting with implants for twenty years, most of which failed and killed the recipient. Serafino's is one of a more advanced designs."

"Wonderful. For Serafino, that is. At least his won't malfunction—"

"It is. The fact that he's able at times to bypass the implant means it's in the early stages of breaking down. When it finally does, it'll kill him."

"Okay, then not wonderful. How do we fix it so we can remove it?"

"That tidy bit of information isn't in the stuff you sent me. Any more?"

Sass made a quick scan of the files. "Nope. Don't see anything here that looks like that. Maybe it's inside one of these."

"Let's hope so." Eden sat in the chair opposite the desk.

"Can you work with what I've given you?"

Eden sighed. "I can, to some extent, delay the inevitable, based on what I know. I'm sure I can increase Serafino's telepathic access time, perhaps up to two, three hours. But I can't remove the implant with what we have, no."

"Is it possible Kel-Paten doesn't have that answer?"

"It's possible," Eden agreed. "We still have more than we had before, Sass. And if Serafino can be more of, well, himself, maybe he can help, too."

"Hard to help from inside a Panperran prison. Or from Ren Marin," Sass noted.

"Ren Marin?"

"My perusals of some of Kel-Paten's files gave me other information. Remember I told you I thought the Triad had a prison world like Lethant? They'd denied that, of course, during the peace talks. Wanted to appear more civilized than us, you know," she added haughtily. "Anyway, they do. It's called Ren Marin, way the hell out in Sector 814. A desert world; red desert. One hundred fifty degrees during the day, fifteen below at night. At least Lethant was a constant, humid ninety-five."

"You think they'll send Serafino to Ren Marin?" Eden asked.

"If they let him live that long. And, according to Serafino, we may be included in that little party as well."

Eden stood. "Lovely."

"I'll send you my next download shortly," Sass told her as she headed out the door.

"Give me five minutes," Eden said, glancing at her watch. "I need a cup of Orange Garden. Desperately."

"Got it." Sass turned back to the comp and resumed scanning the files. The medical terminology meant nothing to her but she dutifully unencrypted what she could and sent it to Eden.

Two hours later, they were no further along except for an added appreciation of the deviousness of Psy-Serv.

This time when Eden appeared in her doorway, she had both tea and coffee.

"I can now understand why telepaths kill themselves rather than be recruited," Eden said.

"I'm sorry." Sass blew across the top of her mug. Small steam clouds swirled. "I really thought we'd find the answers here."

"We did," Eden reassured her. "Just not all of them."

"What do we do now?"

Eden thought for a moment. "I already let Cal go off shift. We won't attempt surgery on Serafino until we have more data. And what I've learned from the reports I can do with a sonic-laser tomorrow on him, before we dock with Panperra. That should increase his access time and slow down the implant's deterioration."

"What about this Faction he talked about? About what about the admiral's involvement?"

"Those are command decisions, Sass," Eden said.

"Command's bloody damn tired," Sass growled. "I don't like this, Eden. I don't like this at all. It was so much easier before the Alliance. At least we were relatively sure who our enemies were. Now," she shook her head. "I don't know. I used to have this great respect for the Tin Soldier. I actually looked forward—and I know this sounds silly—but I kind of hoped that after time, he and I could be friends. As much as anyone could be friends with a 'cybe. I've even tried kidding with him, lately. Sharing a joke and all that."

"He must have looked at you pretty strangely. He's not known for his sense of humor."

"No, he seemed to get it," Sass told her, remembering their exchange about Homer Kel-Farquin. "He has a pretty dry wit. Or should I say, his programming has a dry wit." She looked at Eden. "I never thought to ask this: can you read him empathically? Being he's not human?"

"It's confusing," Eden admitted, "because he is half-human. I thought, well, the first couple of months on board I thought I was picking up some definite emotional readings from him, which surprised me. I sort of mentioned that to you."

Sass nodded.

Eden sipped her tea. "Anyway, it wasn't until I had a talk with Serafino that I realized everything I thought I was sensing might be garbage; scrambled emotional output designed to throw any telepaths, or empaths, off the trail."

"You've hinted that he's more human that we all think," Sass said.

"I know. I might be wrong. That might be what he's programmed to transmit as a cover to whatever is really going on."

"Wonderful. So you're telling me you can't read him at all."

"Not reliably."

"Can Serafino?"

"Once I get him fully functional, certainly better than I can. I've asked him the same questions, by the way."

"Because you're concerned you can't read Kel-Paten."

"Because I'm concerned," Eden told her, "that what I think I'm reading might be wrong. In which case he's masking something serious. But if I'm reading him correctly..."

"If you are?" Sass urged her.

"If I'm right, we've seriously misjudged *him*. It's not an easy position."

"You're saying there's a chance Serafino's wrong and he may be on our side in this?" Sass asked.

"Yes."

"When will you know? What we're finding here could lead to a mutiny on board. You do realize that, don't you?"

Eden nodded solemnly.

"Then I need to know whatever you know. Don't let me work on the dark in this. It's too dangerous for all of us."

Eden turned her mug in her hands before speaking. "By tomorrow I should have Serafino's telepathic time increased. See if you can't schedule a conference with him and Kel-Paten. I'll get Serafino to read whatever he can from him. We'll have to go from there."

"You seem to have a specific focus for this. There's one issue here, isn't there?" As tired as she was, Sass picked up on that.

"Yes."

"Which is?"

Eden closed her eyes. "You," she said finally. "The issue is you."

"With Kel-Paten? *I'm* the issue?"

"That's when I get the conflicting readings. When he's focused on you."

Sass glanced at the comp screen. "Eden, he's got a whole set of files on me, a whole directory. I haven't even looked at them yet. It didn't seem important. But now...now do you see why you have to tell me what's going on in that devious brain of yours?"

"What kind of files?"

"I don't know. I didn't bother to open them because I thought Serafino was the issue here. But Serafino did say that he thought I was brought on board for Kel-Paten to handle. If what we have here are marching orders from the Triad, or a list of acceptable fatal accidents with my name on them, then that might be enough right then and there for me to contact the U-Cees for assistance when we get to Panperra."

It was almost 0300. "You want some more coffee? I assume you weren't thinking of making it an early night," Eden noted.

"Yes and yes. I was hoping to pack it in after we decided there was nothing more with Serafino, but we've just opened up a whole other can of frinkas, and this one's got my name on it. Mahrian blend, black. But you know that."

Sass sipped the hot coffee and opened up the files, one after another. Most she recognized as her official U-Cee Personnel Files and even— Gods, was he thorough!—a report on her academy coursework. Just how long had he been keeping tabs on her...and why?

A chill ran up her spine. Had the Triad issued a termination order years ago and never rescinded it? Is that why she'd ended up on the *Vax*, to make it clean and convenient, all under the cover of "killed in the line of duty"?

Or worse, did Kel-Paten know, not who she was, but who she wasn't? His files on her were only the 'official' ones; the ones designed to create Tasha Sebastian. She found nothing on Sass. That was of little comfort, however. Just because she hadn't found them, didn't mean they didn't exist. Or that he didn't know about Lethant.

The next group of files contained transit-tagged downloads from different times and sources. They were coded in such a way that new data automatically appended to the parent file whenever it entered the system. It was a common method. Most Sickbays downloaded transit-tagged files from their med scanners automatically into a patient's main file. Most officers used hand-held datacorders to dictate logs that were later appended to their personal logs on board.

But why Kel-Paten kept a transit-tag file on her was a mystery. Until she opened and read it.

Then she was on her feet, lunging towards Eden's office, swearing.

SICKBAY, DR. FYNN'S OFFICE, THS *VAXXAR*

When Eden saw Sass striding through the main area of Sickbay at 0345 hours she knew something was wrong. For one thing, it completely blew Sass's cover story of being sick. And second, there was always that remote chance Kel-Paten would come in. Eden's glass fronted office provided no place to hide.

Sass didn't try to hide. She plopped down into the chair across from Eden's desk, her eyes wide in amazement. "This is unbelievable. It makes no sense." She waved one hand in the air. "But then again, it makes perfect sense."

"What?" Eden asked.

Sass picked up Eden's teaspoon and pointed it at her. "I thought, you know, I thought at first that this might be part of his cover. That he created all these log entries, all these letters, I don't know, in the past few weeks. But they go back years, Eden. Years! I mean, we're talking since I was on the *Sarna Bogue*!"

"What entries?"

Sass ignored her question. "And he'd have to have a phenomenal memory. Oh, granted, he probably does, but not that phenomenal. Besides, he would've also had to assume that I'd break into his systems and download and read these files, just to throw me off the track. That would be assuming a lot, even for Kel-Paten. Wouldn't you say?"

"I might, if I knew what you were talking about," Eden replied patiently. Sooner or later she had to get Sass to switch to decaf.

Sass gave her a look as if she couldn't comprehend why Eden wasn't comprehending. "The log entries, of course."

"Oh. The log entries. *What* log entries?" She was too tired to hide her sarcasm.

"Kel-Paten's log entries. The ones he's been dictating. To me. For eleven years."

Eden sat back in her chair. "Oh." Like that should explain everything.

"Yeah. No shit. Oh."

"Sass—!"

"I'm sorry. Here." She tossed a thin crystal disk at Eden. "Here's a sample. Take a look and let me know what you think."

Perhaps 'log entries' wasn't the most accurate description, Eden noted as she read. 'Love letters' might be more like it. Most written as 'captain's personal logs' as he'd been a captain when he'd first seen Sass, on the *Bogue* eleven years before. They were very personal observations of what he was feeling, what he was dreaming, what he was hoping for:

Captain's Personal Log, Stardate 351904.2...encrypt code SBSTN...subsequent encrypt code SASS...transit tag this and all subsequent coded logs for delivery to TransGal Marine Depot 31 UPON MY DEMISE...Append...deliver to United Coalition HQ Varlow attention Lieutenant Sebastian...Append...deliver to U-Cee Huntership Goldstar *attention Commander Sebastian.....Append...deliver to U-Cee Huntership*

Regalia *attention Captain Sebastian...Append...deliver to Captain Sebastian, Alliance Huntership* Vaxxar ...

It's been four days since I've seen you, four days since we first met and I still don't know more than your last name. That I learned from the patch on your jacket: Sebastian. Gods, woman, I need to call you something more than that. My green-eyed vixen? Do you know how you haunt me? Do you know how I've damned myself for not removing you from that U-Cee patrolship four days ago?

The Kel aren't kidnappers—how many times have I heard that? But this wouldn't have been a political action, my green eyed lady. This would've been personal. Purely personal. But in that area my cowardice is rivaled by none. So I walked away. It is an action I will regret for as long as I live.

I cannot accept that I will never see you again. I cannot permit that. I will find you. If it takes the rest of my life, I will find you.

Captain's Personal Log, Stardate 350508.6...encrypt code SASS...

You have my hearty approval for your transfer from the Bogue*! Sass, I'm so proud of you, I wish there were some way I could tell you. Eventually you'll read these letters. You'll know that I've been following your career. Then know that today I learned you've received your first assignment on a U-Cee huntership. I could tell you they're not half as good as the Triad. But you suffer because of my cowardice. Would you have hated me if I'd pulled you from the* Bogue*? Possibly. But there's so much I want to share with you. Maybe someday. In the meantime, you can run circles around the U-Cees. I know you will. Hell, woman, you ran circles around me on that patrolship.*

I've read your personnel files, your academy records. Top of your class, all the way. You have no idea how much I respect that. Your family's money could have paved an easy route for you, but you've chosen the harder one. In the Triad, family name equates respect. I'm so proud you've taken your grand one, and made it even more so.

I miss you, Sass. I miss the way you wrinkle your nose. I miss your smile. It's been four months since I've seen you and the holos my agents bring back to me don't carry your energy.

I may have to engineer an attack on the Goldstar *just to see you again.*

Captain's Personal Log, Stardate 381022.2...encrypt code SASS...

I'm sitting here in the bowels of Antalkin Station and I don't know if I'll ever see you again. I'm recording with an overlay note that it should append to my personal files, all of which will be sent to you. Very shortly, I think.

The Illithians staged a brilliant ambush. I know what they're after; what they're always after. My head on a silver platter, as the saying goes. I don't know if we received bad information or I was just being more stupid that usual. In any case, they almost took the Vax *but my ship maneuvered out of their reach. As it's me they're after; I stayed behind on what's left of Antalkin. Waste of metal anyway, in my opinion. Bloody backward station!*

But that's...that's not the point. The point is they managed a couple good shots at me. I'm not so indestructible as Triad intelligence would lead you to believe. Though you and the U-Cees probably have that figured out by now as well. Sometimes, sometimes I wonder just who we're fooling with all this cyber shit.

Things don't look optimistic at the moment. I've found a hiding place but I'm sure it's only temporary. They've got a couple of teams out looking for me. I'm flattered. Twenty to thirty Irks combing a dead station looking for me. I've kept moving as long as I could, but I've run out of energy. And time.

Sass, Gods, Sass, I've run out of time with you, haven't I? I've had these dreams, all these years, I've had these dreams. I want to take you to T'Garis—we could play the tables. I know you're hell at Starfield Doubles.

But it's not going to happen now.

Sass, I'm so tired. I miss you so much.

I have to move again. I hear...something.

I love you.

And then, a more recent selection...

Admiral's Personal Log, Stardate Forty-Six0310.9...encrypt code SASS...

I don't know where you found that 'No No Bad Captain' shirt. Nor do I know where you found those pink shorts. But Sass, you don't know how close I came to totally losing it all and making more of a fool of myself than I already have.

It seems all I'm able to do in your presence is stare at you like a complete idiot, like some stupid schoolboy. I just want to talk to you. I've been trying so hard to reach you but I'm so afraid, and the Gods know if you found out you'd probably think it hysterically funny...but I'm so afraid of losing you. I don't know how close I can get. I don't know if I can get close at all. I tell myself, Gods, Sass, I tell myself all the time that you're here with me, on the Vax and I should be thankful for that! It's more than I ever thought I deserved. I know where you are, I know you're safe, I know I can protect you.

And I know to some extent I'm driving you crazy. You think I'm following you around. You're right. I am. I need to be with you, Sass. Don't you see? I need just to be with you.

After we handle this Serafino situation, we'll go to T'Garis. I know. I know. I've been saying that for ten years. But I mean it this time. I will ask you. I will ask you and we'll go to T'Garis and you can break the bank on the Starfield tables.

I've dreamed about this, Sass. I really need to make it come true. I have to talk myself into this. I have to ask you. And I have to figure out another way to keep you from playing racquet-lob with that Gods-damned lieutenant whatever his name is! Damn it, Sass, don't you know what he wants from you?

I mean...that is, I want the same thing, but Sass, I love you and I don't care what he tells you, he doesn't. He couldn't. Not as much as I do. And not for as long as I have.

Eden looked at Sass. The captain distractedly twirled the teaspoon on the desktop. Eden cleared her throat.

"Heavy, eh?" Sass asked but the flippancy in her tone didn't quite match the seriousness in her eyes.

"I'm relieved to know I'm not as bad an empath as I thought," Eden replied.

"You knew. This is what you were talking about a couple days ago. And earlier, when you said I was the focus."

Eden nodded. "I had a suspicion. Kel-Paten has a hard time controlling his emotions around you."

"What you're telling me is that it's possible...that there's a part of him that feels, that has emotions..." Sass closed her eyes, leaned back in the chair. "Eden, what do I do?"

"Depends on what you want to do, I guess. But I think this sort of answers one of our questions as to whose side he's on."

"These log entries." Sass pointed at Eden's comp screen. "They're tagged to be sent to me only after his death. I had no right reading them."

"You didn't go looking for them. There were circumstances—"

"The hell with circumstances!" Sass rasped. "These Gods-damned things tore me apart, and I haven't even read them all! I can't. I can't read them. They're...I don't know. I feel like a total shit for some of the things I've said and done to him."

"From the sound of them, he might be relieved to hear that. You could always ask him to go to T'Garis."

Sass held her hands up in front of her. "Wait, wait. I just said I feel like a shit. I didn't say I was ready to get involved with him. I mean, he's my CO. He's a pompous, annoying, overbearing bastard."

"He's a 'cybe," Eden added.

"That, too." Sass agreed, then added: "It's been said it was a damn shame the Triad wasted such a nice body on such a shitty personality. If only he didn't scowl so much."

"You remember the old U-Cee theories about him and Rohland Kel-Tyra," Eden said. It was rumored they were brothers, genetically speaking. Or cousins. Rohland Kel-Tyra, son of recently retired Admiral Rafe Kel-Tyra, was unequivocally drop-dead gorgeous. He also had a personality to match and rarely scowled. Kel-Paten was taller and several years older. And had a distinct tendency to scowl.

"Oh, Gods." Sass covered her face with her hands. "How do I deal with him tomorrow? Today. Whatever it is."

"The same way you always have?"

"I'm either yelling at him or trading barbs with him. Neither of these is real productive right now."

"Yeah, I think that 'dinner by starlight' quip almost got to him the other day."

Sass groaned. "I'd forgotten about that! See, this is exactly what I mean! What in hell do I do now?"

"You could probably earn the eternal gratitude of the crew by seducing him," Eden suggested.

"Very funny."

"He'd probably stop scowling."

"Ver-y funny."

"Then let me suggest you carry on as you usually do, but with a little more tact," Eden said.

"Like he's not going to know something's changed?"

"Not unless you switch to decaf," Eden intoned.

CHAPTER FIFTEEN

SICKBAY, THS *VAXXAR*

At 0850 Kel-Paten strode in, broadcasting, as far as Eden was concerned, apprehension and anticipation. Apparently, he couldn't wait any longer to drag his 'green-eyed vixen' out of Sickbay, back to where he could keep an eye on her.

At least, she hoped that's what it was. Serafino's warning still echoed in her mind: there were several layers to Kel-Paten's emotions. Some of which may have been very expertly manipulated by Psy-Serv.

"The captain will be ready to leave in a few minutes," Eden told him as she retrieved Sass's file from the cart. "The earliest she's allowed to go back on duty is late this afternoon."

And that went double for herself, as well. Neither of them had had more than three hours sleep. Three cups of Mahrian blend, black, and Sass looked as ready as she always did. But Orange Garden just didn't carry the same punch and Eden was strongly looking forward to discharging the captain and heading straight for her own cabin and some serious sleep.

"I'll make sure no one disturbs her," the admiral told Eden.

Tuck her in and read her a bedtime story, will you? Eden thought. "Very good," she said out loud. "I'll just—"

"Don't be ridiculous! I don't need that thing!" Sass's forceful complaint flowed out into Sickbay as soon as her door opened. Inside, a young nursing tech—a young, rather attractive male, as Eden couldn't resist, knowing Kel-Paten would show up—was trying unsuccessfully to talk Sass into sitting in a wheelchair. SOP for discharging patients, he was telling her.

"Screw SOP. I wrote most of the damned SOPs and—" She looked out the open door, saw Kel-Paten and immediately clammed up.

Oh, great, Eden thought. *Sass, this is not acting normally. Keep yelling. Do something. Have another cup of coffee.*

Kel-Paten was already at the doorway. "What seems to be the problem?"

The ensign looked from the admiral to the captain and back to the admiral again. "Captain Sebastian, sir, isn't cooperating in regards to Sickbay dismissal procedures."

Kel-Paten glanced at the service bar on the young man's lab coat. "Ensign. You will learn that Captain Sebastian rarely cooperates in regards to any policies. The day she starts is the day I resign my commission." He looked at her. "Sebastian?"

Pause.

It was, Eden noted, a familiar phrase Sass needed to hear.

"Kel-Paten." Sass nodded in return and then breezed past him and headed for the corridor. "Thanks for the hospitality, Doc!" she called out to Eden.

"My pleasure," Eden replied, but it was automatic. She was still trying to tune into, and sort out, the emotional readings from the Tin Soldier.

They were there, oh yes, they were there. She had more faith in her abilities after seeing his personal logs. And if the admiral were full human...

But he wasn't. Psy-Serv and Triad Bio-Cybernetics had to seen it that.

Eden chewed absently on her bottom lip and went back to her office to log off duty. She needed some serious downtime. Very serious. She had to talk to Jace Serafino. And she wasn't sure he was going to like what she had to say.

MAIN LIFT, THS *VAXXAR*

Sass heard Kel-Paten's hard bootsteps come up behind her just as the lift doors opened.

"You're off duty until I tell you otherwise, Sebastian," he said as they stepped inside.

"Ah. And who died and made you CMO?"

"If I see you on the Bridge any time today I will forcibly carry you back to your quarters."

Could be interesting, Sass noted. Then: *Nah.*

"You don't have to keep looking at me," she told him after the lift doors closed. "I'm not going to keel over on you again."

"I should've realized you weren't well yesterday."

"You shouldn't have realized anything. You can't keep track of all four hundred fifty of us on board. That's Eden's job. If anything, I should've checked in with her earlier when I didn't feel well." Those letters. Those damn letters and the way he'd looked at her when he'd walked into Sickbay. It made her stomach tense and she knew it was guilt knocking at her conscience's back door. He'd thought she was dying. Cal Monterro had hinted how miserable Kel-Paten had looked.

"All the more reason you are not to be on active duty today."

"Kel-Paten—!"

"There's been...a lot of stress accompanying this transition with the new Alliance," he said, ignoring the daggers she visually flung at him. "We've only this Serafino situation to wrap up right now and when that's finished, well, I think you might want to take some time off."

Oh no. Oh no. This wasn't heading where she thought it was heading. Not now. Not so soon! "I really don't think—"

"Perhaps just a couple of days. Some light R&R." He wasn't looking at her, but watching the digital deck numbers flash on the wall of the lift.

No. No, Sass pleaded. *Please don't mention T'Garis. Please. I can't handle this right now!*

"Have you ever been to T'Garis?" he asked just as the lift doors pinged.

She stepped out onto the Deck Two Corridor.

"No, I've never been to T'Garis," she said through clenched teeth. "You wouldn't let me, remember? Something about a little inconvenient war going on. Damn tough to bust through the neutral zone with the *Vax* on my tail all the time."

She laid her hand against her door scanner. "But," she continued brightly as the door slid into the wall, "I'll probably get there sometime. I know Eden wants to go. I'll mention it next time I talk to her." She nodded at him. "I'll be in my office after lunch. Not on the Bridge, admiral. In my office." And she hit the manual override on the inside of the doorframe, closing the door in his face.

From his position on the back of her couch, Tank perked up his fluffy ears and *murrupped* several times.

"Don't ask, fidget, you don't want to know," she told him, then stripped off her jacket and fell promptly asleep on her bed.

NOVALIS

Jace reached for Eden's hand and drew her down beside him on the bench. *So what's the news?*

As you suspected, there's not enough for me to risk surgery to remove the implant right now. There were references to what I need to know, but the data wasn't there. Eden shook her head. *I'm sorry.*

Don't be. I'm a great believer in all things in their right time. Like your coming into my life. I have to believe it's more than just that you want to dig a hole in my head.

She swatted at him playfully. *The medical profession hasn't dug holes, as you put it, in centuries. Besides, with you, I'd be afraid if I did so, all kinds of gremlins would leak out!*

Jace responded with a comical growl and drew her against his chest, nuzzling and nibbling at her neck. Eden shrieked, laughing and finally managed to break free.

She wiped at her eyes. *Jace, stop it! I still have something serious to discuss with you. Just because I couldn't find the data I need to remove the implant doesn't mean I didn't find anything at all.*

I'm listening.

I think I can increase the amount of telepathic access time. In fact, I think I'll have to. She flashed to him all she had read about the implant's inevitable deterioration.

Damn. He was definitely not pleased with the news. *How much time to I have before I self-destruct?*

You're not going to self-destruct, not if I have anything to do with it. As for time, you still have several months before any serious deterioration sets in. Now that we'll have Kel-Paten's cooperation—

The Tin Soldier's cooperating with you? This is news. What the hell happened?

She hesitated a moment, indecisive about something so personal; something, as Sass had said, wasn't supposed to be public knowledge. She wanted to trust Serafino—he'd been honest with her so far, even about his own failings. She just hoped his long-standing feud with Kel-Paten didn't override his good sense.

What happened started about eleven years ago. She hesitated, needing information before she went further. *Jace, I need to know more about a statement you made. You said that this Faction wants Sass out of the way, and that they put her on the* Vax *with Kel-Paten to accomplish that. What leads you to believe that?*

This Faction has been in place longer than the Alliance, he said with a wry grin. *From what I've been able to piece together, there are several key 'players' that this faction wants either to control, or to neutralize. Captain Sebastian's name was one that came up on several occasions.*

Why do you think that Kel-Paten's involved?

Because of some transmissions some associates of mine intercepted. The Tin Soldier was adamant, during the peace negotiations, that she be assigned to the Vax. *He made a few threats, and then a few concessions, and here she is. Given that Kel-Sennarin is one of his superiors, we couldn't think of any other reason.*

She could, but if she hadn't read the admiral's private logs, she'd still doubt her own empathic readings of him. She didn't know if simply telling Jace what she knew would be sufficient. *Do you remember what happened in the session in the Ready Room?*

Mostly. Why?

You said, at that time, you sensed a 'heat' from the admiral. Do you remember?

He frowned, his blue eyes darkening. *Not really. No. I...there are a number of blanks in my mind. I'm sorry.*

She damned the implant. So that had been Serafino, and not Jace, picking up on what was going on between Kel-Paten and Sass. Evidently he'd always had a low-level empathic ability, even with the implant. But until she could get Jace talking to Serafino, as she had started to think of his two existences, the full story on anything wouldn't come out.

Eden?

I'd like to explain what I think is going on with Kel-Paten, but I'd really rather have you see it for yourself, she told him, laying her hand reassuringly on his arm. *Because, well, I don't think Kel-Paten himself understands what's happening. I could use your telepathic guidance, Jace. And your experience with Psy-Serv.*

Right now my telepathic guidance is limited.

I'm going to disable the implant, or at least weaken it. That should give you more control and give us some more answers. Believe me, we need answers.

Okay. He nodded slowly but she saw, and sensed, a tension in his smile. And he felt her question. *Eden. I don't...I don't know what's going to happen when you put me 'back together'. I feel sort of like that silly egg in the children's story, that fell off the wall, you know? I don't want to lose your friendship. Your respect. I've come to value that.*

He brushed his thumb gently across her cheekbone. *No matter what happens, don't give up on me, Doc. Please. Promise me.*

A lump formed in Eden's throat at the intensity, and fear, in his words. She knew if she had to answer him out loud at that moment, she wouldn't have been able to. But there were advantages to telepathy. *I promise. No matter what happens.*

The gray mists cleared. Reilly's furry presence was warm against her arm. Eden Fynn stared at her cabin's ceiling in the darkness and wondered about her promise.

No matter what happens.

She knew he was worried about his 'evil twin', the flirt, the rogue. That part of him he thought Eden wouldn't want to know. Not like she did the gentle, mystical Nasyry warrior.

But which Jace Serafino emerged from surgery wasn't even on her mind. As long as one of them did.

Eden's real fear was that in trying to save one, she might kill them both.

CAPTAIN SEBASTIAN'S OFFICE, THS *VAXXAR*

Sass sipped at her coffee. She found it a necessary action when all her instincts demanded she jump down Kel-Paten's throat. It was difficult to sip and yell at the same time, so she chose sipping.

He'd barged into her office, without so much as a 'by your command' less than ten minutes before. He was angry, of course, that she was back on duty. And angry, of course, that she'd also been in contact with Kel-Farquin's office on Panperra Station and told them she and Dr. Fynn would, unequivocally, be part of any interrogation involving Serafino on Station.

She did not know, however, which action of hers made him the more angry.

Not that it mattered. He'd taken up residence in the chair across from her desk and made no motion to leave in spite of the fact that she told him she and Eden would handle Serafino's transfer. And that she had a lot of formwork to do before that, none of which would get done while he glared at her.

And glared at her, she decided, in a very possessive manner. She could see it now, see it behind any number of his actions—or reactions—around her. He damn well felt he owned her!

Well, he was damn well wrong.

But she couldn't bring herself to tell him so, because behind all the glaring and all the scowling and all the possessiveness, she saw something else. Something very lonely and very afraid...that used the advantage of his rank to keep her near him.

She kept remembering reading that admission: *I know to some extent*

I'm driving you crazy. You think I'm following you around. You're right. I am. I need to be with you, Sass. Don't you see? I need just to be with you.

And then she'd take another sip of coffee to keep from saying something stupid. Something hurtful. Because she really didn't want to hurt him.

"There's been more reported Illithian activity out by the Drifts," she said, wanting to change the subject. "When do you think HQ's going to let us loose on that?"

"Sebastian." Pause. "I'm not going to discuss that until we've resolved the Serafino situation."

"Kel-Paten," she replied and paused as well. "There is no Serafino situation. I told you. I've been in touch with Kel-Farquin's office. They want a re-run of what we know. Given your...history with him, I thought it best if I handle it." She didn't want to bring up his recent actions, but he'd backed her into a corner and she felt she had no choice. "If you feel I'm not capable," she offered, remembering the old adage about 'the best defense'.

"Or do you feel I'm not capable?" he asked her quietly. Too quietly.

So much for the best defense.

"I feel," she said, choosing her words carefully, "that Serafino will do all he can to drag you into a pissing contest." Or maybe he won't, she considered, knowing that as they sat there, Eden was tinkering around with the implant. Either way, she didn't want Serafino exposed to Kel-Paten until she and Eden were sure which Serafino they were dealing with. "He has no history with me," she pointed out.

"Except at Queenie's."

"That's ancient history."

"I've reason to believe Serafino has a long memory."

"So? You think he's going to challenge me to a game of Starfield Doubles?"

He studied his gloved hands, fisted in his lap. "There are other issues here," he said finally.

She almost said 'So?' a second time, but stopped. She knew what the issue was. It was a who. And she was the who and that was something she definitely did not want to discuss.

She sipped her coffee again. It was cold. "I'll make sure you see everything on Serafino before it goes out, and all that comes in," she conceded, or at least, tried to appear as if she were conceding. There were things she could not, would not let him see. His infatuation with her notwithstanding, there was much she didn't understand about Kel-Paten;

much she didn't trust.

Not as long as Psy-Serv was involved.

"You can even take over all communications with Homer," she added.

That rated a slight raising of one eyebrow. And a relaxing of the tenseness around his mouth. "And deprive you of the pleasure of his oratory skills?"

"Deprive me." She stood, cup in hand. "I need coffee." She didn't offer him any as she made her way past his chair to her office's small galley niche.

Evidently, her lack of manners made Kel-Paten finally realize he was extraneous. He shoved himself to his feet while she leaned against the wall, waiting for the dark liquid to brew.

"We'll handle Serafino together." His pale gaze pinned her and his words were no question.

She smiled, her smile fading as her office door closed behind him. She hated lying to her CO. She hated being in a position to have to lie to her CO. But if the Triad really was dealing with this 'Faction' Serafino had warned about, then they'd violated the treaty and there was no Alliance. And if there was no Alliance, Kel-Paten wasn't her CO.

It was convoluted, circuitous logic but that, and a hot cup of Mahrian blend, black, made her feel one hell of a lot better.

She turned back to her deskscreen and pulled up notes on Serafino and Panperra's layout that Kel-Paten would never see.

BRIDGE, THS *VAXXAR*

Branden Kel-Paten sat in the command chair, one elbow on the armrest, his chin in his hand and watched, without watching, the movement of his senior officers at their stations. No one spoke to him, which was just as well. His mind rehashed other things.

Sass thought he still doubted her allegiance to the Alliance, because she'd known Serafino when she'd worked undercover on Farside. That Sass knew more about a darker side, a very much less legal side of life, he had no doubt.

That that also created an ease between Sass and Serafino was also a logical conclusion. They'd spent time in similar circumstances.

But Kel-Paten was afraid there might be more than just that. Everything about Jace Serafino when he was around Sass—the way he moved with a controlled grace; the way he talked as if every word were intimate; the way he looked at her with anticipation—everything said something more was going on.

What that something more was, he couldn't prove, yet. Other than the one thing he did know: that Serafino would, given the chance, strip Kel-Paten of whatever he valued, whatever he held dear.

Because he'd been the one who'd found Serafino's sister. He'd been the one who'd relayed that same information to the Defense Minister, all the while uncomfortably knowing that the young woman and her son were innocent bystanders.

He wanted very much to believe that they'd been taken into protective custody and were safely relocated.

But he'd never been able to prove that.

Serafino had never mentioned that. But he knew; he knew Serafino knew he'd been the one to find his sister.

And he also knew Serafino would stop at nothing to get revenge.

CHAPTER SIXTEEN

SICKBAY, THS *VAXXAR*

"How are you feeling?" Eden asked, though she already knew the answer. There was a dull, throbbing pain on the side of his head; empathically, she could feel his discomfort.

Jace Serafino grinned at her from his reclining position on the diag bed. "I feel like I hit a brick wall with my head. And I'm hoping you'll tell me the brick wall looks the worse for it."

"No, but you should be the better for it," Eden said and routinely checked the panel readouts. Everything appeared normal.

Other than that damn thing in your head, you're disgustingly healthy, Serafino, she said telepathically.

Dark blue eyes moved upwards quickly to meet hers. *Well, hello! How did you...oh!*

Eden saw and felt a series of images, memories really, flow through his mind. Memories of Novalis, both the ship and the place; memories of her, of a light kiss placed on her wrist and the accompanying warmth that had flooded both of them; and memories of another woman, dark-haired, and a young boy. Bianca and Jorden. Jace was integrating, merging memories and events for the past four years, and to some extent, even more than that. There were older memories, age-old memories shared by all the Nasyry. Eden saw and felt only the edges of those; her fledgling telepathic skills couldn't handle their full impact.

He'd pulled himself to a sitting position on the bed and had reached for her before she realized what he was doing. But he only touched her face, three times, temple, cheek and chin, in the ritual blessing. He was marking her, again, but this time it was for real.

She pulled his hand away, held it lightly in her own for a moment.

"Captain," she said, a slight, very slight warning tone in her voice.

"Doctor," he replied, his voice low and enticing.

It almost reminded her of Sass's "Sebastian—Kel-Paten" routine and she had to shake her head, chuckling slightly. "You're feeling just fine, I think," she said, releasing his hand.

She picked up the chart from the nearby table. He tried to grab it from her and pull her back to him.

"Tell me, Doc, do you kiss as passionately here as when we meet there?" he teased softly. He had no need to explain 'here' or 'there'. His audible words were accompanied by an equally loud telepathic sensation that woke up those damned butterflies in her stomach again.

She looked at him with narrowed eyes. "I was right. There *were* gremlins in there and they've escaped. Behave yourself, Serafino. I still have a healthy supply of rectal thermometers."

"Eden—"

"Jace, let's put these silly flirtations aside for a moment, okay? We have a lot more serious things to tend to." She glanced out the open door into Sickbay and saw only Cal and other personnel she could trust. Still, she lowered her voice. "You're back together, in a sense, but we won't know for how long, and to what extent, for several hours yet. We, and by 'we' I mean Captain Sebastian and I, need to know everything you know about this Faction that's infiltrated the Alliance. We're only a few hours out from Panperra. We don't know what's going to happen there. Whatever information you have could be crucial."

His expression sobered immediately. "I thank you for your trust. And for believing me."

"You still have to convince the captain."

"And the Tin Soldier?"

Eden sighed. "That job we may relegate to Captain Sebastian."

"Kel-Paten," he told her, "will not credit anything I say. I just want to warn you about that."

"I know. We've already had one experience in that area."

"Ahh." He shook his head, his eyes closing momentarily. "The conference in the Ready Room the other day. There was something...odd. A number of layers of issues, if I remember."

"Do you? Remember, that is?"

He thought for a moment. "Not clearly. Is there something in particular—?"

"Yes, but it's not an immediate concern. Your talking to Captain Sebastian is. Do you feel up to it?"

Her question elicited an immediate devilish grin. "Well, I don't know, Doc. Why don't you feel—"

She groaned loudly. "I'll get the captain," she told him as she exited through the door.

She reached Sass in her office and, not knowing who might be in there but assuming the worst, she went through their agreed upon routine: "Captain, this is Dr. Fynn. I'd like to see you now for those final tests I had mentioned earlier."

"Of course," came Sass's voice over the com. "I'll be there in five."

Jace Serafino watched Eden thread her way through bustling med-techs as she headed for her office. It was a rather pleasant view, the soft curve of her hips apparent even under the shapeless lab coat. Not as pleasant, of course, as from the front—she had the most incredible flower-blue eyes, a wonderfully pink mouth and the most delightful way of blushing...and a quick mind, an equally quick wit and a determination that he had seen in very few women in his experience. Compassion, competence and a very womanly body, well-padded in all the right places. That was Eden Fynn. She intrigued him. She fascinated him. She tempted him.

And she made it clear that she was also off-limits. Oh, she'd tease with him, but that only made it worse. She could flirt, she could smile and then she could go right back to being the Chief Medical Officer, leaving him hanging on a proverbial limb, so to speak.

He was definitely not used to that. It was he, Jace Serafino, who would take control of the flirting. It was he, Jace Serafino, who would decide upon whom he would bestow his charms. And it was he, Jace Serafino, who would decide when to withdraw them as well, and move on to the next interesting little flower.

But Eden was more than an interesting little flower. She was a whole garden. A bouquet of endless delights. He felt as if he were locked outside the gate, unable to gain access, but drawn by the sweetness of her scent.

It had all come together in the few minutes after he woke up—all the memories of touching her, kissing her in their telepathic meetings. All the memories of speaking to her, flirting with her in Sickbay. He'd put together the warmth with the woman, finally.

And she wasn't to be had. Not by him. He felt that very clearly. It was a 'take your business elsewhere' feeling under the smile and the laughter. He was mystified how she could enjoy his company so much, and yet be so willing to let him go.

He knew he was charming. He knew he was good-looking. Well, let's be honest. He knew he was gorgeous. Scores of women had told him so. He knew he was intelligent. And he knew she knew all that.

And she was still willing to let him go.

Damn!

He'd have to correct that notion very shortly.

A flash of movement in the corner of his hospital room caught his eye. He turned, tensing slightly, always on the alert. But nothing was there. At least, nothing he could see. But yet...

He reached out, telepathically. *Something* was definitely there. And it was laughing at him.

A noise. He looked around, quickly. Nothing. Yet he could feel it, feel the presence...

Then a large black furzel jumped on his bed, landing gracefully at his feet.

"*Muurup!*" said Reilly.

"Murrup yourself," Jace said, badly imitating the furzel's noise. He reached for its soft head but the yellow eyes narrowed.

Okay, Jace said. *What's the deal here?*

The answer came more in feelings and images than in words: *Eden. Warmth. Love. Protect. Eden. Safe. Safe. Eden. Cuddle. Protect.*

You're the doctor's furzel?

Again, images and feelings: *Eden. Love. Stroke. FOOD! Eden. Protect. Protect.*

I won't hurt Dr. Eden. We're friends.

Eden. Love. Protect. Trust.

Jace saw his own image, slightly skewed, from the furzel's point of view: *Mistrust. Not know. Strong feelings to Eden. Danger! Danger! No bring danger to Eden. Love. Protect. FOOD!*

I promise. I won't hurt Dr. Eden. Ever. She's my friend, too.

Reilly cocked his head. *Maybe. Maybe. Not know. Sense danger. Sense danger. Protect. Protect Eden. Love.*

With a flick of his tail, he was gone.

Something distant, yet uneasy, lingered behind. Jace had sensed it through his link with the furzel. He tried reaching for it, probing, but his head pounded. The damn implant had him worried, a bit cautious.

And the furzel, too.

Something was on this ship, or near this ship. He couldn't tell. It was more than just the headache stopping him. He could faintly sense the jagged outlines of a psychic block.

But who, or what, on this ship could do that? It wasn't another Nasyry. He'd know a Nasyry mind signature immediately. No, this had Psy-Serv written all over it.

Psy-Serv.

Kel-Paten.

SICKBAY, DR. MONTERRO'S OFFICE, THS *VAXXAR*

Sass leaned back in Cal Monterro's office chair. "Okay, Serafino, we don't have much time. I need answers, and I need it without the usual lubashit."

"Of course." Serafino unlaced his fingers and gestured casually at her. "Why do you think I came looking for you, for the *Vax*, in the first place?"

"I have several theories, but I'd rather hear your version," Sass replied.

"You're U-Cee," Serafino said, with a glance at Eden as well.

They were the only three in Cal's office: herself, Eden and Jace Serafino. Cal was poised in Sickbay to alert them to any "incoming", which included at this point any Triad officer other than medical staff. She and Eden figured the ruse about the medical tests would last about forty-five minutes at most before someone—most likely Kel-Paten—would come hunting.

"Everything I've been able to uncover about the Faction has been closely tied in with the Triad," Serafino was saying. He was all business, all seriousness now. "It started long before the Alliance was formed; I'd say as long ago as ten to twelve years. Kel-Sennarin wasn't their first contact. Kel-Adro was. But he's dead. Now."

"Unfortunate shuttle accident." Sass remembered the reports.

"Timely shuttle accident," Serafino corrected. "I gather he wasn't cooperating as they felt he should."

"The purpose of this Faction?" Sass asked.

"Total control. I think that's obvious. The Illithians tried at first to dominate the U-Cees and the Triad separately. But you know as well as I that didn't work. They had to wait...they were counting on this Alliance to meld us together. Now, they have total access and inevitably, total control."

"Don't they see that the people will resist?" Eden asked.

"They won't," Serafino answered, "because this time the Illithians aren't attacking with hunterships. They're infiltrating by securing the allegiance of politicians and big money corporations." He named several intergalactic concerns where the Illithians had already made their presence felt.

"They came to me, years ago," he continued, "because of my, shall we say, underground connections. I had a pretty good set up in arms trafficking across the Zone, plus the other usual stuff. I let them pitch me because I needed to know who they were, what was going on. Did a few minor deals just to let them think they could trust me. All the time, I was working as well with Dag Zanorian."

Sass knew the arms runner well. Very well. Another little tidbit that wasn't in her personnel files. "Zan worked with Gund'jalar," she put in, naming another mutual friend. "And through Gund'jalar you knew I'd been on Lethant." She saw the trail clearly.

Serafino nodded. "If you hadn't been a student of Gund'jalar's, I wouldn't be here now. That's how widespread the Faction is. I don't know who I can trust anymore."

"So you did come looking for us?" Eden asked.

"I knew from my sources that the *Vax* was in the quadrant; knew the Alliance would send Kel-Paten on my trail. I needed to contact you," Serafino said to Sass, "in a way that the Faction wouldn't deem as suspicious. Though in a way, by making sure you were on this ship, they sent you after me. That's the only thing that surprises me. They know, I'm sure they know, about your stint on Lethant. If I know, they know."

"It's not in my records; the Triad has no knowledge," Sass said.

"Are you sure?"

"I had a recent occasion to take a look at Kel-Paten's personal file on me. They have my connection with Farside. But the time I spent on Lethant is still recorded as Official Leave and Sabbatical, showing me on Varlow and Trillas."

Serafino considered that for a moment. "Then they may not suspect you as much as I thought they did, which right now would be to your advantage. Me, I have no doubt that if you release me to Kel-Farquin I'll be dead before you even get back to your office."

"Exactly our thoughts," Eden said. "I've not written your medical release yet. When I spoke to Kel-Farquin's office, I relayed a pretty sad med file on you. As far as they know, you're borderline comatose. We want them to assume you're not in fighting shape when we get there."

Serafino grinned. "Ah, beautiful and devious! What a wonderful combination!"

"Serafino." Sass had to bring his attention back to the situation at hand. "The Doc tells me you're a high level telepath. Is that correct?"

"Except when the damned implant kicks in, yes."

"And part Nasyry?"

"Courtesy of my father."

"Any other talents? Telekinesis?"

Her coffee cup rose in the air and hovered about a foot above Cal's desk.

"Cute," Sass intoned dryly. The cup settled gently down. "We're going to have to do some fancy dancing when we get to Panperra. The Doc and I have already been in touch with people, former U-Cees, who'll help. I need you back on the *Vax*, Serafino, but without Kel-Farquin or Kel-Paten knowing about it. For all intents and purposes, it's going to look like you're on a long trip to Ren Marin."

"Do I get to choose whose cabin I hide out in?" he asked, flashing a wicked grin at Eden.

Eden had mentioned to Sass that there was a slight attraction between Serafino and herself. Now, seeing him in action, Sass wondered if the good doctor hadn't underestimated things. Well, it was something she could use to her advantage. If he wanted to be near Eden, so be it. As long as Eden had no problem with it. At least she knew now that someone would be able to keep the rather rambunctious mercenary in line.

She decided, however, not to reward him with that information yet, and instead spent the next fifteen minutes going over just how they were going to engineer his escape from Panperra and return to the *Vax*. How they would contact Zan and Gund'jalar and the rest of the assortment of professionals that, if all Serafino prophesied came true, they would need. That and a few good ships.

When she felt they'd covered all eventualities, she stood and nodded to Eden. "You and I can leave now, just in case there's a certain problem up front." She pulled her extra service pistol from under her jacket and held it out to Serafino. "You may need this. I hope to hell not. But you may need this."

He took it and tucked it in the back of his pants. Then touched her arm lightly as she walked by. "It's good to be working with you, Lady Sass. Master Gund'jalar always had high praise for you."

"A lot of what I know, I owe to him," she replied. "Watch your back, Serafino."

Sass didn't miss Eden's questioning look as they exited Cal's office. She hadn't told her CMO she'd intended to arm the mercenary captain. Her decision to do so violated at least a half dozen Alliance regs and probably twice as many Triad ones. Eden, being Eden, would've no doubt quoted a few of those just to make sure Sass was really certain that's what she wanted to do: arm a man labeled, and for good cause, a dangerous and volatile mercenary.

It was. Those were Alliance legs. And she was starting to suspect that the alliance between the U-Cees and the Triad no longer existed.

CHAPTER SEVENTEEN

CAPTAIN SEBASTIAN'S CABIN, THS *VAXXAR*

Sniff. Sniff.
Greeting! Friend.
Friend. Greeting!
FOOD?
FOOD!
The two furzels touched noses one more time before Reilly followed Tank into Sass's small kitchen. Tank sat and looked up at the counter top. Reilly leaped gracefully, landing next to a shallow bowl of cream.

Tank scrunched his pudgy body against the floor and pushed with all his might, managing only to scramble against the cabinet doors before falling.

Shtift-a! he swore.

Reilly looked down at the pudgy fidget then indicated with his nose the other side of the counter and two tall stools. Obediently, Tank trotted around and, paw over paw, grunting audibly, managed to pull himself up to the counter level. Reilly had graciously left a bit of cream for his friend.

FOOD!
FOOD!
Sweet. Cool.
Cool. Sweet.
FOOD!
FOOD!
A noise at the cabin door drew their attention.
Sass. Friend. Love, said Tank. *Mommymommymommymommy!*

133

Friend. Sass, agreed Reilly.

"Well, aren't you two a sight!" Sass pulled off her uniform jacket and threw it carelessly onto the couch. "Out of cream, hmmm?"

Two pairs of golden eyes followed her movement to the small 'fridge. Two noses twitched at the buttery smell as more cream was poured.

FOOD!

FOOD!

Sass patted both heads affectionately as they lapped up the cream. "Have to talk to Eden about how you get in here, Reilly." She peered at the air vents in the wall. They seemed intact. "May have to commbadge you both and let the computer track you one of these days," she continued as she entered her bedroom and dragged a medium size duffel bag from the closet. She stuffed the usual items inside; enough for an overnight stay on Panperra and then something a bit more unusual: a long dress that spoke of times several hundred years past. And a metal sword. And a few other things that completed one of her and Eden's favorite pastimes—Olde Legend Fairs. There was one scheduled on Panperra for the next few days.

And conveniently enough, it was the Fair's usual pandemonium and plethora of people in costume that she and Eden were going to utilize to get Serafino off-station and back on the *Vax*.

She heard the thud of Tank jumping off the stool and the muted thumpety-thump of his over-large paws as he ran into her bedroom.

Mommy leave? Mommy leave? No! No! Take Tank! Take Tank! No Mommy leave! He pushed his wet nose against her hand and then proceeded to dig under her clothes in the duffel.

Reilly heard his young friend's distress and sauntered in to see what all the commotion was about.

"It's just for one night," Sass told him, guessing at the meaning behind his burrowing. "You and Reilly can have the place all to yourselves. Eden and I will be back before you know we're gone."

No Mommy leave! No Mommy leave! Tank go with! Tank go with!

Friend. Reilly sat on his haunches and stared at Tank. The little fidget frantically rooted through the clothes.

Friend!

Tank stopped, ears perked high.

Friend. Safe. Safe. All go. All go with. Plan. Go with. Secret.

"*Muurrrup?*" said Tank.

"*Muurrrup,*" said Reilly.

"Good boys." Sass ruffled Tank's fur. "Now, go play. Go play! Mommy has some work to do."

Tumbling over each other, the furzels raced from the room.

CAPTAIN SEBASTIAN'S OFFICE, THS *VAXXAR*

Sass had just logged off her office comp when her door chimed. She glanced at the overhead read-out.

Kel-Paten.

"Damn," she said softly. Then: "Come."

The door slid open.

"Admiral, what can I do for you?" she asked, standing and touching the mag-seal on her slim briefcase.

"When were we denied permission to dock?" He leaned his gloved hands against the back of one of her two office chairs.

"About an hour ago."

"Why wasn't I informed?"

She met his gaze levelly. "You were. I left that information on your office comp board when I didn't get an answer."

"I was in my quarters. You could have reached me there."

She'd known that. That's why she'd left the message where she had, knowing it could easily get buried under the usual deluge of information every ship's officer received upon arriving on station.

"It's not a critical issue." She shrugged. "We weren't actually denied dockage. With this Fair, Panperra's heavy docks are full. I've already allocated a shuttle to transport Serafino in and alerted Kel-Farquin as well."

"What shuttle did you reserve?"

"*Definator.*" She'd turned away from him to sift through some files on her desk, hoping he'd interpret her body language: I'm busy. Leave.

"The command shuttle is the *Galaxus*," he reminded her.

She knew that, too. And, given Serafino's warnings, she'd thought it best not to advertise the status of those on board by using the larger craft.

"I thought you might be using her," she offered.

"I will. We will," he corrected. "I'll accompany you to Panperra."

She'd figured that was unavoidable. Though she'd had hopes. "If you do, it'll be on the *Definator*. I've already loaded—"

"Then I'll order it unloaded." He took her briefcase from her hands as she tried to step past him. "I see you've put in for a stay-over on Station."

"My schedule's clear—"

"Good." He looked down at her. She tried to tug the briefcase out of his hands. "The Triad maintains an excellent Officers' Club there. I'll arrange a dinner meeting with several of the more influential merchants

135

as well as some of Kel-Farquin's key staff."

"Ede—Dr. Fynn and I had plans." She stubbornly continued to hang on to her briefcase as they moved towards the door.

"Yes. This Fair. I've never been to one. After dinner, we can take a walk through the Fair compound."

We will do nothing of the kind! Sass finally relinquished her efforts to regain her briefcase. All she needed was Kel-Paten traipsing along after her while she and Eden maneuvered Serafino back to the *Vax*. She'd have to think of some kind of diversion for him.

She thought of one. Actually, Eden had thought of it earlier as a means to stop Kel-Paten from scowling so much. It would also, she knew, keep him from uncovering their deception.

Though it would take her out of the action for a while.

She glanced up at him as they entered the lift and tried to put together the passion in the logs she'd read with this always-in-control Tin Solider next to her. It didn't make sense.

Until he glanced down at her in return.

People often compared his pale blue eyes to ice. But they were wrong. It wasn't the cold blue-white of ice they resembled, but the white-hot blue of the center of a flame.

There was no way, she knew, seeing the intensity reflected there, she was going to be able to avoid him on Panperra. And his presence would create a big problem in getting Serafino safely off station.

She had no choice. She trusted Eden; they'd worked far more dangerous situations than this. She'd just have to let Eden and Serafino handle this one on their own. It was their only chance of success.

"Dinner sounds wonderful." Sass tried to put the right combination of enthusiasm and seductive suggestion in her voice. "Actually, Eden has plans to see someone special at the Fair. I'd have only been a tag-along." She gave him a small, confidential smile. "Are you sure you wouldn't mind my tagging along with you, Branden?"

He almost dropped her briefcase. "No, I wouldn't mind." He swallowed hard. "I think it would be nice. Very nice."

He'd moved closer to her. She turned her face up towards his. In the back of her mind she monitored the muted ping as each deck passed by. She waited until the lift was just a few pings from her destination before she deliberately stepped up to him, one hand resting lightly on her briefcase that he clutched against his chest.

"I think that would be very nice, too," she whispered. Parting her lips slightly, she leaned towards him, her eyes half closed.

"Oh, Gods, Sass." He breathed her name and brought his head down to close the few inches that separated them. The lift pinged, twice this time and the doors slid noisily open.

She snatched her briefcase out of his hands and sprinted through the doors, pivoting after only few steps and grinned at him.

"Shuttle Bay Three. Half hour, Kel-Paten," she called and touched her fingers to her temple in a mock salute.

He stood in the middle of the lift, his mouth half open in surprise, his arms raised as if holding on to a briefcase...or a woman...who was no longer there.

He was still standing that way when the doors closed in front of him.

Sass trotted the short distance down the corridor to Sickbay, chuckling.

"You look like the fidget who caught the slitherskimp," Eden said as Sass entered her office. "What now?"

"A slight change of plans, once we get on Station." Sass drew a thin datadisk from the briefcase and handed it to Eden. "Here's the layout of Panperra. Serafino shouldn't need more than five minutes to memorize it. Meet us in Shuttle Bay Three in twenty-five minutes."

"Us?" Eden questioned.

Sass signed. "Long story. But yes, us. As in Admiral Kel-Paten. You were right. I am the issue here, and the issue's going to have to keep him busy while you get Serafino back to the ship.

"Busy?"

"Don't look at me like that, Eden. This is duty. Lives are at stake."

Eden's grin was decidedly wicked. "You mean you're going to—"

"Have dinner with him. Engage in some slight flirtatious conversation. Take a long, slow walk through the Fair. Give you time to find Gundja'lar's contact. He'll make sure Serafino's on the right med shuttle, purportedly going to Ren Marin. Our shuttle. Coming back here."

"And you'll be?"

"Keeping the Tin Soldier as far away from our shuttle bays as I can until the *Vax* heads out again."

SHUTTLE BAY THREE, THS *VAXXAR*

Shuttle Bay Three was a cavernous, well-lighted bay in the mid-aft portside section of the *Vax*. It housed two of the huntership's five shuttles: the larger *Galaxus* and the smaller *Definator*. Both were elliptical in shape, silver in color, emblazoned with the *Vax's* signature dragon and slashed lightning bolt symbol. When Sass arrived, cargo 'droids were transferring luggage from the smaller shuttle to the larger.

Admiral's orders.

She glared at the young lanky ensign but held her tongue. One of her U-Cee crew would have commed her before taking such action, but this still wet-behind the ears boy was pure Triad and purely terrified of the Tin Soldier. Kel-Paten no doubt had known that and chosen the ensign specifically. Because he also no doubt knew Sass would be less likely to countermand his orders. The poor kid had enough problems and it wasn't his fault the admiral had his knickers in a knot. Again.

She sighed. "She's fully fueled?" She laid her hand against the shuttle's fuselage.

The ensign saluted smartly. "Yes, ma'am! I double-checked myself. She was last in for maintenance just ten days ago, so everything else should be good as new."

"Thank you, Ensign..." she looked at his name tag. "Kel-Nortin. Carry on." He turned back to an anti-grav flat as it floated the luggage towards the *Galaxus'* underbelly. A Strata-class shuttle, the *Galaxus* could comfortably seat up to ten people with a commensurate storage area aft. She was similar in design to a medium sized luxury-transport, with a large cockpit area forward of the main cabin. Like a luxury-transport, she had a small galley and full san-fac. Unlike a luxury transport, she also had a full weapons array and an enhanced shield and scanner system.

Sass was about to start a pre-flight check when the sound of the corridor doors alerted her to Eden and Serafino's presence. Well, Eden, Serafino and a small security contingent headed by Garrick.

"Everything secure as per your orders," Garrick told her as Eden and Serafino climbed the short flight of steps to the shuttle's interior.

"Thank you, lieutenant." What Garrick had just told her was that the pistol she'd given to Serafino was still in his possession and that the sonic-cuffs that bound his hands in front of him were programmed to appear locked, when in fact they were not.

Garrick had worked with her long enough to know that when she asked for the unusual, there was always a damned good reason. As her crew on the *Regalia* used to say, there were rules, and then there were Captain Sebastian's rules. The latter usually won out.

Sass had the pre-flight completed, luggage loaded, her passengers seated comfortably and herself ensconced in the pilot's seat when Kel-Paten arrived, promptly on time. She heard his heavy footsteps on the stairs and then his muted acknowledgment to Eden. She heard the cockpit door whoosh open and, when she heard nothing more, she looked away from the datascreen to find him standing in the doorway, a questioning expression on his face.

She could guess at part of it: she was in the pilot's seat, a role he normally would have assumed for himself.

Grow up, flyboy, she wanted to say but didn't. Now was not the time, especially if she were going to have to convince him that she wanted to be in his company on Panperra. So she only gave him an enigmatic smile.

"Ready when you are, Kel-Paten," she said and turned away to check the latch on her safety straps. Let him interpret that as he would!

"Sebastian." He slid into the co-pilot's seat, clicked on his own straps and activated the instruments without further comment.

"Bridge, this is Captain Sebastian. Requesting departure clearance, Shuttle Bay Three."

"Clearance granted, captain," came back the answer on the cockpit's overhead speaker. "Initiate departure sequence."

"Initiating." Her mind clicked into its piloting mode as her fingers tapped the codes. Inside the bay, a small siren wailed. The lights over the corridor doors went from green to yellow, signaling to any personnel inside they had to leave the shuttle area immediately. The ship's computers scanned constantly and when no more life forms were sensed in the bay, the corridor door lights changed to red and the door sealed.

Directly in front of the *Galaxus*, a ring of red lights delineated the outer bay doors. They flashed and departure systems confirmed their imminent opening.

Sass activated the shuttle's anti-grav thrusters just as the air was sucked from the bay.

The wide doors disappeared into the wall, revealing the immense black starfield beyond. Panperra Station wasn't visible; the shuttle would have to clear the huntership first then drop below her before the multi-level artificial world could be seen.

"Main thrusters on line," Sass said.

"Confirmed," Kel-Paten replied. "Full power in ten seconds. Nine. Eight. Seven."

She and the admiral worked in practiced synchronization as the shuttle glided through the bay doors then made a sharp bank to starboard.

"*Galaxus* to Bridge. We're clear." She relayed their heading, making adjustments on her console.

"Acknowledged. Turning you over to Panperra Approach Command. Have a nice time, captain!" said Timmar Kel-Faray.

"Thanks, Timm. See you in forty-eight. Don't trash the *Vax* while we're gone!"

"Oh, the admiral would put a stop to that right away!" Timm's voice clearly held a smile.

It was then Sass realized that the First Officer—and no doubt the rest of the crew—didn't know Kel-Paten was gone. She had only a moment to puzzle over that before Panperra Approach was on the overhead, requesting her ship ident and clearance codes. She relayed that information and then waited for the docking instructions in return.

"Theta level security docks," Kel-Paten read out loud as the data scrolled over his screen. "ETA thirty-five minutes, given the current traffic."

The current traffic was the problem. At least fifteen freighters waited for docking clearance and another five commercial transports reported on an incoming heading through the jumpgate.

Sass listened, unconcerned, to the pilot-to-pilot chatter on the overhead. At a thirty-five minute ETA, she knew the *Galaxus* had been bumped ahead of some of the freighters, the captains of which were none too pleased. But they all understood, having seen the familiar silhouette of the *Vaxxar* in the distance. Rank had its privileges.

But the *Galaxus* hadn't been bumped ahead of the commercial transports, as those spaceliners had tight schedules to keep.

It was a routine situation.

Until an alarm erupted loudly. Five Illithian fighters came screaming through Panperra's jumpgate, weapons signatures hot. They veered suddenly, dropped into their kill-or-suicide formation, and headed straight for the *Galaxus*.

CHAPTER EIGHTEEN

ALLIANCE COMMAND SHUTTLE, *GALAXUS*

The *Galaxus* was already more than halfway to the Station. That was the first thing Sass checked when the shuttle's alarms wailed. As much as she would have loved to respond aggressively, her primary concern had to be Eden and Serafino. The *Galaxus* was a shuttle, not a fighter craft.

"Panperra Command, this is Captain Sebastian. I need an emergency commlink to Commander Kel-Farquin. Now!" While she spoke those words she activated the shuttle's shields. Kel-Paten, she noticed, had brought the weapons system on line. And was checking something else.

"The *Vaxxar* has them," he told her. "She's powering up."

But it would take, Sass knew, at least five minutes for her to come to full power. The large huntership had been in stationary orbit around Panperra for over three hours; her main drives off-line per standard Fleet procedure. This was not a war zone; this was a Triad station, a 'friendly' station. Given the proximity to the station, her torpedoes couldn't be fired without endangering the commercial and freighter traffic, as well as Panperra's inhabitants.

"What's Station's defenses?" Sass asked, then, before Kel-Paten could answer: "Damn! Why the hell hasn't Kel-Far—"

"Vidcomm Link One open," the shuttle's computer intoned.

Sass slapped at the instrument panel before her. Kel-Farquin's fleshy face appeared on the small vid screen. He looked distinctly troubled.

"Captain, I—"

"Commander, we need emergency access to Theta Bays. We'll be coming in hot, full power." She tabbed the thrusters to sixty per cent as she spoke. "The *Vax* is in position to render support. In the meantime, the admiral and I—"

"The admiral?" Kel-Farquin's face jerked as he noticed the dark-haired man seated next to her. "Kel-Paten? What are you—?"

But Kel-Farquin's question was lost as the vid link dissolved under a burst of laser fire from one of the Illithian fighters.

"Irk at five o'clock." Kel-Paten responded by activating the aft lasers and returning fire. "Shields holding at ninety-five per cent. No structural damage. What's our ETA?"

"We're still ten minutes out. But I think we can—shit!"

The shuttle jerked as another round of laser fired slashed her shields. "Damn it! How'd they know we'd be here?"

Several thoughts clamored for her attention. Serafino's warning that the Faction wanted both her and Serafino terminated. His suspicions that Kel-Paten might somehow be the agent for that. Kel-Paten's insistence on using the command shuttle to transport Serafino. And both Timm Kel-Faray's and Commander Kel-Farquin's ignorance of Kel-Paten's actions. But more than that, Kel-Farquin's surprise at finding Kel-Paten on board.

The shuttle dipped harshly as Sass tried to shake the three Irks now on their tail. Kel-Paten seemed to be intent on targeting them. Still...

She tapped at the shuttle intercom. "Serafino! Get your ass up front, now! You, too, Fynn." She knew that would alert Eden to the seriousness of the matter. She rarely called her friend by her last name except in the direst of circumstances.

Serafino burst through the cockpit doorway, Eden in tow. "What the hell's going on? Who'd we pick up?"

The shuttle rocked again from laser impact. "A handful of unfriendlies," Sass said quickly, aware the admiral stared at her. "Irks. Who seem to know more than they should."

"What's Serafino—" Kel-Paten began but she overran his question with a forceful one of her own.

"You tell me, Kel-Paten. You tell me just what's going on! You're the one who insisted on transporting Serafino in the *Galaxus*. And you're the one who didn't tell Kel-Faray of your plans. Just whose side are you on, anyway?"

"Whose?" He looked from her to Serafino and back to her again. Eden, no doubt knowing someone had to mind the store while these three fought it out, slid into the navigator's seat to the right of the admiral and brought her instruments on line.

"Why did you change to the *Galaxus*?" Sass asked angrily.

"It's the command shuttle! What are you getting at?" His pale eyes narrowed.

"I'm getting at the fact that you made sure we're transporting a highly controversial prisoner in a highly visible craft, admiral. We're doing the expected. Or is it the requested?"

"Are you implying—?"

"No, sir, I'm *stating*. I'm stating that these changes were made to accommodate those who want both Serafino and myself out of the way. Isn't that how you put it?" Sass turned to Serafino standing behind her. He grasped the back of her chair as the ship dipped to port again.

Before Serafino could answer, Kel-Paten grabbed her armrest and swiveled her chair in his direction. "Tasha! Do you really think I would—?"

"We've got incoming, three o'clock," Eden said loudly. "Shields eighty per cent and holding. Sass—"

"Taking evasive action, Doc, and thank you!" She returned her attention momentarily to the shuttle's instruments. They were still eight minutes from the Station. Why the hell hadn't Panperra sent assistance?

"I don't know, Kel-Paten." She replied to his question through clenched teeth. "But if you've set me up, and if I live through this, I promise you I will dismantle you, piece by piece and sell you as scrap."

Something painful flashed across his face. She knew the vehemence of her words had cut him. To another man she might have threatened to kill him. But to a 'cybe, and only to a 'cybe, she would threaten dismantling. Like an unusable Kessie unit. Or a malfunctioning bar 'droid.

He released his hold on her chair and sat back abruptly. "You're wrong." His voice was strained.

"Am I?" She glanced at Serafino who'd strapped himself in at the small weapons station next to her and worked with the data Eden fed to him. "Scan him, 'Fino. I need to know everything, and I need to know now!"

"Scan?" Kel-Paten focused on Serafino, then suddenly jerked back as if he'd been hit. "Thought-sucker!" He spat out the word and whipped his head to the right as if by so doing he could break the probe.

"Nasyry thought-sucker," Serafino said quietly and in a voice filled with pride.

Kel-Paten turned back to him, unlatched his straps, started to rise.

"Sit down, admiral." Sass's tone brooked no argument. Neither did the Ryker 857 in her hand. She pointed it, not at his head or his chest, both areas cybernetically protected through layers of microfine but impenetrable plasteel, but at a small, vulnerable area at his throat. U-Cee Intelligence was thorough.

He took his seat again, slowly.

"Sass, I need you." Eden's voice had a firm, but singsong quality designed to get her friend's attention.

It did. Sass reholstered the Ryker, glanced at her instruments and made the necessary corrections. The *Vax*, she noted, was already on the move. At least someone was on their side!

She felt Kel-Paten staring at her. When she turned slightly, she caught the undisguised pleading look in his eyes. He could, she knew, have moved with such speed when she drew her Ryker that he could have killed her, and Eden, before Serafino would have even had time to react. Or he simply could have grabbed her arm and, with a thought, ended her life.

But he hadn't, nor had he even tried, and that very fact—coupled with the pain she now saw on his face—made her temper her words, and offer him a half-hearted apology.

"If I'm wrong about you," she told him quietly as the shuttle jerked again in response to another incoming barrage of laser fire, "then I'm sorry. But circumstances right now are a bit strange."

"Tasha, I'd never hurt you." His voice rasped.

"He's clean," Serafino said. "That is, I can find no trace of loyalty to the Irks. Or the Faction."

"Eden?" Sass looked past Kel-Paten to where her friend sat at the nav station. She knew Eden would have been running a perfunctory 'truth scan' as well, empathically.

"He's telling the truth," Eden said. "I'm not sensing any duplicity."

"But he's also," Serafino pointed out, bringing Sass's laser pistol from the back of his pants and clicking off the safety, "one of Psy-Serv's prized projects. He might've set this up, he may have set us all up, and not even been consciously aware of it. Had any tune-ups lately, admiral?"

That Psy-Serv and the Faction could have implanted subliminal commands in Kel-Paten was a fact Sass had considered. She heard his sharp, angry intake of breath at Serafino's words.

But any comment—or threat—he might make was lost as the shuttle jolted violently to starboard. Lights flickered. The horrifying squeal of metal straining under impact filled the cockpit. Kel-Paten reached for the instrument panel before him, tried to throw more power to the shields and at the same time locate the hull breach. Serafino was back at weapons, returning fire, swearing loudly.

Sass worked to coax more power out of the shuttle's engines. Panperra Station was so close! If they could just make it to...

But they couldn't, as two Irks peppered the port side of the shuttle with laser fire, forcing her to turn away, to turn off course.

"We've feeder valve failure in the port thruster," she told her shipmates over the wailing of the sirens.

"Working on it," Kel-Paten said.

"'Fino! I need some room!"

The Irks forced them out into open space, away from the Station.

"Can't seem to break through their shielding," Serafino replied, a note of frustration in his voice. Sass saw the shuttle's lasers doing only minimal damage to the Irks.

"Try a reverse phase modulation in a gamma-delta pattern!" The shouted suggestion came from Kel-Paten.

"Bloody damn!" replied Sass as the shuttle jerked and cockpit lights dimmed again. Suddenly everything went red as the emergency override power supply kicked on.

"On back-ups!" Sass quickly tapped in the adjustments on her instrument. "Switching to manual on Five. Four. Three. Two. On manual."

Around her, Kel-Paten, Eden and Serafino mirrored her movements.

"Navigation on line," Eden said.

"Shields at seventy per cent but dropping. We have an aux-line leak in section four," Kel-Paten added.

"Weapons off-line," Serafino said angrily. "Ladies and gentlemen, we're toast."

"Shit!" Sass looked quickly from Kel-Paten to Serafino.

"I can seal the cockpit, pull life support off line in the cabin and add power to the shields," Kel-Paten said, already starting to make the changes.

"Re-routing life support takes five minutes. We don't have that." Sass turned to Serafino. "Well?"

He hesitated only a second. "Throw all power to the engines. Head for the jumpgate. The section four thruster will blow bad. We'll just have to deal with that."

"Agreed." Sass nodded and moved to implement his idea.

"You can't make a blind jump!" Kel-Paten shouted. "We'll never—"

"It's not blind. He's Nasyry," Sass reminded him. She unlatched her straps, stood and reached across to tap instructions into his instrument panel "Go, 'Fino, go! You've got the con."

She stepped swiftly away from her seat and Serafino slid in, his hands moving rapidly over the panel. The shuttle lurched forward, pounded by laser fire.

"I'll drop aft shields last as we cross the gate!" Serafino said.

"Then we can kiss our asses good-bye," Sass said ominously as she grabbed the back of Kel-Paten's chair to keep from falling over. She watched as he synchronized his movements with Serafino's, and felt more helpless than she had in years. Irks on their tail, spitting death. No help from Panperra. The *Vax* unable to respond in time. Their only chance at escape didn't guarantee survival. The ship could very possibly be torn apart by the fierce currents of a blind entry into the gate.

As if he could read her thoughts, Kel-Paten glanced over his shoulder at her, his gaze as desolate as she felt.

Then she heard Serafino chuckle. It was an odd, almost cruel sound.

"Be careful if you do." Serafino looked at Kel-Paten. "Lady's got a mean right hook."

Kel-Paten took his attention from the instruments just long enough to send a look full of hatred at Serafino. "Go to hell."

Mind reading. Serafino had read something in Kel-Paten's mind and responded out loud. His answer clearly angered Kel-Paten but what Serafino had sensed, and who it involved, suddenly held little interest to Sass.

The ship burst violently through the perimeter of the jump gate, a ship on a mad mission, raked by energy currents. The *Galaxus* shuddered wildly as Serafino and Kel-Paten fought to keep it under control.

"Grab the closest fix!" Sass shouted, knowing Kel-Paten already scanned for one. But he was such a Mr. Perfect she knew he'd look for one that fit a long list of acceptable parameters. They didn't have that kind of time.

They needed a fix—a secure energy trail that had an active guidance beacon at both ends. A jump gate was nothing more than a hole in the fabric of space-time, like a long tube whipping about in the wind. Unless someone was holding the other end of that tube when you entered, you were in for a rough ride.

Two active guidance beacons provided that secure trail. Right now, they had only one. At Panperra behind them.

"Serafino!" Kel-Paten said. "Code in a fix at—!" The ship dropped suddenly as if into an endless cavern, throwing Sass almost over Kel-Paten's seat. Eden pitched sideways, her straps tearing. She ended up on the floor just as an overhead nav panel exploded in a shower of sparks.

Serafino yanked off his straps and lunged for her, pulling her away from the falling debris. He managed to grasp her wrist as the ship was thrown to starboard this time, rolling up on one end as if slammed from below. Eden slid rapidly into him and he locked his legs around hers to keep her from careening into the bottom of the weapon's station.

Kel-Paten grabbed Sass around the waist and pulled her into his lap, holding her tightly against him. Another panel blew and he turned quickly, shielding her from the spray of hot liquid. He unhooked his safety straps, fumbled to wrap them around her.

Then something yanked her and the admiral out of the chair. Sass swore as they slammed against the wall.

Or the floor.

Or the ceiling. She couldn't tell.

The emergency lights failed. The cockpit plunged into darkness.

The last thing Sass saw from over Kel-Paten's shoulder was the green glow from the instrument panels winking out.

<^>

Serafino unlocked his legs just long enough to pull Eden beneath him, his hands securely on her shoulders, his mouth hard against hers.

We're not going to make it. I'm sorry... Regret, frustration and passion all washed over her as his tongue seared the inside of her mouth. Beneath her, the *Galaxus* bucked and with each movement Serafino pressed the hardness of his body more insistently against her.

Eden kissed him back fiercely, let her mind flow into his, no longer caring about protocol or patients. She felt his desire, physically and telepathically, felt the tension and the tenderness, felt him fill her mind with his fervor as he wanted to fill her body with his physical being. The latter would never happen, but the first, the first granted her a few moments of something so pleasurable that she gasped out loud as a thousand butterflies coursed through her veins. She arched against him in an eternal, primal response, her hands threading tightly through his long, dark hair.

He whispered her name in her mind just as the shuttle rolled over one last time. He was torn away from her and thrown against the weapons station wall. It responded by buckling in half, the stack of power units jarred loose from their couplings and raining onto his body like large, metal boulders.

"Jace!" She screamed his name, reaching for him. Another wave of energy whipped the shipped around. Her head connected with the metal cylinder under the pilot's chair. Pain crested just as Eden heard was the sound of bodies thudding against the forward viewport, accompanied by Sass's very familiar, "Bloody damn!"

Then her world went black.

So she didn't see other bodies that tumbled just as the *Galaxus* began a violent ass-over-teakettle spin.

Friend!
Friend!

CHAPTER NINETEEN

It was a familiar dream and one that always left him with an empty ache upon awakening. He fought the rise in consciousness and held more tightly onto his fantasy, taking in the sandalwood scent of her hair, so soft against his face. And the warmth of her body, so neatly fitted against his, two spoons curved together. In his dream she sighed, arching her back and her round bottom pressing against him caused an immediate reaction of heat and hardness. He groaned her name, drawing her closer, his hand finding the swell of her breasts as he did so. He could feel the outline of something lacy through the fabric of her uniform and then his thumb found a gap and his fingers slipped inside, past the lace...

She stirred, let out a ragged breath as his finger traced that taut peak and he didn't know if it was the sound of her pleasure or the ever-present yellow data readout across his mind that alerted him to the chance that this might not be a dream:

Tactile Data Input—Subject female humanoid—approximately 38 years of age—body temperature 98.6—respiration fast—metabolic rate normal—

Kel-Paten's eyes flew open. In his field of vision was a tangle of short, pale hair and an immense black starfield. And not another ship or station in sight.

"Oh Gods, Sass." He said her name softly, carefully, remembering the bastard Serafino's comment about Sass's 'mean right hook'. Serafino had telepathically caught Kel-Paten's own fantasy of making love to Sass, and his fear that, with death imminent, he'd never have a chance to.

Yet he didn't feel dead. But he knew if Sass woke up now, finding his hands placed where they were, there'd definitely be that mean right hook to worry about. Still, the intimacy of their position afforded him the opportunity to assure himself of her well-being. He opened his hand, slowly, let it rest against her chest and dropped quickly into full 'cybe function, running a cursory med diagnostic on her through the sensors linked though his gloves. No internal injuries and only a slight bruising on her shoulders and back, probably from impacting the viewport. She'd be sore for a while, but nothing more.

He simultaneously ran his own diagnostics, expecting no damage and finding none. His brief lapse into unconsciousness, and hers, was due no doubt to a sudden drop in air pressure as life support had shut off and recycled back on.

He withdrew his hand, letting it come lightly to rest on her hip as she let out a small, "Oh!" then a louder "Oh, Gods!" and rolled over to face him.

Her eyes fluttered opened. Her face wore a slightly lost expression. "Hey."

"You okay?"

She seemed to study him. "Yeah. Must have been a helluva bar fight. Who won?"

"I think we did." He had the distinct feeling she had no idea who 'we' were.

"Hmpf!" She gave a short, low laugh. "Then the other guys must feel like shit." She sighed, snuggling against his chest.

She *definitely* had no idea who he was.

The feel of her pressing so intimately against him destroyed what little prudent restraint he had left. He clasped her to him and was drawing her face up to meet his own when he felt her tense, her arms stiffening, He knew that she'd just realized who—and what—he was.

"Bloody damn!" she said.

"Are you all right?" He tried to make his voice sound as normal as possible, hiding the hard edge of passion in it much better than he was able to hide the hard physical response of his body to hers. He shifted position away from her, let his hand fall from her face to the slick surface of the viewport on which they lay.

She followed the movement of his hand. It looked as if they were lying suspended in deep space.

"Gods!" Sass sat up abruptly.

He pushed himself up as well, reaching for her as she wavered slightly. The cockpit of the shuttle was bathed in a red glow, casting eerie shadows on the total disarray of cables and floor tiles—floor tiles?—and seat cushions and panel covers and Doctor Fynn's boots—

"Eden!" Sass clambered over him onto the instrument panel before sliding to the floor. The CMO was curled peacefully around the base of the pilot's chair.

He pushed himself off the viewport and saw a suspiciously damp section of Fynn's shoulder length hair. He grabbed a medkit from a nearby panel.

"Let me take a look," he told Sass as she searched for the med scanner. He laid his hand flat against Eden's face and then chest, much as he had with Sass earlier, and relayed to her what his diagnostics found.

"No major internal injuries. No broken bones."

Sass flicked the scanner on, confirming his words with the unit's data.

"We lost life support briefly," he told her, seeing the worry and concern on her face even in the dim lighting. "That's most likely why we lost consciousness. She'll come to shortly."

Sass looked at him, her eyes a little wild. "Okay. Okay." She drew a deep breath and nodded in what he understood were her thanks. "Okay. Let's get this ship stabilized. I can't work and walk on walls. I'll secure her."

The *Galaxus* was only slightly skewed. A minor adjustment to her internal gravs—thanks the Gods that still worked!—fixed the problem, though there were a few strange clanks and thuds.

Together they moved Eden from under the chair and arranged the loose chair cushions around her. She'd already begun to stir, much as Sass had minutes before.

"Serafino? Where's—oh, shit!" Sass grabbed his arm and dragged him to the back of the cockpit where Serafino lay under a pile of rubble. "Wait 'til I scan before you move anything!"

He crouched next to her, glanced at the data on the med scanner and then back at the man called Jace Serafino. A telepath. A Nasyry telepath. A thought-sucker with who-knew-what capabilities. He would've like to have believed Serafino was dead, but his brief glance at the scanner plus his years in combat told him he wasn't going to be that lucky. Serafino was alive. Injured but alive. Man had the proverbial furzel thirteen lives.

"Only a broken arm to worry about, so I think we can move this stuff," Sass was telling him. She turned unexpectedly, caught the expression on his face before he could mask it.

"Don't look so damned disappointed that he's alive, Kel-Paten. He just saved your unworthy ass back there."

She was defending Serafino—not only defending him, he thought as he carefully moved the debris, but had obviously taken Serafino's side even before they'd boarded the *Galaxus*. The laser pistol Serafino had pulled was Alliance issue, Alliance *command* issue and he doubted the doctor owned such a weapon. Sass had ordered Serafino to telepathically scan him, and he had, without question, without hesitation. Sass had known Serafino was Nasyry.

He had questions, a thousand questions, including whether Serafino, or Fynn, had told Sass about his feelings for her. But now was not the time.

Besides, he hadn't forgotten her comment about selling him as scrap. That, in many ways, told him all he really needed to know.

They supported Serafino's body in much the same way they'd secured Eden's. Sass collapsed awkwardly into the pilot's chair. It squeaked in complaint.

"What's our situation?" She ran one hand through her hair then turned to the damaged instrument panel at her station.

He leaned against the back of her chair, studied the data as she did. It told him virtually nothing that he couldn't discern with his own eyes through the viewport. They were alive and in deep space. Somewhere. Life support functioned, but minimally so, and only in the cockpit. The ship's structural damage was unknown, as was fuel reserve, engine status, their supplies.

The only good news was that the Illithian attack squadron had disappeared.

Sass turned her face towards him. "Can you spike in, or are the systems too far gone for that?"

He eased himself down in the co-pilot's chair, faced her and rested his elbows on his knees. "I can try. No promises."

"Will it damage your systems? Kel-Paten—"

"No!" He turned abruptly away. Systems. Your systems. Not *you*. Your *systems*. He heard the words and hated them. "No," he said again, suddenly exhausted. "There are safeguards. But I need to sit there," he added, nodding to the pilot's chair.

She changed seats with him; he tried to forget she watched as he tugged down his right glove, sliding the small plasteel flap that covered his dataports to one side of his wrist. The arm of the pilot's chair housed an extendable pronged input line which fit neatly into his wrist and he pushed it in place with his thumb, his eyes momentarily closed as he put his 'cybe functions fully on line.

When he opened them again, he was there, in the pilot's chair, but he was also in the ship—in the cabin, the engine compartment, the small storage bays. And outside where the vid monitors continuously scanned the ship's exterior. He let the data flow into him, scanning and sorting as need be and, at the same time, watched Sass from all different angles. He imprinted, as he had many times before on the *Vax*, imprinting her form into his cyber memory, into subdirectories of subdirectories he'd created that no one—not even Psy-Serv—could find and erase.

The image, this time, was a Sass he'd never seen before. Disheveled, tired and in pain. Worried. About Fynn, he surmised, as she kept glancing towards her friend on the floor. Once or twice she looked at him but he was in profile to her, seeing her not through his physical eyes but through the various monitor lenses in the cockpit.

Finally she unfolded herself from the chair and sat on the floor next to Eden, taking her friend's hand in her own and patting it absently.

He went back to work, very aware that the damaged, malfunctioning shuttlecraft he was linked to was the only thing keeping them all alive.

NOVALIS

The gray mists seemed a bit thicker this time. Eden telepathically felt him before she actually saw him. And when she did, her relief was so great that she ran across the short expanse and threw herself into his arms.

Jace! What's happened? Did we make it? Can you tell?

He held her tightly. *We're fine. We got through, though I'll be damned if I know how.*

Eden looked up at him, brushed a stray tear from her cheek. *Are you okay? I remember you falling—*

Broken arm, that's all.

She stepped back. *You look fine...* She touched both his arms and he laughed.

This isn't my physical self, love, though we can still have fun.

She blushed. Of course. She still had a difficult time adjusting to two worlds. And two existences. *Can I start the healing process from here?* She lay one hand on his chest. *Which arm?*

He held his left arm out to her. *We can join our energies in healing. It may surprise you at the power you'll find there.*

She ran her hand up his arm, wincing when she sensed the location of the break. *I...I can feel it! I can feel the break. How odd.* Then she closed her eyes and sent healing energy to that area.

Jace lay his hand over hers, adding his energy to her own. A warmth flooded her. She'd never shared a healing before.

Then his hand traveled up to the back of her neck. *You've got a bit of a lump there, Eden.* He applied a light pressure. She was aware of the pain and then not. It was if he'd drawn it out of her.

I think I hit the bottom of Sass's chair, she told him.

Ummm, he agreed. *She's worried about you.* He looked over her shoulder as if seeing something but she knew there was nothing there.

The Tin Soldier's working on the ship, he continued. *He's spiked in, making himself useful though he's most uncomfortable doing it around her.*

Around Sass? Eden questioned. *I've noticed that, too.*

Jace nodded. *Poor Tin Man. If only he had a heart, isn't that how the ancient children's fable goes?* He drew Eden back against him, lightly kissing the top of her head.

I thought I lost you, he said suddenly, his voice rough. She felt an ache in him, a frisson of fear, an anger at being caught so helpless.

She held him tightly then sighed as his mouth left a hot, wet trail down her neck. He was breathing heavily—odd how even an incorporeal body could exhibit those sensations!

Eden, I thought I'd lost you! he repeated, but this time his voice cracked. He pulled her against him with such force that she let out a small, startled cry. He held her that way for a long time, his face in her hair and it was only when she finally began to pull away that she realized he, too, was trembling.

She thought it was just herself.

She gently touched his face. It was wet.

He'd been crying.

Jace— she started, but he hushed her and kissed her fingertips.

You tell a soul about this, young lady, and I'll pull down those pretty lace panties of yours and give you a good spanking! He smiled, but it was a watery one.

Don't tempt me, she teased softly.

You tempt me, he told her and then kissed her fully, in control again, the pressure of his mouth on hers insistent, demanding.

She nibbled on his lower lip and he groaned. *Oh, Eden, Eden. There's work to be done and all I want to do is play with you.* He looked in the distance again. *Your friend's worried. We shouldn't do this to her. The Tin Soldier, well, he's wished me dead a hundred times already. But Sass is upset. So go wake up and tell her we're fine.* He touched her face three times, temple, cheek and chin.

And ended by brushing his mouth lightly across hers.

It was getting to be a rather nice ritual.

GALAXUS COCKPIT

Sass saw Eden's blue eyes flutter open.

"Hey," Eden said weakly.

"Hey, yourself, Doc. No more Wine Fizzles for you. You're flagged." Sass grinned. "How's the head? You have some tomato juice leaking out there."

"Throbbing, but it's getting better. I...we took care of that."

"Ah-*hah*." Sass glanced back at Serafino's quiet form. "Wondered what took you so long. He has—"

"A broken arm. Left. I know." Eden struggled to sit up. "We're working on that, too. And you?" She accepted Sass's hand in assistance. Sass knew it was for more than just support. Her CMO often did quick med scans with a touch. Her next words confirmed that had been part of her reason. "Last time you felt like that was in that bar fight in Port Bangkok. The one where the Garkal hit you with the bar stool."

"While my back was to him, coward!" Sass said and then sighed. "Wondered why this felt so familiar. Odd how the mile markers in my life are a collection of bar fights."

She stood, and pulled Eden up with her. "He's checking on the damage," she said with a nod to where Kel-Paten sat behind them. "Can you wake Serafino up? Maybe he can give us a hand, even if he's only got one useable one."

She held the med kit out to Eden, who accepted it with a nod and turned her attention to Serafino. Sass went back to the front of the cockpit and sat again in the co-pilot's chair, her legs crossed underneath her. Kel-Paten watched her, his eyes that luminous blue-green.

"Doctor Fynn is fine." His voice, when he was spiked in, was always a bit softer than normal, yet oddly monotone. And he was more prone to make statements than questions, even when those statements *were* questions.

Sass nodded, understanding. "She's fine. Bit of a headache, but she can deal with that, as well as Serafino's arm." She motioned to the back of the cockpit where Eden knelt.

"Good."

"She reminded me...she felt the injury in my back and remembered the last time I'd had that was after a bar fight on Port Bangkok. That's where I thought I was when I came to. Just now." Sass remembered too clearly waking up with her face nuzzled intimately into Kel-Paten's chest. She felt she owed him an explanation.

"I see."

Did he? Bloody damn, she hated when he was so mechanical. "Look,

I just didn't want you to think...well, I was pretty disoriented. Kind of a flashback. You know?"

"Of course."

She tried to smile. "Could be worse, you know. I've been known to wake up swinging."

"So he said."

It took a moment for Sass to grab the connection. Serafino had said something about a 'mean right hook' just before the shuttle hit the jumpgate. Had he been referring to her? Evidently, Kel-Paten had thought so. Anger had flashed briefly in his luminous eyes.

Because he thought the only way Serafino would know that Sass had been prone to wake up swinging a mean right hook was that he'd been in her bed.

She was about to explain that it had been Dag Zanorian she'd clocked when she realized *that* explanation might not help, either. Now wasn't the time to piss him off. Not when he was under full power. She looked away, ran her hand over the lifeless instrument panel. "So. What's the situation? Do we need to send out a distress signal?"

It took a moment before he answered. She hoped it was just because he was reassessing their data. "We've sustained major damage to engine section four. It's inoperable at this time. I'd estimate at least four to six hours to repair it. Life support is functional, two of the three replicators are back on line and the scanner array is functioning with only minimal damage. In essence, we have enough food, water and power to last us approximately two to three weeks, should we require it.

"That's the good news," he added.

She turned back to him. She didn't like the way he said that last sentence at all.

"The good news? Meaning?"

"Meaning there is bad news, Sebastian."

"Which is?"

"I have no idea of where we are, or how to get back to Triad Space. Or even Illithian space, for that matter. Nothing in our nav files matches what I find out there." He looked out the viewport and nodded.

Sass leaned back in the chair and regarded him in disbelief. "You're kidding."

"I do not kid."

No shit, she thought. "There's nothing familiar out there," she waved her hand at the viewport.

"No."

"Nothing. Not a star. Not a constellation. Not an asteroid belt we can get a fix on."

He was kidding. He had to be kidding. But the finality in his voice when he answered made her stomach clench.

"Nothing."

Bloody damn and lubashit on a lemon. They were lost.

CHAPTER TWENTY

GALAXUS

Lost.

In a damaged shuttle.

Not a sturdy, functional Raider-class transport, but a bloody, Gods-damned luxury command shuttle! If it hadn't been such a frightening realization, Sass would've laughed.

"That can't be!"

"Why not?" Kel-Paten asked her. "We've not charted our entire galaxy, let alone the universe."

"Yeah, but, we've charted—and by 'we' I mean, you, me, the Irks, the Kalfi, the T'Sarii and a handful of others," she ticked off the names on her fingers as she spoke. "We've charted a really big chunk of it. You'd have to go damned far to get to a point where nothing, and I mean nothing, correlated with even the edge of one of the star charts."

"I believe we have."

"*You* believe?" she repeated, her voice rising.

"Sebastian..."

"Don't 'Sebastian' me, Kel-Paten. You *could* be wrong."

"I could. But the *Galaxus*'s nav comps are intact."

"That's impossible." She glanced to the back of the cockpit. "Maybe Serafino can help. The Nasyry have been around a lot longer, and a lot farther, than any of us."

The bright glow in his eyes flared briefly. "How did you know he's Nasyry?"

"Eden told me," she replied after a moment, knowing he wouldn't be satisfied with that answer, and knowing they were opening a can of frinkas here.

"Dr. Fynn—"

"Is a telepath, too. Yes." Might as well cut to the chase.

"Her personnel records—"

"Don't reflect that because she didn't know until recently. Working with Serafino uncovered it. She confirmed he's Nasyry, or half-Nasyry. And if Eden says so, then it's so." She tried to look sternly at him but failed. She was too damned tired.

Evidently, so was he. With something that was a cross between a sign and a groan, he initiated his shutdown, closing his eyes briefly as he spiked out, letting his head rest against the high back of the seat.

"You okay?" she asked softly after a few minutes.

He turned his head towards her, his eyes once again their familiar pale hue. "No. But it's something I've gotten used to."

She ran her hands over her face, his soft, apologetic tone tugging at her. That, and the realization that he more than likely wasn't behind the attack by the Irks. Kel-Paten was nothing if not a perfectionist. He would have foreseen the possibility of escape through the jumpgate; something the Irks hadn't. Had Kel-Paten orchestrated the Irk attack, they would have succeeded. "I'm sorry. I shouldn't yell at you. I know you're just doing what you have to do." She hesitated. "Are we really lost?"

"Technically, no. I know exactly where we are. It just doesn't relate to anything in our nav comps, that's all."

"So we're lost." It sounded ludicrous, even to her own ears.

Still, she was surprised when he responded with a small, crooked smile. "Yes."

She was even more surprised to find herself returning it with one of her own. "Well, hell. Let's look on the bright side, then. That means there's a whole galaxy of pubs out there that haven't banned me. Yet."

"If Serafino can't help us, finding those pubs may become your full-time job," he said. "We're going to need supplies, eventually."

True. "Did your scans pick up any habitable worlds?" It would be nice to know there were a few places they could bunk in with breathable air and potable water. "Or how about a Station, any Station?"

"No Stations, not even a subspace radio transmission in this quadrant, no. But as for habitable worlds, a few possibilities. I'll know more once we get the engines back on line."

Sass looked out at the silver points dotting the blackness of the starfield, hoping that a planet would suddenly send up some sort of welcome flag, something like "Beer Here! One Credit Shots 1900 hours to Closing!"

Kel-Paten's voice cut into her wishful thinking. "Go check on Serafino. Sounds like he's functional now. I'm afraid I won't be able to make the proper appreciative noises at his survival."

She gave him a wry smile, surprised at his candor. "Sure, admiral. Will do." She left her seat, thinking that sometimes he wasn't quite that intolerable.

Sometimes.

Friend? Sleep. Sleep. Tank hurt.

Friend. No sleep. Sleep bad. Alert! Alert! Help friend. Help Sass. Help Mommy.

Friend...hurt....

Reilly hurt, too. Friend. Alert! Help. Soon food. Soon.

Food?

Food. Soon.

"Though the admiral may never tell you so, we're both appreciative of what you've done."

Sass sat cross-legged on the floor next to Jace while Eden activated the small bone regeneration device she'd attached to his left arm.

"What I've done," Jace said from his position propped against the bulkhead wall, "is get us into a blind jump. I did not, and I tried to explain this to Eden, I did not get us out. I thought he did," he continued with a nod to Kel-Paten in the pilot's seat. "Thought he might have spiked in and taken control. But evidently not, from what you tell me."

"Then who pulled us out? Someone had to initiate the deceleration sequence on the engines. The computers were off-line; we were on manual," Sass said, remembering their wild ride.

"Could you or the admiral have done that by mistake?" Eden, briefly glanced up from the med scanner. "Hit something when the ship inverted and you ended up on the viewport?"

"Unlikely," Sass replied. "The only other possibility is the emergency shut-off, and that's not even up front. It's back..." and she turned towards the rear of the cockpit, towards a long access panel whose door was skewed on its hinges. There was a broken air vent directly above it. And a collar, a bright blue furzel collar, torn in half, snagged on a jagged edge of the vent.

This time her stomach clenched and her heart stopped at the same time.

She sprang to her feet. "Kel-Paten!" She didn't know quite why she called for him. Except she was afraid that if she found what her sinking heart told her she was going to find, she was going to need something large and immovable to pound on in her grief. He was the largest and most immovable thing she knew.

She yanked on the access panel door as he strode up beside her.

"The panel door's stuck!" she cried. "I need in there. Now!"

He didn't question her request, but tore the panel off its hinges.

And there, hanging by their front paws on the long metal emergency shut down handle, were two furzels—one rather large black one with a white tuxedo blaze, and a smaller, furrier black and white one. A fidget, really.

"How in hell—?" Kel-Paten's question ended abruptly as he was roughly shoved aside by two laughing and crying women.

"Tank!"

"Reilly!"

"Mommy mommy mommy mommy!"

"Mommy mommy mommy mommy!"

Kel-Paten had never heard of furzel massage before. But it had been Eden's suggestion, no, medical direction. He watched from the pilot's seat as Sass, her face still damp from tears, gently and methodically rubbed the front paws and legs of the pudgy creature that fit nicely in her lap.

The one in Eden's lap didn't fit so well, but received the same loving attention.

When I die, Kel-Paten thought, noting the adoring look Sass bestowed on the small furzel, *I think I know exactly what I want to be reincarnated as.*

They're traditionally neutered at six months, though. You might not find that as rewarding. Or maybe you might not even notice.

Serafino's voice in his mind hit Kel-Paten like a bucket of ice water. Which was, he realized, exactly what the younger man had intended. He shot Serafino a look of pure venom, but Serafino only shrugged, unconcerned.

Then he caught the narrowing of Fynn's eyes. Had she heard the comment, too? Sass had said the CMO was a telepath; something he didn't want to hear. Not now.

Or had Fynn only sensed an exchange of emotions, as she often did?

And just what had they told Sass?

He could've sworn something passed between Fynn and Serafino as well. And was pleased to note Serafino finally looked a bit chastened as he reached out to ruffle the furry ears of the creature in Fynn's lap.

"They knew what they were doing." Serafino adjusted his position against the bulkhead with a small wince of pain. "The furzels," he added, when Eden looked at him. "You can scan him and know for yourself, but since Sass and the Tin—Kel-Paten can't, I'll explain.

"Animals, especially domesticated ones like furzels, form a bond with their humanoid counterparts. A telepathic and sometimes even psychic bond. Reilly," he said with a nod to the large black furzel now purring loudly in Eden's lap, "came to me in Sickbay with a warning. With all else that was going on, I don't know, I didn't take it as seriously as I should have. So I accept blame there."

"A warning?" Sass asked, echoing what was in Kel-Paten's mind. "They knew the Illithians were going to attack us at Panperra?"

"Nothing that specific. Just that something felt very wrong. And because of their bond to Eden and you, they decided to take things into their own hands. Uhh, paws." Serafino grinned.

The fidget, Tank, sneezed a small sneeze that could have been mistaken for fidget-giggles.

"They stowed away," Serafino continued, "first on the *Definator*, then they moved to this ship when the luggage was brought over. And hid out, up there." He pointed to the ceiling. "What I seem to get from Reilly is that he pretty much had free run of the *Regalia*, is that correct?" he asked Sass.

She nodded.

"He's very intelligent," Serafino said. Reilly purred louder. "He'd been through enough drills with you and Eden to understand certain basics. When trouble started, he and—Tank, is it?"

Tank stretched one paw towards Serafino in acknowledgment. Kel-Paten didn't know if it was happenstance, or if the small creature understood the conversation.

Serafino nodded to Tank as if he were acknowledging something said. "Tank and Reilly knew they'd have to shut down the engine to drop us out of the jump. They don't have the knowledge to initiate a shut down via the command panel. But Reilly remembered seeing the emergency shut off handle. And, of course, it's labeled."

"You want us to believe they can read Standard?" Kel-Paten hadn't wanted to address Serafino but *someone* had to inject some rationality into this insane recounting.

"Of course not." Serafino looked pleased in his denial. "But they can recognize the same symbols or patterns. It's image retention, not reading.

They don't actually understand the word t-u-n-a but when they see that combination, that shape of letters on a can of furzel food, they know it's something they like."

Food? Reilly's head shot up.

Food! Food! Tank wriggled in Sass's lap.

"T-u-n-a," Serafino repeated.

Fynn stood and handed Reilly over to Serafino. "I'll check the replicator and see what it can provide for them."

The 'menu' was somewhat limited in the cockpit, the larger replicator being aft of the cabin, which at the moment, with life support still going through recycling procedures, was off-limits. But the CMO returned with a meat stew she said she thought they'd like, and when the furzels were happily slurping away in a corner, the humanoid contingent of the *Galaxus'* crew turned their attention to more pressing matters.

Like survival.

And getting home.

Serafino ran through the available data at the nav station. "Sorry," he said. "Nothing in my memory, collective or otherwise, ties in to what I see here."

"So we could be two quadrants or an entire galaxy away from Alliance space and we wouldn't know," said Fynn.

"Well, not two quadrants." Serafino turned his chair to face Fynn at the weapons station. "At two quadrants there'd still be something recognizable. A constellation, a star cluster we could home in on. That's not the case."

"So what do we do?" Fynn looked from Serafino to Kel-Paten and back to Serafino again.

"Regardless of where we are, Doctor," Kel-Paten told her from the pilot's seat, "we have to first assure the integrity of this ship. We have to get the engines, life support and the computers back to optimum—or as close to optimum as we can manage. That's something Captain Sebastian and I, and to some extent Serafino, can handle." He had no intention of gracing the mercenary with the title of 'captain', or any kind of title unless it was one that couldn't be said in polite company. "Our second priority is to find a habitable world. We cannot stay in this ship forever, not much past two weeks, and even that will strain the *Galaxus's* facilities. I'd prefer to find a space station, but since at this point that doesn't seem to be an option, we have to look for a habitable planet.

"That," he said to Eden, "is definitely your job, Doctor. You have the knowledge to ascertain habitability and biological compatibility."

"Most importantly," Sass put in with a smile, "they have to be capable of brewing damn good beer. And a damn good cup of coffee!"

"We also," Eden added, "need to get some rest. None of us, and that includes you, admiral, are in perfect condition after what we've just been through. If you could make the main cabin one of your first priorities, I think we all might benefit from a little more room."

"Understood, Doctor," Kel-Paten said. "We should have life support back in the cabin within three hours."

He glanced at Sass. His 'we' wasn't the 'inclusive we' but the 'we' that meant Sass and himself.

She seemed to understand. "Where do you want me to start?"

"I've already started the preliminaries." He transferred to her comp screen the data he'd worked on while spiked in. He leaned on the arm of her chair, about to close the distance between them in order to bring her attention to the results of a diagnostic scan when a small, furry body thrust itself under his arm.

Tank positioned himself on the edge of Sass's chair and looked up at Kel-Paten with a noticeably determined and possessive expression.

Mommy. Mine.

Sass wrapped one arm around the fidget and snuggled him closer against her. "Does it bother you he's here?"

"No," he lied. He angled back towards his console and tried to concentrate on the problems at hand: they were lost, in a malfunctioning shuttle, out of range of help from any sort of civilization as they knew it.

That should be the problems he needed to address. Not that he was on that same shuttle with a woman who'd never love him, and two telepaths who knew exactly how he, and that woman, felt.

Even her damn fidget wouldn't let him get close.

All he'd need to find out now was that there was something wrong with the shuttle's engines. Then Fynn wouldn't need to file a Section Forty-Six on him. He'd do it himself.

CHAPTER TWENTY-ONE

"Jace..." Eden said his name softly, but not without an underlying tone of warning.

It wasn't that she was angry, though the Gods knew she could have been, would have been, if it had been anyone other than Jace Serafino whose fingers now oh-so-innocently traced a trail along the side of her breast, sending small shivers of excitement—and distraction—up her spine. She sighed.

"Jace!" She said his name a bit more emphatically this time, turned her face away from the scanner and tried to look at him. But his chin rested on her shoulder—which was how his arm had snaked around her waist and eventually, his fingers explored upwards—so all she could see in this almost nose-to-nose position was an out-of-focus Serafino. But even in such a position she could see he was smiling his usual devilish smile.

"Ummm?" he questioned.

"You're distracting me."

"Ummm." This time the deep voice dropped an octave to respond in a low growl.

"How am I supposed to locate a habitable world with...oh!" Eden gave a little ticklish squirm. "You're making this...oh my! Difficult."

"Oh my," Serafino repeated in her ear. "The Tin Soldier's not here." For the past two hours, Kel-Paten and Sass had been working on the shuttle's engine, accessible only through a small aft hatchway. Their return, when it happened, would first be proceeded by a series of loud noises as that hatchway groaned back into place, and then the sound of their footsteps through the main cabin.

"You're incorrigible," Eden told him.

"I've never denied it." He suddenly swiveled her chair around and dragged her to her feet, his mouth on hers, hard and demanding, yet at the same time teasing, as he kissed her. He nibbled on her lower lip, then covered her face with small kisses again.

She was laughing giddily by that time.

"You get," he told her when they both gasped for air, "too serious, love. I've been watching you. Yes, we have to find someplace to put this bucket down to finish repairs. And get fuel. And food. And the Gods know what else.

"But there's something else," he said, stroking her face lightly. She moved her hands up to encircle his neck. "You're worrying. I know why you're worrying." His voice became softer now, his smile more faint. "I've been apart from people I love, too. For a long time now. It doesn't help, Eden, it doesn't help keeping that worry in the front of your mind all the time. Trust me. I know. I've been there. I'm still there."

She leaned against his chest, grateful for his warmth and his words. Her cousins on Varlow, who'd been her constant childhood companions and had also been as constant in their encouragement of her when her ex-husband decided he wanted 'wife with a smaller dress size' and one who couldn't empathically sense his dissatisfaction. Cal, back on the *Vax*, who'd never voiced the prejudice some had about working with an empath. Others she'd worked with on the *Regalia*, who were almost like family. They were, as he said, in the front of her mind, and had been in the almost thirty hours since the *Galaxus* ended up in this unknown and distant galaxy. They had to believe she was dead, and their useless grief pained her.

"How do you deal with it?" she asked quietly into the soft fabric of his shirt.

"One minute, one day at a time." He kissed the top of her head. "I've been doing better since I met you. I don't really know why. It's just that...everything's different now. There's a connection between us, maybe our loneliness. I just don't feel as lost when I'm with you."

She looked up into deep blue eyes. "Thank you."

He smiled. "No, I—" The back of the shuttle resounded with a thunk and a clank. He raised his eyes in a pleading expression. "The troops return," he announced and let her regain her seat.

There was a smudge of something grayish on Sass's right cheek. She looked, Eden thought, distinctly annoyed as she stepped into the cockpit and took her seat in the captain's chair. Kel-Paten followed moments later, looking equally as rumpled but more confused than annoyed.

Eden looked from the admiral to Sass. "Bad news?"

Bad news, Jace told her telepathically.

Sass wiped her sleeve over her face, smearing the gray streak. "We've got a fuel leak."

Okay, not good news, Eden thought, tamping down her initial alarm. *But workable, if—*then Jace pulled further information from Kel-Paten's thoughts and relayed it to her.

It was more than a fuel leak. It was a *major* fuel leak. Their estimate of being able to survive in the shuttle for two to three weeks had just been drastically shortened. Jace picked up the engines' visuals out of Kel-Paten's mind. He explained the basics to Eden. Something had ruptured going through the jump gate. They had maybe three to four days before the *Galaxus* would cease being a shuttle and become a coffin.

"How much fuel do we have left?" Eden asked.

"Thirty-six to forty-eight hours." Kel-Paten's voice showed no emotion but Eden sensed his frustration loud and clear.

His words chilled her. She swallowed hard before giving her own report. "There are three possible planets. Two of them are at least fifty hours from our present location. That leaves us only one choice. Unless you can get the warp drives—"

"Negative," Sass told her. "Sub-light power only. So," she leaned over and lifted the chubby fidget into her lap. Tank murruped appreciatively. "Tell us about our new home."

Eden brought the data up on her screen, simultaneously transferring it to the other workstations. She'd designated the world as Habitable Venture-1, based on its coordinates and bio-scans. HV-One, or 'Haven-One', as she'd nicknamed it, had two large sections of land mass and one smaller one. However, the larger sections occupied the polar regions; the only temperate climate, and the best place to try to land would be on the smaller land mass. She ran through the other pertinent data: water regions, mountain regions, the small desert region in the southernmost tip. And the three moons orbiting the planet, which created frequent coastal flooding.

"Life forms?" Sass asked.

"Unknown at this point, captain. We're too far for this scanner array to detect anything accurately. In another twelve hours, though, I should have more data. I can say, however," Eden continued, "that I'm definitely not picking up any evidence of technology."

"Great. You mean we might be digging for sharvonite crystals with our bare hands." Sass shook her head wearily.

Eden felt Jace's concentration shift. She glanced at him. His eyes were shut. She could feel him reach out across the blackness of space, probing, sensing. Yet she couldn't see what he did. He'd temporarily shut her out, putting all his energies into finding out what he could about Haven-One, picking up on the life threads that all physical things emitted.

She was distantly aware as he probed the world, felt its oceans, its mountains, its small and hot desert region. And...something else.

Something that didn't know they were there—but if it did, it wouldn't have liked Jace's probing one bit.

But they were too far for Jace to be able to define just exactly what that something was.

And fortunately, too far for that something to know they were about to drop in unexpectedly.

Jace pulled back, gave his head a light shake, much as Sass had minutes earlier. *I think we should be careful,* he told Eden. *There just may be a serpent in paradise.*

Sass swiveled abruptly in her chair, jerking Eden out of her connection with Jace. "Talk to me, 'Fino."

He glanced up, amused. "Do you have telepathic abilities I don't know about?"

"Hardly. But I've known her," Sass said with a nod to Eden, "long enough. That little dip of her mouth, that twitch of her foot—that's not good. And she was looking at you."

"Jace sensed something in or on Haven-One," Eden explained quietly. "It could just be the three moons creating a gravitational flux."

"Or?" Sass prompted.

"Or," Jace explained, "it could be a form of intelligence with a level of telepathy. There's an energy there. Not overwhelming. More of an erratic pulsation. And yes, it could be natural, a residual from a flux. But it feels slightly different. And not overly happy."

"You can't be serious—" Kel-Paten's words halted as Sass raised her hand.

"It knows we're coming?" she asked.

Jace shook his head. "Not at this point. But we should be careful about putting out any calling cards as we get closer."

Eden clearly saw, and felt, the admiral's disbelief as he turned back to the data on his console. Sass's face showed thoughtful interest. Unlike Kel-Paten, she wasn't going to discount anything, especially not in an unknown, uncharted quadrant.

We'll handle whatever it is when the time comes, Jace told her.

That time, Eden knew, would come more rapidly than she'd originally thought. Forty-eight hours was all they had left. Forty-eight hours, to get this shuttle stable and functional enough to make a dirtside landing.

The unknown energy form seemed the least of their problems at the moment.

<^>

Kel-Paten noticed everything about them, feeling like a *voyeur* yet at the same time knowing there probably was no better instructor on female seduction than Jace Serafino. The way he lightly caressed Eden Fynn's neck as he leaned over and talked to her; the way he touched her hand. The looks they exchanged; the small smiles, the meeting of gazes. There was so much involved, so many 'moving parts'....

Kel-Paten's own inclination after thirty-six hours with Sass in the close confines of the shuttle was to pin her up against the bulkhead, press his body against hers and kiss her until neither of them could think straight anymore.

But he knew that wouldn't work. If nothing else, his own mind ceased to think straight whenever he got within a few feet of her, let alone up against her. Plus he believed that her reaction would be to think him straight...to hell.

But he'd been aware of Serafino's effect on his CMO since the renegade captain had first come on board the *Vaxxar*. He'd watched Eden's demeanor go from cold to professional concern to friendly compassion to passion. If Serafino could break through the well-known barriers of the Zingaran healer—a feat no other male on his ship had been able to do—then surely Kel-Paten could apply the same tactics to Sass.

Maybe.

There were, he knew, other issues. Like, Serafino was full human. And he wasn't. Like, Serafino was known for his charming personality. Kel-Paten was known for his arrogant attitude in keeping with his nicknames: the Tin Soldier. And recently, the Ice Admiral.

Cold. Unyielding. Uncaring.

How little anyone really knew him.

They were still a few hours from the world they'd named Haven-One and Serafino was bent over Eden's station, speaking to her in low, intimate tones. Kel-Paten heard her soft chuckle; caught, in his peripheral vision, the brief tilt of Eden's head against Serafino's shoulder. And the corresponding light kiss Serafino planted on her hair.

Kel-Paten refocused on the woman in the captain's chair next to him in the cockpit. For a moment, he let his mind overlay Serafino's actions as if they were his own and saw himself leaning over Sass, his voice low and caressing in her ear...she would turn her face slightly and he would catch that impish grin she had...and perhaps then he would lean closer, brush his mouth across hers, tasting her smile...

Fantasizing again, are we?

Serafino's voice, loud and harsh in Kel-Paten's head, shattered the pleasant image of Sass and replaced it with another one—a grim, hurtful one. The bitter face of a sloe-eyed prosti, sneering at him in disgust.

He was out of his chair in one swift move. He turned, arm raised to grab at Serafino who'd already straightened and stood, arms folded across his chest, laughing.

That'll really impress Captain Sebastian.

Narrowed eyes met narrowed eyes only inches from each other. But one set of narrowed eyes had taken on a distinct luminescence.

"*What* is going on?" Sass's question was a definite command for information.

Kel-Paten couldn't tell her. And he'd kill Serafino if the bastard said one word right now.

It was Eden who spoke up. He'd forgotten she could read him, and Serafino, too.

"Gentlemen." She swiveled in her chair. "Now is not the time. We have work to do." He recognized her "Mother's at the end of her rope" tone.

He was at the end of his proverbial rope, too. What he felt for Sass was private, personal. Not to be used as evidence of a Section Forty-Six by his U-Cee issue CMO. Not to be used as fodder for that Nasyry thought-sucker. Who'd discovered more than just his feelings for Sass.

He'd stumbled onto Kel-Paten's hidden pain.

He spun on his heels and marched through the cockpit doorway and into the main cabin, slamming his fist on the bulkhead wall as he went.

Sass let out the breath she'd been holding. "He puts a hole in this ship and we're going to have real problems," she muttered and then looked up at Serafino. "Whatever you're doing, *can* it, mister."

He gave her his most charming smile. "Me? I'm not—"

"Lubashit, 'Fino. Once we get dirtside, you two can pummel the hell out of each other with my blessings. But until then, I really need his expertise and your cooperation. Do you read me, captain?"

"Yes, ma'am."

"Good," Sass replied.

But it wasn't. Things were far from good. Serafino and Kel-Paten were at each other's throats. The shuttle was running out of air and leaking fuel. She needed the cooperation of both men to get this shuttle functional. Just so, she realized grimly, they could land on a planet that housed some kind of malevolent energy form.

If they landed at all. The *Galaxus* wasn't built for heavy air duty, even in the best of conditions.

This was far from the best of conditions. Their attempt at landing might well turn into the last one they ever try.

GALAXUS, AFT CABIN

Kel-Paten leaned over the small galley sink and splashed cold water onto his face.

He could've killed Serafino.

Wanted to kill Serafino.

But for Sass and Eden Fynn, he would have.

He'd evidently underestimated Serafino's telepathic abilities. How he'd found that deep memory of the prosti, he didn't know. But Serafino had dredged it up from the darkest corners of Kel-Paten's mind as if he'd known just where to look. Shore-leave on Mining Raft 309 in the Drifts. He'd been a mere lieutenant and alone, as usual. His fellow crewmembers had all gone to find what amusements they could in that Gods-forsaken locale that didn't even qualify for a casino license. Just a scattering of dirty pubs, two eating establishments that promised a healthy dose of intestinal parasites with the food, and one nighthouse, with a crude sign that advertised both male and female prostis.

He would never even have considered going inside had it not been for a conversation he'd overheard at the dingy bar where he'd sat, bored and restless. There was no casino license on the Raft, but there were games. Or a game, to be more specific, an illegal poker room in the nighthouse.

The only way he was going to survive the next thirty-six hours on this hellhole would be to keep his mind challenged, and busy, with gambling.

What he, in his twenty-three year old innocence, didn't realize was that the nighthouse, in order to ensure its profits, routinely spiked the gamblers' drinks with any pharmaceutical concoction that was cheap and handy.

When the young, taciturn, dark haired Kel lieutenant started winning, the bar manager started slipping drinks laced with Heartsong into his black-gloved hands.

Then his mind could no longer concentrate on anything except the heat in his body, a heat that crested when a sloe-eyed, skimpily clad prosti draped herself in a chair next to him.

And he forgot about the cards in his hand and the stack of chips at his place on the table and followed her up the back stairs and into a musty room that smelled of cheap perfume.

But he didn't care, didn't care about anything except removing his uniform and that thin bit of lace that was sloppily wrapped around her...

Then she saw the scars on his chest and arms. And as his hands moved to cup her heavily powdered face, she saw the two small holes at the base of his palms.

She jerked back, her mouth pursed as if she'd just tasted something sour.

"Yer that *thing*, thass 'cybe, ain't you? Whassyer name?" she drawled.

"Kel-Paten," he answered automatically, swaying slightly towards her.

"Yeah, thass right." She looked him up and down. "Yew may look like real people all right, but they ain't payin' me enough to do the likes of yew, 'cybe." Her face filled with disgust. "Thass wrong. They should'na make yew look so real. Thass sick."

She'd snatched her lace robe from the bed and bolted out the door.

He'd stood there, shaking, pained. Shamed.

Killing Serafino wouldn't have erased the pain or the shame. But it would have helped.

GALAXUS, COCKPIT

Do you need to hurt him that badly, Jace?

Eden sipped at her cup of hot tea and focused on Serafino seated on the cockpit floor next to her, Reilly sprawled across his lap. They were taking a break from staring at the scanners and, as far as Sass in the captain's chair knew, were sitting quietly with their respective drinks: her Orange Garden and his Roast Java.

They were sitting. And sipping. But they were far from quiet.

Jace gave a mental sigh. *It goes way back. An eye for an eye, you know.*

Bianca?

And my nephew, yes. You know that.

So you have to...do this to him? Make him feel this hurt?

Hurt? Jace laughed tightly in her mind. *Pain, Eden. He has to feel pain. I want to break through that icy fortress he's locked himself in and make him feel what it's like to be human, to suffer a loss. Don't damn me because of it.* He reached over and stroked her hand. *In the long run, he'll be the better for it. Maybe he'll think twice next time before acting to ruin someone's life.*

I think he already feels the pain. Jace, there's something you should know—

About the Tin Soldier? You mean that he's got the hots for Sebastian? I picked up on that from the start. That's why I know my methods will work.

He stroked the furzel's soft head.

It's more than the 'hots'. He's...been in love with her for a long time. Over ten years.

He gave a surprised chuckle. *No shit? That's wonderful!* he added sarcastically. *So we have a real full blown obsession here.*

This isn't something to toy with. You don't understand this. Or him. I've done some...digging in his mind. The way he feels about her isn't an area you want to mess with.

All the more reason, love. All the more reason.

Jace! Eden shot him a feeling of strong disapproval. *I don't understand you when you're like this. I don't...like this in you. I really don't.*

He leaned his head back against the metal panel and closed his eyes. *Eden, try to understand. This is not...an element of my personality I would ever turn on you. Ever. But what he did to me, what he did to Bianca goes too deep. Cuts too deep. I can't...I can't let it go unavenged.*

And if you push him too far?

I won't. Not on this ship, anyway. When we're dirtside...? And he shrugged.

Eden shook her head. *He'll kill you. Don't you realize that?*

Eden. He said her name with such finality, such force that she physically turned and looked at him. His eyes were still closed but she knew he could see her. *There are things about me, about being Nasyry that you don't know. I can...well, let's say it would be very difficult for Kel-Paten to kill me. That was one of the reasons Psy-Serv was so insistent on tracking me down. They knew, you see. They knew that if anyone was a match for their prize 'cybe it was me.*

He opened his eyes, his dark blue gaze on her now. *It never mattered before. Before I met you. I didn't care if I lived or died. But I want our life to be perfect, Eden. I want to make all the wrong things right. And this is where I have to start.*

And he brought her hand to his lips. *Trust me on this one.*

Even if I feel you're being cruel?

It's not cruel, love. And it's more than just vengeance on my part. Remember, he's a protégé of Psy-Serv. Until I break him down, until I peel away those impenetrable layers he's concocted, I don't know whose side he's on. I don't know if we can trust him.

I've dealt with him before. And I've never been able to 'read' him, until now. Whatever has happened to him because of Sass has opened a hole in his defenses. Because of her, he's let down his guard. That's my only way into his mind, and his only way out of whatever programming Psy-Serv has imbedded in there. Do you understand now?

She did. But it was a frightening and dangerous route he'd chosen.

It had been almost an hour since the admiral had challenged Serafino and then stomped off to the main cabin. Sass had no interest in chasing after him when he fell into one of his royal snits and so had let him simmer down, or stew, whatever the case may be. But when he'd not returned after what she felt was a reasonable time she decided to go after him—not out of concern for whatever had sparked the tiff, she told herself, but because they had to make some important decisions about getting the shuttle dirtside. Decisions she knew the admiral wasn't going to like.

Serafino was placing both his and Eden's empty mugs into the recyc panel when she stood. "You have the 'con, 'Fino. I'm going to brief Kel-Paten on our landing preparations."

Jace started to head for the captain's chair. Sass put out one hand to stop him. "No, no." She laughed. "Over there." She pointed to the co-pilot's chair, the one Kel-Paten had been seated in. "I'm still in charge here, big boy."

"Just wanted to see if you'd notice," he drawled with a wink.

"My ass," she quipped back.

His laughter followed her as she stepped through the doorway.

Kel-Paten was seated in the last row, staring out a small viewport. He didn't turn when the hatchway whooshed open, nor at the sound of Serafino's deep laughter, nor when the hatchway closed. He didn't turn when her footsteps came down the aisle towards him. And he didn't turn when she took the seat next to his.

He was in a *royal* snit. She'd witnessed the signs before. It was if he'd crawled in somewhere deep and dark and locked the door after him.

And locked everyone else out.

When she'd first been assigned captaincy of the *Vax*, she'd watched how his First Officer had handled the Ice Admiral: *"Sir, if you don't mind...Sir, can I get you some coffee...Begging the Admiral's pardon, sir..."*

Kel-Faray may have been with Kel-Paten for almost twenty years, but Sass decided right then and there that his methods stunk. And that was during the average on-board crisis that occurred with familiar regularity on any huntership.

Now, with less than seven hours of fuel on board and stuck in some Gods-forgotten remote corner of the Gods-knew-what galaxy, Sass had even less time to mollycoddle him.

"Serafino and I will take the shuttle in," she announced without any preliminaries. "We both have considerable heavy-air time and he's got more freighter experience than any of us. And this thing, once we hit heavy air, is going to fly just like a ten-bay freighter."

That got his attention. His head jerked towards her and she was surprised to see the bleakness in his eyes. She'd expected anger, after what had happened in the cockpit. Or perhaps, even by this time, righteous indignance. He and Serafino were always engaged in some game of one-upmanship, it seemed. Though over what exactly she'd yet to fathom.

So the bleakness, the surrender she saw made no sense. Though his question did shed some light on the subject.

"You think I'm losing my mind, don't you?"

She thought of the way he'd lunged at Serafino and how he'd done almost exactly the same thing during their interrogation back on the *Vax*—was it only days ago? She'd physically intervened then. Later, he'd admitted to her he'd lost control. Not the usual admission for a highly trained officer.

And definitely not the usual admission for a highly trained 'cybe.

And it had happened again. The thought that he might need a tune-up had crossed her mind.

"Serafino pushes your buttons," she said. "And you, no doubt, also push his. We're all stuck in a rather small shuttle with very little fuel left. Whether or not you're losing your mind is the least of my worries."

"Then why did you decide to have Serafino assist without consulting me?"

She shrugged. "Because I knew you wouldn't agree. And we don't have time to argue."

"Am I arguing now?"

His tone was too bland, too calm. It had her worried. But, as she'd pointed out to him, she didn't have time to worry right now.

"No," she said.

"Do you think I don't trust you?" he asked quietly.

She'd thought that for quite some time. Until she'd read those damned personal logs of his. Logs she'd been trying hard to forget every time she caught him looking at her with that almost pleading look in his eyes.

Like now.

She picked at some non-existent lint on her sleeve. "I think there have been a lot of misunderstandings on both our parts. You and I, we operate from different command methodologies." She looked back at him. "I didn't ask Serafino to fly right seat to undermine you, Kel-Paten. He *has* the heavy air experience and we don't. It's not like we're going to get a second chance at putting this bucket down."

"You made a wise decision," he told her softly.

She tried unsuccessfully to keep the look of surprise from her face. "Thank you."

"If the engines do start to blow, I can do a lot more good hands-on with them than I could in the cockpit," he continued.

Being down in the engine compartment below the main cabin would also put the necessary space between himself and Serafino. "You don't sound overly optimistic."

"I'm not," he admitted. "You saw the same damage I did. The *Galaxus* is a deep space craft, not made to deal with the effects of gravity. When we hit the planet's atmosphere we could encounter additional problems."

Sass understood now what was so odd about Kel-Paten. It was as if he'd deleted that part of him that was human. His responses, his phrasing was automatic, mechanical. And, save for the still humanly strained look in his pale eyes, he was all 'cybe. Unemotional. Reporting the facts.

We are probably going to die. Oh well. I'll be below decks if you need me.

Swell.

"Are we talking total engine failure here?" she asked.

"Do you want probabilities?"

She had to keep herself from raising her eyes to the mythical Five Heavens. He was definitely into a mechanical mode now. "Why not?" she replied grimly.

"There's a seventy-six point five percent chance of total engine failure. A forty-three point two percent chance we'll experience more than a fifty percent loss of power upon atmospheric entry. A—"

"Miracle, Kel-Paten," she cut in. "What's the percent probability for a miracle?"

He regarded her plainly. "I don't believe in miracles."

"I base my life on them," she challenged.

He seemed shaken by her statement, a small spark of human emotion flashing briefly in his eyes. "Do you?"

"Bet your ass I do." She stood, braced one hand on the back of his seat and looked down at him. "Any landing you can walk away from is a good one. We're all going to walk away from this one. I'll give you a one-hundred percent probability on that, flyboy."

She hadn't called him that in a long time. He closed his eyes but not before Sass saw the undisguised heat in them.

She straightened and stepped back. She was so used to interacting on a personal level with her friends, her crew. Sometimes she forgot and did the same thing with Kel-Paten. Only things weren't the same. He was a 'cybe. And he wanted her, in a way a 'cybe shouldn't.

She tossed a light parting comment over her shoulder as she returned to the cockpit. "When we land, you get to buy me a beer, Kel-Paten. And if we don't make it," she stopped at the hatchway and turned. "You still get to buy me a beer. In the hell of your choice."

"Ready to initiate entry procedures." Serafino called to her.

She took the seat he vacated, tried to forget the bleakness in Kel-Paten's pale eyes. And the exactness of his probabilities: seventy-six point five percent chance of a total engine failure.

Seventy-six point five percent chance that three hours from now, they'd all be dead.

And she'd be sipping hot beer in hell.

CHAPTER TWENTY-TWO

"Let's take her in, 'Fino."

Sass tapped a command into the console before her. The *Galaxus* responded, her sub-light engines cycling off and, with a slight jolt, the emergency heavy air engines kicked on.

She coordinated landing data with Serafino. Eden had designated a southern area of the largest landmass as the most likely and most amenable area for them to put down. The CMO's scans had shown a sizeable fresh water supply, lush vegetation and more important, it was adjacent to a mountain range that contained a possible fuel source if they could mine and convert the natural ore. But that was a distant problem. Getting this bucket down was the immediate one.

"Engines at max," Serafino told her. She watched their speed and temperature carefully. Coming through the planet's atmosphere they could encounter any number of problems, not the least of which would be in response to the damage the vessel had already incurred.

She tapped open the mike on her headset. "Status, Kel-Paten."

"Holding our own," came back the reply from the engine compartment below deck.

"I'm keeping this line open," she told him. "First sign of any trouble, I repeat, any trouble, you talk to me, got it?"

"Affirmative."

The shuttle shimmied slightly. Sass glanced over at Serafino. "We're getting some vibrational feedback from the deep space shields."

"Ummm." He keyed in a few adjustments. "I don't want to reduce them more than that. Not yet."

She noted his changes. "Agreed."

"ETA fifteen minutes thirty-four seconds," Eden said from her post at navigation.

"Fifteen thirty-four," Sass repeated. "You hear that, Kel-Paten?"

"Affirmative."

"Talk to me about the drop in coolant level," she continued.

"I'm on it."

She knew that; knew he saw what she saw in the cockpit. What she wanted to know was how serious it was.

"What's our rate?"

"Moderate," came back the reply.

"Moderate, my ass. I need numbers!" Next to her, Serafino adjusted the craft's attitude as the shimmying had started again.

"Your job is to bring this thing in, Sebastian. I'll keep the engines on line."

"You can be very annoying sometimes, Kel-Paten, you know that?"

"Thank you."

Serafino raised one eyebrow. "Sometimes?" he said loudly enough for her headset mike to pick up.

"Fuck you, Serafino," Kel-Paten's deep voice growled over the speaker.

"You're not my type, Tin Soldier," Serafino shot back.

"Enough, boys!" Eden voiced her displeasure before Sass could.

The black starfield outside the forward viewport had been replaced by a deeper blue, then a lighter blue as the shuttle hurtled through Haven-One's atmosphere. Hull temperature had increased; not critically but worth watching. Serafino worked the shields, but Sass could tell by the frown on his face that they weren't responding as he would have liked.

"Thing flies like a rock," he muttered when for the third time in less than a minute the shuttle had shimmied almost out of control, her engines straining audibly.

"Worse than a ten bay freighter," Sass agreed. She needed to be able to buffer their descent with the thrusters. But given the damage they'd received, she didn't dare bring them on line until she absolutely had to.

Gravity exerted a more potent pull on the shuttle, warning messages flaring correspondingly.

"We have to reduce those shields," Sass told Serafino.

"I don't like this, but..." He made the adjustments.

"I know. Eden?"

"Twenty-two minutes, fifteen," Eden replied wiped her hand over her brow. The interior temperature of the shuttle had increased dramatically in the past few minutes and would get worse as the shields came off line.

But it had to be. The *Galaxus* wasn't a heavy-air craft. The only way the ship would be able to negotiate in that foreign environment would be to reduce power to the shields and siphon it to the engines and thrusters.

Suddenly, the grating whine of the engines crested, then died. The shuttle veered sharply to port.

Sass held on with one hand and frantically keyed in adjustments with the other.

"Kel-Paten! Talk to me!"

The response that came back was strained. "We've got...thruster failure...feed lines one and two out...doing what...I can."

"Shit!" she said. "'Fino?"

He was already rerouting the remaining power feeds. "It may not be the smoothest of entries," he said through gritted teeth.

"Seventeen minutes, ten!" Eden told them over the ship's rattling and groaning.

They broke through into the cloud layer, the brightness almost blinding.

"We're coming in way too hot!" Sass tried to alter the angle of their descent with no success.

"Braking vanes will shear off at this speed," Serafino noted tersely.

As if in response, the shuttle shuddered violently again, prompting a flurry of activity in the cockpit. Sass watched the readouts with a critical eye. She had no doubt they were pushing the shuttle to its design limits. She was surprised there hadn't been more systems shutdowns than the ones already...

Then she knew. She knew what was keeping them together at this point.

"Fifteen minutes even," Eden said.

"Damn him! Bloody fool's spiked himself into the ship's systems!" Sass thrust herself to her feet, ripping the headset off and throwing it into her chair. "'Fino, you have the con. Just do what you can!" She bolted through the cockpit hatchway and ran towards the rear of the craft.

Sass scrambled down the ladderway into the engine compartment, one look confirming what she'd guessed. Kel-Paten sat on the floor next to the dismantled main engine panel, datalinks snaking from the panel to the small ports in his left hand. His head was bowed, his breathing ragged.

She hunkered next to him and grabbed his forearm. "What in hell do you think you're doing? Spike out, now!"

His face, when he turned to her, was covered with a sheen of sweat, his eyes a bright luminous blue. "Desperate...times." His voice was thin, raspy.

"Spike out, Kel-Paten. Or I'll rip those things right out of you!" she said harshly.

"Feed links...are blown. No other...way."

"Damn it, this'll kill you!" She shook his arm. "Spike out!"

"No...links..."

"Forget the links!"

"...No."

"I don't have time to argue." She reached for the datalines. His right hand clasped her wrist.

"No. Sass..." His voice was barely above a whisper and the hand that held her wrist trembled.

She stared at him. He was going to kill himself. She knew that, knew the energy requirements of slowing and landing the shuttle would take every bit of life from him. He was willing to do that.

She wasn't willing to let him. And there was no time to argue.

He was choosing to die. She had to make him want to choose to live.

She kissed him, with a passion born of desperation and fear and anger, taking advantage of his gasp of surprise to let her tongue probe his mouth, then raked his lower lip with her teeth. As she withdrew he leaned towards her, wanting more, needing more, his mouth still against hers.

He'd released her wrist. She placed her hands on either side of his face. His luminous eyes blazed like a white-hot flame.

"Spike out," she told him softly, her thumb against his lips, stilling his attempt to claim her mouth again. "You're no use to me dead."

He closed his eyes briefly, cycled into a shutdown. He pulled out the datalinks before she could. She wrenched him to his feet.

"Move it, Kel-Paten!" she barked and shoved him towards the compartment hatchway.

He hesitated at the foot of the maintenance ladder, a questioning look on his face as she stepped in front of him.

"Sass—" he started.

The ship bucked, hard. She fell against him, then he was shoving her up the ladderway, swearing, his voice still raspy.

She clambered back into her seat, raking the safety straps across her chest, as Serafino fought to control the bucking shuttle that seemed to want to do nothing more than drop like a rock out of the skies.

Kel-Paten, at the station behind her, manually adjusted what he could of the failing engines. She hadn't looked at him since she'd returned to the cockpit; his one glance at her at the foot of the maintenance stairs had told her she was playing a dangerous game here. But she'd read his personal logs and if manipulating his feelings for her had saved his life, so be it. He could be pissed at her all he wanted, later.

If they survived.

Sharing a beer in hell was beginning to look more and more like a realistic possibility.

"Fifteen hundred feet...twelve hundred feet...one thousand..." Serafino read out their descent as he manipulated the controls.

"Eight hundred. We're still coming in hot," he said.

"Got to chance the braking vanes," Sass told him.

"Try a steep bank first." This from Kel-Paten.

"Hard to port," Sass said and the shuttle's frame groaned under the pull of gravity.

"Five fifty," Serafino said. "Starting landing sequence."

"Extending vanes," Sass noted a lot more calmly than she felt. A lot more calmly that the shuttle reacted.

"Heading corrected," Eden said for the third time as the craft slipped out of control.

"Hope you found us someplace soft!" Sass managed a tense grin.

"Like a baby's bottom," Eden replied.

The forward viewport filled with deep greens and browns of a forest and a long expanse of meadow below.

The meadow. They had to make the meadow. The engines—

—died.

"Brace for impact!" Sass grabbed her armrests just as the shuttle carved a deep furrow into the soft, green carpeted ground.

REGNAND'S FARM

The loud rumbling and subsequent thunderous boom didn't go unnoticed by Farmer Regnand, who turned from his cattle stall at the first and jumped noticeably at the second. Gray, weathered eyes searched the skies—it was but midday and not the season for storms.

Then he saw it, something silvery and fiery at the same time, streaking through the white clouds and behind the mountaintop. It was there only for a few seconds and had it been night, he would have thought it to be one of those falling stars.

But it wasn't night. And somehow he knew it wasn't a star.

The soft mooing of his cows brought his mind back to more immediate concerns. Still later, sharing a plate of stew and fresh baked bread with his plump wife, he mentioned what he'd seen and heard.

She shook her head solemnly. "'Tis him, the Wizard, then. He be doin' his dark magic."

Silently, Regnand agreed and a morsel of bread stuck in his dry throat. He washed it down with a draught of cold, bitter ale.

If it were the Wizard, then things were not good. They were not good at all.

CHAPTER TWENTY-THREE

HAVEN-ONE

"Helluva baby's bottom," Sass rasped, untangling herself from the shredded safety straps.

Tank and Reilly stared wide-eyed at her from their safety kennel under her station. She shoved herself out of her seat and flipped open the kennel's latch. Behind her, she heard Eden's responding chuckle as the furzels bounded out, tails fluffed and flicking.

Gods' blessed rumps, they'd made it!

Four forms surged to their feet, groaning and swearing and in between all that making sure the shuttle's systems were safely locked in full shutdown.

"Main feed off line," Kel-Paten said.

"Off line. Secondary off line," Serafino responded hoarsely.

"Initiating final shutdown!" Sass leaned over the pilot's con, gently pushed a murruping Tank out of the way, and tabbed at the last of the pads. Shutdown completed, all systems on safety. She spun about and grabbed Eden around the waist and hugged her hard. "We did it, we did it!"

There was a loud whoop and Eden was dragged from Sass's embrace into Jace's arms.

"Son of a bitch!" Serafino shouted. "Damn, but we're good!"

Laughing, Sass slapped him on the back, shared a congratulatory handclasp with Eden again before turning.

And bumped directly into Kel-Paten's broad chest. Her right hand caught him on the shoulder and as she stumbled against him, his arms snaked about her waist. He held her there, his pale gaze locked onto her.

Her laughter subsided into a hiccup. Her hand slid down his shirt, coming to rest on the lightning slashed emblem of the *Vaxxar*. She patted it absently, drawing a breath. "Looks like we made it." She gave him a nervous smile and tried to step back.

But he had no intention of releasing her.

Behind her, she could hear Eden's throaty giggle and caught a few words of Serafino's recounting of their rather unceremonious descent and landing. Those two were caught in their own world of relief and rejoicing; unaware at the moment of Kel-Paten's hold on her, or of the heat in his eyes as he looked at her.

Of course, they had no idea she'd kissed him earlier. Nor how much she was regretting her unorthodox methods right now. Clearly that was an avenue he wanted to pursue; his private 'love letters' to her assured her of that much.

As did the way his hands slowly made their way up her back, caressing, pressing her closer to the hard heat of his body.

"I think we should check for structural damage," Sass said quickly. This time when she stepped back he loosened his grasp slightly, enough to put some space between them. She used that space to try to turn away. He caught her by the wrist. She looked up at him.

"Sass, when you found me in the engine compartment—"

"Desperate times, desperate measures," she told him quietly, echoing his own excuse for his actions earlier.

He gave a short sigh of frustration before releasing her.

She retrieved a tool kit from storage locker, looking to escape the results of something she admitted she'd started.

And had no intention of finishing.

She wasn't allowed to get away. Kel-Paten plucked the stress analyzer from her hand as she stepped through the hatchway into the main cabin. "You'll need some help."

"Sure." *Business. Let's keep this strictly business.* She followed him to the rear airlock that led outdoors and prayed he wouldn't ask further about desperate times, and desperate measures. Or how she'd known such measures would work.

She damned the day she'd ever seen those damned love letters.

The *Galaxus* was in surprisingly good shape, considering the 'gear up' landing she'd just been through not even an hour before. Sass watched the data cascade down her scancorder, confirmed her readings with Kel-Paten then marched up to the airlock to shout instructions to Serafino in the cockpit. The communications system was one of the things that had gone inexplicably offline when they crashed.

Landed, she reminded herself. She was still walking. They'd *landed*.

"Let me see your 'corder." Kel-Paten held out one black-gloved hand towards her. She trotted down the stairs, puzzled, but handed it to him.

Unexpectedly, he turned away from the shuttle. "We've a significant ore source not far from here."

She glanced over his arm. Not far if they'd had a hovercar or two. A long walk, though.

"Some possible secondary deposits closer." She pointed to a highlighted area on the screen.

"I saw that before, but the next reading showed it in error." It was his turn to frown. "We probably should've recalibrated these units to this world before using them."

Energy fluctuations danced across the screen.

"Ummm," she said out loud and thought of Serafino's words: an unknown, malevolent energy source. Beckoning them.

Playing hide and seek, from the looks of things.

Or else it was only what Kel-Paten said: they should've recalibrated the units before coming out here. Each world had its own signature. Unfortunately, they had no Alliance issue datapack on this one.

"It'll take me about an hour to set up a recalibration." Kel-Paten almost echoed her thoughts. "We'll worry about that mountain range later." He flipped his unit back to close range and turned to the shuttle.

Sass stared at the distant mountains for a few seconds longer. They looked lush, green, peaceful. Certainly nothing to worry about.

A small energy spike flared on her screen, then disappeared.

Calibration incompatibilities. That's all it was. They'd fix that…later.

Jace Serafino put his hands on his hips and surveyed his surroundings—this was paradise, though he had a feeling neither Sass nor the Tin Soldier would agree. He pushed aside that odd, discordant sensation, that energy source; his serpent in paradise? It seemed quiet, tame at the moment. What he saw was more vivid. Lush green forest ringed the long meadow that had served as their landing strip. Over the treetops, the deep purple of a mountain range could be seen. A range that contained, according to Eden's science scans, sufficient raw crystalline ore to power the shuttle.

In the opposite direction was a large, placid, clear blue lake. He and Eden, hand in hand, with furzels behind them, had already been there, following the readings on her 'corder. It was a fresh water lake, no doubt filled by runoffs from the mountains. Eden had been testing a water sample through her unit when he'd taken a deep draught of it from his cupped hands.

She'd shrieked, admonishing him about potential poisons and he'd only laughed and splashed water back at her. Which had required, of course, that she kick water at him.

And so, splattered and damp, they'd returned to the shuttle. Eden had gone inside to find dry clothes from the jumble of luggage they had been able to retrieve from the storage compartments.

Serafino removed his damp shirt and threw it carelessly over a nearby small bush to dry. The warmth of the sun felt good on his skin and he closed his eyes, leaning his head back and let the heat soak into his tired body.

No, no evil serpents now. Maybe he'd misread. That damned implant might be disconnected, but it was still there.

Hearing soft footsteps on the ground behind him, he turned, his long hair swinging over his shoulder. He caught the bright gleam in her blue eyes and grinned. Damn, but she was beautiful! The way the sunlight played through her honey colored hair, wisps of which now brushed her cheeks and lips as she walked. He envied those wisps, wanted to kiss every place they touched...

A breeze caught the light fabric of her tunic, outlining the soft curves of her body, the fullness of her breasts and the sweet lushness of her thighs. A sweetness he very shortly intended to explore.

"Its...kind of a mess down there," she said, stepping up before him.

Down there? Well, yes, his thoughts were definitely 'down there' though he doubted they were talking at the moment about quite the same location.

"Hmmm?" He transformed his desire for her into a sparkling, tingly mental shower that he rained on and through her mind.

"Oh!" Her bright blue eyes shot wide open in response.

He laughed and, grabbing her by the waist, spun her around. "You're right," he told her. "I am incorrigible. And it's all your fault. Now tell me, what's the problem?"

She blinked a few times. "The problem—? Oh, yes. The luggage. When we decided to plow the field here, we did so with the storage compartments. The luggage is basically intact but, well, all over the place." She motioned with her hands. "Shirts here, shoes there. Tank and Reilly are having a wonderful time, crawling under and through everything."

"Glad someone's enjoying it." He drew her closer to him, planted a kiss on her head and watched the movement of two forms on the far side of the shuttle. Sass and the Tin Soldier, discussing repairs that needed to be done. Useless, he knew, unless they could convert the fuel ore. Far more important, in his estimation, was his and Eden's project: survival here on Haven-One.

"I gather we're in charge of dinner," he continued. "Replicator's functioning?"

She smiled. "Yes, but better than that," and she wriggled away from him and drew out her scancorder, "we have fresh vegetables!" She pointed the unit somewhere behind him. "I saw the readings earlier. Looks like fruit *and* vegetables. Not furzel fare, of course, but I think they'll find what they want. But for us, at least, something with some real flavor."

"No meat?" He wrinkled his nose in mock disgust.

"That's your job, O Great Hunter!" she teased back. "Just keep in mind that I do not pluck, skin or gut."

He took her hand. "But you do dig! C'mon, then. We'll start with the salad course and go from there."

<^>

It had been a satisfying, if not interesting, first meal. Sass left Eden to categorize some of the unused vegetables into the bio-logs and found Kel-Paten outside the shuttle, pulling on his dark flight jacket. She frowned but knew he hadn't seen her in the darkness, so she put her question into words.

"Going somewhere?"

He turned abruptly at the sound of her voice. "I thought it would be a good idea to scope out our surroundings."

He started towards the dark edge of the forest and she caught up with him. "Eden's scans showed the closest settlement to be almost ten miles away. You intending to take a long hike?"

"I'd rather see than be seen."

"You'll run smack into a tree, Kel-Paten. You're not used to this terrain," she said then noticed the luminous glow in his eyes. He was on cybe-power. Night scope. *Well, that'll really give a warm and friendly feeling to the natives,* she thought. *Demon from hell invades local village at night.*

"C'mon." She waved her arm in the opposite direction. "I have a better idea."

She'd seen the equinnards—some cultures called them horses—

earlier in her trek, while Eden had worked on dinner and Serafino and the admiral had tinkered with the ship's systems. They were obviously wild yet not skittish of humans—at least they weren't when she'd held handfuls of sweetgrass out to them.

How they'd view a bio-cybe, she had no idea. But sweetgrass was known to work wonders.

As were companion animals. Tank had trotted up alongside her as she led Kel-Paten to the base of the mountain range, just a short distance from the shuttle.

She picked him up, massaged his furry ears and prayed he wouldn't fart. That wouldn't go over well with *any* species.

The small herd of equinnards looked large and shadowy in the pale light of the rising moons. She softly clucked her tongue at them and, setting Tank down, grabbed a handful of sweetgrass from under a nearby bush.

A hushed snorting sound came from the herd.

"Here, Prancer boy. Here, Prancer. Good boy. Come here. Come see what Sassy has for you." She held the sweetgrass stalks flat in her hand.

Kel-Paten came up behind her but she stuck out her arm and stopped his progress while he was still a few feet away. "Wait," she told him quietly. "They can't take too many new people at a time. Let Tank talk to them first."

The small furzel had already made his way towards the herd, looking cautiously up at the giant animals. One gray stallion lowered his head, snuffling the fidget. Tank raised his mottled pink and black nose and snuffled back, purring.

"S'okay. S'okay," Sass crooned, walking towards them both. She lay her hand on the gray stallion's side, then stroked his long head as he munched the sweetgrass. After a few minutes, she waved to Kel-Paten.

"C'mere. This is Prancer. I think you two ought to be introduced."

The only equinnards he'd ever ridden had been on simdecks. Digitally reproduced forms, they'd responded to whatever program had been requested and none he'd ever tried had felt as large and foreign as the one on which Kel-Paten sat now.

Prancer. Thumper was more like it. He had a feeling there might be an even worse name come morning, when his rear end fought back with a description or two of its own.

As usual, Sass seemed immediately comfortable seated on her own smaller equinnard, a cream colored animal with large dark brown eyes. 'Bailey', she'd called her, after the sweet liquor the same color as the beast. He watched her post as they traveled through the thick forest; moving up and down in time to the rhythm of the beast's movement. There was something inherently sexual about it and if he hadn't been so damned uncomfortable at the moment, he probably would've let his mind wander into a more than pleasant fantasy.

It took all his attention just to keep Prancer under control. With no saddle and no reins, the equinnard wanted to run. He could feel the animal's muscles ripple with tension under his legs.

They came to a small clearing and Sass slowed as he did, seeing the dim glow of lights in the distance.

"Land ho," she said softly.

He nodded. "Dr. Fynn said it was a small settlement, about one hundred or so life forms."

"Eden," she told him, not without a small note of irritation. "She has a first name, you know. It's Eden. I think we can start to dispense with some of the formalities here, Kel-Paten."

"So do I," he replied and when she looked at him he continued: "Have a first name."

"You *are* Kel-Paten. You always will be Kel-Paten," she said, overriding any further comment from him. "The only thing we may have to drop here is 'admiral'. It might create too many questions right now."

She nudged Bailey forward.

"Is it Sebastian or Sass, then?" he asked, coming alongside her.

She gave him an enigmatic smile. "Sass. It's always been Sass. There is no Sebastian." She kicked at Bailey's sides before he could question her further.

They emerged from the forest onto a wide graveled road, rutted from the wheels of many wagons. Or what he had to assume would be wagons as Dr. Fynn's—*Eden's* scans had shown only a low level of technology on Haven-One.

The small town twinkled brightly, candles flickering from first and second story windows. Only in one or two instances did there seem to be a third story

"Is that a watch tower?" she asked.

He turned his enhanced vision on the object of her scrutiny. "Not a watch tower," he said after a moment. They were closer to the town and the clop-clopping of the equinnards' hooves were answered by other sounds coming from the source of the flickering lights: metal and wood clanking, like doors slamming. Voices, muffled but carrying in the night.

Other animal noises, the low mooing of lubas, the high whinny of stabled equinnards.

He saw movement in Sass's lap as Tank perked up his ears and sniffed the air. He caught the scent, too. Food. Meat grilling.

"Behave," he heard her tell the fidget.

He fought the urge to warn her in a similar fashion.

They passed through a wide wooden gate without attracting any notice.

VILLAGE OUTER ROAD

Torches set in metal-wrapped sconces jutted out from the brick and plaster walls of the commercial establishments of the village, illuminating wooden signs colorfully decorated in a manner befitting the trade: an anvil and iron for the blacksmith; a table laden with food and drink for the pub and eatery; and a bosomy female, flat on her back, skirts hiked around an impossibly narrow waist...

Sass chuckled at that one when Kel-Paten averted his eyes.

"It's the galaxy's oldest profession," she reminded him.

"I'd heard second oldest, politicians being first," he replied. "And not dissimilar."

"Umm. I heard there was no love lost between you and the Defense Minister."

Actually, it was more like a deep-seated hatred, from what U-CID had discerned shortly before the signing of the peace treaty. Sass knew that at times it was only the Prime Councilor's strong support of Kel-Paten that had kept him out of serious conflict.

But that was, for now, not even worth thinking about. They were the-Gods-only-knew how many light-years away from the Kel Triad, or U-Cee space, or anywhere familiar. Kel-Paten seemed to realize that, too, as he responded to her comment.

"I'm sure he's rejoicing over my disappearance," he said, referring to the minister. "Not that it matters, here and now. What matters," he said, guiding Prancer towards an empty railing near a large fountain, "is finding out a bit more *about* our here and now."

He swung one leg over the stallion's wide back and dismounted gracefully, but she caught a slight wince. Not used to riding, evidently. She hadn't been either, until Lethant.

She started her dismount but he held up one hand, stopping her.

"With all due respect, Sebastian, I think it best if you wait here for now. From what I've seen, you're not quite properly attired for the

typical female. I need answers more than I need questions at this point."
He patted Bailey's neck gently. "I'm going to ask a few questions in the
pub across the square. Try to stay out of trouble, okay?"

He turned, the rapidity of his movement and the surrounding darkness
affording substantial cover for her response, which amounted to her
sticking her tongue out at his retreating back.

But he was right. She'd seen a few women entering and exiting some
of the residences and all were in long skirts and shawls. Her black flight
pants, boots and fitted shirt were certainly not the current mode of
fashion. Nor was her short cropped pale hair.

She remembered what she and Eden were supposed to have been
doing by this time—besides getting Serafino free of trouble, that is. The
Fair, the Olde Legend Fair. All those costumes they'd painstakingly
recreated from the simdeck programs. The long, full skirts. The
embroidered full sleeved blouses. The colorful shawls and wide-brimmed
flowered bonnets. Clothes, it seemed, would not be a problem. She'd
have to inform Kel-Paten of that as soon as—

An anguished terrifying scream split the air, halting her thoughts.

She flung herself off her equinnard and charged blindly into the dark,
narrow alleyway, only a few feet behind her.

CHAPTER TWENTY-FOUR

VILLAGE ALLEYWAY

The bloodcurdling notes faded as abruptly as they'd started. But Sass heard other sounds, grunts and thuds. Sounds more masculine than the scream.

The alley zigged to the left. Sass skittered to a halt at the corner and felt something small and soft thump into her leg. A quick glance confirmed the fidget had followed her. Sass was more interested in what the dim light of the moons revealed ahead. An older woman, her bonnet askew, clutching her torn shawl as two burly men shoved her to the cobblestoned ground. A basket of wrapped breads lay nearby, upended and trampled. One of the men, in a thick and drunken voice, made reference to the old woman's wares as he tried to force her legs apart.

"Yer gort somethin' hot 'n fresh fer me, biddie, do ye?"

The old woman screamed again and tried to push him away. Sass grabbed a handful of rough woven shirt.

The shorter man jerked around. "Wot this?"

Sass's fist connected with his jaw, soundly. The short man staggered sideways, bumping into a taller, thinner man, equally as drunk and equally as surprised at her appearance. The tall man pushed his friend back in her direction.

Sass brought her clasped fists down hard against the back of the man's neck and with a loud grunt, he collapsed to the ground. His weight pinned the legs of the old woman, who screamed hysterically again.

"Hey!" The taller man reared back, arm raised. Sass braced for the blow. But the arm halted in mid-air, its progress stopped by the black-gloved hand clamped on its wrist.

"Not a good idea," Kel-Paten told him calmly.

"Huh?" the man said, just before he was tossed against a nearby wall as easily as if he were a paper doll.

Sass tried to push the limp weight of the short drunk off the women's legs.

Kel-Paten grabbed the unconscious man by the collar of his shirt. "I think he'd like to join his friend." The man landed behind them with a loud, gurgling groan.

The old woman was crying, tugging her skirts down while at the same time grasping the shreds of her shawl around her.

"You're all right, you're safe," Sass crooned softly, her arm around the woman's shoulder. "Can you stand?"

The woman hiccuped softly and nodded. "Aye, thank ye...I thank ye, lass. I should, I should ne'er ha' come doon this walkway. But I was late, and M'Lord gits in sooch a state."

She struggled to her feet, with Kel-Paten holding one elbow and Sass the other. Her faded gray eyes looked from right to left and back to Sass on her right again.

"Ye be Warrior's Guild, ain't ye? Mistress, I am honored ye should coom to me aid. But I canna pay ye—"

Sass shook her head. "You don't owe me anything. You don't have to."

But the woman had already searched her pockets and pressed a small coin into Sass's hand.

"'Tis all I have, Mistress, but I honor the Guild, I do. Surely, I'd be a sight fer trouble wit'out ye." She sighed raggedly. "But should ye be hungry, ye coom to the baker's stall in the market, on the morrow or any day. I owe ye, I do. I—"

At the sound of footsteps in the alleyway she stopped. The footsteps became more hurried.

"Talla!" a young man's voice shouted. "We was worried, we—"

"'Tis all right, Edric," the old woman said. "Now." She fell into the younger man's arms, sobbing softly as she explained how she'd been attacked and then rescued by the two from the Warrior's Guild.

It was only after some cautious discussion that Sass and Kel-Paten figured out that 'Talla' was a title, much like Aunt (Talla's first name was Elgartha). And that Sass's garb, while unusual for village women, was indicative of women who were members of the Warrior's Guild, a small but respected collection of mercenaries.

Later, on Prancer and Bailey and heading back through the forest, additional coins pressed on them by Edric jangling in their pockets, Sass and Kel-Paten discussed what they'd learned in their few hours in the village.

Things were not well in LandsDown, as the small village nestled among the hills was called. Once a prosperous site, blessed by the stewardship of several noble families, LandsDown had experienced a series of inexplicable deaths and unsolved disappearances. Lord Crenmar had died suddenly, his daughter was missing. Sir Argo and Sir Raimund, both young men with bright futures, had also disappeared. There'd been bouts of crop failure and pestilence in the past six months since their disappearance—and over it all, rumors that a Wizard was at large.

"The Edict of Nonintervention," Kel-Paten reminded her, "forbids us getting involved with developing civilizations."

"That Edict," Sass replied, "is several hundred thousand or maybe even million light years away from here. Kel-Paten, we don't know how long we'll be here, or what the outcome is going to be. We're going to need the help of these people if we intend to be able to mine those mountains for fuel. Surely the least we can offer in return is a little assistance in finding out about this Wizard character."

"This is a low technology world—"

"I'm not talking about technology," Sass said as they passed along the edge of a bubbling stream in the darkness. "I'm talking about Serafino. And Eden. We have two telepaths—well, one full-fledged telepath and one empath with serious telepathic leanings. This Wizard shit sounds right up their alley."

"Serafino's alleys," Kel-Paten countered tersely, "have always been paved with the stones of self-aggrandizement. For obvious reasons, he's far less anxious than we are in getting the shuttle functional, in returning home."

And to resume the role of fugitive, Sass knew. If what he'd said about the Faction was true, she, Eden and even Kel-Paten were on the list of the hunted as well.

"How can we be sure," Kel-Paten continued, "that any information Serafino claims to find on this purported Wizard is factual? And not designed to establish a little kingdom for himself here?"

"Eden—"

"—has an obvious bias," he cut in.

Sass felt her jaw clench at Kel-Paten's insinuation that her friend's allegiance, and veracity, could be compromised. She'd known Eden Fynn a long time and they'd survived more than a few narrow escapes together.

"Eden," she started again, "is trustworthy."

"Eden," he answered, "is in love."

"And that makes her untrustworthy?" she shot back. Too late she remembered his secret letters to her.

"No," he said quietly. "But sometimes love can make a person do desperate things."

Like almost sacrificing his life to keep a damaged shuttle functioning. To save her life at the risk of his own.

"Not Eden," she said. She shoved her heels into Bailey's side and urged the equinnard forward. Tank murruped his complaint at the sudden movement. She ignored it, just as she ignored the inexplicable tightness around her heart.

GALAXUS

Friend? A mottled pink and black nose snuffled soft fur.

Reilly stretched, slitted one eye open and inspected the fat young fidget anxiously nosing his face.

Friend, he replied sleepily. *All...well?*

Yes! No!

Tell yes first.

Friend! Friend! New smells, new scents, friend. New! Tank paced back and forth. Reilly reached out one paw and playfully but firmly swatted Tank's hind leg.

Tank immediately sat.

Tell, commanded the older furzel.

Images flooded Reilly's mind. The equinnards. The forest, traveling on the equinnard's back. The denseness of the leaves. The stream. The village. A cacophony of sounds; a pungent texture of smells.

And then 'MommySass' running down the alleyway, Tank huffing and puffing to keep up with her.

Badmans. Badmans!

Reilly saw the confrontation and the arrival of 'Tinsoldier'. And the return trip through the darkened forest, cradled against the warmth of MommySass once again.

Foodsmells! Foodsmells! Tank excitedly returned again to what he'd sensed in the village: cooking meats, thick stews, salty pickles. Port Bangkok born and bred, the stray fidget much preferred 'man cooking' to 'ship cooking'. Replicator-created meals just didn't seem as good.

Reilly's own pink mouth watered as they shared the memory. He, too, preferred when MommyEden cooked things fresh from the hydroponics garden. He'd been long enough in her sheltered and loving care to find his recent meal of griztard and bug not quite to his liking.

Badmans is only badthing? Tank had said things were well and not well when he'd awakened Reilly. But his shared memory of the confrontation in the alley didn't match the disquiet he still sensed from the fidget.

Badmans silly. Not good is Bad Thing. Bad Thing. The fidget's tufted ears flattened against his head.

Bad Thing. Reilly had sensed the Bad Thing too, while still on the Big Ship with MommyEden. He listened for something deep and distant, his whiskers quivering.

Yes, Bad Thing. Bad Thing was here. Like a color-changing griztard, camouflaged in deep foliage, Bad Thing was here but not here. Seen but not seen. Heard but not heard. To look directly at Bad Thing was not to see it at all.

Protect. Protect MommyEden. Protect Sass.

The fidget's ears lifted slightly.

Protect.

He flexed his front claws, raking them against the shuttle's hard floor.

GALAXUS AFT CABIN

"Well, what do you think?" Eden twirled around in front of Sass, who inspected her from her seat in the rear of the cabin. "Will I fit in?"

Sass watched the full skirt billow out as her friend moved gracefully, revealing a layer of lace underneath. 'Fitting in' was critical, not only to survive, but to gather information on this Wizard plaguing LandsDown. A mission Kel-Paten finally agreed was necessary as well.

"From what I saw, it's perfect. Except for the military-issue boots, that is!" She laughed. "Maybe you could wrap some lace ribbons around them."

Eden sighed. "If anyone questions, I don't know. I'll say they're riding boots, I guess."

"Just keep those top two buttons undone on that blouse, Doc, and they won't be looking any farther than your cleavage, I promise!"

Eden glanced quickly down where the small pearl buttons had popped through the thin holes again. "Oh, damn!"

"At least the vest will keep the rest of your charms from spilling out!" Sass grinned. "Keep it laced or you might be in a whole new business when we get to town."

"The Humping Healer?" Eden suggested in a sultry tone.

"Now that would be an interesting sign to see hanging outside a doorway there." Sass pulled herself out of the softness of the seat with a small groan. "Gods, been a while since I've been on an equinnard. I've got aches in places I didn't even know I had places!"

"I'd recommend a long hot bath but that's not possible right now; at least, if there's a tub on this tub," Eden teased, "I've not seen it."

"No, no tub on this tub. No booze, either. Damn! That would help too, you know." Sass rubbed absently at her behind. "Couple of nice pubs in LandsDown."

"They allow women in them?"

Sass walked over to the bulkhead and, leaning her hands against it, proceeded to try to stretch the cramps out of the backs of her legs. "No, but yes," she said, pushing against the wall. "No, not unescorted. But with your trusty escort from the Warrior's Guild," and she shot a smile over her shoulder at Eden, "you can go just about anywhere."

"My trusty escort, eh? Does that mean I'll be giving you orders, captain?"

"Damn! Didn't think of that." Sass chuckled. "Be easy on me, Doc. I'm not used to following orders, you know."

<^>

Kel-Paten had been standing in the hatchway of the main cabin and caught the last few sentences in the exchange between the two friends. He also used the time to admire the length of black clad leg Sass showed, and the firm roundness of her behind. He'd been quiet up until that point, but at her last comment about her disinclination to follow orders, he felt compelled to reply. "That is an unquestioned fact."

Eden twirled, a blur of pale blue satin and white lace. Sass only peered from under one outstretched arm. "Thank you very much, Kel-Paten, for your vote of confidence."

"I'm sure it's not something the Doctor doesn't know," he replied. He ran his gaze over Eden, who was adjusting the small buttons on her blouse again. "Remarkably appropriate," he told her. "Though most of the women also have capes. Did you pack something like that as well?"

Eden shook her head. "A cape would have been hot and cumbersome on Station. Looks like we'll have to do some shopping in town to update our wardrobes."

They fell into a discussion of their further needs in order to appear authentic, as well as the problem of what they would use for money. The small amount Sass had received from the old woman wasn't going to go very far. Kel-Paten hadn't yet been able to coax the ship's replicator into duplicating the local coinage.

Serafino joined them at this point, grumbling about what still needed to be repaired on the shuttle, and immediately agreed that funds had to be a top priority.

"Fortunately, we're dealing with a society that also accepts barter, or trades," he said. "Granted, Sass here or Kel-Paten can claim membership in the Warrior's Guild. But unless there's a fight you can break up every hour on the hour, I don't see that as a reliable source of income in a village as small as you say it is.

"But Eden, as a healer and an herbalist, that's different," he continued, lightly stroking the back of Eden's head. "There's probably a lot more ills than ill will," he said with a grin. "With a little help from some discreetly hidden medicorders, we might just be able to pull off some medical miracles."

"And the problems with this Wizard?" Sass asked him.

"I've been poking around a little, telepathically, while I worked on the shuttle's systems," Serafino explained. "There's something out there. Quite possibly what I sensed before we arrived. I can't really tell more right now without letting it know I'm here, too. But yes, it's something I think I can deal with."

Kel-Paten had been leaning against the back of Sass's seat during the entire discussion. This Wizard could be nothing more than coincidence fueled by superstition. But assigning Eden and Serafino to the problem kept Sass on his own team, so to speak. Still, as Serafino talked about the possible problem with the entity called the Wizard, he let the skepticism—and distrust—he felt show clearly on his face.

Neither Sass nor Eden, because of where they were seated, noticed. But he'd forgotten about Serafino's talents until a memory, deeply buried, surfaced unbidden in his mind. It was a memory of himself as an adolescent, still gangly and unsure with his new cybernetic limbs. Awkward. Ashamed.

Who's going to patch you up out here if we get into a real battle, Tin Soldier? Serafino asked. *Spare parts from the shuttle?*

Kel-Paten straightened abruptly, anger flooding his body before he got himself under control. He couldn't let Serafino goad him like that. After all, the man had only voiced—albeit mentally—what he himself had had to consider when they came dirtside: he was out of his element here. Any injuries to Sass (Gods forbid!) or Eden or Serafino could be handled in a normal human fashion, most likely by Eden.

Damage to his cybernetic systems was out of anyone's expertise, except for maybe Sass's. He didn't want her to know that side of him intimately.

He appeared full human, knew he looked full human. As long as he maintained that appearance, as long as she never saw the layers of plasteel under his synthedermetic skin, he believed, given time, Sass would view him as human.

No, there would be, could be, no accidents on his part. And maybe for all the irritation Serafino caused, it was just as well that he was once again reminded of the fact.

He leaned his arms back down against the top of Sass's seat and gave Serafino his best deadly, cold half-smile.

Serafino only replied with a raised eyebrow, and slipped his arm around Eden's waist. "It's getting late, milady Eden."

"That it is," Kel-Paten replied. "Serafino, you have first watch. I'll relieve you in four hours." He didn't need Serafino's telepathy to know that the man had intended to spend the next few hours very intimately with Eden. His assigning Serafino first watch just short-circuited those plans. And sent a clear message to the Nasyry: Branden Kel-Paten was still in charge.

Serafino seemed unconcerned, accepting the assignment with a shrug. His voice sounded in Kel-Paten's mind as he stepped towards the hatchway: *You won't win, Tin Soldier.* An image of a beautiful dark-haired young woman accompanied his words.

Kel-Paten recognized her immediately: Bianca Serafino.

I know everything, Serafino's voice continued. *And I will not forget.*

CHAPTER TWENTY-FIVE

OUTSIDE THE *GALAXUS*

The night had not yet faded to dawn, but it wasn't far off. Eden automatically touched the laser pistol strapped to her hip as she finished her last inspection round of their campsite. Four hours earlier, she'd relieved the admiral, who'd relieved Jace. Now, she waited for Sass to arrive and take up the last quarter of the watch into daylight.

It had been a quiet watch, as expected. The data she'd been able to coax out of the working science scanners confirmed nothing overly large and dangerous in their corner of the land mass. The watch schedule had been set up more to warn of the curious than the carnivorous.

Eden had been scanning for something else, something Jace had felt and then later admitted he wasn't sure about.

He wasn't *unsure*, either. So she kept a close, but closed, mental watch as well.

That front, too, had been quiet.

Minutes later, she heard Sass's familiar feminine yet throaty tenor voice softly singing the refrain from an old tune. It was the captain's way of letting Eden know she was approaching; sneaking up on someone carrying a weapon was never a productive activity.

Eden joined her in the final refrain.

"All quiet?" Sass asked after they finished their impromptu duet.

Eden nodded. "Unless you count Reilly and Tank's murderous attack on a griztard colony about an hour ago, nothing to report."

"Is that what that was?" Sass groaned.

Eden frowned. "They didn't make any noise."

"No, but Tank came into my bunk a little while ago, proceeded to give himself a full bath and then farted. Bad! I think it's the griztards he's eating. You're going to have to have Serafino talk to Reilly about that."

Tank did have a particularly potent brand of fidget farts. Eden made some sympathetic noises before turning the remainder of the watch over to Sass. She'd reached the hatchway of the shuttle when a low whistle to her right floated through the darkness. She froze. Then a mental sensation of warmth and reassurance cascaded through her and she smiled.

Jace stepped away from the shadows of a tree and held out his hand. "My lady? I require a bit of your time. I've something to show you."

"Now? I was looking forward to about an hour's nap before diving into a cup of hot tea."

"You may prefer this instead. Come."

"Jace, it's still black as pitch out."

"Come."

She took his hand and followed him into the forest just as the first weak rays of light added a pale color to the sky. The denseness of the trees were still creating shadows so it wasn't until they were almost upon it that she saw the small grotto nestled against the side of the hill.

It was almost too beautiful—the lush green ferns surrounding the glass-like pool of water on which floated small white flowers in odd clusters. More flowers trailed down the rocks on her left and in the dim light she could only begin to guess at their colors. Purples, perhaps. Or deep blues.

Jace drew her against him, kissed her lightly and then pulled her down into a kneeling position beside the pool, guiding her hand into the water.

"Gods, it's warm!" Eden said, surprised. "It's—"

"An underground hot spring," Jace supplied.

"It's wonderful! Sass will—"

"Find it later, love." He grinned at her. "Right now it's for you and me."

Hadn't she just been talking to Sass about the missing luxury of a hot bath? Eden skimmed her hand across the surface. "If we had some towels and some soap, it would be perfect."

"Your wish is my command," he told her with a light kiss. "Go on in. I'll be right back."

His footsteps faded into the forest as Eden quickly stripped off her flightsuit, draping it over a low tree limb. The early morning air was damp and slightly chilled against her bare skin but as she slid into the silky, warm water of the pool she forgot that, forgot everything except how blessedly wonderful she felt.

The sky brightened, sending sparkles of golden light across the surface. She dipped her head below for a moment then resurfaced, and brushed her wet hair back from her face. The warmth of the water seemed to work deep into her shoulders and back and she felt her body relax as she moved with a light stroke to the other side of the pool, and a small rocky ledge ringed with flowers.

Purple. They were a brilliant purple and had the most wonderful scent...

She inhaled deeply and let out a long sigh.

A sudden splash made her turn, quickly. She caught a glimpse of a taut male body arching through the water, and then a dark head appeared.

Jace shook his head like a dog shedding water, sending droplets in an outward pattern. Then he ducked under again and when he resurfaced, he ran one hand through his long, dark hair, pulling it away from his face.

He grinned at her. "Well?"

"This is wonderful! Incredible!"

He swam over to her. "Take one of those and crush it in your hand."

Eden had been leaning with one arm against the low rocky ledge, her toes just barely brushing the sandy bottom of the pool. "One of the flowers?" she asked, motioning with her free hand.

"Umm-hmm. Crush it in your hand."

"Why?" They were so lovely. It seemed a waste.

"Because," he said and when she made no move to comply reached around her and grabbed a handful of purple blossoms, his body brushing against hers as he did so.

She could feel the lean muscle of him, the soft yet bristly hair on his chest, and drew an involuntary breath. He'd been her patient, then her friend and then something more. They'd kissed—oh, how they'd kissed! And he'd teased her and nibbled her neck...and she'd felt comfortable with him, so comfortable that she hadn't given a second thought to sharing this pool, naked with him.

Until now. Until the hardness of his body against hers spoke to something deep and primal inside of her. Until the look in his eyes suddenly contained more passion, more desire than she'd ever thought possible.

Taller than her, Jace stood on the sandy bottom of the pool, rubbing the crushed, fragrant blossoms between the palms of his hands. Their sweet aroma was intoxicating, tantalizing...

And then he touched her. His large hands, slick with the oil from the flowers, gently grasped her shoulders and his fingers began to knead the potent oil into her skin. His hands moved down her arms, massaging her muscles tenderly but insistently until he reached her hands and, clasping them in his own, brought them to his lips and kissed her fingers.

He pressed a handful of blossoms into her hands. She crushed them, releasing their scent, then threaded her perfumed fingers through the mat of dark hair on his chest and up over his shoulders til her arms wrapped around his neck, her body slippery against his.

He covered her mouth with his own, kissing her deeply, his tongue hot and probing as his own male hardness rubbed against her thigh. His hands worked their way up her back, his thumbs making small circles on her spine, and when she finally pulled her face away, he encircled her waist with one arm, using the water's buoyancy to hold her against him.

He'd taken another handful of crushed flowers. His free hand cupped her breast, slick and slippery, his fingers teasing her nipples into taut rosy peaks.

Eden sighed raggedly, arching against him and then his mouth was on her neck. He groaned her name, softly.

"Gods, woman, how I've wanted you..."

Eden found herself unable to reply but let her hands and lips speak for her, exploring him, tasting the salty sweetness of his skin.

His hands grasped her thighs, lifting her and yet pulling her closer. She knew instinctively what he wanted and responded by wrapping her legs around him.

His kisses were more passionate, more demanding. When he slid into her, hot and hard and throbbing, she could do little more than gasp into his mouth, a gasp that turned into a low sigh of pure pleasure.

They moved together in an ancient rhythm, sending small ripples outward through the clusters of pale flowers floating around them.

As dawn broke over the mountain horizon, Jace's own control broke and he thrust deep inside her, letting his passion explode in an intensity that left them both clinging to each other, wanting more yet feeling at that moment more was simply not definable.

"I'm sorry." His voice was husky. "I wanted the first time to be...better. But it's been so long. I wanted you so badly. Eden, I—"

She took his face in her hands and kissed him, silencing his useless apologies. She couldn't imagine a 'better'.

Then later, when he led her out of the water and proceeded to towel her down on the small beach, he taught her just how limited her imagination really was.

BACK AT THE SHUTTLE...

Sass, seated on the low metal step at the base of the shuttle's rampway, accepted the cup of hot coffee from the admiral with a nod. "Have you seen Eden or Serafino?"

"Isn't she napping? She usually—"

"Pops in for a quick nap after her shift, yes, I know. I checked about ten minutes ago to see if she wanted me to brew some tea as I was going to start the coffee anyway…and her bunk's empty. Not been slept in."

Kel-Paten sat down next to her, not too close, she noticed, but not too far away. "Are you worried?"

Sass shook her head. "If there was a problem, Reilly would know. Both furzels have come a long way since Serafino's worked with them." Which was true, though it hadn't done anything for Tank's propensity to fart.

"Perhaps we should—"

The sound of low laughter stopped Kel-Paten's words. There was a rustling of leaves and snapping of twigs and a moment later Jace and Eden emerged, hand in hand, out of the forest's edge and into the morning sunlight. Their faces were flushed, their hair was wet and both had wide grins on their faces.

"Oh-ho! Looks like mom and dad are waiting up for us, darlin'!" Jace drew Eden closer to him.

Eden blushed shyly. "We, ummm, there's this wonderful pool. A hot spring, actually, just about a mile or so from here. It's…quite nice." She looked up at Jace.

"Wonderful," he intoned.

"Very…relaxing," Eden added.

"Quite. Restorative, even."

"Therapeutic." She was starting to giggle.

"Energizing." Jace fought to keep a straight face.

"Okay! Okay!" Sass held up one hand. "If I need a thesaurus, I'll call on you two!" She swatted at Eden as she approached. "Go get some tea. We have a full day ahead of us. And get into costume, and out of that flightsuit."

Kel-Paten waited until the shuttle hatchdoor whooshed closed.

"I think she's already been out of that flightsuit," he stated evenly but not without a small note of derision in his voice.

Sass shot him a questioning glance. "This concerns you, admiral?" she asked. Then, before he could reply, she continued: "I mentioned it before. We have to forgo a lot of the military protocol here. It's just the four of us and HQ is the Gods only know how many parsecs away. Or quadrants away. Or systems away."

"I didn't mean it—"

"Didn't you? It's no secret to me, or anyone—you hate Serafino. As long as you held rank over him on board, that was fine with you. But like I said. We're not on board the *Vax* anymore. You can't dictate what Serafino, or even Eden, do with their personal time."

"Sebastian." Pause. Emotion flared briefly in pale blue eyes. "I never dictated what anyone did with their personal time. Not on the *Vax*. Not now."

Yeah, and fidget's don't fart, Sass thought, not even bothering to bring up all the instances where Kel-Paten had assigned her to this-that-or-the-other-thing just when she was due some R&R. Or while she was *on* R&R.

She downed the last of her coffee and stood. "I've got to change my clothes too," she told him then turned and walked quickly up the ramp.

<^>

He sat for a minute after she left, disturbed that she once again had defended Serafino (the fact that Sass had also defended her friend, Eden, was dismissed in his mind). And that she'd felt it necessary to give him a dressing-down, albeit a small one. Yet in one sense, if he allowed himself to try to read between the lines, it wasn't that bad. She seemed to be suggesting that they drop any hierarchy based on rank. That was fine with him—he really wanted to see the day she called him Branden and not 'admiral' or 'Kel-Paten'. He wanted her to see the man and not the legend.

It was all he'd really ever wanted since she'd come on board. Which was why he'd taken up so much of her time; even her off-duty time. Which, he knew, was what she'd alluded to a moment ago.

And not very happily.

He bit back a frustrated sigh. Every time he felt he might be getting somewhere with her, he'd find they'd only taken another step backwards.

Let's drop military rankings, she'd said, and then followed it with: *Let's not get personal.*

He didn't know how to do that. Military protocol and professional ethics were the only things that had kept him from grabbing her and kissing her senseless more than once.

A noise from behind him made him pull abruptly out of his thoughts and turn. What he saw almost made him fall over backwards.

Sass stood at the top of the rampway, clad in tight black leather pants that laced provocatively up the outside of her legs. A white, filmy long-sleeved collarless shirt was held against her by an equally form-fitting black leather vest, also with lacings up the front, drawing his eyes to an enticing show of cleavage. A long sheathed sword hung by her left side; the silver hilt of a dagger peeked from out of the top of her right boot. She moved down the ramp with a sinewy, almost furzel-like grace until she came to stand before him, arms crossed over her chest.

"You said you wanted to get to LandsDown before noon. Eden and Serafino are almost ready."

Right now he didn't give a damn about Eden and Serafino. Right now he wanted throw her into that soft green bed of flowers over there and take her outfit off...with his teeth. He licked his lips, unconsciously.

"Admiral—?"

He closed his eyes briefly. Admiral. He was Admiral Kel-Paten in the Triad Fleet. Right. And she was Captain Tasha Sebastian. Okay. Okay.

"Okay," he said out loud, opening his eyes. "I...I just have to change my shirt." His Triad black uniform pants would suffice for his costume. He stood, let his eyes rake over her once again. He was only inches from her. Mere inches. He could smell her perfume, a heady, musky scent of sandalwood...

"I left the other broadsword on your bunk," she was saying.

He watched her mouth move. She'd kissed him, once. He remembered that, remembered the feel of her mouth on his. Hell, he remembered it nightly. And twice at noon.

"Eden didn't think the sword would fit with her image as a healer."

"Oh?" He knew who Eden was but couldn't even picture her at the moment. All he could see in his mind was the dark and cramped engine compartment of the shuttle behind them, and Sass, her face full of emotion and concern, yelling at him, grabbing him, and then the heat of her lips on his, the taste of her, a mixture of his sweat and her tears...

"...but we figured we should all carry stunners concealed, in case..." Sass paused, as if she'd suddenly realized he was staring at her.

A light morning breeze rustled through the branches and brushed by his face, but it did nothing to cool the heat he felt between himself and Sass. He stepped closer, closing those few inches that had separated them and she responded, tilting her face up towards his, her hands somehow finding their way splayed against his dark shirt—

The shuttle hatchway whooshed open again and Serafino clomped noisily out onto the metal platform.

"Yo, ho, ho and a bottle of rum!" he bellowed, holding his arms out and shaking his fists at the sky in mock anger. "Is this a great shirt, or what?"

Sass sprang backwards quickly. Serafino was stomping around in a kind of war dance on the ramp platform, his gauzy, full sleeved white shirt billowing around his outstretched arms. Then Eden appeared, laughing, tying a laccy blue ribbon in her hair.

"Hold still, Jace, damn it! Hold still!" she admonished him as, finished with her own tresses, she worked on tying his hair at the nape of his neck.

"Tasha." Kel-Paten said her name softly, the deep ache in his body making his voice rasp. She glanced at him. "Tasha, I—"

"You'd better go get changed," she told him. "We've got a lot to do before nightfall. I'll go find the equinnards."

She turned abruptly and headed towards the edge of the forest.

HAVEN-ONE'S FOREST

What in hell had come over her? Sass plunged into the forest with anger at herself pounding through her footsteps. Gods' feathered asses, what had come over her? She'd almost...almost kissed Kel-Paten. The Tin Soldier. Her C.O. and a major royal pain in the ass.

Okay, so she'd kissed him once before, but that was different. That was a diversion, a move out of desperation to stop him from doing something stupid.

But this...this was just a balmy morning with no major concerns or worries and she'd just about fallen into his arms.

Something was very wrong here.

Granted, it had been a while since she'd been involved with anyone. But hell, she was almost forty and her pub-crawling, stud-seeking days were long behind her. She'd had her fill of military-groupies and officer-groupies and whatever other title turned on the male spaceport bar griztards. Plus, there'd always been Zan, her friend and confidant and sometime lover since they were kids on Farside Station.

But it had been, what, almost a year since she'd seen Dag Zanorian? Then involved with wife number four at the time, he hadn't been what she would have called 'available'—though he seemed to think so. But then, Zan was known for many things, and fidelity wasn't one of them.

Which was why they'd gotten along so well for so many years. Her career had always come first and commitment was something she understood only in military terms. The thought of spending the rest of her life with only one man frankly scared the hell out of her; she had a short attention span when it came to the male of the species. In other words, she bored easily.

'Sass the Non-Committed', Eden had once chided her. Don't get involved for fear they'd want to make it permanent. And don't get involved because you're afraid of the permanence, and the hurt in their eyes when you tell them so.

Because permanence meant intimacy. And intimacy meant answers she might not be able to give, to questions she didn't want to hear.

And that's maybe just why she was so afraid of Kel-Paten. Not that he was a bio-cybe. Not that he held the exalted position of Fleet Admiral. Not that more than half of civilized space lived in fear of him.

None of that really bothered her. It was the way he looked at her. It was the way he was always there. It was the way he would've given his life to save her. And the way he'd loved her for more years than any sane male should have.

But it wasn't Sass he loved. It was Tasha Sebastian, the totally fictitious orphan of totally fictitious wealthy parents. Without which, she'd never had been granted admittance to the academy, never have achieved the rank of captain.

If she let him get close to her, sooner or later, he'd know. So the best she could offer him would be a brief fling before she moved on.

And it would come to that. Sooner or later with Sass it always did. Love 'em and leave 'em, Eden would chastise her. And she had, for years, because it had been necessary. It never really bothered her.

Until now.

CHAPTER TWENTY-SIX

LANDSDOWN

Their entry into the rustic village was heralded by no fanfare, no scrutiny and barely even a nod. Of course, no one watching the two men and two women ride past the main gate could discern they were being visited by people from another galaxy. Probably, no one watching even *knew* there were other galaxies, Eden mused as they slowed their progress to allow a heavily burdened cart to pass before them. They'd traveled more than just hundreds of thousands of parsecs away from Triad Space. From her viewpoint, they'd traveled hundreds of years back into the past.

Following directions from a street corner flower seller, they wound down narrow cobblestoned lanes until they saw the large square sign swinging from a metal rod on the outside of a red brick two story building. The sign was that of the local healer; an elderly man, they were told, who'd taken over the practice after his sister's death. He didn't have his late sister's patience—or patients! And when Eden introduced herself as a traveling herbalist and healer willing to assist in his practice, he spent a good fifteen minutes kissing her hand in gratitude.

Evidently satisfied that her CMO was in good hands, literally, Sass took her leave with a nod to Master Grendar. "The adm—Kel-Paten and I will be at that pub later. We're going to seek out the local Warrior's Guild."

Grendar seemed much more at ease after the leather clad, small but obviously dangerous woman left. "You, my dear Lady Eden, are the answer to a tired old man's prayers!" He ushered her towards an overstuffed yellow couch. The couch, like most of the furniture in the dimly lit drawing room, was surrounded by jars and vials and small boxes that held a wide variety of herbs and potions. Eden stepped gingerly over the cluttered piles. The couch was surprisingly soft and comfortable. Perhaps, she thought as Jace took the seat next to her, few had been able to traverse the mess far enough to sit on it.

My thoughts exactly, love!

She felt Jace's warm smile in her mind. *Grendar really needs some help,* she told him as a plump housekeeper bustled in with a tray of tea and cakes.

"M'lord Jace? M'lady? Please help yourselves. Nordra is not much of a tidier, I'll admit, but she does brew a wonderful cup of tea." Grendar smiled broadly.

It *was* a wonderful cup of tea, Eden noted appreciatively and for all the mess and all the disorder, Grendar was a relatively accomplished healer. But she and Jace could do more, much more, which would provide them not only with a source of income, but also help out the small and friendly village.

Jace was reaching for his third fruit tart drizzled with a dark chocolate sauce when Grendar's tinny brass bell jangled. A young stablehand had fallen from a hayloft—fortunately landing on several bales of hay or he would have had injuries more serious than a dislocated shoulder and the usual bruising. Eden mentally felt for more serious internal injuries and, finding none, realigned the boy's shoulder and sent him on his way with a small jar of salve to relieve the pain and aid in healing. Along with that Jace admonished the lad not to add strong drink to his lunch on work days. The stablehand responded with a wide-eyed stare.

"How'd you...I mean, yes, m'lord. I will. Ye be sure I'll be right as rain from nigh on in, I will, sir." He nodded, backing out of the door, clearly surprised at Jace's uncovering of his secret pastime.

"I was a bit unruly as a youth," Jace explained as Grendar looked questioningly at him. "He's at the age when having a few pints with the lads at lunch is a sign of prowess."

"Aye, been years since I was a lad, but I remember how we was a bit wild, too." Grendar nodded understandingly and then shuffled off towards the kitchen to ask Nordra to brew more tea.

Eden smiled at Jace. "When did you *stop* being unruly?" she teased.

"So it was just a small lie." He kissed the back of her neck lightly.

Lightly, Eden knew, because Jace sensed Grendar was returning— just as he had known what had really precipitated the boy's fall. Ever since she'd disconnected the implant in his head, his telepathic powers had returned strongly. It took very little effort now for him to pick up on the thoughts and emotions of others—and very little effort to send his own hot and passionate emotions to Eden. Like right now.

Her hands momentarily froze over the boxes of dried herbs she was sorting as he sent her some very strong, very erotic images of what further pleasures awaited her by their little pool.

She sent back an equally arousing visual response.

Only Grendar's return stopped then and there from throwing themselves onto the yellow couch. She had a fleeting glimpse of Jace's intention to cover her with some of Nordra's delicious chocolate sauce.

It would ruin the couch, she scolded him with a grin.

I'd buy the old man a new one. I'd buy him ten couches!

"Well!" Grendar looked from a smiling Jace to a naughtily grinning Eden. "It certainly is nice to work with two such happy people!"

Jace lay one hand affectionately on the old man's shoulder. "Trust me, Master Grendar, there is no one happier in the entire village of LandsDown than Lady Eden and myself right now."

LANDSDOWN MAIN STREET

Branden Kel-Paten was miserable. Somehow, he'd lost track of Sass. He wasn't quite sure how.

They'd sought out the local Warrior's Guild only to find the headquarters empty. Several conversations with street urchins later, they surmised that the Guild was predominantly inactive in LandsDown. The village was a quiet and peaceful place, populated by shopkeepers and farmers who, for the most part, got along. What warriors had once resided in the village had long since moved on to larger—and more lucrative—cities.

Oh, there was the occasional drunk, like the ones Sass had stumbled over accosting the old woman. But that was the exception, not the rule and one rescue was not going to afford them saddles and clothing and other items needed at this point.

Like a Hyperlinked Transconductive Recompositor. Or whatever raw materials they could find to construct an HTRC so they could convert the raw crystalline ore Eden's science scans had confirmed in the mountain range into fuel for their shuttle. So they could get off this Gods-damned dirtball that was firmly ensconced in medieval history, and get back to where they belonged. To where he and Sass belonged—on the *Vax.* Or even T'Garis. He'd almost forgotten his promise to ask her to go there. Right now he'd even settle for Port Bangkok, or anywhere in civilized space. Anywhere their commbadges operated so that he wouldn't be wandering around this damned village with no idea of where she was, and no way to find her. Except by looking in every shop and market and tailor and pub...

It was in the fifth pub that he found her, after striding up and down rough and dusty alleyways for almost two and a half hours, his equinnard, Prancer, plodding patiently behind him.

He probably could've covered more ground riding, but his rear end was too sore and with no saddle and no saddle blanket, Prancer's hard spine was less than inviting.

So he'd walked, trudged and poked until it was well past noontime and he'd not even had lunch.

And then he found her. Or rather, heard her. Her voice—used to issuing commands—carried out into the street from the dark depths of a rather disreputable looking pub.

"Seven, seven, seven! C'mon baby, roll 'em now, roll 'em! Give me a sweet seven! Momma needs new shoes!"

The biofilters in his eyes immediately adjusted for the change in light when he stepped inside. He saw her at once, kneeling on the floor, surrounded by a motley looking group of farmers and tradesman. And one man who appeared, by his dress, to be wealthier than the rest.

They formed an elongated circle with Sass at one end, and the pale flash of the now tumbling dice at the other.

He watched the cubes fall and stop with five dots facing up on one, and two dots on the other.

"Lucky Seven!" someone called out.

A female voice whooped in glee. The only female voice in the room. He stepped up next to her.

She looked up. "'Lo, Kel-Paten."

"Sebastian," he said and paused, waiting for the usual rejoinder. It never came. She was too busy collecting her winnings.

"Okay, boys, okay. Pay up, now." She held out her hand. Coins rained into it. She was transferring them into a small leather pouch when her progress was stilled by the well-dressed man kneeling next to her. He took her wrist, lightly but firmly, and brought it to his lips.

Something in Kel-Paten went white-hot and then cold.

"I request a rematch, Lady Tasha," the man was saying. "You win, I'll triple your winnings."

"And if I lose?" Sass asked. Kel-Paten noticed the man still held her hand. And noticed also the decidedly hungry gleam in the man's eyes.

"I would hope," the man said smoothly, "that you would not view losing to me as a loss. I would propose...dinner. Perhaps a nice bottle of wine or two. I am asking only for your time, lady."

"I'm flattered, your lordship, but I'm not for sale," Sass replied with a measured sweetness.

A low chuckle moved around the group.

"My lady, forgive me." The man bowed his head briefly. "I didn't mean to imply—"

"She's not for sale." Kel-Paten's voice thundered and the room immediately hushed.

Sass swiveled around. The well-dressed man was already rising, his luxurious cape falling gracefully about his broad shoulders. If he were bothered by the fact that Kel-Paten was several inches taller than he, the calm and controlled look on his handsome face gave no clue to that. Nor did the way he genteelly extended his hand.

"I don't believe we have been introduced. I'm Tristan Dalbaran, Duke of LandsDown Keep."

Kel-Paten glared at the sandy-haired man and ignored his outstretched hand. "She's not for sale," he repeated tersely. "Captain Sebastian—"

"Captain?" Lord Tristan turned to the small blonde standing between them. "I was not aware of any woman ever—"

"It's a long story," Sass cut in smoothly with a quick and decidedly irritated glance at Kel-Paten. He knew immediately why: captain. He'd used her title and shouldn't have.

"And a fascinating one, I'm sure," Tristan replied. He bowed graciously to Sass. "Let us forget this minor diversion, then, my lady. I extend only the most honorable of offers. Would you care to dine with me, at the Keep? Squire Ferbtil and his wife share my table most Fourthday evenings. Your presence would be a delightful addition to our threesome."

"No," said Kel-Paten.

"I'd love to," said Sass.

"Your...associate would of course be welcome as well," Lord Tristan told Sass with a cursory glance at Kel-Paten.

Sass sighed. "I'm afraid, my lord, that if your generous invitation is also to include Kel-Paten, I would have to impose on you further by advising you I am traveling with two more companions: Lady Eden of Fynn, an accomplished healer and her consort, Lord Jace Serafino."

"I would be delighted to meet your traveling companions," Lord Tristan said warmly.

Kel-Paten knew that whatever dislike he'd felt at first spotting the man had now grown into a full fledged hatred.

"Tomorrow night, then, Fourthday? At the Keep?" Lord Tristan took Sass's hand once more and grazed her knuckles with a light kiss.

"I look forward to it, m'lord," Sass said.

"Not as much as I, my lady captain. Not as much as I."

With Lord Tristan's departure the show, as far as the gamblers in the pub were concerned, was over, and they ambled in small groups towards the bar. A fresh platter of meat pies was just now being brought out by a balding barkeep who was no doubt only too glad a fist-fight had not ensued.

Sass glared up at Kel-Paten, arms folded across her chest.

"I thought we didn't interfere in someone else's personal life," she said in a quietly angry tone.

"My officers are not for sale," he replied after a moment of tense silence.

"I wasn't offering myself!" she snapped back. "Damn it, power down! Those Gods-damned eyes of yours are going to have someone calling in the local priest to have you burned at the stake, if you're not careful."

He'd powered up the minute Lord Tristan had touched her, then forgotten about it. He closed his eyes and briefly turned his face away.

When he opened them again, she was already striding towards the door, head held high, shoulders back, a decided swagger in the unmistakable feminine sway of her hips.

She was pissed. She was royally, royally pissed. At him. Just as she had been so many times on the *Vax*.

There she'd sought her comfort in the gym, or in Dr. Fynn's office. Or in the lounge, nursing her mood through a tall glass of iced gin with some of her staff from the *Regalia*.

But now she had somewhere else to go, someone else to go to. Someone who would no doubt be very glad to tell her what an uncivilized, unmannered, uncouth bastard Branden Kel-Paten was.

It was nothing, Kel-Paten knew, Sass hadn't heard—or thought—before.

However, this time it would be Lord Tristan Dalbaran telling her. The Duke of LandsDown Keep. A full human, virile, very available male.

So as far as Kel-Paten was concerned, a full scale intergalactic war was more than preferable to dinner at the Keep tomorrow night.

At least with the former, he had a chance of winning.

CHAPTER TWENTY-SEVEN

Kel-Paten caught up with her a few doors down, in front of a candlemaker's shop. She tugged up her sleeve and glanced discreetly at her watch as he strode up beside her. "We're meeting Serafino and Eden at a pub about two alleys away."

He knew that. It had been one of the reasons he'd been looking so diligently for her. Not that he thought she wouldn't make the appointed meeting time. A memory of Sass, in her 'No! No! Bad Captain!' shirt, colliding with him in the corridor as the red alert sirens blared, then handling the subsequent crisis with her usual aplomb, flashed briefly through his mind. No, he knew she'd show for their prearranged meeting.

He just wanted to be by her side when she did so. After Serafino's strident warning last night, he knew he couldn't afford to let Jace speak to Sass alone. Not for the first time, the Nasyry had accessed memories he had no right to see. And no right to share. And share he would with Sass, Kel-Paten believed. Given the chance to do so. Because of what he thought Kel-Paten had done to his sister, Bianca.

Kel-Paten had no intention of giving him the chance to do so.

They turned left at the second alleyway. Sass had said nothing more since he'd caught up to her. Her usual playful sarcasm would be preferable to the silence. There were a thousand things he wanted to say, but no idea where to start.

And no time, because a few feet in front of them was a low, wide doorway with a wooden sign swinging overhead. 'The Laughing Cow' was lettered in red on the sign; letters that were similar to Triad Standard, just as the language spoken in LandsDown was similar to Triad Standard. Though the local accent, and cadence, was different. He didn't know the word 'cow' but a crudely drawn but colorful depiction of a luba was in the center.

He ducked his head as he entered, his eyes adjusting immediately to the change in lighting. His nose caught some surprisingly delicious aromas.

Sass slowed, blinking. Her eyes couldn't filter the lighting as his could. He wanted to take her arm, guide her, but the hard set of her shoulders told him she was still angry. His touch wouldn't be welcome, and not just because of what he was.

So he pointed, past the two burly men in well-stained tunics, arguing loudly; past the well-endowed barmaid in the brightly beribboned apron threading her way towards them, a large metal tankard in one hand; past the thin old man seated on a bench in front of the low-burning fire, his gnarled hands wrapped around the bulbous end of a cane. "There. By the back wall."

Serafino and Eden sat on one side of a rough-hewn table, a loaf of bread on a wooden tray in front of them. Eden wiggled her fingers in the air. Sass waited until they were closer then tossed a small sack in the air. Serafino caught it, hefted it and let out a low whistle of appreciation.

"Would have done better at Starfield Doubles." Sass accepted the small sack back from him, taking the seat on the bench across from Eden. "But they don't know the game here. Yet."

Kel-Paten caught her mischievous grin as he sat next to her, but it was directed at her friend, not himself.

"What were you playing?" Serafino asked, including Kel-Paten in his question with a short nod.

"It was kind of like Two Cube, but more like it's played on Kesh Valiir. Not like you play it in the Triad," Sass said before he could explain he hadn't been there. But wished, after seeing Lord Dalbaran's interest in Sass, he had been. "Or like it's played in the sanctioned casinos. I had to watch for a game or two to catch on."

"Or to identify the patsies," Eden said with a low and knowing laugh.

"It's not like a fight breaks out in this village every half hour, you know." Sass briefly outlined their earlier findings and the reasons behind the absence of the Warrior's Guild in the village.

A serving girl placed a plate of hot meat and vegetable stew on the table.

"Jace ordered some food," Eden said. "Hope you don't mind."

Kel-Paten didn't though no one seemed interested in his opinion. The menu offerings appeared to be nothing short of delicious. Or maybe he'd just had replicator food for too long.

A large shank of meat on a platter came next, followed by a smaller platter of shellfish.

Sass groaned. "I don't know if I can afford your tastes, 'Fino."

That started some good-natured teasing back and forth. Only Kel-Paten was quiet, sampling his dinner without any comment. Sass wasn't speaking to him. With Serafino at her side, Eden barely noticed him. And Serafino...well, Kel-Paten had no idea how much Serafino knew or, worse, was telepathically and empathically picking up on. He just knew that whatever Serafino had to say, he was in no mood to hear it.

Eden briefed them on what had happened at their first day at Master Grendar's.

"Were you able to learn anything about this malevolent energy source?" Sass asked Serafino pointedly.

"Neither Eden nor I picked up on anything unusual. And we thought it better not to ask things like that on day one. Once we know the villagers a bit better and have their trust, we'll be able to get answers."

"A few days, perhaps," Eden volunteered.

"Tomorrow," Sass said. "We have a dinner invitation from a duke. Command performance, you know." She filled in the details of her meeting Lord Dalbaran.

"Well, well, well!" Serafino said.

Kel-Paten refused to raise his eyes, refused to look anywhere but his dinner. He'd heard definite undercurrents in Serafino's brief comment and he knew the mercenary captain wasn't wondering about tomorrow night's menu.

Eden's thoughts traveled in a more practical vein. "We'll have to present very tight cover stories. In a setting like that, it's only natural for people to ask where someone's from, who they know."

Serafino speared another roasted rib with his knife. "I asked Grendar if I could borrow a book of maps he had, and took one on history as well. That should help."

"We won't be Lord Tris's only guests," Sass said. "He mentioned a Squire Ferbtil and his wife."

Lord Tris. Lord Tris. Kel-Paten heard the familiarity in the shortened name. Not Lord Tristan or Lord Dalbaran or even Duke LandsDown. Hell's ass! Eleven years he'd known Sass and he was still Kel-Paten. A few hours this silk-shirted pretty boy knows her, and he's already 'Lord Tris'.

Serafino seemed interested that Ferbtil would be there. "Grendar mentioned him briefly. He said Ferbtil's a bit of a, how did he say it? Oh, a ninny wit, but basically harmless. Ferbtil's popular, like a scatter-brained old uncle. And coming from Grendar," he added with a smile, "that must be something!"

"Did he mention Tris?" Sass asked, nibbling thoughtfully on a large vegetable floret.

Kel-Paten's grasp on his fork tightened until it threatened to snap. Tris.

"Not specifically, but he did mention the Keep a couple of times. Now I know what he was talking about."

"Umm, yes. I remember." Eden pushed a large part of her shellfish to one end of her plate. She automatically cut it into small portions for the furzels. "Grendar said that the Keep helped the village repair the water system. And had acquired new stones for the roads leading northward last year. I thought at the time he referred to the local government, but I guess now he meant the Duke's family. Did Lord Tris mention any family?" she asked Sass.

"His mother, the Dowager Duchess. I gather she lives quite a distance south of here. Better climate or something like that."

"So they have their luxury destinations, too, hmm?" Eden asked teasingly.

"And there was," Sass continued, "a cousin that Tris—"

The metal fork snapped in Kel-Paten's hand with an audible crack.

"—said he'd been close to years ago. But I really don't know more than that."

The conversation—without Kel-Paten's input—drifted to the general political layout of the village and what little had been learned about LandsDown in particular that day, when all of a sudden, as tea was being served, Eden sat up straight and stared at Sass.

"Oh my Gods!" she gasped. "We have nothing to wear!"

GALAXUS STORAGE BAY

Sass sat cross-legged in the middle of the storage bay, satiny fabrics to her left, muslins to her right and all around a rainbow of colors: crimsons and violets, pale blues and cream golds. Lace peeked out here, a row of pearly buttons there. She sighed and looked plaintively at Eden. "There's nothing to wear."

Eden turned from the mirror where she'd been holding a pale violet gown trimmed in slate blue up against her shoulders. Had they had the replicator system of the *Regalia* or the *Vax* at their disposal, their limited selection of costumes wouldn't be a problem. But they didn't and the shuttle replicators were programmed to dispense only the basics, and in military mode at that. Out of the five gowns now strewn about the floor (and the one in Eden's hands), four were Eden's from past Old Legend Fairs. Only two were Sass's size. Eden was a good six inches taller than Sass, decidedly full-figured and with a fuller bustline. No amount of last minute pinning would do.

"You're going to have to wear the silver one," Eden told her. The only other choice was a green muslin and that was far too casual for dinner at the Keep.

Sass narrowed her eyes. "Oh great. I'll look like a damn bride. Or a ghost, with this pale hair of mine!"

Eden grinned. "Ooohhhh!" she crooned, making ghost-like noises. "Maybe the Keep is haunted!"

Sass reached back and threw the first thing she lay her hands on. Tank yowled as the object was ripped from his teeth. Eden unraveled it after it hit her in the stomach and held it out for Sass's inspection.

"This might work."

"A sweater? Eden, this isn't the Red Light district of Port Bangkok. I'll need more than a shaliswool—"

"The fur collar. I can tack that to the neckline of that silver dress. That'll take away the severity of it and, well..."

"Thank you very much, I know I'm rather small up top!" Sass glared at Eden in mock sternness. "So the fur will add a bosom, eh? Hey, tack Reilly to my chest and I'll be a real knock out!"

At the sound of his name, Reilly stuck his head out from under a pile of lace and murrupped. Tank promptly pounced on him and the next few minutes were taken up with a game of Furzel Tussle.

Eden gathered what she needed. Clothes were only a part of the problem of life on Haven-One. But they were one of the easier ones. Mining the mountain range for the needed ore for fuel, repairing the shuttle and gaining the trust of the villagers while doing so were the more difficult.

As was keeping Jace from baiting the admiral. She understood his reasons, but his methods disconcerted her.

And worried her. She loved Jace. Loved him more than she ever thought possible.

That worried her, too. Because Haven-One or not, she was still a Fleet officer. She'd never had her loyalty, and her love, so at odds before.

GALAXUS

Sass had opted not to return to the Village with Eden and Jace the next morning, which was fine by Kel-Paten. He accepted her comment that to try to increase her gambling winnings so soon after her last win would no doubt cause some resentment in the small village. He really didn't care what the reason was. He was just glad to keep her away from the village, away from Lord Tristan and away from the rest of the hungry male eyes that turned her way every time she walked into a pub or a shop.

Not that the village men didn't stare longingly after Eden as well. They did and Kel-Paten had noted it. But he also had noted the way Eden stayed by Serafino's side; how Serafino protectively and often possessively had his hand on her arm, or around her shoulder. That they were a couple was very clear to anyone who could see.

Not so with Sass, who forever walked ahead of him, or took detours to the left and right, her small form slipping easily in and out of the crowds with a grace, he suspected, honed by her undercover training. Or perhaps her parents' wealth had provided her with classical dance lessons. She moved like a dancer, her motions fluid.

He turned his attention back to his repairs on the auxiliary thruster. It kept him from thinking about that dreaded dinner at the Keep tonight. He hated social engagements, but at least at ones in the Triad most people knew to stay away from him.

Yet oddly enough, just before this whole situation had unfolded, he'd actually been looking forward to a proposed social engagement—taking Sass to the casinos on T'Garis. And later, to the ritual parties celebrating Rohly Kel-Tyra's impending nuptials.

At least there no one would have dared approach Sass once he'd defined himself as her escort.

The frantic beeping of the analyzer in his hand brought his attention back to the mechanical matters before him. He adjusted the power levels. But thoughts of Sass crept back into his mind again.

For so many years he'd wanted a chance to be with her without his reputation, without his infamous pedigree interfering. Here, on Haven-One, he had that chance. And yet now he found himself wishing he could broadcast that pedigree, tell this Lord Tristan just who and what he was and thereby keep this interloper away from Sass.

It was a totally nonsensical wish. That was the only thing that cheered him. It meant that part of him still had the ability to act and think like a human.

LANDSDOWN

The afternoon in the village brought a sprained wrist, some minor lacerations from a careless cook and a visit to the home of a small child with a high fever. Nothing that Eden and Jace couldn't handle; and it was a relieved and grateful Grendar who willingly gave the majority of the coins over to their keeping in payment. The old man was now free to do what he liked—sleep late in the morning, spend the early afternoon cataloging his various herbs and powders and then retire to The Laughing Cow for a pint or two with some of his old cronies.

They talked fishing—aye, the redfin were running particularly big this year—and the local games; jousting and log-rolling were two of the more popular events. Midlar's lad had grown big and would be a contender, that was for sure. But there was always Tredmin, a brawny man with an unlikable attitude. And an unbeatable stance.

It would all remain to be seen.

"And this new lass, a sight fer sore eyes, she is," one of Grendar's neighbors commented, drawing deep on his pipe.

Grendar's lined face crinkled as he smiled. "Sweet as sugar, that one. Name's Lady Eden. Quality, finely bred but has more than enough in the brain box, I'll tell ye! Knows her herbs and potions."

"Married?"

"If not, will be shortly. Her suitor is that broad shouldered one. Says his name's Serafino," Grendar explained. "Regular kind of fellow, though a bit cocky. Still, I like 'im."

Heads nodded around the table in the smoky air. "Southerners?" came the question.

Grendar shrugged. "Ne'er did say, other than they were travelin', yes. And not been in these parts afore, yes. But that description fits only a hunnert or so others."

Again, heads nodded. LandsDown was a place traveled *through*. Not to, for most people.

"Thought there was another gal." Grendar's neighbor again. A retired judge with too much time on his hands and a large front window.

"Friend of her ladyship's. Warrior guild."

An understanding murmur went around the table. Quality often traveled with protection.

"And the dark man with her?" the judge continued.

"Didn't see him," Grendar answered honestly. "Her ladyship mentioned she is traveling with friends, in the plural, you know. I don't inquire. Not m'place to."

"Mean lookin' bastard," the judge noted. "This big dark one. Dressed in all black. Black gloves on his hands, too. Like a Night Rider."

"They're not....with the Wizard?" The last question was asked softly, fearfully, by old Derwin the shoemaker.

"Nah, have no indication of that!" Grendar reassured him. "At least, not her ladyship and Lord Serafino. Peaceable, they be. And kindly. Gentle-spoken, even if he is a bit of a snap-wit."

"That Warrior gal, I seen her with Lord Tris. They be friends, do tell." That was Egbard, an old stablehand with a strong love of gambling.

"Lord Tris? Aye. Aye."

A uniform nodding of heads around the table. If Lord Tris were involved, then all was well.

"Seemed quite smitten with her, with the Warrior gal," Egbard continued. "The pale haired gal. Looks at first like a lad, she does, til she turns. Then," and a broad, wily grin split his thin face, "then she's all female. If ye be knowin' what I do mean. And I know that ye do, gents!"

Low laughter rumbled around the table. They might be collectively and individually grizzled and gray-haired and well past their prime, but not a one gathered there still didn't appreciate a fat redfin, a well-bred horse or a pretty woman.

Another pitcher of ale was called for and the topic turned from women to horseflesh. After all, the games would be starting next week.

Then one by one, they wandered back home, or to their sons or daughters for a hot meal, until it was only Grendar and the judge left with the last tankard of ale.

"Think he's moved on? Lost interest?"

Grendar glanced left and right over his shoulders before answering the judge's question. The tavern was empty enough, but he kept his words pitched low. "The Wizard, you mean? Aye, it's been quiet. Don't know if it be good news, that, or bad."

"Like he's waiting for something?" The judge tapped the bowl of his pipe against the palm of his hand.

"Or someone. Could be waitin' for someone. That's what the squire's wife says."

"Bluebell?" The judge snorted but then his expression sobered. "Never gave much credence before to those visions of hers. Bad omens."

"They're only bad because we didn't heed them in time."

"So what's Bluebell's latest prediction?"

"Not clear. A man with blue eyes is all she knows." Grendar looked troubled. "That could be any one of a dozen of us here."

"Aye." The judge sucked noisily on his pipe. "Damn shame to be marked for death for the mere color of your eyes. You ain't told Derwin this, have you?"

"And set the village to panic?" Grendar shook his head. "Just heard meself this mornin'. No, the squire's talking to Lord Tris, as is proper. The Keep's handled this afore. They will, again."

"As long as the Keep stands, we're safe. But the Gods help us the day the Keep falls."

CHAPTER TWENTY-EIGHT

OUTSIDE THE *GALAXUS*

Eden felt Sass's surprise at about the same time as she saw her friend's eyes widen. She bit back a chuckle. In her blue muslin gown, perched as she was on the carriage's high front seat with Jace at the reins beside her, she probably did look as if she belonged in a museum. The contrast with the deep space shuttle behind them was a bit jarring.

"It was Grendar's idea," Serafino explained to Sass, holding one hand out to Eden as she climbed down from the square wooden conveyance. "He felt it would be more appropriate to arrive at the Keep in a carriage than on horseback, especially as we still have no saddles."

"And especially since you and I will be dressed in our finery," Eden put in. She bent down to retrieve Reilly who had bounded up to meet her. She cuddled him against her. He purred loudly.

Serafino was reaching for Tank when Sass put out her hand to stop him. "I wouldn't do that right now if I were you. I've watched him eat two griztards in the past hour."

Serafino laughed and squatted down next to the round-bellied fidget. "Getting a bit fragrant, are we?" he asked Tank as he scratched a proffered chin.

Eden gave Sass a brief rundown of the afternoon's medical adventures as they walked towards the shuttle. The villagers were already comfortable with her and Serafino and willingly accepted some of Eden's ideas on cleanliness and disease prevention.

"When I took that seminar three years ago on the medical needs of emerging low-tech societies, I never dreamed I'd actually be putting it to use! Then I just viewed it as another way the military had of eating up budget money." She shook her head. "Speaking of the military, where's the admiral?"

"Last I saw, a few hours ago, still working on the auxiliary thrusters."

Eden heard—and felt—the studied indifference in her friend's response, and knew the tension that had been building the past few days between Sass and Kel-Paten—hell, the tension that had been building the past few months, or even years!—had not yet reached any kind of resolution. She'd seen a change starting in the admiral since they'd come to Haven-One; an attempt to relax and let his human side come through. He was trying to open himself up to Sass, Eden knew, but in doing so he was also becoming vulnerable. Letting himself feel things for perhaps the first time in his life, he was feeling them almost too intensely.

When Eden was around Kel-Paten, she clearly sensed his ups and downs. And even though Sass wasn't an empath, Eden knew she felt it too. Especially as a lot of it was directed at the petite blonde.

Eden had noted the same instability in Kel-Paten when they were back on the *Vax*. She and Sass had even discussed it in Eden's office. But on the ship they'd had their respective cabins and offices to withdraw to. Here, with only the small shuttle, there was little privacy, emotionally and physically.

"Are you talking to him yet?" Eden asked quietly. Serafino was occupied several feet away with two pouncing furzels and a long tree branch. As much as he'd backed off irritating the admiral, per Eden's pleas and requests, she still didn't want him privy to her conversations about him with Sass.

Sass shrugged. "We talk about what is necessary."

"That's not what I mean. Sass, you know how he feels—"

"Don't remind me!"

"I think I have to. I watched him last night at The Laughing Cow. Every time you mentioned Lord Tristan...well, you've got to cut him some slack."

Sass glanced at her friend, her eyes narrowing. "He's got to grow up."

"He is, he will," Eden protested. "But it's going to take time. I don't know, I've never had a chance to review his psych profile, or his emo-patterns, but we've discussed this before. What he's going through, about you, is completely new to him. He—"

"He has to grow up," Sass repeated and kicked at a pile of moss with the toe of her boot. Obviously, she didn't want to be reminded about how Kel-Paten felt or how she could or was hurting him. She was, Eden knew, too aware of it already. And too confused.

Eden sensed that confusion. "I'm not criticizing you."

Sass sighed. "I know. I'm sorry. It's just that...I don't know. He's got me on edge. Every time he looks at me, I feel like I should apologize, but I don't know what for. For being human? For being female?"

"He thinks you hate him," Eden told her. Serafino had informed her of the shame Kel-Paten felt.

"I wish I did, Doc. It would make things a lot easier."

Eden looked questioningly at her as they neared the rampway of the shuttle. "Do I sense a softening of the heart?"

"Towards the Tin Soldier?" Sass's laugh was brittle. "No, just...I don't know." She shoved her hands in her pants pockets and looked skyward, as if pleading with the deities for answers. When she looked back at her friend there was a tired sadness in her eyes. "I've dealt with crewmembers who've had crushes on me before. Hell, so have you!" She grinned. "There was that lieutenant in security who kept leaving roses outside your door, remember?"

Eden raised one eyebrow. That she did.

"It comes with the job, you know? There are always the dirtsiders who find us attractive because we're female and we're spacers and on top of that we hold military rank. The fleet groupies and all those kind. You've had 'em, I've had 'em..." Sass waved one hand as she spoke. "But this is different. There's an ...innocence about him that scares the hell out of me. Which is strange to say, considering he's one of the most powerful individuals in the Triad Fleet. Hell, in Triad *and* Coalition space. He says 'jump' and the fleet says 'how high and when'," Sass explained.

"But you don't," Eden pointed out.

"True." Sass grinned at her friend. "Me, when he says 'Jump', I say 'Up yours and the equinnard you rode in on.'"

"A classic Sass line if I ever heard one," Serafino said, coming up behind Eden. He planted a light kiss on the top of her head and Eden knew nothing more was to be discussed with Sass on the subject of Kel-Paten.

"Finished tormenting the furzels?" Eden leaned back against him and tried to look up into his eyes.

"Can't say I was outclassed there, but I was definitely out-gassed!" he answered with a low chuckle.

"Tank," Sass said knowingly.

"Griztards," Serafino added.

"Maybe I should look for some digestive herbs," Eden said with a nod to Sass. "Or else one particular fidget may find himself sleeping outside for the rest of his life."

"I'm sure Grendar has something. We can ask him tomorrow. Are you coming inside?" Serafino started for the rampway.

Eden nodded. "In a minute." Only after Serafino's tall form disappeared through the hatchway did she turn and pick up the thread of the conversation with Sass.

"So what are you going to do?"

"Hmm? I don't know. I guess it depends on what herbs—"

"No, not that." Eden frowned. "About Kel-Paten."

"Oh. That." Sass made an aimless motion with her arms then let them fall back to her sides. "Just because I think I understand him more now than when we were on the *Vax*, doesn't mean, well, you know. If he wants to be friends, fine. I don't have a problem with that. Never did, actually. But anything more..." She shook her head. "Even if he weren't Fleet, and you know the risk there." She shot her friend a meaningful look. Eden knew of Sass's concerns. Sass had never taken a lover in the U-Cee Fleet; someone who might know her well enough to see the holes in her personnel record. "I just don't want to be involved with anybody right now."

"And Lord Tris?"

Sass gave a short laugh. "You don't get involved with men like Tris. You flirt with them. That's all.

"But with Kel-Paten," Sass continued, lowering her voice after a quick glance at the hatchway, "Eden, you've read some of his letters. He's not a quick flirtation. He's, I don't know. He's a project. One thing I don't need right now is another project."

"Then I think you'd better have a talk with him. Honestly," Eden advised her. "Because everything I sense from him points to an increasing possessiveness towards you. I'm not saying you're leading him on, but he has to know what you feel, or don't feel. Or there're going to be big problems ahead."

<^>

Sass reflected on Eden's words as she rounded up the furzels, taking care not to hold Tank too tightly. She'd tried to distance herself from Kel-Paten as much as she could since they'd come to Haven-One, but it wasn't always possible. For one thing, out of necessity they had to work together. With Eden and Serafino pairing off, it was only natural that she'd end up with Kel-Paten in many situations. More than that, she had to grudgingly admit she'd grown to like him. She enjoyed his company and intelligence. There was a quiet strength, a sense of power she admired.

But he wanted more than her friendship. And more than her friendship she wasn't willing to give.

She'd thought that perhaps a light flirtation with Tris would send the message, but she saw now, after talking to Eden, that would only hurt him. In spite of the fact that he was an arrogant, pompous, royal pain in the ass at times, she really didn't want to hurt him.

She found the object of her thoughts watching her as she climbed the rampway to the shuttle, a furzel tucked under each arm. He had his usual unreadable expression, only the intense blue of his eyes hinting at his emotions.

"Keep away from me, Kel-Paten," she warned and immediately regretted her comment. She saw the tension in his face as he thought she was still angry over his behavior in the tavern. It was such a ridiculous supposition on his part that she wanted to shake him, but he'd no doubt misunderstand that, too. So she just smiled and nodded to the smaller bundle of fur nearest him. "Tank just ate another griztard. His third."

Understanding dawned on his face. Kel-Paten stepped back quickly, intending to let her pass in front of him, but she motioned with her chin for him to go first. "Downwind of this fidget is not a safe place to be."

"I appreciate the warning," he intoned and stepped inside through the airlock and into the main cabin.

Sass let Reilly jump from her arms, then gently placed Tank on the cushion of nearby seat.

"Dr. Fynn said she'd shower first," Kel-Paten told her as Sass slowly back away from the black and white bundle.

Tank looked at her, tilted his head to one side and let out a small belch.

"Oh no," Sass said. Kel-Paten grabbed her elbow and pulled her towards the front of the shuttle.

"Perhaps we should wait in the cockpit," he suggested quickly.

"Excellent idea, admiral." She made a dash for the front hatchway and tumbled into the pilot's seat, laughing, just as Kel-Paten palmed the hatchway shut behind them.

"I should warn Eden...and 'Fino," she said between giggles, stretching her arm out across the instrument panel for the intercom button.

Kel-Paten leaned towards her and the life support panel. "We could kick on the air filtration system and—"

Their arms and shoulders collided. Sass, half-kneeling, half standing at the pilot's seat, lost her balance. Kel-Paten's arm suddenly wrapped around her waist, pulling her upright against him. They tottered for a moment then fell backwards into the copilot's seat.

Sass ended up in Kel-Paten's lap, her face on his chest, her thighs straddling his hips in a rather intimate posture. She was very aware of one hand intimately cradling her rear end, and another that had snaked up her back, holding her firmly against him.

She raised her head quickly, pushing against his shoulders.

Big mistake. Her movements made the chair tilt back. Kel-Paten instinctively tightened his hold on her, so she ended up grazing his face with her cheek. Their mouths were inches apart.

"Oh," she said, her voice a whisper. "Sorry. You okay?"

No, he was *not* okay. He was definitely not okay. His body was hot and pulsing and tingling, especially where she touched him with her body. His respiration had increased; his cardiac rate had risen and had he so desired he could have visually monitored all these things in the yellow print out in his lower field of vision.

But that's not what Kel-Paten was looking at. Or thinking about.

He was looking at Sass's mouth. And he was thinking about kissing her.

CHAPTER TWENTY-NINE

GALAXUS AFT CABIN

Eden Fynn was thinking longingly about her comfortable and roomy shower back on the *Regalia*. Even the somewhat smaller one on the *Vax* would do right about now. The shuttle's shower—the shuttle's everything!—was a scaled down version of only what was absolutely necessary, and in the Triad designers' minds (no doubt Kel-Paten's, she mused) a roomy san-fac (or bathroom as she knew dirtsider's called it) was not a top priority. Neither were wide bunk beds, a large galley or even comfortable seats in the main cabin. Strictly military issue, and Triad military at that.

The shower water cycled lukewarm again and as a breeze drifted over her bare skin, she shivered. The san-fac shared the same life support systems as the rest of the shuttle and consequently when things heated up, for example, in the cockpit or the main cabin, everything cooled down at once. And the constant comings and goings through the hatchway to the outside was driving the temperature systems crazy—the shuttle was designed as a sealed, deep space transport. Not a temporary dirtside motel.

When the water heated up again she leaned her head back into its comforting stream and closed her eyes. At least the pressure was good. She reached for the slim shampoo bottle but her hand found only empty air. Odd. She knew she'd placed it in the soap dish. But with water in her eyes...

A cool liquid oozed through her hair and before she could yelp in surprise a warm, wet mouth covered hers as large hands firmly massaged the shampoo through her hair.

Hands—and a touch—she was getting very familiar with. Her aborted yelp turned into a giggle as a hot, hard and wet male body pressed against hers in the small confines of the shower.

She peered up at Jace through damp lashes. "We could get stuck in here, and then what?" she murmured against his mouth.

A low chuckle rumbled in his chest. "We'd just have to lather each other up and slide right out!"

"Mmmm. Sounds like a great idea." She took him up on his suggestion, exploring and massaging the firm planes of his body.

"I think..." he said somewhat breathlessly after a few moments, "that we could...reinvent the meaning...of good...clean sex."

Whatever verbal response Eden may have had was lost as his mouth found hers again, and his hands found the length of her back, then her waist until his hands cupped her bottom and drew her hard against him.

She felt her knees weaken as moist and slippery fingers explored even more intimate areas.

"I think..." she whispered.

"Ummm?"

"Maybe...we should...." She knew she was trying to say something, but her brain wasn't cooperating.

"Ummm." He was in total agreement, whatever it was.

"Oh yes. Oh my!" Eden exclaimed softly. Then: "Oh!"

The water cycled to lukewarm.

Jace laughed quietly. "Never fear, dearest. I have an alternate plan."

He picked her up and carefully backed out of the shower stall, laying her gently on a large pile of towels on the floor.

She nestled down into their warmth as he lay on top of her, his large body covering hers in just the perfect way, his mouth blazing a trail of kisses down her neck.

She responded by arching against him, her nails raking lightly down his wet back and he groaned her name out loud.

And then her concerns about showers and san-facs and none-too-soft bunks were forgotten as only the sensations of Jace—his muscular hardness, the soft bristly hair on his chest, the spicy smell of soap on his skin, and the hard and hot feel of him inside her —were all that Eden could think about.

That and the ripples of sheer pleasure cascading through her body as he possessed her, lovingly yet insistently, not hiding the intensity of his desire.

A thousand butterflies seemed to flutter through her veins as he climaxed inside her. Only his mouth against hers quieted her moans of pleasure. He held her tightly against him, cocooning them both within the soft, fluffy towels, until their breathing returned to normal.

"If we're late for dinner, it'll be your fault," she teased.

He looked at her in mock horror. "My fault? But my dear, you wantonly flaunted your beautiful body at me. What was I to do?"

"Exactly what you did, Captain Serafino," she replied. "Exactly what you did."

GALAXUS COCKPIT

The harsh lighting in the shuttle's cockpit only highlighted the unmistakable glitter of desire Tasha Sebastian saw in Kel-Paten's gaze. She knew, without a doubt, that if she didn't do something and do it quick, the Tin Soldier was going to kiss her.

Surprisingly, that wasn't an altogether uninteresting option; perhaps Eden's friendly advice was getting to her.

But it was an unworkable one, at least as far as Sass was concerned. First, he was her Commanding Officer. Her boss. Secondly, even though they were the Gods-only-knew how far from Fleet HQ, he was Fleet and knew her personnel file, her *falsified* personnel file, far more intimately than she wanted him to. Though for a moment a small hope whispered it might not matter. Of all the people she knew, he might truly understand why she'd done what she had. She shoved it away. Because thirdly, he wasn't, as she'd explained to Eden, someone you could lightly flirt with. Branden Kel-Paten was a project.

Right now she was not in the market for a project at all.

She grasped the arms of the chair and pushed herself back just as he leaned towards her, which helped as it rebalanced the pilot's chair. She half-slid, half-tilted out of his lap and hauled herself into the captain's chair.

"Sorry," she said again. "I lost my balance." She turned from him and busied herself with the life support monitors to her left. "Water pressure's back up. Eden must be out of the shower. I'll head there now."

She swiveled her chair around and stood with a wave in the direction of the cabin. "I'm sure Tank's contribution has, umm, faded by now. Have to risk it anyway or we'll never make it to dinner on time."

She glanced quickly at Kel-Paten. He sat upright, his dark gloved hands clasped on his thighs. He looked briefly at her and nodded. "Yes. Of course." Then he immediately resumed staring out the forward viewport at the greenness of the forest beyond.

She palmed the cockpit door open but not before she took a deep breath of air into her lungs.

With Tank, you never knew for sure...

Only after the door had cycled shut behind her did Kel-Paten let his head drop forward and rest against his waiting hands.

He was losing his mind. Day in, day out in such close proximity to her, he had no choice but to lose his mind. Little by little his military training, his rigid self control, was chipped away by her every smile, every laugh, every wrinkle of her nose.

And she was oblivious to it all.

Which only made it worse. If he could just talk to her, tell her how he felt, then he knew he could find a solution. Logic decreed that if he told her and she was horrified, or worse, found his admission of love ridiculous, then he'd accept that, know he could never have her, and go on.

Which was exactly why Kel-Paten couldn't tell her. Because it would force a resolution and it would put an end to his dream —however small it might be. As long as he didn't tell her, they both existed in the realm of 'possibility'. It was possible she could care for him. It was possible she would let him love her. It was possible she would respond....

But take away those possibilities and he had only harsh reality. And no Sass. And no dreams.

He lived in a limbo of his own making, and he knew it. He lived for a tomorrow that might never come. But at least he could dream about that tomorrow.

There was always that hope...

Then there was tonight. And Lord Tristan.

He didn't know what he'd do if this feudal barbarian made serious noises about Sass. A few months back, he'd considered putting a pompous ambassador through one of the *Vax's* bulkheads just for flirting with her. Now he had no rank to consider and no military codes to stop him if Tristan tried to take his dream away from him.

Logic and his heart decreed something else: he wouldn't lose her to another man, without a fight.

GALAXUS AFT CABIN

Eden and Serafino strolled off to bring the carriage to the shuttle when Kel-Paten went to find Sass. She was not, Eden had intimated, overly happy with her attire. When Kel-Paten, more than a little innocent regarding the eccentricities of women, had given Eden a quizzical glance, the CMO's explanation of it 'not being quite Sass's style' made even less sense to him. He didn't know what 'style' had to do with it. He assumed, like his outfit of shirt, pants and vest, it would be appropriate to the date and time and customs of the locale. What more could possibly come into consideration?

He stepped to the rear of the shuttle, where the moveable interior partitions had been rearranged to create four rooms with some modicum of privacy.

"Sebastian?" He heard a rustling sound from the corner that housed Sass's cubicle. "The Doctor and Serafino are ready."

Something between a sigh and a curse floated through the air. Then: "Okay. Okay. I just wish I had a shawl or something."

At the sound of her footsteps, Kel-Paten turned from the life-support panel he'd been studying on the far wall of the main cabin—and stared.

This was not the Sass he knew. This was not the Captain Tasha Sebastian, whose boots had more than once found their way insolently onto his desktop; whose arms were more often than not clad in wrinkled, rolled up uniform sleeves...who thought nothing of crawling through dark and musty maintenance accessways...or crawling through a wide variety of disreputable spaceport pubs.

This was...he wasn't quite sure who this was poured into this liquid silver dress, with hair like moonlight fluffed out from a face slightly tinged with pink on her cheeks; a darker pink staining lips wet and glossy with color.

She raised her face to meet his gaze. Her eyes were a luminous green; the color he recognized but not the darkness or length of the lashes. Or the way they seemed to fill her face, lending an air of innocence, of fragility to her.

No, this was not the Sass he knew. This was someone different, someone totally feminine, totally elegant, demure....

"If I don't make a total asshole of myself in this bloody damn outfit tonight, it'll be a bloody damn miracle," she said as she strode past him.

No. Correction. This was definitely the Sass he knew.

LANDSDOWN SOUTH ROAD

Sass tugged at the fur-edged neckline of her dress as the carriage jostled its way to the Keep and tried to ignore the fact that the admiral stared at her.

It wasn't Eden's fault—she'd done her best to alter the silver dress and in truth, it no longer hung like a wilted sack from her shoulders. But in giving the dress some form, Eden had also given it much less of a neckline. Something that hadn't been apparent in the alteration procedures but now that Sass was living, moving and breathing—or trying not to breathe—in the dress, it was an obvious problem.

Reassurances from Eden didn't help. Nor did the fact that Eden's own gown was equally as low cut. For, as Sass was quick to point out and Serafino was as quick to snicker about, Eden had more with which to hold it up.

"If you can find an equinnard blanket in that carriage somewhere, I'll be grateful," Sass had called out to the pair as they'd gone to fetch the carriage. But they hadn't returned with one and the next noises she'd heard were Kel-Paten's.

So she'd squared her shoulders, grabbed a handful of skirt which constantly threatened to trip her, and marched into the main cabin. The look of surprise on his face only underscored in her mind how foolish she looked.

Now, seated next to her, he'd barely said a word. Any other time, whether riding through the forest together or cruising through the star-lanes together, Kel-Paten was always one to review the current plan of action for whatever it was they headed towards. She'd fully expected, sensing his dislike of Lord Tris, that he'd lay down some serious rules and regulations for the dinner tonight.

But she'd rated nothing more than a calmly offered, "You look very nice tonight, Sebastian," as he'd ushered her up into the carriage.

She'd fought the urge to clock him with a quick right cross. She did not look nice tonight and she knew it. She looked and felt silly. Like a child dressing up in mother's clothes. And the hair didn't help. She'd kept it short because in her position as a Fleet officer, it was easy and convenient. Now, it looked too easy. And too casual, in spite of all the fluffing Eden had done.

She not only looked like a child dressing up in mother's clothes, she looked like a boy child dressing up in mother's clothes!

LANDSDOWN NORTH ROAD

In another carriage, coming from a different direction, were Squire Hagar Ferbtil and his wife, Bluebell. Far from being discomforted by her new dress, Bluebell was quietly pleased. The bright orange and purple colors, she felt, complimented her curly red hair. She couldn't understand why no one in the dressmaker's shoppe had purchased it after so many months! And considering all the extra material it contained—why the two rows of huge purple and green flounces along the bottom hem and again around the neckline were worth the price of the dress alone.

She had Driznella, her chambermaid, wind some green and gold ribbons through her frequently unruly hair. Then she'd pranced down the front steps of their small manor on her way to the waiting carriage, nodding happily at the wide grins of the stableboy and gardener who once again were astounded at the cacophony of colors bedecking their mistress.

Her husband patted her thin hand affectionately.

"You certainly look one-of-a-kind tonight, my dear," he drawled. "A true original."

"Thank you, Hagar. I find I'm feeling much better. Very much better."

"A new dress will do that."

She brushed at her sleeve. "Yes, but it's actually because of the visions."

"Not more?" He leaned towards her, frowning.

"None at all, the past two nights." Bluebell took a deep breath and smiled. "Perhaps you were right. Perhaps they were just indigestion."

"Don't want me to mention them to Lord Tristan, then?"

Bluebell cautiously sought that cold, evil chill that had hovered on the edges of her dreams for weeks now, and found nothing. Blessedly, nothing. "Let's just enjoy our evening."

The squire nodded. "Couldn't agree with you more."

THE KEEP

Lord Tristan greeted them both warmly, long used to Bluebell's outlandish apparel.

"Sorry to be a tad early." Squire Ferbtil clasped Tristan's outstretched hand.

"No problem, old friend," Tris replied, leading them, as he always did when they were early, to the drawing room where an impressive selection of the best his cellars had to offer was laid out. To arrive on time, both Hagar Ferbtil and Lord Tristan knew, would seriously cut into the Squire's drinking time.

"Oh, just a wee bit for me, as usual," Bluebell said sweetly. Tris poured her the usual full goblet of sherry and stood by with the bottle as she gulped it down in one swallow.

"I must have been thirsty," she chirped and batted her sparse eyelashes at him as he refilled it, chuckling.

It was a comfortable scenario and one repeated weekly.

But this week, things were different. It wasn't that Tris wasn't glad to see old friends; he was. But he found himself unusually nervous about meeting a new one. This Lady Captain Tasha; this small but at the same time overwhelming package of pale moonlight energy. He hadn't been able to stop thinking about her since he'd met her...was it only yesterday?

Every once in a while, in one of those thoughts, he'd also see the shadow of a tall, dark man. It was not a pleasant intrusion. He didn't understand the presence of this man she call 'Kilpatten'. It was not a name he'd heard before and to be honest, not one he'd care to hear again. There was something quietly deadly about the man.

And something strange, though exactly what it was Tris didn't know. But tonight he'd have a chance to study him, if he so desired.

He just had a feeling though that he'd prefer to study Lady Captain Tasha more.

The sound of hoof beats on the graveled drive caught his attention through the open windows of the drawing room. Tris bowed politely to Bluebell. "If you will excuse me, my dear." He nodded to her husband also. "Squire Ferbtil. I believe I hear our other guests arriving."

<^>

Jace brought the carriage to a stop before the wide planked doors of the Keep and looked up.

"Damn nice piece of architecture," he commented, taking in the heavy stonework, impressive turrets and long slate roof. "Wonder where they keep the dragons?"

"There are no flying reptiles indigenous to this world," Eden replied with a smile, then paused and turned to Sass who leaned forward in the seat behind her. "Actually, we haven't seen any reptilian avians since that time we got shit-faced in Port Bangkok and ended up—"

"No, we haven't, that's for sure." Sass stood and gave giving her friend more than a warning glance.

"Sounds interesting," Jace intoned, hopping down from the front seat of the carriage and extending his hand to Eden. "Tell me about it sometime."

"Just don't believe everything you hear, 'Fino," Sass warned.

The former mercenary looked up at her, grinning devilishly.

"Actually, your and Eden's adventures have become rather legendary," he teased.

"Oh, great," Sass replied but she was smiling.

Kel-Paten, who'd been standing quietly beside her, stepped down from the carriage before Sass could and held out his hand.

Sass took it and, Jace noticed, didn't pull away when moments later when Kel-Paten's other hand rested against her waist. He could feel hope blossom through Kel-Paten but then, so could Eden. She turned her face coquettishly up to his, but her mental admonition was stern. *Don't start.*

He shelved the disparaging comment he'd intended to send Kel-Paten's way with a short sigh. *Yes, ma'am.*

Then something shot through his mind, fierce, intense. Only when Eden's hand tightened on his arm did he realize she'd sensed it as well. *Jace?*

Whatever it was dissipated as quickly as it had appeared, leaving no trace, no trail. Only a mild, rapidly fading sense of unease.

Not sure, he told her. *There may be dragons hiding here after all.*

Lord Tristan Dalbaran stepped through the great doors of the Keep in time to see the man called Kilpatten rest his hand against Lady Captain Tasha's waist. And he saw, as well, the decidedly possessive look on the man's face.

As much as Tristan preferred to have Sass be the object of his study, he'd first have to find out just who this pale-eyed man was. And what threat, or what leverage—for Lady Captain Sass didn't look overly pleased—he held over the small blonde.

But for now, he'd play the host as he'd been born and reared to do.

"Welcome, dear friends." Tristan sketched a slight bow and motioned the group towards the door. "Please, come in. You're most welcome at my humble home tonight."

Both Jace and Eden had already been aware of his presence before he spoke. And aware of his immediate dislike and distrust of the admiral. But he wasn't the negative energy they'd sensed.

Jace lightly stroked the nape of Eden's neck as she moved in front of him. *It's going to be an interesting evening, my love,* he told her. *Our dragon notwithstanding.*

It should be fine, Eden told him soothingly. *I've already warned Sass to behave.*

It's not Sass I'm worried about.

Tristan's too well bred and Kel-Paten's too well trained, she countered.

Don't count on it, love. Don't count on it.

THE KEEP DRAWING ROOM

Helluva dress if you've got a hangover.

Eden caught Jace's comment as he bent over Bluebell's hand during their perfunctory introductions to the Squire and his colorful wife. Fortunately, the social situation was such that her wide smile was easily interpreted as her pleasure at meeting the couple. No one but Jace and herself knew it was really in response to Bluebell's clownish costume.

But it was also a kindly smile; she could sense no meanness in the thin, oddly attired woman. And hell, she and the captain had known more eccentric types. Especially at that one pub on Kesh Valiir...

Another story I'd love to hear! Jace reminded her as he picked up on her train of thought.

But then Squire Ferbtil was bending over her hand as Lord Tris performed the introductions and she could only send Jace a fleeting mental roll of her eyes.

"Worth gettin' sick if Healers were all as lovely as you, my dear," the Squire offered her. "Pleasure to make your acquaintance." He turned to Sass, eyeing her thoroughly before grasping her hand next.

"Ahh, Warrior's Guild, Lord Tris tells us, eh? You bust 'em up and your Lady Healer puts them back together. Quite a business you have there!" He guffawed loudly, looking from Sass to Eden. Then his gaze traveled upwards to Kel-Paten standing behind Sass and he cleared his throat nervously.

Tristan stepped forward and continued with the introductions. "And may I present Lady Tasha's...associate, Master Kilpat—"

Bluebell's scream cut off his words.

The Squire caught his wife as she staggered back. "My dear! What is it?"

Jace dropped his shields, went on a wide telepathic scan. Images and sensations from the garishly dressed woman's mind flooded his, but he sensed nothing further than that. Nothing evil, nothing other than what Bluebell was remembering: a tall, dark-haired man with pale blue eyes, a miasma of death and destruction wrapped around him like a thick cloak.

The man looked like the Tin Soldier, yet something was different. Jace tried to hang onto the images, but Bluebell's intense emotions lay over them like a cloudy haze.

Jace? Eden's concern touched his thoughts as her fingers brushed his hand. *How could she know the admiral?*

She's remembering a dream, or what feels like many dreams.

Lord Tristan held a glass of sherry to Bluebell's lips. Kel-Paten had backed up several steps. Sass's frowning gaze focused on Lord Tristan, the Squire and Bluebell.

Bluebell's hand shot out, knocking the glass away. "You!" She pointed at Kel-Paten. "You've come to kill us all!"

A servant in a blue velvet jacket stepped into the drawing room, a small hand bell on a tray.

"Dinner is served," he said, punctuating his words with the bell's tinkle.

Bluebell collapsed in a heap on the floor.

CHAPTER THIRTY

THE KEEP LIBRARY

Sass managed not to trip on her long skirt as she hurried across the stone floor of the wide hallway. The library was the second door on the left, Tristan had told her. Kel-Paten stood in front of a large fireplace, gloved hands clasped behind his back. He turned slightly when she came in, his face shadowed. His eyes were their usual pale blue. No glow. No luminescence.

"Did you power up, not know it?" That had been her first thought when the Squire's wife had recoiled in abject fear at the sight of Kel-Paten. But Tristan had escorted the admiral—banished him, she realized belatedly—to the library before Sass had had a chance to verify her theory.

Tristan had also seemed none to happy to direct her to the library. But Bluebell's mournful pleas as she lay on the couch attended by Serafino and Eden, and the way the Squire kept trying to tug Tristan off into a corner, had permitted Sass to escape.

The library door clicked softly as she closed it.

Kel-Paten's harsh sigh was audible even over the crackle of flames in the fireplace. "I have no idea why that woman thinks I meant to kill her."

"Eden said Serafino couldn't pick up a whole lot from her thoughts yet, but evidently she's been dreaming about you."

"Me?" Kel-Paten started visibly. "But how, why? I've never met her before."

"That's why I thought maybe you'd powered up—"

"No."

"You remind her of someone in her dreams, then. Visions, actually. I heard the Squire mention something about her visions." Sass shrugged. She hoped that as Bluebell calmed down, Serafino and Eden would be able to make some sense of this. Having the admiral labeled as a killer wasn't going to help them gain the cooperation of the villagers in LandsDown.

Kel-Paten turned away, his fists clenched at his side. "I should leave." There was an odd tone in his voice. It took her a moment to place it.

Hurt. He was hurting, genuinely upset that he'd frightened the woman. An odd reaction from a 'cybe who was a professional soldier, whose purpose often had been to attack and defeat.

And protect and defend. She thought of how he'd responded immediately when the *Vax* had been threatened by the vortex. How he'd intercepted T'Krain's hand when the T'Sarii had suddenly grabbed for her.

And how he'd been willing to sacrifice his life when the shuttle's engine had faltered.

Branden Kel-Paten was a lot of things, but he wasn't a heartless killer. If anything, she was only too aware he wasn't heartless at all.

Thunder rumbled ominously in the distance. "Scared of a woman with a bad wardrobe, flyboy?" She pursed her lips into a small grin when he looked at her.

"More likely, she's afraid of me," he said but some of the tension she'd sensed in him was gone.

She stepped over to him, let her gaze travel up his chest to his face. "You scowl too much." As she said that she remembered Eden had suggested a fix for that problem.

But Kel-Paten wasn't a light flirtation. He was a project. She had enough projects at the moment, on this strange world in an uncharted galaxy. Though this was one project, she grudgingly admitted, that might be a bit fun to take on...

Nah. A grumble of thunder echoed again. She rubbed her hands over arms in response. Not that she was cold, but the thunder reminded her of the storms on Lethant. Reminded her of things she didn't want to think about.

"You all right?" Kel-Paten asked.

Bloody damn! Her smile had faded. He must have caught that, caught her movements.

"You're the one scowling now," he continued. Lightning flashed through the tall library windows.

"I hate storms." Her words came out in a rush. She forced herself to laugh. "At least, I hate them dirtside."

"You don't strike me as someone who'd be afraid of anything, Sebastian."

"Why don't we go see what Eden and Serafino have found out?"

That had been why she'd come to the library looking for him. Bluebell's hysterics had to be just that—hysterics. The woman, this whole damned planet, had no idea what a bio-'cybe was. Even if Kel-Paten had powered up, and he hadn't. The glow in his eyes could be nothing more than a reflection from the fire in the fireplace. Or the bright flash on lightning, like just now.

She jumped in spite of herself.

Kel-Paten's hand on her arm was oddly reassuring. "I'll apologize to Lady Ferbtil for frightening her. And I promise not to scowl."

Tristan met them at the closed doors to the drawing room, delaying their entry. "You've heard, I gather, that this region has of late been plagued by a malevolent Wizard."

Sass noted an expression of distaste cross Tristan's features as he spoke, but whether it was from the mention of the Wizard, or because Kel-Paten's hand cupped her arm, she didn't know.

"We've heard," Kel-Paten said as the door opened behind Tristan.

Serafino stepped through.

Tristan glanced at Serafino then back to Kel-Paten. "Lady Ferbtil maintains you're that Wizard."

"That's nonsense! We—" *Aren't even from your planet.* Sass caught herself before the words were uttered. She looked pleadingly to Serafino to intervene. But the Nasyry was damningly silent. He hated Kel-Paten and was probably enjoying Tristan's accusation.

Tristan continued. "She doesn't say you, Lady Sass, are in any way involved. Nor your friends. She maintains you're all unaware of Master Kilpatten's true identity." Tristan straightened his shoulders, glared up at Kel-Paten. "Ensorcelled. Her visions tell her so."

"Her visions are wrong," Kel-Paten said. "She's mistaken me for someone—"

"She says if we were to cut your arm, there would be no blood."

Oh, bloody damn! No, bloodless damn. Unless all the intelligence the U-Cees had on the admiral was in error, Bluebell was right. At least about that one thing: Kel-Paten's limbs were cybernetic. There wouldn't be any blood.

"May I?" Serafino asked smoothly. He held a small, thin knife in his hand.

Sass almost clocked him, then and there. What did he think he was doing? Their survival and their eventual return home, however far away that might be, depended on their combined talents. They needed Kel-Paten for his knowledge of the shuttle, for his ability to spike in. For his unerring, rapid analysis of data. For his unwavering dedication.

She—*they* needed him, damn it!

"Shadow." His nickname hissed between her teeth and only the slight shake of his head, and the fact that Kel-Paten didn't seem as upset as she was, stopped her from making her threats known.

Thunder crashed, rumbled. Jagged flashes of light pulsed through the hallway's tall arched windows, danced across the stone floor.

You'd better know what you're doing, Shadow, she told him silently, having no idea if he could hear her or not.

Kel-Paten extended his right arm, pushed up his sleeve. Serafino touched the point of his knife against the admiral's pale skin—synthederm, Sass knew. He drew the knife down in a line.

A thin red trail beaded up in the knife's path.

"Well?" Kel-Paten's voice was harsh as he pulled his sleeve back down.

"Well?" Serafino wiped the knife on his pant leg.

The flare of Lord Tristan's aristocratic nostrils was the only indication of his emotions. "I'll inform Lady Ferbtil she's in error. My apologies, Master Kilpatten."

Sass waited until the door closed behind Tristan before pinning first Kel-Paten with her gaze, then Serafino. "Well? Gentlemen?"

"A Nasyry can plant images in your mind," Kel-Paten said, his voice low. "Among other things."

Gods' sacred asses, she'd forgotten about that. That he'd levitated a coffee cup for her.

"Thank you," she told him.

Serafino shook his head. "Thank Eden. I didn't do it for him." He shot Kel-Paten a narrowed eyed glance. "Bluebell's not lying. You are what she's seen in her visions."

Kel-Paten tensed. "What are you talking about?"

Serafino reached back, laying his hand against the door as if to insure it wouldn't open unexpectedly. "There is something here, on this world. Something very dark, very dangerous. It's killed already, we've heard the stories. And lately, it's come to that woman in visions. It has your voice, your face, your eyes, right down to the power-glow. It's shown her your body. Right down to those access ports in your wrist."

Sass couldn't believe what she was hearing. "Impossible! They don't have that kind of technology here."

"They don't have to," Serafino answered. "These visions started a little more than a week ago. Just at the time we arrived. What have you been doing on your nightly watches, Kel-Paten? Guarding the shuttle? Or terrorizing the locals?"

Kel-Paten's fist moved in a blur. But Serafino's hand was surprisingly as quick. He held Kel-Paten's wrist firmly, his arm shaking with the strain—but he held it.

It took Sass a few seconds to realize what she'd just witnessed. Jace Serafino had stopped the unstoppable Branden Kel-Paten.

CHAPTER THIRTY-ONE

THE KEEP MAIN DINING ROOM

It was the worst dinner Kel-Paten had sat through in his life. The food, he was sure, was delicious. He hardly tasted what he put into his mouth. He was far too aware of Bluebell Ferbtil's terrified glances from across the table. Far too aware of Lord Tristan's suspicious glances from down the table. Far too aware of Serafino's barely perceptible sneer.

And very aware of Sass's position at the head of the table, next to Lord Tristan. With the Squire and Eden as further buffer.

He couldn't look at Sass without catching his lordship's cold gaze. The few times he tried, there was a decided puzzlement in her eyes.

He could well understand that. Serafino's ability to challenge him, physically, had surprised him as well. Oh, the Nasyry's arm had trembled from the effort; his face had paled from the strain. But he'd held his own for a few moments...long enough for Sass to step between them, shove them apart with a brusque command.

He didn't doubt that he could kill Serafino, if need be.

It just might take him a bit longer than he would have anticipated.

Yet, the man had intervened on his behalf. Because of Eden, he'd admitted. Doctor Fynn was the only one who'd smiled at him, spoke to him pleasantly all through that hellish dinner.

Serafino, Kel-Paten decided as tea was served in delicate cups, didn't deserve Eden Fynn. She was far, far too good for the likes of the Nasyry bastard.

Outside the tall leaded-glass dining room windows, the wind whipped the rain through the trees. Branches thrashed, hitting the outer walls, scraping the windows. Unless it stopped soon, the drive back in the borrowed open carriage would be hell. The perfect end to a perfect evening.

"I fear the storm shows no signs of slowing." Lord Tristan signaled for a second pot of tea. "You're all more than welcome to spend the night. I'll have the guest rooms freshened."

"There's no need—"

"Don't trouble yourself."

Sass and Bluebell Ferbtil spoke out in unison. But it was to Sass, Kel-Paten noted, that Lord Tristan turned his concerned countenance. "I'd never forgive myself if something happened to you, my dear."

The Squire cleared his throat. "'Preciate the offer, we do, m'lord. Terrible night out. Best to stay safe and dry inside."

Bluebell nodded at her husband's words, her voice wobbling as she spoke. "If we are to stay, would you mind if I had another glass of wine?"

She had three before the table was cleared, then tottered unsteadily against her husband as he led her from the dining room, a newly opened wine bottle clutched in her hand.

Evidently she needed more than a bit of alcoholic fortification in order to spend the night in a castle with Kel-Paten, the evil Wizard incarnate.

More servants appeared in the Ferbtils' wake.

"My staff will show you to your rooms," Tristan said, rising. He'd taken Sass's hand, drawn her up with him.

Something hot and cold roiled through Kel-Paten's chest. If this pretty-boy aristocrat thought he'd lead Sass back to his own rooms, he was sadly mistaken.

He rose quickly, but not quickly enough. A thin-faced older man stepped forward before he could reach Sass and Lord Tristan.

"Master Kilpatten? I'm Durward, the butler. This way, sir."

He went that way, but only because Sass and Lord Tristan went that way, too.

THE KEEP SECOND FLOOR

Kel-Paten's room was at the farthest end of the long second floor hallway. He lingered openly in the doorway, ignoring Durward as he bustled around inside, lighting the fire, fluffing the pillows on the four-poster bed. He acknowledged the location of the water pitcher and washbasin with the barest of nods. Lord Tristan lingered as well, talking quietly with Sass in front of her doorway at the base of a second set of stairs. Stairs that led, Kel-Paten guessed, to Tristan's own rooms, one flight above.

Durward departed. Eden and Serafino retired to side-by-side rooms midway down the hall. Kel-Paten had no doubt one of those rooms would be empty that night. So be it. At least that would keep the Nasyry away from him.

Now all he had to do was keep Lord Tristan away from Sass. He stayed in his doorway, scowling his best scowl, until he saw Sass retreat into her room and close the door.

Lord Tristan climbed the stairs without looking back.

Thunder crashed, the wind wailed and Kel-Paten stayed in his open doorway. He could switch to his full 'cybe function, last a long time without sleep. Between the moans of the wind and the thrash of the trees, he listened for the telltale creak of floorboards from above. The telltale footstep on the stairs. He fully expected Lord Tristan to creep down the stairs, decanter of something potent in hand, before the hour passed.

Which was why he was surprised when Sass's door cracked open, first.

His heart, or what he thought of as his heart, plummeted. Dear Gods, it'd never occurred to him she might seek out that pompous pretty-boy on her own.

She faced him before he had a chance to duck back in his room, hide his pain. After all, she'd been the one to berate him for meddling in the personal affairs of his officers and crew. A meddling he'd denied.

He couldn't deny where he stood now, caught, shamefaced.

She softly closed the door behind her and hesitated. He held his breath. He couldn't stop her from climbing those stairs. He wouldn't. But neither could he watch her.

He started to turn away when he realized she hurried towards him, silver gown swirling around her bare feet. To lecture him, no doubt. For meddling in the personal affairs of his officers.

No, only one officer. One particular green-eyed captain. He waited, fully prepared for a volley of words.

Fully unprepared when she threw herself against his chest, wrapping her arms tightly around him. She clung to him as if for dear life.

He tugged her inside his room, shutting the door without letting her go. And wondered if he'd indeed fallen asleep, and was dreaming.

Eden nestled back against the bed pillows, alone. Well, not quite alone. She could feel and hear Jace in her mind as he prowled through the shadows of the Keep's rooms below. The servants were in their quarters. Their host was one floor above, in his rooms. But it wasn't physical persons Jace Serafino sought.

It was an essence, an evil essence. He'd sensed it once, twice during dinner, when the storm battered the walls outside. So had Eden, though not as clearly as Jace had.

He couldn't sleep until he'd assured himself it wasn't also inside. Seeking, perhaps, the 'cybe admiral. Neither Eden nor Jace gave complete credence to Bluebell's visions. But they couldn't discount them, either. They'd seen her visions as she'd remembered them. And they felt the presence, too.

Jace?

Nothing yet, love. Just a few more things I want to check. Then I'll be right up. Keep the bed warm.

She snuggled further down into the soft mattress and hoped the furzels were safe inside the shuttle.

The wind howled.

Jace prowled.

Something felt very wrong in LandsDown.

<\^>

Kel-Paten thought Sass felt very right in his arms, even if the next two crashes of thunder made her tremble. He brushed his face against her hair, rested his mouth next to her ear. "It's okay, Sass."

"It's not okay." Her voice was muffled in his chest.

He slid his arm under her legs, bunching the fabric of her skirt and picked her up easily. Her arms curled around his neck, her face burrowing into his shoulder. There was a long couch in front of the fireplace. He sat, still cradling her, still not sure he wasn't dreaming. Rain thrummed against the windows. The fire flickered, crackling.

Her hair against his face felt like silk, smelled like sandalwood. Everywhere her body touched his felt alive, electric. He wanted desperately to push her down into the soft cushions of the couch and kiss her senseless. Except he wasn't sure if that's what she wanted; he honestly didn't think she did. She probably just needed a friend. The storm frightened her, as illogical as that was to him. She needed not to be alone.

He was willing to be that friend; anything she wanted, anything she needed.

She shifted in his lap. Her breasts, almost spilling out of her low-cut gown, pressed against him. Her fingers played up the back of his neck, into his hair.

He bit back a groan. His mind might be willing to be her friend, but his body intensely wanted to be her lover. "Sass—"

She leaned her forehead against his. Her voice rasped. "Lecture me, yell at me. Do something to me! I. Hate. Storms."

He kissed her. Friendship be damned, his mouth came down hard on hers and he kissed her.

For a moment he thought she might pull away. Then her lips parted, letting his tongue explore her mouth. He sucked in the sweetness of her, the soft, warm, hot everything of her.

He moaned when she kissed him back, her teeth raking his lower lip. Her tongue teased his and threads of heat shot through his body.

He pushed her back against the couch's cushioned arm. Or maybe she pulled him down on top of her. He wasn't sure. It didn't matter because he felt her leg snake up around his thigh and she arched against him, pressing into his hardness, making his breath come out in something that was cross between a gasp and a growl. It ended in another kiss, deeper, harder.

His left hand cupped her breast, his fingers searching past the edge of the fabric 'til he found a taut nipple. He circled its peak with his thumb. Her small whimper of pleasure tore through him like an entire bank of ion torpedoes. He dragged his mouth off hers and let his lips take over where his thumb had been.

"Oh, Gods!" She thrust her hands through his hair as he teased, sucked.

He licked the curve of her breast, then ran his tongue up to the hollow of her throat. Her pulse beat frantically against his lips. He kissed her neck, the line of her jaw, claimed her mouth again. She raised her hips, pressing, moving wantonly against his throbbing hardness. He reached under her, closed his hand over the soft swell of her rear, pushing her more intimately against him. His tongue thrust into her mouth.

She kissed him back with a passion he'd only dreamed about. Her body, her hands touched him, caressed him. Heat surged through him, made him catch his breath. Made him realize that if he didn't slow this down, it would be over far, far too quickly. They had all night. He wanted to make love to her slowly, thoroughly, passionately all night.

He pulled back slightly, stroked the side of her face with a black-gloved hand that trembled as she'd trembled in his grasp a little while before. Her eyes glittered in the firelight. Her lips curved in a small, almost secret smile. "You're not scowling, Branden."

Branden. His heart swelled with joy. Dear Gods, she did know he had a first name.

"I've loved you for so long, Sassy-girl."

A softness played over her features. It made him ache. She gently touched his mouth with her fingers. "Branden, I—"

The bedroom door crashed against the stone wall behind him. "Fire! Fire!" Durward stood in the open doorway, his white shirt hanging in sooty shreds from his shoulders. "We've been hit by lightning! Fire!"

And then as quickly as he had appeared, the butler disappeared, the only proof of his existence the continued pounding on the doorways as he ran down the corridor.

"Fire!"

Branden Kel-Paten stared down at the beautiful woman in his arms, taking in the flush on her cheeks, the moist and swollen lips, and the unmasked terror in her wide, green eyes, and wondered, not for the first time, if some potent and pissed-off deity had put a curse on him the day he was spawned.

He swore volubly as he dragged Sass to her feet then propelled her towards the door.

CHAPTER THIRTY-TWO

OUTSIDE THE KEEP

Fully involved.

It was a term, Jace noted as he jogged back towards the line of servants forming a meager bucket brigade, that often applied to a raging fire. But it was also one that could have just as aptly described himself and Eden when Durward had pounded on her bedroom door.

Talk of *coitus interruptus*!

The scenario might have even been humorous had the situation before him not been so dire.

The storm had passed as quickly as it had appeared, leaving not even a trace of rain to assist in firefighting efforts. The entire west side of the Keep was engulfed in flames. The bright reddish glow cast eerie shadows on the forms of shouting men and women moving in what looked like controlled confusion around the mansion's perimeter. Jace saw Squire Ferbtil, a nightstocking on his head, waving his arms, shouting orders. Orders no one listened to.

Jace pulled up short, shaking his head, his thoughts suddenly echoed by a familiar deep voice.

"Fire's out of control," Kel-Paten said, stepping out of the bucket line. Soot smudged his face and his shirt.

Sass appeared by the admiral's side, looking equally as disheveled, her silver gown ruddy in the fire's glow. "We found three servants trapped in the hallway, had to guide them out. Then we've been doing what we could here." She nodded to the line behind her. "Where's Eden?"

Jace motioned to the stables. "She set up a sickbay, a triage area for any injured."

She nodded and turned back to the conflagration, her brow furrowed. "The Keep has a tile roof. Stone walls. To get this far, a fire this intense...it's not like they had high-voltage wires to conduct a charge."

"The storm didn't cause the fire. At least," and he closed his eyes briefly, no longer sensing what he had minutes before, "not directly."

Kel-Paten tensed visibly. "What did?"

"Something that wants our attention. *Your* attention." Jace felt the anger surge through the admiral at his words. Anger and a twinge of fear. He understood. This wasn't an area normally covered in Triad Fleet training.

"Well, it's got it," Kel-Paten said tersely as Lord Tristan strode up, wearing the same dark pants he had at dinner, but bare-chested. His short quilted robe, blackened and stained, hung open.

"A miracle, but I believe everyone's out. Alive." He seemed deeply shaken, not at all like the suave, self-assured man who'd presided over dinner. "I am so sorry. I don't understand how..." His voice trailed off. "Excuse me. I must speak to the Squire."

Jace turned back to Kel-Paten as Tristan headed away. "If Bluebell's had any more visions, you're in trouble."

"And if you put the suggestion in her mind?" Kel-Paten shot back.

"Then Eden would tell you." Which was true. Eden had turned out to be not only his soul-mate, but his conscience. Had he not met her, had her love and compassion not soothed the jagged edges of his heart, he would've gladly challenged the Tin Solider before they'd left the *Vax*. And he would've gladly used any opportunity to cause the 'cybe pain, in any way he could.

But Eden would know and his pain at losing Eden would be greater than his pain over Bianca and Jorden.

"You and I," he told Kel-Paten, "have a situation to straighten out. You know it. I know it. But this isn't it. And this isn't the time."

The time would come. Jace Serafino would make sure of that. They just had a Wizard to deal with, first.

THE *GALAXUS* AFT CABIN

Sass woke to the heavy weight of Tank on her legs and the acrid smell of smoke in her nose. She sniffed her arm cradling her head. Her skin smelled slightly barbequed. Her arms and back ached from hauling bucket after bucket of water the night before.

Noises told her someone moved about the ship but she saw no one as she padded to the san-fac. She tabbed on the shower, and though the streams of water washed away the stench of the fire nothing could clear the memory of the flames, the smoke, the storm, the…

Dear Gods, what *had* she been doing with Kel-Paten just before the Keep caught on fire?

Causing more than a bit of heat of their own, that's what.

She toweled off, rearranging her thoughts. The ride back in Grendar's carriage had been full of arguments, and information, about this malevolent energy Serafino and Eden sensed. Nothing further of an intimate nature had happened, or been mentioned. They'd all been exhausted, angry, perplexed.

She pulled a comb through her short, damp hair. Serafino and Kel-Paten had continued their arguments when she'd trudged back to her cubicle and collapsed onto her bunk, dislodging her fidget. She barely remembered removing her silver gown.

When she'd awakened, Tank was still the only creature sharing her bed.

Gods' blessed asses, what *had* she done with Kel-Paten?

Assigned herself a project, that's what.

Her project was bent over the science console in the cockpit, data lines spiked into his left wrist. He gave no indication he was aware of her presence. She stayed back from the open hatchway, sipped her coffee and studied his profile for a moment: the strong line of his jaw; the thickness of his dark brows, drawn down in concentration; the sheen of his tousled dark hair.

He was scowling. Which only made him slightly less gorgeous than when he smiled.

When Branden Kel-Paten smiled, she'd learned last night, he was downright devastating.

She'd always known that, always felt it. But he'd been her adversary, then her CO. He was an admiral. He was a bio-cybernetic construct. She was…not who he thought she was. If she were finally to be honest about it, that's what had kept her away from him, more than any other reason. He didn't know who she was, what she'd done. He didn't know about Lethant. He just might rescind all those love letters if he did.

He turned as she raised her coffee cup to her lips, his eyes luminous. He was under full 'cybe power, which meant she couldn't read his expression. She wished she had Serafino's ability to read his thoughts.

"Sass." His voice had that oddly soft quality it always did when he was spiked in.

"'Lo, Kel-Paten." She tilted her cup in his direction. "Need coffee?"

"Sure."

"Be right back." She refreshed her cup, filled one for him and wondered what she should say, if anything, about last night. Wondered if she should wait for him to say something first. For all she knew, he was under the impression she'd wantonly and brazenly thrown herself at him.

Well, she had. The storm shared some of the blame but not all of it. She sealed the coffeepot, set it to brew again. It was a small cockpit up front and just the two of them. Maybe she should wait to see if he said anything first.

Serafino almost mowed her down as she crossed through the main cabin. Hot coffee sloshed on her hand.

"Got it!" he shouted.

Kel-Paten appeared in the cockpit hatchway. No data lines dangled from his wrist. He'd spiked out. "You have a fix?"

"Strong one. We move, now."

Sass had a feeling their conversation revolved around the Wizard. It looked like her discussion would have to wait. She chugged a mouthful of coffee, handed Kel-Paten his cup and turned. "Clue me in, 'Fino."

"You know that Wizard he said doesn't exit." Serafino thrust his chin towards Kel-Paten, behind her. "I just found him."

"An unstable energy field is not a Wizard," Kel-Paten countered.

"Energy fields don't have a sentience. This thing does."

"You can't be sure—"

"I can."

Sass left them to their argument, which sounded suspiciously the same as last night's, and went outside in search of Eden.

"I don't have the same talents as Jace," Eden admitted as she disconnected the portable generator from an assortment of scanners. A small griztard scurried up the cable and out of sight. "But I think he's right. There's a sentience there, a consciousness that has intent."

"You found it with this?" Sass pointed to what appeared to have been some kind of makeshift science lab on the edge of the clearing.

"Jace and the admiral put this together last night. They took turns monitoring."

Sass heard footsteps behind her, then Kel-Paten's voice. "The field's instability precluded a direct tracing scan. A dual system was the only option."

"The Wizard likes to play hide and seek." Jace seemed almost gleeful. "It's time for us to seek. Save the village and all that rot."

Sass watched Serafino load the equipment onto the small anti-grav pallet. *He's hiding something.* The fire at the Keep had disturbed them all, as had the stories they'd heard about dead animals and missing villagers. All attributed to this Wizard.

Altruism and Serafino were not completely incompatible concepts. However, revenge and Serafino seemed more likely. Revenge for the recent destruction would make most people solemn, not prone to whistling, as Serafino was now as he guided the pallet back to the shuttle.

Unless, of course, this revenge also provided vindication. And the destruction of someone Serafino hated even more than this purported Wizard.

Sass could think of only one person who fit that description: Branden Kel-Paten.

GALAXUS MAIN CABIN

"Carriage is packed." Jace Serafino leaned on the back of Eden's seat and plucked the mug of cold water from her hand. He took a long sip. It was a warm day outside and promised to get warmer. At least the ride to the foothills wouldn't be physically taxing. From there, however, they'd have to continue on foot to the southern side, where their sensors had located a nest of caverns. Supplies and equipment would have to be carried.

Supplies, equipment and weapons. He accepted the rifle and spare powerpack Sass handed him. Lights blinked green. He adjusted power levels, raised the rifle to his eyes, squinted, brought the shuttle's open hatchway into his sights. The Tin Soldier ducked his head slightly as he stepped into the main cabin. Jace followed his movements, keeping the 'cybe in the crosshairs.

A ripple of annoyance washed over him. It wasn't Eden, but Sass. Sass didn't trust him. He assumed that would be the case after what he'd sensed between Sass and the Tin Soldier last night. Something had shifted in the small blonde's attitude towards the 'cybe. Something the 'cybe was very happy about.

This meant that what he'd learned might make both of them very unhappy.

Too bad.

You don't have proof.

Eden's admonition sounded in his mind. He lowered the rifle and sighed. *I'm an unholy bastard, love. Get used to it.*

This sentience may have sought Kel-Paten but that doesn't mean Kel-Paten's involved.

Involved enough that it knows the Tin Soldier intimately. You saw

Bluebell's visions as clearly as I did. She knew about the powerports in his hands.

None of us, Eden countered as she checked her rifle's powerpack, *have been here before. That includes the admiral. This Wizard sentience was here before we were.*

But we are *here. Almost as if we'd been guided. Once we find, and disable, this Wizard, I'm going to go over the shuttle's nav logs. Remember how insistent he was that we take this shuttle? Want to bet he had our destination pre-programmed?*

And he pre-programmed the Irks to attack? Eden's mental snort was most unladylike.

I put nothing beyond the capabilities of the Faction.

And that's why he's going with us to stop this energy field? The one you say *he created.*

Or it created him. Jace gave her a mental shrug as Sass distributed four small, but lethal, combat daggers. Standard Triad dirtside survival gear.

"Just in case this energy field tries to mess with our energy fields," she said.

Jace was about to comment that metal knives would have little effect on an incorporeal substance but decided against it. After all, it was the Tin Soldier's belief the Wizard was incorporeal. Jace wasn't sure. The Nasyry had legends of things that were, yet were not. He'd lived long enough to know anything was possible.

The admiral wouldn't be going with us if he were part of this Wizard thing, Eden persisted.

Jace hesitated. He loved Eden but her loyalties were obvious. He hated being the one to destroy them. Nevertheless, he'd be damned if he'd let anything harm her. She had to know. *He would, if Psy-Serv and the Faction programmed him to do that. I told you this on the Vax. It's very possible his cooperation is a set-up, a trap. One he might not even be aware of, until he hears the right code word, sees the right image. Then that Tin Soldier you think is so brave and true may turn out to be an enemy, programmed by the Faction to kill me.*

He felt horror shudder through her.

And Sass?

I'll do what I can to keep her alive. Because if he intends to kill me, then his primary mission is to kill her, too.

CHAPTER THIRTY-THREE

LANDSDOWN FOREST

Kill! Kill! Now, kill!
Friend...
Fat griztard! Stalk! Kill!
Friend!

Tank quieted his wriggling rear end and twitching tail and peered through the underbrush. The older furzel was two tail-lengths ahead of him. Beyond him, he could see MommySass's boots. But they were now far enough away from their secret hiding place in the back of Rolling Wooden Box that he could only barely scent the equinnards. It had been a long trip from Shuttle Home. Tank was hungry. *Fat griztard, friend. Please?*

Reilly trotted back to Tank and cuffed the fidget's ear with his paw. *Bad Thing, friend. Stalk Bad Thing. Protect MommyEden. Protect Sass. Kill Bad Thing.*

Fat griztard later?

Later. Follow MommyEden. Follow Sass. Follow Tinsoldier and Shadow. Kill Bad Thing.

Tank bounded ahead, his large paws scattering twigs and leaves. *Kill Bad Thing! Kill Bad Thing! Later, food!*

<^>

Kel-Paten adjusted the sensitivity on his datacorder again and frowned. It was picking up interference from somewhere or something. He suspected the high concentration of crystalline ore in the mountain range was part of the problem. The other was the fact that, as he and Sass had discussed, they had no base data on Haven-One; nothing to use for calibration parameters.

Then there was Serafino. He had no idea if a half-Nasyry could skew a datacorder. But he wouldn't put it past him.

So he damned the datacorder, he damned Haven-One and he damned Serafino's theatrical tendencies as he trudged up the winding hillside through the thick underbrush. He hadn't wanted to confront this energy field today. They needed more time to analyze it, study it. It was too erratic, too unstable.

Those were the same reasons Serafino used to insist on action. The thing—Kel-Paten refused to think of it as a Wizard—was unstable. They might not get another chance.

The only positive note was that Sass was at his side. But she'd been uncharacteristically quiet since last night's events. She'd offered him coffee but called him Kel-Paten.

Not Branden.

He wondered what had happened to Branden. But with Serafino only a few feet ahead, now wasn't the time to ask. He angled his 'corder towards her. "I'm still getting random spikes. What do you have?"

She sidestepped a low bush and showed him her screen. "I'd give anything for one of the *Vax*'s science stations. Or the *Regalia's*. Manually integrating this stuff is a—holy lubashit!"

Eden, ahead of them, stopped and turned. "What?"

He would've asked the same question, but when Sass put her 'corder side by side with his, he saw it, too. What they would've seen had they been on the *Vax*. What they might have seen had Serafino not split apart the *Galaxus*' meager science scanners, dragging half out into the forest because of the damned crystalline interference.

Sometimes less is more. The smaller, held-held 'corders stripped away all the superfluous data and left only the basics. Basics that looked incredulously familiar to both him and, judging from her outburst, to Sass.

"Vortex." He couldn't believe he was saying the word. He couldn't believe what the data told him. But data didn't lie. "This Wizard of yours, Serafino, isn't a Wizard at all. It's a vortex, a rift, forming somewhere in this mountain."

Serafino grasped Sass's 'corder. "Impossible. It's…"

"A vortex," Kel-Paten repeated, feeling suddenly a bit more encouraged. Some of the guilt he'd wrestled with lifted. "You claim this Wizard's looking for me. But this vortex matches the energy signature of the rift that brought you to us."

Serafino seemed to catch the implication: all that had happened wasn't Kel-Paten's fault. But he didn't like it, either. "That doesn't preclude your involvement."

"It does preclude your assumption it's some kind of Wizard. We," and he glanced at Sass, caught her nod, "monitored the entire rift eruption. It may have been unexpected, but it wasn't unusual. And it definitely wasn't some kind of sentient life form." Damn, but it felt good to be right again!

Serafino's eyes narrowed slightly. Kel-Paten waited for the customary terse remark to sound in his mind but there was only silence, underscored by the rustling of the leaves and distant hoot-calls of Haven-One's avian species.

It was Sass who voiced what Serafino no doubt was thinking. "Rifts don't form within a planet's gravity well."

Serafino pointed to Sass's screen. "It's shifting again. Let's go!"

It took Kel-Paten micro-seconds to know what he had to do. "I'll meet you at the cavern entrance." He dropped into full 'cybe power and sprinted ahead, cresting the rising terrain effortlessly. He hated leaving Sass behind but he hated more to risk her walking into an unknown situation.

His cybernetics guaranteed he'd arrive twenty, if not thirty minutes before she, Eden and Serafino did. He'd know by then if it was a Wizard they faced...or something worse.

"Why does that not surprise me?" Jace adjusted the rifle strap on his shoulder and picked up his pace. *Think he's going to warn someone?* he asked Eden.

"He's just used to being in command." Sass answered his first question, unaware of his second.

Sass is right, Eden replied but he could almost hear a slight crack in her confidence in the Tin Soldier.

I need you to keep an open mind. In case.

I need you to keep an open mind, she countered.

Then there was only the grunting silence of three people climbing rocky, rising terrain while laden down with laser rifles, stun pistols, datacorders and a variety of dirtside survival equipment.

Haven-One's native creatures hooted, warbled and cawed in the forest around them. Leaves rustled overhead. Branches of low-lying shrubs snapped, cracked as they passed. It'd been about two hours since they left the shuttle. Twenty minutes, perhaps, from where Grendar's carriage sat tucked into a shady grove, with a small stream close by for Prancer and Bailey. Jace focused all his concentration on the energy source ahead, the one that pulsed at him through the rocky walls of the mountain. It knew they were coming. Hell, even without Kel-Paten playing advance scout, it knew they were coming. This close, it had to feel his probes as sharply as he felt its own.

He was only half-Nasyry. He was aware of the limits of his power, his shielding, his abilities. But they'd had been enough to startle the Tin Soldier. Jace grinned to himself, in spite of the fact that sweat trickled between his shoulder blades and his rifle strap chafed against his neck. Kel-Paten would be a little more circumspect around him now. That, Jace Serafino believed, was something he'd be able to take advantage of when the time came.

That time was coming very soon.

Something jolted him, hard. He stumbled, met Eden's concerned gaze as he straightened, leaning against a tree for support. In spite of the heat of the day, he felt chilled.

"I think the Wizard just said 'hello'."

Kel-Paten hunkered down a few yards from the cave opening, breathing hard, and saw the readings spike on his 'corder. At the same time, he felt a slight tremor beneath his boots. Coincidence? Or had his presence sparked the energy surge, the tremor? It was a question he'd never have asked on the *Vax*, never have even considered but for the Nasyry bastard.

He straightened, adjusted parameters on his 'corder again, then swept his gaze over the cave's entrance. His enhanced vision sought physical proof of an inhabitant, or inhabitants. Just in case Serafino was right and they were dealing with a physical sentience. But he saw nothing, no footprints, other than his behind him. No forced chiseling of the narrow rock opening. No debris, no illogically broken branches. Up until the point the Keep had burned, he'd even suspected Lord Tristan—he still gritted his teeth at the name—of playing a prank on the villagers. Creating a Wizard so the Keep would maintain control.

But even that pompous pretty boy wouldn't burn down his own castle for that purpose.

The ground trembled again. He stepped closer to the mouth of the cave. Readings spiked, flattened, spiked. It made no sense. It made no damn sense.

That was the only thing that prompted his next action. He sucked in a deep breath and, feeling like a total fool, addressed the cave in a voice infamous for making crewmembers shake in their boots. "I'm here. What do you want?"

<^>

"How much farther?" Eden asked Sass. The medicorder in her hand was useful for identifying and analyzing organics, not distances. She'd monitored Jace for the past fifteen minutes. His heart and respiration rates were higher than she liked, even with their current physical exertion. Something was going on, something with this Wizard energy source, and Jace had shut her out.

More than what her medicorder told her, that's how she knew something was going on. Jace had shut her out.

"Depending upon how many more boulders we have to go over, or around, I'd say ten minutes." Sass lengthened her stride. "You look like lubashit on a lemon, 'Fino. Want to tell us about it?"

Jace's smile was thin. "I'm handling it."

Not well, Eden told him as, true to Sass's prediction, they came to another cluster of boulders.

"Around," Sass said. They backtracked a few yards to the left and plunged through the underbrush.

Twice Eden felt something strange brush past her mind. It was an odd sensation, not frightening, but not wholly pleasant, either. She wished she knew more about telepathic talents, about her Zingaran heritage. About the Nasyry. Maybe she and Jace should've spent more time talking and less time kissing.

Not a chance! He underscored his comment with a decidedly sexy chuckle.

Jace, what's going on?

If I knew, I'd tell you. Trust me on this, love. This is... I'm still working on identifying on what this is.

Sass stopped so abruptly that Eden bumped into her shoulder. "Up there." Sass held her 'corder out. Lines danced on the screen, converging on a single point. She raised the small unit and used it to delineate a jagged outcropping of rocks.

Jace grasped Sass's wrist, brought the 'corder towards him. "Well, either the Tin Soldier hasn't been able to shut down the energy source, or else it ate him."

"Energy source?" Sass jerked her face towards him. "You said it was a Wizard."

"It is." Jace shrugged. "And maybe it's not."

"He's being equally as evasive with me." Eden patted Sass's shoulder. "I think Captain Serafino's having trouble admitting he may not have an answer."

"If that's so, it'll be a first." Jace's grin had a bit more life to it. "Aren't you two lucky to witness to such a momentous occasion?"

"Spare me, 'Fino. C'mon. Let's see what the admiral's found out." Sass pushed past them.

Eden waited until the captain was a few feet ahead. "You honestly don't know?"

"Let's say I have a couple of ideas. I just don't like any of them."

A low growl rumbled in Reilly's throat.

Friend? Tank hurried to catch up with him.

Bad Thing. Bad Thing comes.

Something foul laced the wind. Something dark filtered through the sunlight. A rare shiver of fear ran down Tank's spine. He flattened his furry ears to his head and suddenly felt very, very angry with Bad Thing. *Protect MommySass. Protect. Scratch. Claw. Kill.*

CHAPTER THIRTY-FOUR

Sass pushed on ahead, her boots slipping on pebble-strewn ground cover. Best to let Eden work on Serafino in private. The Nasyry knew more than he was telling and Eden's interrogation methods were no doubt far more effective than her own would be.

The forest had thinned but the low, bristly scrub brush was still aggravatingly thick. Branches snagged her uniform pants, scraped her hands.

The wildly vacillating readings on her 'corder worried her more.

So did the fact that Kel-Paten's life-signature flickered erratically on the screen. She hoped that was due to crystalline interference. A small, nagging fear made her pick up speed.

Not that he couldn't handle whatever was in that mountain. He was a 'cybe, for the Gods' sakes. Constructed to kill.

He kissed pretty damn well, too. She didn't want to think about that.

The 'corder beeped, signaling she'd reached the coordinates per Serafino and Kel-Paten's calculations. She put one hand on her hip and looked...up. Bloody damn. A ledge, probably fronting the mouth to a cave, jutted out about ten feet over her head.

"Kel-Paten?" she called out hopefully and wished for the hundredth time the commbadge system worked.

One heartbeat, two. Ten. No answer.

And no sign of Serafino and Eden behind her.

But something...something else was. She heard it, in the softest of noises. A rustling. A snap. She drew out her laser pistol, flicked off the safety.

Whatever stalked her was smaller than Eden and Serafino, but far more stealthy. She backed up a step, listening. Watching...

...and saw a black and white furred fidget scamper out of the bushes, his long fluffy tail decorated with twigs and leaves.

"Tank! How in hell?" She shook her head, chuckling and holstered her pistol. "No, don't tell me," she said, scooping the pudgy creature into her arms. "I don't want to know."

Tank squirmed as she plucked the twigs from his tail.

"Where's Reilly?" she asked, as if the fidget could answer. Well, he could, to Serafino or Eden. She put him down, scanned the bushes but didn't see the furzel's sleek, dark form. "Just you?"

As if in answer, Tank shook himself then trotted a few steps away. He stopped, looked back at her. His long tail flicked twice.

"Want me to follow?" Gods, she was in love with a 'cybe and having a conversation with a fidget. The U-Cees, or the Alliance, or whoever the hell they were now would no doubt Section Forty-Six her when they got home.

If they got home.

Tank disappeared around a scrawny clump of bushes. Sass followed, her mind playing back what she'd just said.

In love with a 'cybe. With Branden Kel-Paten. Was she?

Nah. Not her. She argued with herself as she followed the fidget to a stack of boulders that, with a little effort, provided a sharply sloping stairway to the ledge.

She'd always *admired* Kel-Paten, she told herself as she secured the 'corder. They were friends. Well, maybe a little more than friends.

She assessed her current location, which was preferable to the journey her mind was making. The only way up those rocks would be fidget-style, on all fours. Her knee scraped against a jagged edge of the rock as she climbed.

Tank had much less trouble navigating.

Sass crawled onto the ledge. Round yellow eyes blinked at her as if to say, well, what took you so long?

She brushed herself off as she stood, then flipped open the 'corder. "Kel-Paten?"

No answer, and his life-sig still blinked on and off.

"Think we should wait for—" she asked the fidget but he bounded ahead of her into the mouth of the dark cave. Pistol in one hand, flashing 'corder in the other, she followed.

It wasn't a cave, but a cavern. It opened before her like a black-filled maw, smelling damp and dusty. Her bootsteps echoed. "Kel-Paten?"

She hesitated, listening, straining. Heard nothing but Tank's furry paws scattering pebbles as he trotted in front of her. She moved forward, grayness closing around her. Reluctantly, she shoved the 'corder back in its holder on her belt and replaced it with the slim glowlight. The pistol she wasn't willing to relinquish.

"Tank?" His black tail blended with the cave's murky interior. She played the beam over the shadows, looking for the fidget's white hind leg. Something wavered on the edge of her vision to the right. She jerked the beam, saw only a blackish green color. Mossy rocks?

No. It moved.

She flicked the light to wide beam. A giant griztard lunged towards her, mouth open, fangs glistening, slime dripping.

She sucked in a harsh breath of fear—and fired.

White streaks split the misty grayness. Splinters exploded from the cavern's walls. Damn, she'd missed it! She swung the light in an arc, right, left. Nothing. Heart in her throat, she spun around. The thing was enormous. It couldn't have gotten behind her. Nothing that big could move that quickly!

The cavern's entrance formed a pale yellow glow, absorbing her light beam. The monster griztard wasn't behind her. It wasn't in front of her. That meant—

She spun again as a pounding, crunching noise echoed over her right shoulder. A shadow wavered. She targeted—

—and almost shot Branden Kel-Paten.

"Sass!" He dropped to his knees as laser fire burned past his head.

"Shit!" She holstered his pistol and bolted towards him. "Branden!" He was up on one knee when she reached him. "Gods damn! There was this griztard. Huge! Did you see it?" She grabbed his arm, hunkered down and only then realized how close she'd come to killing him. "You okay?"

He stared at her, his eyes luminous. He was on full 'cybe power. Because she'd almost shot him? She hoped not. Still, she didn't pull away when he reached out and touched her face. His 'cybe systems also enhanced his low-light vision. "You're real this time."

"This time?"

"You own a red dress?"

"A red what?" She rose as he did, not quite sure who pulled whom upwards.

He shook his head. "I should know better than to think you'd be traipsing around in a cave in a red dress."

She played the light over his form. He looked okay. "You hit your head in here?"

"No, I think…" He frowned. "I think *in here* affects our heads. You saw, what, a giant griztard?"

"Huge sucker! Had to be eight, ten feet tall. It—"

"Was wearing a red dress?" His mouth curved in an odd smirk.

"Don't be—oh. You're saying it was an hallucination?"

"You shot at it. Did you hit it?"

"No."

"That big. That close. You're a damn good shot."

She was. Fortunately, Kel-Paten had damn better cybernetic reflexes.

"Hold this." She shoved the pistol at him, tucked the glowlight in her armpit and pulled out her 'corder.

"It doesn't work," he told her as the readings flared and disappeared.

"I saw a griztard." Her voice was firm.

"I saw you, in a red dress. Bottle of something in one hand. Never did get close enough to read the label."

"Murrupp," said Tank.

She gently nudged the fidget's ample hind end with her foot. "He's real."

"You brought him?"

"As usual, he brought himself. So what's in here, beside me and my red dress? And a nasty griztard. Did you locate the energy source?"

"I couldn't get anything useful from the 'corders. I hoped that my, um, my own systems might be more reliable." He let out a short, frustrated-sounding sigh.

"What did you find?"

"Nothing." He glanced to his left, where Tank sat diligently cleaning his white hind foot. "I, my systems function normally relative to my own diagnostics. But all external data is as skewed as this." He tapped her 'corder. "We need Serafino."

He wasn't happy about that, Sass could tell. He didn't like being powered up around her. He didn't like not having answers. And he didn't like having to rely on Serafino. "He and Eden were a bit behind me."

He glanced over his shoulder again. "Probably be best to wait for them outside."

She wouldn't argue with that. The dark shadows of the cave seemed to be excellent hiding places for giant griztards.

Suddenly, the rocky floor beneath her boots trembled violently. Sass stumbled to her left. Kel-Paten caught her against him as they fell against the rough wall. Dirt and debris rained on them from above and a groaning, tearing sound echoed through the cavern.

"This way!" He grabbed her around the waist and propelled her forward towards the entrance to the cave. The ground lurched. Rocks tumbled.

Something latched onto her shin, something needle-like and sharp. Sass swore, stumbling.

"Tank!" she reached down to grab the fidget. But just as quickly the small animal detached himself and bounded in the opposite direction, back into the dark heaving maw.

Her heart plummeted. "I can't leave him!" she cried to Kel-Paten.

"Damn it, you can't—"

"No!" she tore out of his grasp and ran after the fidget. "Tank! Come back!"

"Sass!" Kel-Paten pounded after her.

Tank's solitary white hind leg flashed in and out of her glowlight's beam. Sass skittered unsteadily, the ground shuddering. The fidget careened to the left, into a narrower tunnel. Sass followed, her breath coming in hard gasps. She couldn't leave Tank to die. There had to be time to catch him, and get out.

The fidget sprang onto a low rock ledge. Swearing, Sass grabbed him, dropping her glowlight in the process.

Then Kel-Paten grabbed her, almost crushing them both against his chest.

Behind them, an ear-splitting screeching echoed, then a great roar. Kel-Paten shoved her into a crouch, his body shielding hers. He rasped her name, his mouth against her ear. She wrapped her free arm around his neck, turned her face and as dust and pebbles showered down, kissed him with every bit of energy she had.

The ground jolted. Then all was quiet. Except for the pounding of her heart, the sound of her breath and his, mingled with kisses…and purring.

The fidget was purring.

She pulled back slightly. Kel-Paten's eyes were like the center of a candle's flame.

"Sass." His voice was rough, not at all the flat, emotionless tone she was used to hearing when he was under full 'cybe power.

She brushed her hand down the side of his face, feeling the grit from the cavern. Something in the way he said her name made her ache inside. "You okay?"

"Desperate times, desperate measures?"

It took her a moment to place his question. It had been her excuse for kissing him when he'd been spiked into the shuttles engines, willing to die to keep her alive. "Selfish measures. If I'm going to die, I want to do so smiling."

He pulled her to her feet and took the wriggling Tank from her arm.

"Then yeah, I'm okay."

She bent down to retrieve the glowlight. "We should probably head—oh, shit!" The light spilled out into the main tunnel, illuminating a wide chasm in what had once been the cavern floor. She strode towards it, seeing more bad news. The mouth of the cavern was blocked with rubble.

"He knew." She turned back to Kel-Paten. "We'd never have made it out alive that way."

They would've fallen into the chasm, or been buried under the rocks.

Kel-Paten stared at pile of boulders.

"Any chance it's a hallucination?" Sass asked.

He carefully lowered the fidget to the ground, then picked up a stone and hurled it at the blockage. It made a very real cracking sound when it hit.

"Damn." He turned back to her. "I don't trust the stability of this cavern. Think this fidget also knows a way out of here?"

"There's only one way to find out." Sass clapped her hands lightly. "Out time, fidget, out!"

CHAPTER THIRTY-FIVE

She didn't seem to mind that his hand cupped her arm as they plunged into the darkness after the fidget. Kel-Paten took that as a positive sign, as well as the fact that she'd unequivocally, willingly, kissed him.

Okay, she thought she was going to die. But she'd been willing to die with her lips on his. That was definitely a positive sign.

He needed something positive right now. His external cybernetics were useless, they were trapped inside a mountain cavern prone to earthquakes and their entire lives rested on an overweight furry creature.

And, oh yes, on a Nasyry bastard who hated his guts.

He had no doubt Serafino, if he chose to do so, could telepathically locate Sass and himself. The fact that Serafino might permit Sass to die just to ensure Kel-Paten's death ranked right up there on his list of possibilities.

He only hoped Eden Fynn might sway Serafino. She was Sass's longtime friend. Plus she seemed fond of the damned fidget.

"There's light up ahead." Sass motioned to the right, her voice excited.

He'd seen it already, his enhanced vision picking up the light source before she could. His filters didn't scan the light as natural, though. For that reason he'd slowed, pulling her back with him. "It doesn't register as sunlight."

She angled her face towards him. "Sure it's not a false reading?"

"No, but considering all that's happened, I'd advise caution."

"Tank seems okay."

"How can you tell?" The fat, furry creature looked like it always did. He'd never been able to discern its moods.

"His tail's not fuzzed and his ears aren't back." She focused the beam of the glowlight on Tank's body.

He agreed with her assessment of the ears. The fidget's tail, however, resembled a feather duster. He acknowledged her expertise in the matter and followed the fidget into the light.

The light was a large room, or rather, a large almost circular cavern. He tested his external sensors again, found them useless and watched Sass bring out her 'corder and come to the same conclusion. The room glowed, yet there was no apparent light source. No hole in the roof or walls. No exterior access at all.

Yet it glowed.

Something prickled across his skin. Whatever this was, he didn't like it.

"It's better than stumbling around in the dark," Sass countered when he mentioned that. And the fact that they were still trapped inside the mountain.

The fidget walked in a wide circle, sniffing the ground. Kel-Paten turned back to Sass. There were smudges of dirt on her face and dust in her hair. He ran his hand through the silken strands, encouraged that she let him, encouraged by her small smile when he did so.

"What's 'out time'?" he asked, remembering her command to the fidget.

"A little game from the *Regalia*. Tank and Reilly—"

He clasped his hand over her mouth, hearing things he knew she couldn't hear. Someone or some thing moved rapidly towards them. He yanked her against his chest. "Hush," he whispered in her ear. "We're about to have company."

She nodded, pulled out her laser pistol as he pulled out his own. He motioned her towards the wall flanking the room's narrow entrance. She flattened herself as he did.

Only at the last moment did he steal a look at the fidget, who was cleaning his right hind foot now as if he hadn't a care in the galaxy.

He relaxed slightly. Maybe all he'd heard was another hallucination. A giant griztard in a red dress, this time.

Tank halted his cleaning and sat upright, eyes wide.

Kel-Paten focused on the small opening. Maybe not a hallucinatory griztard. Maybe this time, they were about to meet the real thing.

The scuffling sounds came closer. He raised his pistol, sighted the opening—

—and missed the chance of a lifetime. But for the fidget's bounding forward and Sass's exclamation of delight, he could've shot Jace

Serafino.

"How did you find us?" Sass grabbed Eden's arm.

"We didn't," Serafino said. "Not totally."

It was then Kel-Paten noticed the larger furzel had joined them.

"Reilly found you," Eden said. "Jace and I just followed him."

"How?" Sass waved her hand in the air. "There was a small earthquake. It closed off the cave's entrance."

"Back door." Eden massaged one shoulder. "A bit tight, though. We used the lasers to carve out some areas."

Kel-Paten watched Serafino wander away from Eden and Sass. His head was tilted slightly, as if he examined something. Kel-Paten could see nothing but rocky walls. He caught up with him at the far side of the room.

"There's something here," he said when Serafino turned. "What is it?"

"What are you reading?"

"Nothing." It grated on him to admit that his cybernetics were flawed. But it was more important to know what they faced, even if he now knew there was a workable exit. He had a feeling they might have found what they'd been looking for. "The 'corders don't work, either."

"When I was a child," Serafino said, his voice oddly soft, "my uncle promised me a wonderful present for my birthday. He left this big box in our apartment three days before. All wrapped and sealed. I poked at the box, sniffed it, listened to it, nudged it. I heard things. But I had no idea what it really was." He turned slowly around, nodding. "That's what this feels like. There's something there. I can feel it, I can nudge it. It rattles."

"But you don't know what it is." Kel-Paten should've been elated at Serafino's admission of failure. He wasn't.

"In the box was a bicycle. I have no idea what this is."

"It's too calm to be a rift vortex."

Serafino arched one eyebrow. "It's calm because it wants to be. That much I can tell you."

A sentient vortex? All he needed now was the griztard to show up in a dress and he'd be number one in line for a Section Forty-Six. "Let's get out of here. Maybe we can recalibrate the 'corders. Or rig a probe shielded from the crystalline in this place." That's what had to be interfering: crystalline ore. Not a sentient vortex.

Serafino shook his head though he didn't seem to be listening. Something on a section of the rock wall captured his attention. And the furzel's as well. The black animal crept forward, ear flattened.

Kel-Paten glanced over his shoulder. The fidget was transfixed at

Sass's feet, ears in a similar mode. Eden stared.

Sass's laser pistol was in her hand. "What's going on?"

He took a quick scan and damned his malfunctioning cybernetics. There was just rock. Plain brown and gray lumpy, jagged rocks, with clumps of dirt in between.

And a luminous blue haze hovering, oozing from the wall. It was about ten feet high, half as wide, elliptical in shape.

"Bloody damn." He heard Sass's soft exclamation.

"Serafino." He growled out the Nasyry's name, wanting an answer.

The haze pulsed, shimmered.

He didn't like this. "Grab Fynn, Sass. Get out of here," he ordered.

"Absolutely not," said a woman's voice behind him. It wasn't Sass or Eden. "I forbid it."

He spun and stared. He was hallucinating. There was no other rational, logical explanation.

She was dead; she'd died years ago. The dark haired woman in the blue jacket couldn't be real.

Then Sass spoke, and with a sinking feeling he realized he wasn't the only one who could see the woman in blue.

"Hold it right there." The angle of Sass's pistol reinforced her command.

His hallucination faced him, her lips pursed, her head tilted slightly to the right. Just as she always had. "P-A Ten. Have your people drop their weapons, and they won't be harmed."

P-A Ten. Not his name. Not Branden. Not even Kel-Paten. She'd staunchly refused to use either. Only his bio-cybernetic designation. P-A Ten.

He caught Sass's confused glance and wondered if she could sense his shame. P-A Ten. Gods, how he'd hated that. "She's not real, Sass. It's another hallucination."

But the woman's footsteps crunched on the rocky ground as she walked towards him. His red-frocked Sass, he remembered, had walked silently.

The real Sass grabbed his hallucination's arm. Shock surged up Kel-Paten's body. Sass's hand didn't pass through but met up with something solid. That something solid jerked back, dark eyes narrowing. "Unhand me, *fregla*."

Fregla. An ancient Keltish expletive for a bastard child. Sass evidently knew its meaning as well.

"Tell me who you are and what you're doing here, and I'll be glad to."

"She's Triad Medical." Eden pointed at the emblem on his hallucination's blue lab coat. "Sellamaris Bio-Cybernetics."

"Triad? The Alliance...the *Vaxxar's* here?" Sass switched a glance from Eden to Kel-Paten and then to Serafino, who'd come up behind Eden.

"P-A Ten—"

"She's not with the *Vax*. Let her go, Sass."

The fabric of the blue lab coat retained visible wrinkles when Sass pulled her hand away. Hallucinations didn't wrinkle. But she had to be a hallucination. Because even if her death had been a lie, she would've aged. And she looked the same as he remembered her, twenty years ago.

"You know her?" Sass asked him.

"Of course." His hallucination answered before he could. "I'm Rafaella Kel-Tyra."

Sass's eyes widened. "Admiral Kel-Tyra's—"

"Sister," Serafino cut in. "Doctor Rafaella Kel-Tyra. Former head of Sellamaris Bio-Cybernetics. She's the Tin Soldier's mother."

Mother. The word was flat. It had no meaning to him. He'd never considered Rafaella Kel-Tyra his mother. His maternal genetic donor, perhaps. But not his mother.

Serafino, however, was clearly pleased with his pronouncement. Rafaella was here, though how and why Kel-Paten couldn't fathom. But her presence would no doubt be taken as proof of Serafino's theory that the Wizard, the malevolent energy source, was his doing. Bluebell Ferbtil had certainly felt that way.

"The Alliance sent you to find us?" Sass asked.

Rafaella looked at Sass and something ran cold in Kel-Paten's veins, both his cybernetic and human ones. "Alliance? To bond with *freglash*, with the unholy mixture of the United Coalition? That is no Alliance. That is stupidity."

She'd always had strong opinions. As a child he remembered her arguing with other doctors, with his fath—with Rafe Kel-Tyra. *The Keltish Triad must be kept pure. We were superior to others. Our purpose was to conquer and rule.*

An alliance would be deemed stupidity in her eyes. But then, she'd been dead more than a decade when the Keltish Triad ceased trying to conquer the Coalition, and instead offered to form a partnership.

Frankly, the Illithians had given them little choice.

"Well, P-A Ten?"

She'd asked him a question. He hadn't heard it. It didn't matter. He had one of his own. "Who are you?" he asked gruffly.

"You know—"

"I know who you appear to be. But Dr. Kel-Tyra's dead."

"Am I?" Her laugh was brittle. "Maybe I choose not to be limited by human concepts of life and death." The blue glow in the room pulsed as if in agreement with her words. "It's why we created you. Why we brought you here."

"To this world, or this cavern?" Sass asked, echoing his thoughts.

Rafaella's smile was smug. "Both. Though you and," she motioned from Sass to Eden Fynn, "that one are inconsequential. Except as *sykari*. You should be honored."

He couldn't quite place the alien word. He knew it; it hovered on the edges of his data libraries, but—

"Sacrifices." Serafino's voice was harsh.

The term came back to Kel-Paten. *Sykari.* An ancient word that depicted the absorption of a person's essence, soul, life force by a mythical demon, so that the demon could experience that life and gain the person's knowledge. *Sykari.* The demons who demanded that were called—

"Ved'eskhar." Serafino pointed at Rafaella. "You're a Ved'eskhar."

Sass shot Serafino a disbelieving glance. "There's no such thing."

"Stupid *fregla*. The Nasyry knows. He's always known. Why else do you think he's here? Why else would we have sent him to you? He fulfilled his role as expected."

Color drained from Eden's face. Sass's pistol wavered from Rafaella to Serafino. She'd just lost her trust in the Nasyry, something Kel-Paten would've taken as a positive sign days ago. Now, it underscored his own failure in discerning his allies.

"That's a lie!" Something dark and bitter crossed Serafino's face. "You can't control me."

"We don't have to. The implant serves that function for us," Rafaella said smoothly.

Serafino glanced quickly at Eden but said nothing. Kel-Paten had no idea what transpired telepathically, if anything. "What implant?" he asked his CMO.

Another glance between the two, then Eden shrugged. "I don't know what she's talking about."

He thought she did but now wasn't the time to press. He had other issues. Like his dead mother standing before him, claiming to be a mythical demon. And claiming to be responsible for their current location and predicament. No, for *his* location. Sass and Eden were useful only as a snack for a demon. Serafino…was an unknown. "You said you deliberately brought me here. Fine. Let them go."

The blue haze pulsed sharply behind him. Rafaella gave a small nod. "He wants them. He's hungry for more souls."

He? It took a moment for Kel-Paten to realize she meant the blue haze. Another demon?

"That's the Ved'eskhar," Serafino said under his breath, but he heard him. Eden nodded, probably sensing his lack of trust in Serafino. Unless Serafino controlled her as well?

No. Eden's voice sounded clearly in his mind. *But we need to let her think Jace's implant still functions. And yes, there's an implant. We'll explain, later.*

Later? He hoped like hell they had a later.

The blue haze, the Ved'eskhar moved, widening.

Rafaella pointed to Sass. "He wants the *fregla*."

Too bad. He wasn't about to let any demon, real or not, take Sass away from him. In half a breath his laser pistol was in his hand, primed, aimed.

The Ved'eskhar lunged. Sass fired as he did, white light spearing blue. Thunder rumbled, crashed. Lightning arced. The demon swelled, expanded. Too late, he realized the thing fed on energy.

"Sass!" He hurled himself forward as Sass screamed. The blue haze enveloped her and she slumped to the floor.

CHAPTER THIRTY-SIX

Another scream ripped through the air of the cavern; a harsh wail filled with Keltish curses. Kel-Paten recognized Rafaella's voice but didn't turn. Other than as an adversary, Rafaella didn't matter. Sass did; she was his entire world. His gloved hands burned as he tried to push through the churning blue haze surrounding her.

It wouldn't let him in. This demon, this energy field felt like solid ice. Solid excruciatingly hot ice. Pain seared his senses but he pushed on, pounding his palms high and low, looking for a break in the field. Anything, no matter how small. If he could just grasp her. He had to pull her free. Sweat trickled in his eyes, down his cheeks.

Kel-Paten. I've...I've got her. Help Jace.

It took several seconds before he recognized the weak voice in his mind as Eden's. She knelt on the floor near the edge of the shimmering haze, hands out but not touching the Ved'eskhar. *Help Jace,* she repeated.

Jace Serafino. Someone else who didn't matter. "I can't leave Sass."

I've got her. Help Jace kill this thing or we'll all die.

Indecision wrenched him. But reality told him he couldn't break through the blue haze. He had to trust Eden. He remembered that Sass always had.

He spun, watching for Rafaella in case she tried to stop him, and saw Serafino standing, arms out, in front of a blue oval glow in the wall.

Another one? No, the haze surrounding Sass connected to that spot on the wall. This had to be the source. He sprinted over behind Serafino. "What do you need?"

The Nasyry's arms trembled. "It's a big sucker." His voice rasped.

"You've seen these before?"

"Only in nightmares. But my people have fought them for centuries."

"Can you kill it?"

"We," and Serafino stressed the word, "might be able to fold it."

"Fold?"

"Collapse it. Upon itself."

"Will that kill it?"

"It's a start." Serafino slowly lowered his left arm. "Take my hand. And no stupid remarks, Tin Soldier. This doesn't mean we're friends."

"No arguments from me on that." He grabbed Serafino's hand. And gasped as something shot through him.

It recognizes you, Serafino told him. *Your essence is similar to your mother's. It will let you in.*

In? He had no desire to become part of that thing. But he had no desire for it to claim Sass.

Send a full charge through your hands.

"That'll kill you." Not that he minded but he seemed to need Serafino's link to the Ved'eskhar.

The feeling's mutual but no, it won't. Not as long as I'm linked to this thing.

He was already powered up, had been since he'd entered the cave. It took only a thought to unleash the fatal energy that resided in him. To be what he'd been constructed, by Dr. Rafaella Kel-Tyra, to be. An assassin. He tripped the code word in his mind.

Serafino barely flinched.

Then the cavern, and everything in it, disappeared.

<^>

Got him, Serafino told her.

Still got her, Eden answered.

But the blue haze, the Ved'eskhar looked thinner. Or maybe she was just being hopeful. She'd never faced and fought a demon before. Neither had Jace, whose instructions she followed. But the Nasyry people had and it was from that collective mind that Jace gathered the methodology.

Look for the life threads, he'd instructed her when they'd realized what the energy source was. A Ved'eskhar demon. An unknown horror. Very real in their midst.

Eden had grabbed Sass's life threads only seconds before the demon had surrounded her friend. That's what she held onto now, fighting the demon for control. Just as Jace held onto Kel-Paten's.

Will he be able to weaken it, collapse it?

I certainly hope so, love. Sooner or later, our physical bodies will need to leave this cave, get food and water. We can't hang on to them forever.

Jace, your implant. She, the Ved'eskhar knew about it.

I told you once how broad-reaching the Faction is. It seems I underestimated them. And their allies. There was a serious note of dismay in Jace's voice.

The Faction aligned with a demonic energy source. The Illithians and possibly even Psy-Serv involved. It was almost beyond Eden's comprehension.

The Ved'eskhar tugged at Sass's life threads again. Eden held on steadfastly, tugging back. *No you don't, you bastard.*

Sass moaned softly, sweat beading on her skin. Eden monitored her life signs and with a start recognized the symptoms: a high fever with no apparent cause and then full body paralysis.

Nar'Relian flu. No, not a flu. Not a virus. But something more heinous, more deadly, more lethal.

A hungry Ved'eskhar, gaining entry into Coalition…that is, Alliance spaceports and stations, wearing the human form of Dr. Rafaella Kel-Tyra. Making a very inhumane meal of every soul she finds, mimicking the symptoms of the Nar'Relian flu.

Alliance Fleet Medical would never believe this. Hell, she didn't think Caleb would believe this. She wasn't sure she did.

Her arms ached and the cavern's rocky ground dug stinging gouges into her knees. She could feel Jace's tension and weariness. Feel Reilly's…

Oh, dear Gods! Reilly and Tank!

The damp chill enveloped Kel-Paten, clinging as if to force its way through his clothes, his skin. It seemed alive, probing. He wiped his gloved hand over his face, surprised to find it dry. Then the world flashed with a bright light.

He was in a hospital corridor, a place he knew intimately. His gut wrenched in spite of the fact that his mind told him it was an hallucination. It had to be. Seconds ago he'd clasped Serafino's hand in a cavern on some strange world. Now he was in Bio-Cybernetics Unit Seven on Sellarmaris. A place he'd never wanted to see again. His own personal hell.

"P-A Ten!"

He whirled around, saw nothing but the empty corridor, its gray walls tilting slightly, illogically. Yellow doors were half open, some at a crazy angle. A medcart rolled slowly away from him, vanishing into a wall.

No sign of Rafaella. Only her voice, sounding hollow, distant. But real enough to give him shivers. He'd hated the sound of her voice.

"P-A Ten!"

To his right, this time. The first open doorway led nowhere. He saw only blackness. The second yellow door had slid three quarters of the way open. He knew the room. It had been his for seven years. He recognized the narrow diag-bed flanked on either side by sensors, monitors, cyber-linkages. Restraining bands arced across the bed. They were open now, but for years they'd trapped him in that bed. The technology to turn a human into a machine was new, developing. Imprecise. Prosthetics often were prototypes.

And painful. Very painful.

His jaw clenched. The desire to destroy the diag-bed and its surrounding equipment overwhelmed him. He could do it. He could draw his laser pistol, obliterate everything. Gods, how he'd wanted to do that for years! He could—

Find the Ved'eskhar, damn it! Serafino's voice, strained, angry, shot through his mind.

"P-A Ten! You listen to *fregla*?"

A surge of energy shot through him, spiraling. The room spiraled as well. Colors seemed brighter. He noted all this with an almost clinical fascination.

Rafaella spoke again. "You're superior to that!"

Energy pulsed like an icy heat in his veins. He was. Gods, he was. Rafaella was right. He had to destroy Serafino, not take orders from him. The man was filth, a half-breed. A rogue telepath.

Sass will die. Find the Ved'eskhar! Serafino sounded impatient.

The room tilted but this time he fought the sensation, fought whatever had pulled him in so easily minutes ago. He watched, instead, the image sent to him by Serafino: Sass, slumped on the floor. His chest felt tight. He shook off the seductive energy Rafaella had aimed at him. That wasn't him. That wasn't what he wanted to be. He was Branden Kel-Paten, an Alliance admiral and, the Gods willing, possibly someone who was more than a friend to Captain Tasha Sebastian. He had to find the Ved'eskhar.

"Destroy me, and you destroy yourself." Rafaella's voice was a harsh rasp. This time, when he turned, he saw her. She leaned against the open doorway, her hair disheveled; her blue lab coat stained, torn. But when

281

she pushed her dark hair out of her face, her eyes glittered as if an infinite energy lived inside her.

"It lives in you, too. P-A Ten, you're my perfect creation. The time has come for you to become what you must be." She held out her hand. "Join me. Together, no one can stop us."

"Don't do it, flyboy." Sass's voice was thin, as if she called to him through a tunnel. Light shimmered to his right. Rafaella staggered suddenly, lunging for whatever was solidifying, taking form.

He moved on instinct, blocking her, grabbing her outstretched arm just as something bumped against his back.

"Sorry." Sass sounded breathless. "Not used to this shit."

He didn't dare turn, didn't dare take his focus from Rafaella. Her skin was almost translucent. Something roiled beneath it, something ugly, desperate.

Was that something also part of him?

"*Fregla!*" Rafaella shoved hard against him, trying to get to Sass. A familiar, searing icy heat flowed over him but he grabbed her arms, restraining her.

"How do we stop her...it?" he asked Sass. Serafino had said something about folding the demon. Somehow he didn't think he was supposed to push down the hospital walls.

"Serafino's not sure. Hell, he wasn't even sure he could get us here."

Us?

A low growl rumbled behind him.

Rafaella stopped struggling.

For a moment Kel-Paten considered that Serafino might be a shapeshifter. Then a small creature brushed by his leg. Out of the corner of his field of vision he could see dark, tufted ears angled backwards, and a long plumey tail that now looked more than twice its normal size.

"His tail's fuzzed," Sass intoned. "He's not happy."

He glanced down at the fidget. It was still the fat, furry creature he remembered. Harmless. But Rafaella backed up a step, snarled out something he didn't understand. The fidget snarled back.

Energy rippled in the air. Around Rafaella, it was blue, frothy. Around the fidget it was pale, almost golden, swirling. Small lights sparkled.

Protect MommySass. Protect.

Kel-Paten didn't recognize the small, high-pitched voice in his mind. But he understood the words, and the sentiment, clearly.

Suddenly the fidget bolted forward. Rafaella skittered aside. The fidget dashed into the corridor.

"C'mon!" Sass grabbed his hand, pulling. "Tank has a plan."

Rafaella's scream echoed behind him as they ran.

The corridor see-sawed crazily. Light flashed in odd patterns, disorienting him. Sass lost her footing, slid to the right. He held onto her arm, kept her by his side as they raced like two drunks stumbling after the fidget. He didn't have to ask where the small creature was headed. As soon as they passed through the first set of wide, double-doors, he knew.

Rafaella's private lab.

"Eden got you out?" he managed to ask at one point.

"Eden and Serafino sent me in here. The furzels," she thrust her chin towards the black and white creature, "they know something. Serafino couldn't explain it. He said just to trust Tank."

"I trust the damn fidget more than I do Serafino," Kel-Paten growled under his breath.

The door to the lab was shut, its seamless metal front undulating in an odd pattern. Not for the first time since he'd found himself transported into this hallucination did he damn his still malfunctioning external sensors. As skewed as it all was, everything looked too real. He'd never felt so blind. For once, he wanted to be PA-Ten, to have all his systems functioning, to be able to break through this nonsensical hallucination.

Tank sniffed along the base of the door.

He felt, more than saw, the pulse of blue energy erupt. He scooped Tank up with one hand, yanked Sass hard against him with the other. They tumbled sideways, landing hard on the slanted floor.

"Damn it all!" he swore as he released the fidget and drew his laser pistol. Rafaella strode down the center of the corridor. He took aim...

No! Bad Thing likes light.

Bad Thing, he realized, was the Ved'eskhar. And the fidget was correct, it liked, it *ate* laser energy.

Tank bounded towards the door then pawed frantically at the base.

"Keep dear old mom busy," Sass said, rising. "I'll try to help Tank."

He chanced a lingering glance at her, tried to send with it all he felt, all he wanted her to know. They were out of their element in this crazy place. He couldn't even begin to calculate their chances of success, or failure, as he had on the shuttle.

All he knew was he didn't want to lose her.

He guessed that Rafaella didn't want to lose him. She and the Ved'eskhar had brought him here. Had manipulated Serafino as well.

He placed himself between Sass and Rafaella. The blue haze swirled angrily around her feet, arching into almost human form behind her, like a misshapen shadow.

"Let my officers go." He motioned to Sass. "Send her and the others in the cave back to the *Vax*. I'll stay and do what you want."

"You're already here, PA-Ten. You'll do as I instruct. *Fregla* is of no consequence."

"Harm her and I'll kill you."

Rafaella's laugh was cold. "Destroy me and you destroy yourself. I told you that before."

She had and it worried him. There were elements of his cybernetic systems that eluded even his comprehension. That there might be an alien energy force involved, a demonic energy force, had never occurred to him.

Maybe it should have. Maybe it was something he could use to stop the Ved'eshkar. Even if it killed himself as well.

A clank and a low curse caught his attention. "Damn it! Almost had the door. There!" Sass sounded positively gleeful.

A bolt of blue energy mushroomed. Kel-Paten ignored personal consequences. He tripped the code word in his mind, uncapped his own fatal energy and stepped directly in the path of the Ved'eshkar's charge.

CHAPTER THIRTY-SEVEN

Sass tumbled through the open doors just as an icy heat cascaded over her. Tank yowled, his tail flicking in anger. She pushed herself to her feet and barreled after the fidget, who'd run under a table and then up and over a chair and a desk. Something that looked like a long shard of crystal lay across a counter behind the desk. Tank arched his back, hissed.

"Kel-Paten, I think we found—" She glanced over her shoulder. The words died in her throat.

Kel-Paten stood in the open doorway, his back to her, his right arm outstretched. The blue haze of the demon spun around him, pulsing, churning. Her breath caught in horror. Dear Gods, that thing had him! It was killing him. Or, once again, he was sacrificing himself to save her.

"Found what?" Kel-Paten called out without turning.

Joy flooded her heart. He could talk. He was alive. When the thing had surrounded her, she'd been paralyzed. "The... the...are you okay?"

"Relatively speaking, yes. What did you find?"

"Something Tank wants us to destroy. But we can't use the laser pistols." The blue energy arced around Kel-Paten's shoulders, traveled down his arm. A ball of blue formed around his right hand. His black glove seemed iridescent. But other than that, he seemed unchanged, unharmed.

"I think I found something we can use."

He wavered slightly in his stance then turned. "Hit the deck, now!"

Sass dropped to the floor. Tank leaped. A ball of blue energy sailed over their heads. Her skin felt as if an icy comb had raked it. She grabbed the fidget, dragged him against her chest.

Light exploded. A woman screamed. Footsteps pounded then black clad arms wrapped around her.

"Hang on!" Kel-Paten's voice rasped in her ear. The floor beneath her rocked, bucked. Tank wriggled and let out a howl.

Out time! a small voice pleaded in her mind.

"Let him go." Kel-Paten tugged on her wrist. "He knows how to get out of here."

The fidget scurried to her left, skittering as the floor swayed.

Sass shoved herself to her feet as Kel-Paten yanked her up. The desk behind them toppled sideways with a crash. She jumped over a broken chair, sprinting after Tank. The fidget sidled through a large gap in the laboratory wall.

A roaring wail sounded behind her.

"Shit!" She angled sideways, scooting through the broken wall, Kel-Paten at her back.

They emerged into a gray corridor. Lights flashed, yellow doors whooshed open and closed in a pounding rhythm.

"Where to?" There didn't seem to be an exit, just more corridor, more slamming doors, more deafening explosions. She didn't know if this world, this hallucination had an outside, and if it did, if it were even stable.

She stumbled, tripping over debris. Kel-Paten grabbed her by the waist. "There!" he pulled to the right as Tank scurried down a side corridor.

They turned the corner and stopped. Sass's heart stopped as well. The corridor ended as if the rest had been ripped away. The floor was jagged, the walls sheared. Beyond was...nothing.

Darkness. Infinite darkness.

Tank pawed her leg. She lifted the fidget into her arms and turned to Kel-Paten. He seemed as startled as she was. The floor swayed. She grabbed him, sandwiching the fidget between them. Tank wheezed but didn't wriggle away.

Jump. Tank protect.

"Jump?" Kel-Paten echoed what she'd heard.

"Yeah, jump." She looked up into luminous blue eyes. "We live through this, you get to take me to the casinos in T'Garis, flyboy."

He pulled her tightly against him. "I love you, Sass."

"I love you, Branden."

Tank purred.

They jumped.

<^>

Serafino careened backwards, landing on his rump. "Shit!" Pain jabbed him where his hands scraped against the rocky floor. He scrambled to his feet. "Eden?"

She was on her side, propped up on one elbow, blonde hair hanging in her face. He helped her to her feet and only then realized the blue haze was gone.

"Where's Sass?" She tugged her shirt back into place. Evidently the same force that had thrown him halfway across the cavern had also sent her for a serious tumble. "You said you had them—"

"I did. Sort of." The ground under his boots trembled. "We have to get out of here."

"No!" She grabbed his arm. "Sass. The admiral. Where—?"

"Safe. They're safe." A rumbling sound echoed through the walls.

"They're outside?"

He pulled her towards the opening. "Not sure. Hope so."

"Reilly!" Eden jerked away from him. The furzel sat, as if on guard, in front of the body of Dr. Rafaella Kel-Tyra. The woman lay face down, her blue lab coat shredded.

Mommy safe. Reilly, friend kill Bad Thing's friend.

"Good furzel," Jace said, knowing Eden had heard the prideful admission as well.

"By the Gods." Eden didn't seem to want to move, in spite of the fact that Reilly headed for the opening, and Jace tugged on her arm. "How... how did they...?"

"Ask later. This place is about to come apart."

The ground shifted but Eden stayed put. "Where's Tank?"

"With Sass and the Tin Soldier. Let's go!" He grabbed her arm, dragged her into the tunnel just as an explosion rocked the cavern. Dust and debris flew, pelting them. Reilly streaked forward.

"Go!" They still had that narrow tunnel to navigate. Jace prayed they'd make it through in time.

Reilly dove through the narrow opening, ears flattened. Jace pushed Eden ahead of him. Cracks appeared in the ground and walls. He constructed a force shield from the latent energy in the cavern. Seconds later, the shield disintegrated. Something much larger than his Nasyry talents moved through the air.

"Damn it all!" He squeezed into the tunnel, watching the soles of Eden's boots ahead. He'd hoped to buy them time. It didn't seem he could do that.

He hoped Sass and the Tin Soldier would be out on the ledge to greet them. If they weren't, Eden, his dear sweet Eden, would be mightily pissed. The rock walls of the tunnel groaned, trembled. He hoped they lived long enough to find out if Eden would be pissed or not.

Reilly made it through. He felt the furzel's delight at the fresh air, the warm sunshine. But he also caught the furzel's plaintive, telepathic *Friend? Friend?*

And no answer.

Light flooded the tunnel as Eden crawled out. He had only a few more feet to go. The ground crumbled under his hands and knees. He lost his balance, slamming his hip against the curved rocky wall.

"Jace!" Light dimmed as Eden shoved herself back inside.

"Get out! Get out!" Dear Gods, don't let anything happen to her.

He shoved himself forward, his hands raw from the sharp stones. The tunnel jolted. He pitched forward, felt something hard crack against his shin…

…then bright light seared his eyes. Eden's hands were in his armpits, tugging, pulling. He tumbled sideways, managed to wrap one arm around her waist and they crashed into something hard yet soft. Branches scraped his face. Leaves tickled his nose. He rolled once, twice, clasping Eden against him. They landed in a heap. The light had dimmed and he found his face burrowed into Eden's ample chest.

"I've died and gone to heaven," he murmured into her cleavage.

"Jace!" She pushed away, sounding truly shocked though he thought that by now, she'd know better. Or rather, had known him long enough. "Are you okay?"

The ground had ceased trembling. And the virulent malevolence he'd sensed was now gone. "I'm alive. Tomorrow I'll probably feel like lubashit on a lemon. You?"

She sat back on her haunches and refastened her uniform shirt. "I ache in places I didn't know I had. Reilly?" The furzel scampered through the bushes towards them.

Jace drew her to her feet. "We need to get back to the equinnards. And the shuttle."

"They're not here, are they?"

Gods, he hated admitting he'd failed. He hated it even more because he had to admit it to Eden, whose approval meant more to him than anyone else's in the universe. The dismay in her eyes wrenched at him. "No."

"Where are they?"

"Alive. Safe. Not with the Ved'eskhar, or what's left of it." He probed as he talked to her and let her sense what he saw: the Ved'eskhar had collapsed. It wasn't dead but it was contained. And neither Sass nor Kel-Paten's essences were within it. But their essences were strong, as was Tank's. He felt the contact through Reilly. They *were* alive.

He just didn't know where.

He relayed what he'd sensed to Eden then threaded his fingers through hers. "We can't do anything more here. Let's go home."

The equinnards, munching on sweetgrass, raised their heads when he approached. They were ready to go home, too. Eden sagged tiredly against him in the cart. "Jace." Her voice held a wary note. Her discomfort she wore like a heavy cloak.

"I didn't deliberately lose them." He knew her concern, knew the one thing she was unsure of. His feud with Kel-Paten. But he hadn't told her what he'd also found out through his contact with the Ved'eskhar. He did so now. "I know now the Tin Soldier's not to blame. The Faction took Bianca and Jorden, because of me. They didn't need Kel-Paten to do that. They knew about Bianca long before. My implant," he glanced at Eden. "For several years they controlled me with it. Through the Ved'eskhar energy that was inside it, they knew all I knew."

"Was?"

He nodded. "Your Zingaran energy worked as a catalyst. Every time you met with me in Novalis, in what you sense as a dream world, it eroded the Ved'eskhar's hold on me. The first few times it fought back, violently."

"The seizures you had. That was it fighting back?"

"If I hadn't trusted you, it would've reclaimed me. Or killed me. But we merged our energies. And it was a very, very small Ved'eskhar. The implant is still there." He tapped one finger on his head. "But the Ved'eskhar in it collapsed. It's dormant. It can't do any harm."

"And the one that has Sass and Kel-Paten?"

"It doesn't have them anymore." He wrapped his arm around Eden's shoulders, hugged her tightly. "I tried to bring them back here. I really did."

Her acceptance flowed over him like a warm, sweet breeze.

"It wasn't safe," he continued as they jostled along the dirt path. "But I can still sense them. And Reilly senses Tank. I think I can use that connection—"

"*We* can," Eden put in.

"—and get back together. Or catch up with them. Whatever we need to do. But first, we need some food. And sleep."

Gods, they needed sleep. He was weary right down to his bones. He'd never fought a Ved'eskhar before. If Eden and, he admitted grudgingly, the Tin Soldier hadn't been there, it would've killed him.

He owed the Tin Soldier a debt of gratitude. And perhaps even an apology. Funny, acknowledging that didn't feel half bad.

Eden, beside him, felt warm and soft. That was another surprise in his life. A woman like Eden, who loved him, understood him. And more than that, believed in him.

He looked forward to teaching her, to exploring her empathic healing abilities, her growing telepathic talents…her delectable, womanly body. He definitely looked forward to exploring that.

The equinnards slowed, coming into a familiar clearing. Jace caught a glint of the shuttle's metallic form through the trees. Reilly jumped down from the carriage, trotted into the bushes with a dismissive flick of his tail. Tank might not be here, but his furzel friend didn't seem worried.

Perhaps that was a good sign.

He helped Eden climb down from the carriage's high seat, then drew her against him. "A minute," he said softly in her ear. "I need this."

She melded, and melted, against him, needing his touch as he needed hers. They'd damn near died. Their friends were missing. But for the moment, just for a moment, Captain Jace Serafino let himself get lost in the warmth and acceptance of the woman he loved. The only woman, he realized, he'd ever truly loved. And ever would.

"We'll find them," he promised.

He knew they would.

After all, because of Eden, he'd found himself.

CHAPTER THIRTY-EIGHT

LOS VALOS

"Ante up! Place your bets!"

Sass jerked upright and smacked her head on the back of the booth. It took a moment for her eyes to focus, for her head to stop spinning and for her fingers to unclench from around the short glass in her right hand. Her heart pounded, but that was okay because there was no way anyone could hear it over the jingling chinkety-clink of the slot machines or the raucous calls of the crowds at the card tables.

Card tables. Slot machines. Bloody damn and lubashit on a lemon. What had happened to the cave? What happened to the hallucinatory hospital? What happened to...?

"Murrupp." Tank jumped onto the tabletop and butted her arm with his furry head.

"Sorry, honey. You can't bring animals in here." A young woman in a tight black dress angled an empty tray against her hip. Her lips were a bright red, her hair a brighter red. She pointed a finger at Tank. Her nails were bright red, too. "You better get him out of here before hotel security nabs him."

"Oh, sorry. Sure." Sass scooped the fidget against her chest and stood. "We were just leaving."

We. Gods' sacred asses. Where was Kel-Paten? She glanced quickly around the u-shaped booth. Other than herself, an empty glass and Tank, there was nothing.

The casino. Just before they jumped into nothing, she'd mentioned T'Garis. The casino. So maybe this was another hallucination. But this wasn't T'Garis. She'd seen holos of the place. This wasn't any casino she'd ever seen. Nor was it any casino bar she'd ever been in, though it was long, dimly lit and flanking a wall, like most. But things were missing. She saw that as she glanced around. No sound mirrors. No holovids. No bar 'droids. No credit screens. There was a menu of daily specials in the middle of her table. It appeared to be made of paper.

Paper?

The woman's glance went up and down over Sass's form. "You with the circus act?"

"Hmm?"

"Your clothes. The cat. You got some kind of animal act, right?"

Cat?

Sass followed the direction of the woman's bright red nail. Tank yawned.

"Looks like your cat's tired.

Oh. Cat. Must be the local slang for furzel.

"Like I said, you'd better scram before they toss you."

"Right." Sass scooted around the edge of the table. "Wait. There was a man, a friend with me. Earlier. Did you see him? Did he leave?"

The woman laughed. "Buys you drinks and then skedaddles, does he? Better check your purse. He's probably spendin' your dough at the tables."

Dough? She was about to tell the woman that Kel-Paten wasn't a baker when a voice called out, "Phyllis! Customer's waitin'!"

"Comin', Joe!" she shouted back. "Hey, good luck with the show." She patted Sass's arm then sashayed quickly towards the bar and the portly man whose arms were folded over his chest.

People stared as Sass strode through the casino. She didn't know if it was because of her uniform—all the other women she saw were in dresses or skirts—or the fact that she held a large, furry fidget in her arms as she tried, none too discreetly, to see if Kel-Paten indeed was at one of the tables.

She didn't see him, though one balding man in a stained jacket loomed drunkenly in her path as she passed by the slots. "Nice pussy."

Sass glared at him, his drawling tone telling her that whatever he'd said wasn't complimentary. She turned on her heel. Two uniformed men strode quickly in her direction. She didn't recognize the uniforms. She didn't have to. She'd grown up on Farside and knew security officers when she saw them.

She whirled again, ducked down a row of slot machines then headed for an opposite door. It opened into a large, high-ceilinged lobby. Crystal chandeliers twinkled overhead. More women in skirts and tight jackets.

Men in loose fitting jackets, dark pants. She didn't recognize the clothing or the hairstyles, nor the paintings on the wall, nor the music tinkling from a large black piano tucked in the corner of the room.

She didn't recognize anything.

This had to be an hallucination. A bad dream. She'd wake up on the shuttle, with Tank lying across her. Or better yet, in her quarters on the *Vax*. It was just a bad dream. She'd wake and have coffee with the admiral, who...

The admiral. She recognized his dark hair, the line of his jaw, the width of his shoulders. His head was bowed, his eyes closed. He was slumped between the two security officers she'd seen earlier, his feet stumbling as they dragged him towards a side hallway marked with an exit sign.

Gods, something had happened. Something terrible had happened. She clutched Tank tightly against her chest and ran after them.

They shouldered open a narrow door. Sass was a few steps behind them. She caught the door with her hip as it closed, jostling Tank, who blinked his bright yellow eyes at her.

She stepped into an alleyway, not unlike the one where she'd rescued the old woman with Kel-Paten's help. Only this time it looked like she'd be rescuing him.

"And stay out, this time! Damn drunk!" The security officers shoved Kel-Paten against a brick wall. His legs buckled and he slumped to the ground.

One of the officers dusted his hands on his pants, stopping when he caught sight of her. "What do you want?"

"Nothing. I..." she remembered what the woman, Phyllis, had said. "He owes me money."

"Yeah, you and every gin joint in town." The officer pointed to Tank. "You with that circus act?"

"Yeah." Sure, why not? "Me and the...cat."

The other officer nudged the one talking to her. "Let's go, Sam."

The one called Sam offered her a dismissive wave of his hand. "Good luck, doll."

The metal door clanked shut. Sass lowered Tank to the ground then knelt in front of Kel-Paten. He'd drawn his knees up and crossed his arms on top of them. His forehead rested in the crook of one elbow.

"Kel-Paten?" She shook his arm then froze. Something had changed. His black gloves were gone. His black uniform was now a dark blue jacket, similar to his pants. She glanced down. His boots weren't Alliance or even Triad issue. She didn't recognize them. She didn't

293

recognize his clothes.

The man she thought was Branden Kel-Paten raised his face. He appeared in every way unchanged from the few moments before, except that his face now looked as if it hadn't seen a razor in days. How much time had passed during their jump from the shattered corridor? He blinked, his eyes the same pale blue she remembered. Not luminous, not glowing. But his powered-down blue.

"Branden?"

He stared at her. "Tasha? But that's impossible." His deep voice cracked as if it hadn't been used in days, either.

Gods, it *was* Kel-Paten. He recognized her. Relief flooded through her. "Tell me about it! This place makes no sense. It's probably another hallucination."

"Place? This place isn't an hallucination." He spoke slowly, his words slightly slurred as if he'd been drinking.

But Eden had said a 'cybe couldn't get drunk.

Hesitantly, he reached out as if to touch her arm. "You're the hallucination."

"What, me and the griztard in a red dress again?" She grabbed his hand. "I'm real, admiral."

He jerked as if startled, then his fingers tightened around hers. "My God, you are. Just like in my drawings."

Drawings?

"What—?"

A loud screeching noise erupted to her left. A boxy vehicle appeared at the far end of the alley. Kel-Paten saw it, too, struggled to his feet. "Damn it!"

A square section of the vehicle opened. "Patterson!" A man stepped out, a short rifle in his hands. "You're dead meat, you son of a bitch!"

Kel-Paten shoved her towards the wall. "Get out of here, now!"

"Like hell I will!" She heard Tank growl as if in agreement. She palmed her laser pistol, flicked off the safety.

He stared at the pistol in her hand. "What's that?"

"A Triad-issue 749. Same as yours. Don't you remember?"

His look of incomprehension was her answer. He didn't remember. Not that it mattered. The man with the rifle raised it. But instead of laser fire, there was a bright flash and a loud, cracking noise.

She ducked, instinctively, Kel-Paten already pulling her down. It took her less than a second to take aim on their attacker. White laser fire streaked from her pistol, catching the man center-mass. He flailed backwards, the rifle spinning from his grasp. He fell to the ground with a satisfying thud.

"What did you do?"

"Don't lecture me about the Edict of Non-Intervention, admiral. It's only set for stun."

"Edict? Admiral? What in hell are you talking about?"

A warning bell jangled loudly in her mind. "You're not Kel-Paten, are you?"

"Patterson. My name's Patterson. I...shit!" He grabbed her shoulder as a second screeching noise echoed off the high brick walls. "My friend has friends. This way!"

She paused just long enough to scoop up Tank. Another boxy vehicle appeared behind the first. This one released three men and three more rifles.

Kel-Paten, or Patterson, or whoever he was tugged her into motion. They bolted down the alley and careened into the street.

CHAPTER THIRTY-NINE

VIX'S BAR AND GRILLE

Sass caught a fleeting glimpse of the name etched on the glass door as Kel-Paten pushed her through. Vix's Bar and Grille. Vix. *Vax*. Kel-Paten. Patterson.

"Back room!" He propelled her past tables and chairs angled down the middle of the narrow bar, past a green topped pool table, past a tall stack of wooden boxes. Faces swiveled in her direction but she didn't recognize anyone. She prayed, when Kel-Paten lifted the latch on the door, that Serafino and Eden would be on the other side.

The door slammed shut behind her, plunging her into darkness. Tank sneezed. There was thud and, simultaneously, "Damn it!"

That was *his* voice. Even with her heart pounding, her head spinning, her breath coming in long gasps, her mind recognized it. Hell, she should. She'd heard him swear often enough.

A light glowed suddenly, like a small yellow moon, illuminating a low desk strewn with papers. A slatted chair was in front, tall metal cabinets in the shadows behind it. No Serafino. No Eden. Damn.

Kel-Paten yanked open the left side drawer of the desk and drew out what she suspected was a pistol. Composed of gray metal with a cylindrical center, it reminded her of something she'd seen in a museum.

He flipped open the cylinder, peered inside, then closed it with a click. "This evens things up. Though I don't think they'll come here. Pretty sure they don't know about this place"

"That's a weapon."

"Revolver." He frowned slightly.

Tank squirmed. She lowered him to the floor. "How do you know who I am?"

"I know you look like, look *exactly* like a drawing of mine."

He'd mentioned that in the alley, before his decidedly unfriendly friends showed up with their rifles. "This drawing told you my name?"

"It? No. I thought, well, I liked the name Tasha. The name fit." Suddenly, he thrust his hand through his hair and angled away from her. "I'm drunk," he announced to the dimly lit room. "This is a dream."

"Considering those people who tried to kill you, I'd label it a nightmare."

He turned back, his mouth curved in a wry smile. "Yeah, well, the Faction doesn't like it when you interrupt their business. But half the cops in this city are on their payroll. Somebody's got to do something."

"Faction." A chill ran up Sass's spine. Was this a nightmare, or had she fallen into another Ved'eskhar trap?

"They've been involved with the casinos for years. No one's cared. It's expected. Then they set up this racket, shaking down the little joints. Cops started finding bodies in the river. If we found any at all."

"Faction."

He shrugged. "You know how it goes."

"Sort of. So you decided to try and stop them?"

"I worked vice for ten years with Metro. I know how they operate."

Sass studied the man before her. He was a cop. An ex-cop, he explained as she sat in the rickety chair in the windowless room. Tank pounced on crumpled balls of paper ringing the base of a metal garbage can. She understood his terminology—cop—by inference. He'd been a sec-officer, fairly high ranking until he'd been fired.

That challenged her theory that he was the Tin Soldier. Dereliction of duty wasn't even in Kel-Paten's vocabulary.

"So these drawings of me. You saw them in your police station?" She used his term.

He sat on the edge of the desk, shoved a stack of papers to one side. His pistol—he called it a revolver—served as a paperweight. "Drawing's a hobby. I've loved comic books since I was a kid. Science fiction ones, with rocket ships. You know."

Comic books? Rocket ships? "You saw a picture of me in a book?"

"I draw them. Comic books. Never sold any, but..." He moved his legs and yanked open a drawer. "I gave Timmy a copy. Here." He handed her a paper booklet.

She held it under the solitary lamp. Her likeness, her exact likeness stared back at her. Written across the top was not only her name, but her title, sort of: Tasha Sebastian, Rocket Ship Captain.

"I made you up. Invented you, eleven years ago. I've been drawing you ever since. That's why I know this is just a dream." He took the booklet from her hand as she rose, tossed it on top of the revolver. "That's why after eleven years, I think I have a right to do this."

His fingers closed around her wrist and he pulled her towards him. Her hips bumped his knees then his legs opened, his arm snaking around her waist. Sass found herself nose to nose with Kel-Paten who wasn't Kel-Paten.

But the look and heat in his gaze was very familiar.

"Eleven years?" Dear Gods, Kel-Paten had had his journal entries on her. Had this one been drawing her picture? He—

—kissed her. His mouth came down hard on hers, his hands splayed against her back, pressing her closer. His tongue teased hers.

An electric heat spiraled up her spine, twirled then rushed back down again. She wrapped her arms around his neck.

He brushed his lips across her cheek. "I've loved you for so long, Sassy-girl…"

She pulled back abruptly, framed his face, his unshaven face, with her hands. "What did you say?"

Startled pale blue eyes stared at her. "I'm sorry. I shouldn't have—"

"You should. You have." In her room at the Keep. That's what she'd been thinking when he'd kissed her. He'd called her 'Sassy-girl' then. Just as he had now.

"Only in my dreams."

"No, for real. On the shuttle, after the Illithians attacked. We had engine failure and I kissed you—"

"That was Issue Three; The Aliens Attack."

"—but we crashed landed on this medieval planet where this energy source—"

"Issue Four. The Wizard of Haven."

"—threatened the locals and burned down Lord Tris' castle. You kissed me—"

"Issue Four again."

"—and called me Sassy-girl."

"I've always called you Sassy-girl. In my stories. In my dreams." His hands slid down her arms until he clasped her hands. He brought her fingers to his lips, brushed a kiss across her knuckles. "This is the best dream I've had yet."

"Wait." She grabbed his right hand, pushed up his sleeve. He was Kel-Paten. He might not remember, but he was. He had to be. She could prove it.

She turned his wrist over. Kel-Paten's dataports were at the base, under a small flap of synth-derm. She ran her thumb across the base of his palm. Nothing moved, nothing slid sideways.

"Damn it!" She grabbed his other wrist, did the same thing.

"What are you—?"

She plopped down on the desktop and dragged his hand under the light from the small lamp. She'd felt something.

The raised knot of a bluish-white scar angled across the top of his wrist. Exactly where she knew Kel-Paten's dataports should be.

"Give me your other hand." Same scar, same pattern. Vaguely she recalled intelligence rumors that Kel-Paten's systems could generate a false covering through the synth-derm as a security measure, in case he was captured. But it could only be rumor. She traced the scar lightly and damned the Triad for not trusting the U-Cees with a full dossier on the admiral.

"I fell through a plate glass window, years ago. Hands first."

"These stories you draw. You're not part of them?"

"Me? No. What does that have to do with my hands?"

"There's a bio-cybe Triad Fleet officer. An admiral."

"Bio-cybe?" He pronounced the word slowly, frowning.

"Half human, half cybernetic construct." She made an aimless motion with one hand as his frown deepened. "Half machine."

"Robot?"

She shrugged. "He interfaces with his ship through dataports in his wrist." She tapped his scar. "Here."

"Inter-what?"

"His name's Kel-Paten. Admiral Kel-Paten. He calls me Sassy-girl. He looks like you. And he kisses me just like you do."

He seemed taken aback. "If you're involved with some guy…"

"You! I'm involved with you!" She fought the urge to shake him. "Somehow, certain things changed when we destroyed the Ved'eskhar. I don't know why or how. But you *are* Kel-Paten."

He had to be. Dear Gods, how else would she get out of this nightmare?

She planted her hands on his shoulders, pinned him with her the-captain's-running-out-of-patience gaze. "You may think you're someone else, but you're…"

"Patterson." He corrected her. "Brandon Kyle Patterson."

Brandon Kyle Patterson. Branden Kel-Paten. Vix. *Vax*. The Faction. Everything, or most everything, was like a slight variation on reality as she knew it. Except, of course, for her and Tank. The fidget had curled into a ball on the chair's cushion, his paws twitching in his sleep.

She and Tank were the keys in this alien game of alternate realities. Until she could convince Kel-Paten of his real identity, survival in and escape from this world rested solely on her shoulders. She had to convince him, had to get him out of here. Rafaella Kel-Tyra had been so insistent Kel-Paten ally with her. This might just be one more trick, one more way, to keep him, to trap him within the energy of the Ved'eskhar.

Or else the Faction and the Illithians would take over the Alliance, destroy the peace the Coalition and the Triad had worked so hard to achieve.

If that happened, she'd be stuck here in Vix's Bar and Grille with Brandon Kyle Patterson.

She relaxed her grip on his shoulders, saw the heat still simmering in his eyes. Felt the heat from his touch as his fingers massaged small, slow circles on her back. And clearly remembered the heat that had flared between them in his room at the Keep. A heat Sass felt very inclined to explore.

There might well be worse things in the galaxy than a lethal alien energy source that had her trapped, for the moment, in some unknown alternate universe. But having the admiral with her, even if he didn't yet know he was the admiral, made things just a little more bearable.

A little more...

He cleared his throat. "Sebastian." He paused, a small smile on his lips.

By the Gods, he *paused*! Her heart quivered with joy. "Yes?"

"After eleven years, I think I deserve more than one kiss."

She wrapped her arms around his neck. "By your command, sir. By your command."

To be continued in...
COMMAND DECISION by Linnea Sinclair
coming soon to an intergalactic bookstore near you!

About the author of COMMAND PERFORMANCE

Linnea Sinclair is a former news reporter, former private investigator and now an award winning author in the science fiction and fantasy romance genres. Her novels, written both under her name and as Megan Sybil Baker, have won the EPPIE, the PEARL and the Sapphire awards and garnered many five star reviews.

A long time "Star Trek" and "Star Wars" fan, she writes what she wishes she could live: adventure and romance in the space lanes. Until she's recalled to active duty in any available space-faring fleet, she can be found in south Florida with her husband and four thoroughly spoiled cats. She's currently working several new novels, including COMMAND DECISION, the sequel to COMMAND PERFORMANCE.

Readers can write to her at starfreighter15@aol.com

NBI

Treat yourself to some good reading from
NovelBooks, Inc.

Desert Dreams by Gracie McKeever   Paranormal
Old World Evil vs. New Age Passion...Can their love survive?

The Anonymous Amanuensis by Judith Glad   Regency
Regency England is a man's world, until one woman writes her own rules...

No More Secrets, No More Lies by Marie Roy   Contemporary
Secrets, lies, and consequences. What consequences does Sydney Morgan pay when all secrets are exposed?

The Blood That Binds by Rie Sheridan   Fantasy
In Ancient Days, when elves were king...the legends tell of wondrous things...

The Dragon's Horn by Glynnis Kincaid   Fantasy
Three Dragons. Three Immortals. One Choice. But what will they choose? Will they rescue their loved ones, or fight to redeem the world?

Escape the Past by K. G. McAbee   Fantasy
Can they escape their pasts and find a future in each other's arms?

The Binding by PhyllisAnn Welsh   Fantasy
He's an Elf Lord trying to save his people. She's a fantasy writer trying to save her sanity. Chosen by the gods to rescue an entire race, they first have to save each other.

Dream Knight by Alexis Kaye Lynn   Medieval
Do you believe in the power of dreams?

Allude to Murder by Emma Kennedy   Suspense
Balkan smuggling conspiracy entangles two Americans

Mating Season by Liz Hunter   Contemporary
One lucky sailboat captain + His fetching first mate + Hurricane Season=Mating Season!

Unlawful by Dorice Nelson   Medieval
Butchery tainted their first encounter... Enslavement separated them... Deception and deceit reunited them... Thus began their struggle of courage and conquest...

Saranac Lake Requiem by Shel Damsky   Historical
Gabriel Levine never dreamed that he would find a new life, true friendship, love, and mortal danger.

Angels Unaware by Priscilla A. Maine   Historical
Is Rebecca's faith strong enough to sustain her through the most trying battles, and help her stand strong in the midst of her adversities?

Enchanted Cottage by Linda Bleser   Paranormal
A story for women who may feel their youth slipping away, but not their zest for life, their taste for adventure, or their ability to recognize and appreciate the power of love—at whatever stage it enters their life.

A Fine Impersonation by K.G. McAbee   Fantasy
Can an incompetent actor take the place of a prince? He can...if he lives long enough to try!

The Choosing by PhyllisAnn Welsh   Fantasy
An extraordinary tale of love, villains and magic!

Apology for the Devil by Stewart Thomas   Thriller/Intrigue
American Secret Service Agent Lia Blaine and Major Robert Garrick of the elite British Special Air Services find themselves thrown together into a violent maelstrom of corruption and treachery which leads up into the White House.

For Baby's Sake by Maralee Lowder   Contemporary Romance
When Rich Jones enters the diner the only thing he wants is a hearty meal and a chance to see his favorite waitress, Anna. What he doesn't expect is a surprise "gift" that will alter his life forever.

Surviving the Novel Experience, An Author's Handbook by K.G. McAbee & A.A. Aguirre
An essential handbook for both established and aspiring authors.

Guarder Lore by Shawn P. Madison   Science Fiction
When a terrorist plot rocks the U.E.N. and thrusts the Guarder Squadron into public view, a history of the ultra-secret is sanctioned for the first time. Now one man, a historian who barely believes the myths himself, discovers the truth behind the legends.

The Last Light by Ana Salazar   Regency
Small and pale, Grace Radbyrne is a timid vicar's widow, burdened by a seemingly impossible dream. Damian Ward, Duke of Carisbrooke, is a bitter man, damaged by betrayal. Failing to locate her missing brother alone, Grace agrees to become Damian's mistress in exchange for his assistance...a devil's bargain only love can break.

The Scent of Stone by Savannah Michaels   Paranormal
Tintagel Castle, secret caves, and a tantalizing scent cause havoc on two unwilling lovers. Shawn Corrigan and Darcy Brannigan find themselves in over their heads as a love potion created in 500 AD affects their lives and hearts. Throw in the magic of Merlin and his delightful sidekick, Aili, and you'll never look at a stone the same way again.

Too Many Spies Spoil the Case by Miles Archer   Mystery
Hard-hitting, quick thinking and an irreverent mouth propel Doug McCool through a tight action thriller with plenty of bodies dropping, bullets flying and, of course, too many spies. Join the hippy detective as he takes you on a tour of San Francisco in the mid-70s.

Married by Mistake by Laurie Alice Eakes   Regency
To protect Stormy from the machinations of her guardian, Dante claims she is his wife and she is by Scottish law. But danger stems from unexpected and far more dangerous sources than Stormy's uncle.

Tyrant Moon by Elaine Corvidae   Fantasy
He had vowed to do no harm. She was born to kill. Can a dying mage and a barbarian warrior put aside their differences long enough to stop a rogue wizard...before time runs out for them both?

The Scottish Thistle by Cindy Vallar   Historical
Rory MacGregor protects her people with cunning and Second Sight. A warrior bound by honor, Duncan Cameron weds her. Will their union survive deposed royalty, vindictive clansmen, and bloody rebellion?